Ten Minutes to Fall in Love

Ten Minutes to
Fall in Love

JULIA LLEWELLYN

PENGUIN BOOKS

PENGUIN BOOKS

Published by the Penguin Group
Penguin Books Ltd, 80 Strand, London WC2R ORL, England
Penguin Group (USA) Inc., 375 Hudson Street, New York, New York 10014, USA
Penguin Group (Canada), 90 Eglinton Avenue East, Suite 700, Toronto, Ontario, Canada M4P 2Y3
(a division of Pearson Penguin Canada Inc.)
Penguin Ireland, 25 St Stephen's Green, Dublin 2, Ireland (a division of Penguin Books Ltd)
Penguin Group (Australia), 250 Camberwell Road,
Camberwell, Victoria 3124, Australia (a division of Pearson Australia Group Pty Ltd)
Penguin Books India Pvt Ltd, 11 Community Centre, Panchsheel Park, New Delhi – 110 017, India
Penguin Group (NZ), 67 Apollo Drive, Rosedale, Auckland 0632, New Zealand
(a division of Pearson New Zealand Ltd)
Penguin Books (South Africa) (Pty) Ltd, Block D, Rosebank Office Park,
181 Jan Smuts Avenue, Parktown North, Gauteng 2193, South Africa

Penguin Books Ltd, Registered Offices: 80 Strand, London WC2R ORL, England

www.penguin.com

First published 2012
003

Copyright © Julia Llewellyn, 2012

All rights reserved.

The moral right of the author has been asserted

Set in 12.5/14.75 pt Garamond MT Std
Typeset by Jouve (UK), Milton Keynes
Printed in England by Clays Ltd, St Ives plc

ISBN: 978-0-141-04817-8

www.greenpenguin.co.uk

ALWAYS LEARNING   **PEARSON**

For Sam and Essie

Acknowledgements

Thanks hugely to Nisha Parti – any mistakes about Punjabi Indians are entirely my own. To the wonderful staff of the Drawing Down the Moon agency (drawingdownthemoon .com) who gave me so much advice: I'd like to stress that they are in every way superior and more professional than the Temperley staff. To Mari Evans, Lizzy Kremer, Celine Kelly, Katy Szita and Ruth Spencer. To the men and women I met in Odessa in 2009, who understandably must be anonymous. To Emöke Denes, you're wonderful and this could not have been written without you. And, as ever, to James Watkins.

Zulekha Forbes opened her curtains and peered out on to the back garden. For the first time since she'd returned to England it wasn't raining and the sun shone clear and strong through the window of her old attic bedroom where she'd hoped to never sleep again.

She pulled up the sash. The panes were filthy, she noted, before reminding herself this was not her problem any more. Leaning over the sill, she had a bird's-eye view of her father Tony's thinning brown crown as he laid out plates and glasses on a trestle table. A large ice-bucket and a collection of Pimm's, lemonade and beer bottles stood on the overgrown grass behind him. The lawn was decorated with a selection of footballs and a trampoline, now rusting and hardly used, which no one had the energy to get rid of.

Zu stretched and yawned. It was tempting to go back to bed, but she knew she should show willing. She turned back to the room, which was like a museum of her teenage self – the self she'd hoped she'd left behind forever. Bob Marley gurned from the wall. In the dressing-table drawer she'd found a dried-out pot of Clearasil. In the bookcase, her well-thumbed Jacqueline Wilsons rubbed shoulders with the titles by Sartre and Camus that had obsessed her during her A-level years when she'd been searching desperately and unsuccessfully for answers to the chaos around her.

So much had happened in the intervening years, Zu thought, sitting back down on the narrow bed with its brightly patterned duvet cover Mum had bought in Debenhams, probably trying to make it up to her after some misdemeanour. It had come in a packet labelled 'Santorini', part of the 'Greek Island' range, she'd told her, which Zu had found wildly exotic.

She dragged a comb through her hair. Last time she'd slept in this room her hair had been spiky and short; a handful of impressive passport stamps later it now grew past her shoulders, though she usually wore it tied in a messy ponytail. Her cousin Anjali, not to mention her naani – or grandmother, to use the non-Hindi word – were always urging Zu to put it in a neat French plait, but really, who could be bothered?

She sniffed: ghee, frying ginger, garlic and onion. Naani must be here and cooking already then. From the twins' bedroom came the thud, thud of their stereo. Zu had no idea what they were playing; in her teens, music had been her obsession, but for years she'd been far too busy to follow it properly. Instead she'd developed not only an embarrassing, middle-aged fondness for classical, but also a sneaky affection for the cheesy Europop that was played in bars all over the former Soviet Union. Roxette's 'It Must Have Been Love' was her favourite. When she was drunk she had even been known to perform a karaoke version that she secretly considered pretty fine.

She dolloped Leela cocoa butter on to her arms and legs. It was one of the bestsellers of her grandmother's beauty range and, annoyingly, it was the only thing that worked on Zu's otherwise dry and itchy skin. Zu prided herself on happily using washing-up liquid when she ran out of shampoo, meaning that most of Leela's beauty range was wasted on her. The little tubes of eyebrow gel and blusher had come in very handy though as gifts and bribes to the Chechen authorities.

Her clothes were still in the suitcases where she'd hastily thrown them when she'd left Chechnya ten days previously. Automatically she reached for her jeans and least dirty T-shirt, but then she reconsidered. Better wear the pink sundress Leela had given her for her birthday.

Zu didn't really understand dresses. Sometimes she wondered if she'd have been more girly if she'd been able to talk to her mother more – if they'd had the kind of relationship where they'd done each other's nails and hair, like her cousin Anjali and Auntie Renu. Zu's mother, after all, had loved to dress nicely when she was sober. You knew she was having a bad day when the sweatpants and old shirts emerged and she didn't bother with the make-up.

Sometimes some guy Zu was having a fling with would urge her to wear skirts, going on about what a tiny waist she had (her teenage self had been chubby from comfort eating but several bouts of dysentery had long put paid to that). 'Fuck off,' Zu had thought, and sometimes said it too.

She squinted in the dusty hand mirror she'd fished out of a bedside drawer. She supposed she should wear make-up, again to keep Leela happy.

'Zu!' Leela's forceful voice came up the stairs. 'Zu-le-kha! Sweetie. Where are you?'

'Coming, Naani!' Zu ran downstairs, glancing into the boys' room. Both were lying on their beds engrossed in their phones; Rohan probably playing some game, Kieran on Facebook. The room smelt sweaty; both were in the T-shirts they'd slept in. Zu remembered them in the cute gingham pyjamas she used to iron because she wanted them to look as neat and innocent as possible in the face of what was happening all around them. Shortly after Mum died they'd rejected them as babyish and Zu hadn't bothered trying to make them change their minds.

'Boys!' Zu tried and failed to sound authoritative. She could coerce strangers to build schoolhouses and repair roofs and undergo HIV tests, but with her own family she was useless. 'Could you start getting dressed, please! The party starts soon. Dad could do with your help outside.'

'Yeah, yeah, whatever.' Kieran didn't take his eyes off the screen.

Rohan yawned and swung his feet on to the ground. 'Tell him I'm coming.'

'Zuzu! I need you to help make the chapattis.'

'Coming, Naani!'

Leela Sangar stood at the bottom of the stairs, resplendent in her best gold and blue sari and matching sandals. She'd aged dramatically since her only daughter died eight years ago, but at sixty-five she was still a splendid woman – less than five-foot tall but straight as a lamp post, with a neat nose, huge hooded eyes and lustrous hair. She scanned Zu thoroughly.

'You're wearing a dress. To what do we owe the honour?' Before Zu could reply, Leela clicked her fingers. 'Come on. There's still a ton to do.'

As usual, she was exaggerating. Everything was well in hand. The curries were sitting under kitchen foil, waiting to be warmed up (golden rule of curry cooking – always prepare twenty-four hours in advance to allow the flavour to emerge). Not that Zu ever made a curry, or cooked at all if she could help it, for that matter.

The rice cooker's red light was on. The bhajis stood ready to be chucked into hot oil and the large ball of cha-patti dough was waiting to be rolled out into round plates. Zu knew she'd make a handful and then Naani would *ttch* at her cackhandedness and take over. Apples, oranges, lemons, limes and a large bunch of mint sat on the table waiting to be chopped up and added to the Pimm's jugs.

'How many people are coming?' Leela asked.

'About forty.'

Leela frowned. 'Hmmm, not so many.'

'This isn't a wedding, Naani, it's a small party to say goodbye to the boys. We can't fit more than forty people in the garden.'

'We should have had it at my house.'

Tony poked his head round the back door. He was dressed in an open-neck lumberjack shirt and jeans. Zu's heart twanged with the mixture of irritation, protective-ness and guilt her father always provoked in her.

On the surface, if you didn't know his history, you wouldn't feel sorry for Tony. He was still a handsome man, albeit on the short side. At primary school Zu had been proud of her good-looking parents. Mum had been so pretty, with her thick raven's-wing hair that she used to spend hours straightening before they went out. Her skin was flawless and she never appeared to be wearing any make-up, though Zu knew she did, because she'd sat at her feet watching her apply it.

Later, of course, it had all been so different: Deepika had spent her days in her flimsy nightie, often not even bothering to cover it with her stained and torn dressing gown. Her eyes were red, her hair matted and her breath stank. Oddly, Zu preferred it when she was like that because she knew it meant Mum wasn't going anywhere. It was worse when she did put on smart clothes and make-up and went out because then you never knew when she'd be back, what state she'd be in and who she might bring with her.

Zu shook her head. Even long dead, Mum was dominating her thoughts when she should have been focusing on what was going on around her.

'Crikey, Leela,' Tony was saying. Zu cringed. *Crikey!* What decade was he living in? 'Are you trying to starve us or what? Why do you never bring enough food?'

Naani laughed and swatted him round the head. 'Get away with you, silly boy.'

Rohan stood yawning in the doorway, in track pants and grey hoodie. 'So what wants doing?'

2

The guests started arriving around noon. Zu stood in the kitchen spooning out the curries into serving dishes and watching neighbours and various friends of the boys talking and laughing through the French doors. Tony had threaded bunting across the rose bushes and hung fairy lights in the elderly elm tree. Too cheesy for Zu's tastes but still very pretty, she had to admit.

The boys were wandering around, clutching beers and clapping their mates from college on the shoulder. Tony was standing by the trestle table. He was holding a paper plate containing an assortment of Naani's curries and chatting to Barry, who worked in his instrument repair shop. Zu spotted Marta from three doors down, looking so pregnant she might pop at any second, and her husband Willem, looking sweaty. Gina from across the road was in a severe grey trouser suit, looking as if she were applying to become the Governor of the Bank of England rather than attending a suburban barbecue. Naani sat on a bench with her best friend, Neelam, plates of dosa on their knees, glasses of home-made lemonade perched on the arms of the bench. Their eyes scanned the crowd, heads nodding happily, as they gossiped about the guests in loud, guttural Punjabi.

Where was Beth, Zu wondered. She was Dad's other employee and, Zu was certain from odd remarks dropped here and there, his bit on the side. She always appeared at the summer barbecue and, although she'd never stayed the night, she habitually stayed on later than the other guests. Zu approved of Beth: she was single, pretty but not too girly-looking and the boys liked her – they said she was a devil on the Wii. Best of all, she wasn't an alcoholic, even if she did enjoy the odd beer.

When she did show up, Zu resolved to engage her in proper conversation for the first time: find out more about her: where she grew up, how she'd ended up working in an instrument repair shop in Edgware, what her dreams were. Beth would be charmed and would eventually reveal what was going on with Tony and – assuming the signs were promising – Zu would give them her blessing. Then maybe Beth would move in and Zu would feel less guilty about leaving again, which she intended to do as soon as possible.

'Wotcha, gorgeous,' whispered a voice in her ear.

'Anj!' Zu whirled round and hugged her cousin. Anjali was Uncle Mahesh's and Auntie Renu's daughter – the only members of Mum's family who'd secretly kept in touch during the wilderness years. She was half a head smaller than the already-miniature Zu, two cup sizes bigger and wearing more make-up than Zu had applied in the whole of her life. Zu didn't have that many close friends – she didn't like people knowing too much about her – but with Anj she felt completely safe.

'How are you?' Zu didn't really notice what people wore, but she computed that Anj was in an orange silk T-shirt over a floaty white skirt and wearing heels that could double as North Sea oil rigs.

'How can you?' Zu asked, indicating the shoes.

Anj laughed. 'Yeah, yeah. We know you've got one pair of trainers and one pair of heels that you only put on when you need to charm a favour out of the head of the KGB.' She sighed at Zu's lack of fashion sense. 'At least you've made some effort today. That isn't mascara, is it?'

'Possibly.' Zu's hand reached self-consciously to her eyes. 'Where's Raman?'

'Over there.' Anjali nodded in the direction of her husband. He was wearing a hot-pink polo shirt tucked into chinos, and was in jovial conversation with a group of neighbours. Zu grinned. Anj had known Raman all her life, their families were great friends. Everyone had always agreed he was an utter buffoon, albeit an amiable one. So Zu had been shocked when Anjali's parents had announced that she was twenty-five and should therefore settle down with him, and Anj had immediately agreed.

They'd had the full Hindu wedding last August: temple, two hundred guests, Raman arriving on a white horse, you name it. Of course, Anj hadn't been a virgin but she didn't sleep with Raman until their wedding night. Zu wasn't sure she'd ever really get her head round what Anj had done. Her mother had brought her up on horror stories about arranged marriages: brides chained to sinks and beaten nightly. But Anj was obviously happy and Raman was clearly no more likely to beat her than start camping outside St Paul's with anti-capitalist protestors, so why worry about them?

'All right, Zu?' he boomed now, as he approached her. 'How is it being back in Edgware? Bit of a change from . . . where was it . . . Grozny? Which is the bigger shithole?'

9

'Rams!' Anjali nudged him as Zu laughed and said, 'Good question.'

'So the recession's hit you do-gooders. Well, about time. What those people need is to learn how to help themselves.'

'What people?' Zu raised a disdainful eyebrow, something she excelled at.

'The starving and needy. They should get off their butts and start growing some food. Or get on the boat. Make better lives for their children. That's what our grandparents did.'

'Oh, stop it!' Anjali slapped his arm. Raman patted her firmly on the bottom.

'And what about your brothers? What are they up to?' he asked.

'Assuming they get the grades, they're both off to uni.' Zu couldn't help the pride that snuck into her voice. Her boys! 'Rohan's got a conditional offer at Salford so he's off on a lad's holiday to Thailand while he waits for his results –'

'Why does that not surprise me?'

'– and Kieran's hoping to go to Sussex. Before that he's spending a year off working in an orphanage in Malawi.' This was like a bag of glass in her stomach. Her little brother far away doing the kind of thing *she* loved, while she festered in Edgware. She had to find another job as soon as possible.

'Like sister, like brother,' Raman said. 'What is it with you lot and saving the world?'

It wasn't anything to do with saving the world, it was about saving themselves. Anyone who'd spent any time with aid workers knew that. Much easier to distract yourself with other people's problems than brood on your own. But Raman wouldn't be interested in such psychobabble.

Leela advanced on them like a purposeful buffalo.

'Raman! You made it from the office.'

'I said I would, didn't I, Leela?'

Leela pinched his cheek. Raman winced as his flesh was scraped by her sharp nails. 'You are a good boy to keep your promises. I know it's hard for you when work's so busy.'

'Did you hear the one about the constipated accountant?' Zu said softly to Anjali. 'He couldn't budget so he had to work it out with a pencil and paper.'

'Just because you're jealous that I've bagged a rich husband and never have to work again.'

'You're not going to stop work, are you?' Zu was aghast. Anjali was a make-up artist specializing in horror films. There was nothing she didn't know about fake blood and the most realistic plastic eyeballs. She loved her job.

'No plans for now,' she said, to Zu's relief. 'But you know. When the babies come along.'

'What are nannies for?'

'I'm not having a *nanny*. What are you like?'

'You'll end up like Marianne. Remember her? Once a wisecracking gal about town.'

'True, and the next it was all, "Oh, I can't come out, it'll mess with Dorrie's *routine*."' They giggled. 'But don't worry, I won't be like that. Anyway, there's no rush. We're not going to start trying for at least a year.'

'A *year*?' That was nothing.

'Now where is that nice young lady Betty?' Leela said, interrupting Zu's disquiet. 'You know, the lady who works with Tony. She's always at this gathering.'

'Beth? I was wondering myself.'

'Zu, love,' trilled Elinor, Barry-from-work's wife. Elinor ran a Weight Watchers franchise and hadn't touched sugar for ten years now. 'Great to see you. I know Tony's thrilled you're back in one piece.'

'Mmm.' Zu smiled.

'He worries so much about you being kidnapped. Or beheaded. Every time I hear a story like that on the radio I say to Barry, "Please God let that not be Zu." ' She took a sip of still water; she never drank fizzy as it gave you cellulite. 'I don't know how you do it, I must say. Isn't it depressing?'

Well, yes, sometimes when drug addicts' babies are dying of Aids, but it's also often a huge giggle back at the compound when every-body's pissed and we're playing nude Twister.

Fun had been another big factor in attracting Zu to that life. She hadn't been much good at having fun before. Far away from home was the only place she could really let loose.

'At least we're trying to make a difference,' she replied blandly.

'Don't you miss home?'

No. If I could never come back to the place where my mother lived, I would be absolutely fine about it. 'Well, you know.' Zu shrugged.

'You must be a saint.'

'Hardly. Ha ha.'

At the far end of the garden, the noise of a fork tinging against a glass could be heard. They all moved out through the French doors and into the garden. As the hubbub died down, Barry cleared his throat.

'Thank you, ladies and gentlemen. Now, I know you've just come here to scoff as much of Leela's delicious curry as possible. But Tony wants to tell you something.'

'No, I don't.' Tony reddened. Zu felt for him. She'd always hated public speaking too, although few would have guessed it from her unflappable exterior.

'Yes, you do, mate!'

'Come on, Tony,' cried Raman, hands cupped round his mouth as if he was cheering on the boat race. Zu shot him her dirtiest look. But, one by one, the guests took up his chant.

'All right, all right,' Tony cried over the din. As it quietened down, he continued. 'You know I don't like to make a show of myself. But since you've all so kindly come along today, I'll say a few words. As you'll all know, this is a knees-up to mark my boys, Kieran and Rohan, finishing their A levels –' scattered clapping and cheering and cries of 'good luck' – 'and starting the next chapter of their lives.'

More applause. Zu looked at her brothers. Rohan had his arm draped round Kieran's neck. How could it be possible that those two children, whose wounds she had cleaned, whose faces she had scrubbed, one of whom (Kieran, obviously) still secretly slept with his old toy gorilla, were heading off alone into the world, armed only with their passports, their iPhones and a packet of Diareze? But then again Zu had done it, as soon as she'd had the chance. The boys had turned out so well, everyone said so, but Zu knew the scars were just well hidden. They were even more eager to escape than she'd been.

'And we're also toasting the return of my gorgeous daughter, Zu. Just in time to keep her old dad company.'

Zu grinned and waved sheepishly as every head turned to inspect her. About time too, she could almost hear the Indian guests thinking. Leaving her poor father to bring up those two boys while she worked with other children in far-off countries. What kind of daughter was she? Another bad one like her mother? Zu tilted her chin defiantly.

'Zu. You've been an inspiration to your brothers. You got a brilliant degree. You've had some amazing jobs. You've travelled to places most of us have never heard of. But it's great to have you home.'

Zu's stomach churned. There he was, putting pressure on her again. Tony had never ever asked her not to do her job, but she knew he hated it – the boys told her so, apart from anything else. But in the past few days he'd talked continuously about how lucky he was to have her back, just as the boys were about to leave. She knew it was heart-felt, she knew Dad loved her – though why exactly she didn't understand – but still, on another level, she hated even the faintest suggestion that she should stick around for a bit. Dad knew why she didn't want to be here. If he didn't want to be left alone, then he was free to go too now.

'To Zu!' Dad yelled.

'To Zu!' everyone cried as Zu smiled and nodded, while thinking how wonderful it would be if an asteroid were to choose that moment to obliterate her.

3

After the speeches, the day dissolved into a whirl of handing out food, topping up drinks, and endless hugs and congratulations. When darkness began to fall, Rohan put on one of his mixes – surprisingly for him, he'd been tactful and chosen a selection even the most elderly could enjoy – and the whole garden, even Leela and Neelam, got down to Gnarls Barkley, to OutKast, to Kylie, to the Jackson Five, to the Killers, to Sophie Ellis-Bextor.

Zu always feared she looked like an electric cable in a puddle when she danced, but after a few beers even she made some silly, over-the-top moves in the hope that irony would hide her lack of coordination.

They were having fun. It was ages since Zu had seen the whole remaining family looking so carefree. Even Tony was do-si-do-ing with Elinor. For a second she found herself wishing that Mum was here to witness the scene. But then she'd have spoiled it all by falling flat on her face or making a pass at Barry. They were better off without her. Zu always told herself that.

It was nearly midnight when the guests began peeling off, children draped over their shoulders, women carrying their heels, everyone sweaty and bright-eyed. When the last guest had finally stumbled out and the music had been turned off (amazingly, the neighbours hadn't complained, but then they'd all been at the party), Tony called a cab for Leela.

'I'll be back early to make everything shipshape,' she protested as he escorted her to the door.

'Don't worry, Naani, I'll do it,' said Zu.

'Don't be silly, darling.'

'Not too early.' Tony looked understandably alarmed as the prospect of his lie-in disappearing.

'Let's say nine. I love you all, darlings. It was a great party. By the way, Tony, why wasn't Betty here?'

'Betty?'

'I think you mean Beth, Naani.'

'Oh. Beth! She couldn't come. I don't know why. Doing something.' Tony reached up and scratched the back of his neck. OK, something had been going on, Zu thought. But now it was over. Damn. Her best hope of making Tony happy receded like the last bus pulling off just as you panted up to the stop.

Leela merely nodded.

'Pity. Nice girl, though I wish she'd do something with her eyebrows. Goodnight then, everyone.'

'Goodnight, Leela.'

'Goodnight, Naani.'

Sun streaming in through the flimsy curtains woke Zu just before seven. As always, it took a couple of seconds to position herself. Edgware, rather than her flat in Grozny. Eleven days ago, she'd been at work, trying to sort out who to bribe to fix the roof of the orphanage when, without warning, she'd been summoned into the head of the programme's office and informed that the British government were cutting aid to Chechnya and therefore fifty per cent of AidInt's staff had to be laid off immediately.

Zu was on a plane that evening and the following afternoon she was on Tony's doorstep. She hated going back to Farthingdale Road – the memories it brought back were just too bleak – but an indefinite stay at Leela's was even more of a no-no, she'd be trying to match her with one of her buddies' grandsons; and Anj's was out too, she was a newlywed and needed space. Anyway, Zu reasoned, it would be good to spend a bit of time with the boys before they flew the nest. Logically, Zu should have resented her brothers, since their birth – or the hormones it triggered – was what sent Deepika loopy. But from the first time Zu had seen them in their little cots in the hospital she'd adored them – adored their banana mouths and thick forests of eyelashes – and with every year that passed she'd loved them more and more for what they'd gone through.

But this time next week they'd be far away. It would be just Zu and Tony in Farthingdale Road, a far scarier prospect than the thought of Grozny under rebel shelling. It was the silence that she dreaded. In Chechnya she'd been surrounded by people all the time at work, and at home too, where the agency flat was occupied by a carousel of Australians, Armenians, Austrians, Americans – and that was just the As – hogging the bathroom and filling the shelves with their weirdly named toothpastes, eating their funny cereals at breakfast. There was permanent company and you never had a chance to be alone with your thoughts, but at the same time no one ever stayed long enough for you to get properly close to them. It was Zu's ideal.

What would the house be like without the boys' music playing, their shouting, their phones pinging? Tony might want to fill the silence by talking about Deepika and that was a conversation Zu was never going to have. What was the point? Mum was dead, it was sad, it was over, they needed to move on.

She rolled over and was just about to plummet back into sleep again when her phone rang. Not unusual, probably one of her mates calling pissed from a bar in a distant time zone. She grabbed the handset from the bedside table. NAANI flashed on the screen.

'Naani? Is everything all right?'

'Everything's fine, darling.' As an afterthought, Leela added, 'I didn't wake you, did I?'

'No, I was –'

'It's after seven. I'd never call anyone before seven. I understand they need their sleep. It's how I got where I am today, by knowing how to deal with others, even though I've never needed more than five hours, like Lady Thatcher. Anyway, Zu, I'm worried. About Tony.'

'Really? Why?' Zu sat up and reached for her cigarettes. Of course Tony said no smoking in the house but she'd open all the windows in a minute and spray the place with Leela Room Fragrance.

'Will he be able to cope on his own?' she asked.

'Of course he will, Naani. He's nearly forty-eight and we've got a washing machine and a microwave.' Zu kept her tone light but a stone had suddenly been placed on her heart as her fears were voiced.

'I was watching him at the party. Your father is lonely.'

'Oh, Naani!'

'He needs a new wife. Is anyone on the cards?'

'Not that I'm aware of.'

'Are you seriously telling me he's been a monk these past eight years?'

'I don't know, Naani.' Zu wasn't going to discuss her father's sex life with her grandmother.

'That's ridiculous. Why not? I know, he was probably trying to protect you. And me. But that's silly. It's been eight years. Deepi wants him to be happy, I know she does.'

'Right.' Zu hated Naani saying she knew what Deepika was thinking. Because (a) Mum was dead and, in her view, vaporized rather than, as Naani believed, floating around reincarnated as a butterfly and (b), more pertinently, Naani had had no time for Deepika's opinions when she was alive.

'Things have obviously fizzled out with that Betty, so I want you to start looking for him.'

'Where would I look?' Zu exclaimed. 'I'm not going to fix up Dad with one of my friends.'

'Just look around you. I'll keep an eye open too. But he needs someone. People shouldn't live alone. It's unnatural. I should know.'

Violins. Hankies. 'You can always go and live with Uncle Amit, you know that.'

'I know, Baccha. I didn't mean it to sound like that. *I* can manage on my own, but women are capable. Men not so. Could you ever have imagined your Naana coping by himself?'

'The world's moved on a bit since then. Dad's British, not Indian. He wasn't brought up with ayahs wiping his bottom until he was ten and rushing around picking up his toys.'

'He still needs a woman's love. I can't believe we've neglected that fact for so long.'

'All right, Naani.' Zu knew she was right. 'We'll put our minds to it.'

'Excellent. How is the job hunting going, by the way? I didn't get a chance to ask yesterday.'

'All sorts of things on the cards,' Zu lied. The aid business was in dire straits. She'd called in every favour, phoned everyone she'd ever met; they were all very sympathetic but they were all saying nothing was out there.

'You could come and work for me,' Leela wheedled.

Leela Sangar was not exactly a typical Indian grandmother. Well, she was in that she'd come here forty-nine years ago, from the Punjab, newly married to a virtual stranger, dreading the English cold, apprehensive about coping without armies of servants, but also certain that Britain held more opportunities than home.

While most Indian wives had been ambitious for their husbands, Naani – spoilt only daughter – had been ambitious for herself. Naana Amit was an enlightened Hindu husband who saw no problem with his wife working, and just months after Uncle Amit was born Leela had set up a business doing facials and massages near their home in Southall. By the time Uncle Mahesh was born, the business had expanded to four more outlets, and by the time Uncle Arun and then Deepika arrived she had opened a West End salon offering full beauty services, as well as her magical facials, a celebrity clientele was amassing and there was a six-month waiting list to be seen by her.

Forty years on, Leela's salon was still going strong and so was her beauty range, including a line sold by Sainsbury's and Waitrose. She had a magazine column, giving advice on everything from cellulite to annoying husbands, she had bought a mansion in Wembley and flew first class six times a year to India to combine new product research with family visits.

Naana, who'd had his own successful career as a cardiologist, had died six years ago, but Naani kept up the role of superwoman, cooking huge feasts for her expanding family at every opportunity and making sure she was up to date with every smidgeon of gossip.

As a small child, Zu had hardly known her. Leela and Deepika hadn't talked since Deepika had run off and married Tony, aged just twenty. Zu was eighteen, away at uni when her mother died, and her first real encounter with Leela had been at Mum's cremation when, dressed head to toe in white, she'd wept throughout the service. At the wake back in Farthingdale Road she'd bustled about completely dry-eyed, offering food and drinks to the guests and, when they almost immediately ran out of supplies, conjuring up more.

Then she'd ushered all the guests out, sent the twins to bed, tidied up and sent Zu and Tony to bed too with herbal sleeping pills (they'd both binned them and taken some proper lovely chemical stuff). In the morning she'd returned with a batch of meals to stuff in the freezer, which Tony and the boys had lived off for months, while she took Deepika's ashes to the airport and escorted them back to India to scatter them in the Ganges.

On her return, Leela had insisted they kept the lines of communication open. Once a month she took Zu out for an expensive dinner. Initially Zu had been frightened they'd talk about nothing but Deepika and how she'd let them all down, but in fact her mother was rarely mentioned – and never critically.

Instead, Leela had talked mainly about herself: how magnificently she'd done, how much more there was to achieve and – after a handful of meetings – had intimated that there would always be a place for Zulekha in the family firm. Although Zu would rather have gnawed through her left elbow than work for a beauty company, nonetheless, wary respect soon mutated into exasperated fondness. Leela was annoying, but there was no doubting her good heart.

Leela had tried to help Tony financially but as he'd pulled himself together he'd told her they could manage and, huffily, she'd backed off. Zu wished he hadn't been so proud. Even though she'd told herself she was not going to let herself be troubled by what went on at home, it still bothered her that the house needed painting and the roof repairing. That aside, Tony needed a decent holiday, but with him having to put the two boys through uni, Zu couldn't see that happening for years. And yet, now the hand was being extended to her, she too recoiled. She loved Leela, she needed a job, but day in, day out at Naani's beck and call? No thanks.

'I really think my skills are best suited to aid,' Zu responded in what she hoped was her most tactful voice.

Leela snorted. 'Well, if you change your mind the offer is still there. Honestly, what would your grandfather say if he knew that none of his grandchildren wanted to join a family business?'

Zu resisted the urge to ask how come Leela knew what Deepika was thinking but not Naana. She stubbed her cigarette out on the window sill. 'Listen, I have to go. Dad's calling me downstairs.'

'I'll be over soon. I love you.'

'OK, Naani.' Zu wasn't very good at saying 'I love you'. She did love Naani, just as she loved Tony and the boys and Anjali, but somehow saying it made her uneasy. Mum had said 'I love you' all the time, but she'd never behaved like she did. So Zu just said: 'See you later. Bye.'

4

Zu was far too alert to go back to sleep, so she went downstairs and unloaded the dishwasher, while feeding herself spoonfuls of cold curries (they were always even tastier the morning after) and dwelling on what Naani had said.

All the niggling fears that had been sloshing around Zu's head since she'd come home were solidifying into icy, lumpen reality. Tony needed a girlfriend – better still, a wife. He was lonely, the boys were leaving home, Zu didn't want to stay, so who else to fill the gap? But given that his social life was non-existent, he was going to need help finding her.

What could Zu do though? Her friends were all at least twenty years too young for him, not to mention the fact that the idea of matchmaking any of them with her father was repellent. Zu shoved the problem to the back of her mind. She'd return to it later, but for now she was going to go out for the papers and buy the ingredients for a proper fry-up. She wanted to spoil the boys while she still could.

It was even hotter than yesterday, the blue sky stretched taut like a tent over their quiet suburban street. Zu clamped on her headphones and fiddled her iPod dial until she found some Debussy harp music that perfectly matched the weather. Zu's iPod was her constant companion; the thought of a journey without it, however short, was like Anjali going out without make-up – unthinkable.

Letting the music wash over her, blocking out the noise of doors slamming, tears, and plates breaking, had always been the best way to keep real life at a distance.

She overtook a woman who could have been any age between twenty and forty, wearing cut-off jeans and a vest top, a cigarette hanging between her lips as she pushed a pram containing a screaming baby. 'Shut up,' the woman snapped and took another drag.

The anger that simmered inside Zu roared up as it always did when she witnessed scenes like this. Mum used to snap at her just like that. Though not when she was a baby, she reminded herself – at least, not as far as she knew.

She tried not to dwell too much on the eight years she'd had with her mother before the boys were born because it made what came afterwards seem even more bleak. But every now and then she'd recall moments of pure happiness, like diamonds in a dark mine. The pair of them snuggling up, interlocking fingers, stretching out both their arms and declaring 'I love you *this* much.' She remembered gazing at the glossy back of Mum's head as they drove to ballet, and standing on a stool in the kitchen helping her mix a cake. She'd never been able to accept that her skin was so much lighter than her mother's, and on one famous occasion had rectified this by covering herself all over in brown felt-tip.

The changes had come subtly. Zu was nine, so the boys must have been one, when she remembered Mum telling her she was far too old to be collected from school and she could walk home alone now. So she had, even though she'd found it scary because she had to cross a main road and cars didn't always stop at the lights. Anyway, she remembered one day walking into the kitchen with her book bag and finding Mum at the table, holding a mug of tea. The boys, in high chairs, were rubbing banana goo into their hair. Deepika's face was twisted and she was sobbing, her shoulders shaking. Zu would never forget the sight of her tears dripping into her mug, the noise of the boys banging spoons on their trays, oblivious.

Another time, maybe six months later, Zu had come home to find the kitchen empty. 'Mum!' she'd yelled, running upstairs. Mum was in her bed under the covers. The boys were gabbling to each other, Rohan's nappy stank and the room looked as if it had been devastated by a tornado.

'Mum, what are you doing?'

'I'm taking a nap,' she'd snapped. 'Is that allowed?'

'But are you OK?'

'I'm fine. Just take them away from me.' She hadn't even emerged from under the covers. A snake squirmed in Zu's stomach, her head felt as if it were being crushed and her breathing slowed down as she grabbed a boy under each arm and hurried down the stairs with them.

Poor Tony, trying and failing to jolly them through it all. As soon as he got back from the workshop he'd take over: make supper, tidy up, put the boys to bed, sign any school forms of Zu's.

'He needs a new wife, he needs a new wife.' Naani's words rattled through Zu's brain like a runaway train. Of course, it wasn't the first time Zu had thought about this, especially when Mum had been alive. Then she'd often harboured disloyal fantasies about her father eloping with one of her friend's mothers – someone like Carina Jackson, Bella's mum, who had apple cheeks and long blonde hair she wore in a plait, who was always in the front row at plays and concerts brandishing her camcorder. Bella had found her behaviour mortifying; Zu had been so envious that even the memory made her stomach contract.

After Deepika died, Zu had felt so guilty that her wish to lose her real mother had been granted and the step-mother fantasies faded away. Sometimes she'd wondered if Tony would like to meet someone but he'd always been so busy – working and then going to parents' evenings and ferrying the boys about from judo to cricket to orchestra practice and their mates' houses – that Zu couldn't see how he'd ever have time.

Occasionally he went to the pub with people from work, but he'd always be home by midnight. As far as she knew, no one had ever stayed the night – the boys would have mentioned it. Zu did not want to dwell on her father's sex life, but – to paraphrase Naani – had he really been living like a monk all this while? Eight years was a long time for a man to exist without a shag; some of Zu's boyfriends could barely manage eight hours. All right, there'd almost certainly been a liaison with Beth, but she hadn't been at the party and if it had been serious they'd surely know by now.

At the corner shop, Zu bought the papers, Marlboro Lights, mushrooms, tomatoes, sliced white bread, sausages, bacon and eggs for her surprise fry-up. Back home everyone was still asleep. Zu sat at the kitchen table with a warmed-up naan and some saag aloo, flicking through the *Sunday Post*.

Nothing about Chechnya, *quelle surprise*, just dull political rows, economic gloom, gossip about someone called Kara Tointon and her potential new boyfriend, no disasters. She flicked through and suddenly on the so-called women's pages – the ones Zu normally skipped, so bloody patronizing thinking women only want to read about make-up and hair – something caught her attention.

WHEN SINGLES TURN TO A MATCHMAKER

With one in five single Britons now paying someone to find them a partner, using a matchmaker is quickly losing its stigma. But is it a route to happiness? Karen Drake investigates.

Zu's scalp prickled. The article was full of examples of people who, not knowing how to meet members of the opposite sex, had turned to a dating agency. 'All my friends were hitched with children and the social scene we enjoyed in our thirties was long gone.' Now they had found love through the agency and were married with several children. Sounded like a living hell to Zu, but she knew most people weren't like her at all, and thank goodness, or the human race would be extinct.

'Perhaps we can learn something from Asian cultures where arranged marriages are still seen as the way forward,' Karen Drake wrote.

Hmmm. Naturally Zu was unconvinced. But a marriage agency was different from Anj and Raman. It wasn't insisting Dad married someone, it was just helping him meet some new friends. Dad, whose birthday was coming up and who was always a nightmare to buy for.

An idea began to dawn.

Juliet, 40, a doctor, used the services of the Temperley Bureau. Based in ultra-hip Marylebone with offices in Monaco and

Geneva, the service was costly (annual membership starts at £1,000) but, she said, unparalleled. 'They really took the trouble to find out who I was and to introduce me to people who shared all my tastes and interests. It was only a matter of time before the chemistry kicked in.' Juliet is getting married next month to Andrew, a 48-year-old lawyer.

Zu bit her lip. Tony was far from being a lawyer; he repaired string instruments. But something like the Temperley Bureau, which had the personal touch, appealed much more than a faceless website. She ran upstairs, found her Mac and turned it on. Straight to the Temperley website. It had a navy-blue background, a logo with a crest and a picture of a gurning bride and groom. Probably off their faces on drugs.

Looking for that special someone? Temperley can find them for you. Scientific research shows it takes less than ten minutes to fall in love. Within seconds of meeting that special someone, your body starts producing 'love drugs', similar to cocaine, like adrenalin and dopamine. But how do you find your soulmate in the first place? Well, that's where Temperley comes in!

There was a page of success stories and within seconds Zu was reading about Georgia and Alan, just about to have their second child, and about Betty and Cameron, ecstatically happy together.

We take the trouble to really know our clients. Prices start from £120 plus VAT for a trial monthly membership.

One hundred and twenty plus VAT. Normally Zu bought Dad something like a DVD box set. She was unemployed. Her bank account was healthyish, because all her expenses were covered in the field, but she didn't know how long she'd need the cash for. But still, but still . . .

The mouse was hovering over *contact us* when Rohan stuck his head round the door.

'Gwaargh. I feel rough. What are you doing?'

'Just surfing.' Zu jumped up guiltily, as if he'd caught her gazing at photos of Dominic West's crotch. 'I've been to the shops. Going to make you a full English.'

'Really? Sweet, Zu.' He rubbed his hands together and patted his stomach.

'But then,' she warned, trying and failing to sound tough, 'you have to help clear up.'

'Whatevs.' Rohan picked up a colour supplement. 'Can I have scrambled eggs, not fried?'

5

Naani didn't leave the house until after five, by which time she'd cleaned it from top to bottom and filled the freezer with half a dozen curries. Now the boys were slumped in front of the Xbox, guiding avatars through wrecked buildings and dilapidated warehouses, occasionally shooting each other in the back with an Uzi, while Tony flapped around them.

'So, you're sure you've taken out full insurance? Because if you get sick it can cost millions to have you flown home.'

'Dad, we're cool,' Rohan growled, frowning as someone on the screen died an agonizing death.

'And you've definitely had all the immunizations?'

'Chill, Dad.'

Tony watched them for a moment, his face twisted with anxiety, but eventually he shrugged. 'I need to sort out the tumble dryer,' he said and disappeared into the minute room behind the kitchen which smelt of steam and soap powder.

He didn't emerge until shortly before dinner. Afterwards, he said he needed an early night and about nine he disappeared to bed, the Sunday papers under his arm.

Suspicions correct. The scab over Zu's heart which had covered up her worries about her father's miserable life was beginning to crack; blood oozing again. Dad was lonely. He had no life. She needed to sort him out, fast. The marriage agency probably wasn't the answer – that would be too easy – but she had to give it a chance. Because if she didn't, she'd feel too guilty to leave home again and she and Tony would grow old together. She'd push him round in his bathchair and the neighbourhood children would jeer at them and put dog turds through the letterbox.

First thing the following morning she looked at her BlackBerry and found – amongst various missives from buddies having fun in far-flung places, lucky bastards – a reply from Temperley.

Dear Zulekha,

Thank you so much for your email, which touched us deeply. Your father sounds like an ideal candidate and we'd love to talk to him further. Would you like to come in and meet us and we can have a real heart to heart about his requirements? I hope so!

Kind regards,

Masha Temperley

Zu called straight away.

'Temperley,' said a husky voice with a hint of eastern Europe.

'Is that Masha Temperley? It's Zulekha Forbes. I emailed you and you emailed me and . . .'

'Zulekha!' Masha Temperley exclaimed. She was Russian, Zu was sure of it. 'I cannot *tell* you how touched

I was by your email. So *sweet*, looking for love for your father. And now your problems are solved. Our clients will be lining up to meet him. So when do you come in and talk some more?'

'Er . . .' Zu hadn't expected things to move this fast.

'Great. Ten this morning OK? Sorry, got to go, darling, phones are going crazy as usual and I'm all alone. My husband, Gary, is in meeting and Lyuba, our old assistant, has eloped with a client to Istanbul. See you at ten. Bye!'

Zu took the Tube down to Baker Street, delighted to have an excuse to escape the suburbs. Temperley was south of the Marylebone Road, in a grid of quiet backstreets lined with quirky little shops you rarely saw any more. There was an old-fashioned ironmongers, a shop that specialized in shoes for large or wide feet and another that sold clothes for tall women (not the best place for Zu, who was five foot two and a bit sensitive to teasing about how this said a lot about her personality).

Another sold Indian musical instruments. Zu gazed at the huge sitar in the window: music and India, a cheesy emblem of her parents' union. She'd have to tell Tony about this place. When he was a child he'd taught her all about obscure instruments – zithers, mandolins, ukuleles. They'd try to spot them while listening to music from all over the world. They'd duetted, her on violin and him on piano. After the twins were born there'd been no more time for that. Maybe it was something they could do together now the boys were leaving. Zu shrugged off the idea. Who was she kidding? Those days had gone forever.

She walked on past several beauty salons, hardly of

interest to Zu; ditto an extraordinary number of wedding-dress shops. Perhaps the Temperley Bureau sent all their clients there. Through the window of one she saw a woman, about her age, twirling in a frothy gown while another woman – obviously her mother – applauded rapturously. Zu imagined such a scene featuring herself and Deepika and her mouth curled wryly.

She rounded the corner into Luke Street. Number twenty-eight was a tall, grey-brick Victorian terraced town house like something out of a period drama, with black railings outside guarding steep steps to the basement. Box trees flanked the front steps and a brass plate displayed a row of buzzers: for a travel agency, a podiatrist, a graphic designer and the Temperley Bureau.

'Hello?' said that husky-accented voice down the intercom.

'It's Zulekha Forbes. I have an appointment?'

'Zulekha! Come in!' The door buzzed open. Zu began climbing the narrow, beige-carpeted stairs. The Temperley Bureau was on the fourth floor and, even though Zu was fairly fit, by the time she reached the top she was wheezing like an elderly pug. Maybe she should cut down on the fags, she thought, as she did about once a week – knowing that would absolutely never happen.

Standing on the landing was a shiny blonde woman, immediately recognizable from the website as Masha. She was a little older than Zu had guessed from her picture, somewhere in her forties, but in fantastic nick with flawless skin and chin-length hair the colour of freshly churned butter.

She wore a floaty patterned top belted at the waist, tight

black jeans over silver stilettos and a quite extraordinary amount of make-up. A row of bangles chunked on her wrist, a sapphire choker twinkled round her neck and a huge diamond on her ring finger reflected the light from the sash window over the stairs.

'I am thrilled to meet you.' Masha Temperley smiled, revealing perfect teeth. 'Your email had me excited.' She ushered Zu into a small sitting room. 'Sit down. Tea? Coffee? I'm afraid I'll have to make it myself. I told you, my assistant Lyuba fell in love with a client and ran off.' She shrugged. 'Strictly speaking, is unethical, but how can you stand in path of true love? As we say on website, it only takes ten minutes.'

'Coffee would be great. Black, no sugar.'

Masha nodded approvingly. 'I hate making white coffee, I never know how much milk to put in. Anyone who not takes it black is crazy in any case. Zero calories! Why wouldn't you?'

Zu tried not to roll her eyes. Typical Russian, obsessed with her figure. Zu's Russian friends had never understood her – how she never ironed, and ate what she wanted, and didn't paint her toenails. They couldn't understand why she wasn't bothered about pulling men and were miffed whenever she did anyway.

Ah, well. Zu still liked them, liked the way that, despite their obsession with appearance, they had read all the classics and could converse about world affairs and loved debating whether God existed, as compared to most of the girls she'd known at school whose most taxing debates had involved whether to have a Brazilian or a Hollywood wax.

With Masha out of the room, Zu looked around. Beige sofa and carpet, pretty vintage posters advertising the French Riviera and a framed certificate announcing that the Temperley Bureau was a member of the Association of Introduction Agencies. Well, that was something, she supposed.

Through the wall, she could hear several phones ringing. 'Hello, Temperley?' Masha said, then she shrieked, 'Jane! I was hoping was you. So how did it go? . . . Fantastic! . . . I am *so* heppy. I just *knew* it.' Lots of *mmms* and *yeahs* followed, then: 'I have to go, Jane, someone's waiting for me. But, truly, you've made my day . . . OK, speak soon. Bye, sweetheart.'

Her sleek head appeared round the door. 'Apologies, Zulekha, but was necessary to take that call. Fantastic news. Jane is lovely woman and Simon is perfect for her. I sense wedding bells.'

The phones had stopped but now one started again.

'*Bozhe moi*,' Masha sighed. 'I'm sorry.' She ran back into the office. 'Geoff,' Zu heard her say. 'Yes, I am looking at paint chart. Is so tricky. Sometimes I think Clunch, sometimes I think Shaded White. Is nightmare. What you think? . . . No! I said definitely not James White. Is too cold. I hate. Listen, I must go. Am with client. We speak later. Do not use James White!'

'Sorry,' she said, returning to Zu. 'Another client.' As Zu goggled at the barefaced lie, she continued, 'We need a new assistant, pronto. I've been asking about but no joy so far. I always do it by word of mouth. I advertised once and got three hundred replies, can you imagine? And all of them useless. Never again. So if you know anyone . . .'

'I'll let you know,' Zu said, absolutely sure she could think of no one.

Masha gave another of her approving nods. Zu sensed she was used to people doing exactly what she told them.

'It really helps if they speak Russian, by the way. A good proportion of our – er, clients – is from Russia and Ukraine.'

'I speak Russian,' said Zu.

'*To tak?*' Masha tried and failed to raise an eyebrow.

'Did my degree in it,' Zu replied in Russian. 'I spent a year in St Petersburg and then the past couple of years I've been working in Chechnya.'

'*Nyet! Nye veryoo!*' I don't believe it. '*Ya ot Odessa.*' I'm from Odessa.

'Ah, so you're Ukrainian. I've always wanted to go there.'

Masha nodded proudly. 'So beautiful. Especially Odessa. Our opera house, second most beautiful in world after Milan.' She eyed Zu suspiciously. 'What on earth were you doing in Chechnya?'

Zu was not surprised at her tone. Most Russians and Ukrainians loathed Chechens, thought they were dirty Muslims. Most thought Zu was a dirty Muslim herself; it had been one of the many downsides about her time there, the whispered remarks, people occasionally spitting at her. She'd had to do a lot of brandishing of her British passport to prove she wasn't 'one of them'. If she hadn't inherited Tony's pale skin it would have been a lot worse; the few black people she knew never travelled on the Metro in big Soviet cities, such was their fear of racist attacks.

37

'I worked in aid,' she said now. 'Helping street children, building them orphanages, making sure they were vaccinated . . .' She trailed off as she saw Masha's expression.

'Very saintly.' Masha sniffed. Well, charity wasn't big in the former Soviet states, it was all about looking after number one – and who could blame them when less than a hundred years ago five million had perished in the great famine? But then Masha smiled. 'Anyway, your Russian is excellent, even if accent a bit wonky. Congratulations. But why you are back in London?'

'I won't be for long I hope. My – er – my contract ended. I'm waiting for another to come up.'

'You *want* to go beck?' Incredulity.

Zu nodded. She didn't expect Masha to understand. After all, the things that Zu herself loved about the former Soviet Republics – the chaos, the corruption, the lack of material goods – were the things that most locals, quite understandably, were desperate to escape. For Zu, however, it was a relief to have to tackle such daily hurdles. If you spent all day trying to get the electricity switched on in your flat, then you went to bed exhausted and grateful for small blessings; you didn't lie awake feeling sorry for yourself for having such a hideous childhood.

'What about you? What are *you* doing here?' she asked Masha, even though she had a very good idea.

'I married Gary twenty years ago. He was in Odessa after fall of communism. I was his interpreter.' She shrugged. 'We came back here and we set up this business because we think if it work for us why can't it work for everyone? People criticize. They say we marry without love. But what is love? Is construct. Different societies define it. In Manu of New Guinea they do not even have word for love. The Marxist argument is we only have this concept to encourage people to mate, breed, raise families, continue to buy things.'

Zu hadn't been expecting this.

'I have PhD in philosophy and sociology, Odessa University,' Masha explained tersely. 'Anyway, what was I saying? Oh yes. Gary and I. All is good. In Ukraine we worry about what to eat that night, here I worry about what colour to decorate kitchen.' Suddenly she shoved two pieces of glass, one violet, one mauve, under Zu's nose. 'Which you like best?'

'Um? That one!' Randomly Zu pointed at the mauve.

'You too? This is Gary's favourite. I am not sure. Is for kitchen spleshbeck.' Masha frowned, then rallied. 'So all is great, except we need new assistant. Anyway, tell me more about your father.'

'Well, he's about to turn forty-eight, he runs his own instrument repair business and he's been widowed eight years.'

'Was it breast cancer?'

People always thought breast cancer. 'A car crash, actually.' So drunk she could barely stand, let alone drive. At least no one else had been killed. In many ways it was a miracle it hadn't happened sooner. One of Zu's strongest memories of her teenage years was the sound of tyres screeching away from outside Farthingdale Road, when Mum had decided to escape again.

'I am sorry.'

'That's OK.' For ages Zu had been furious about having to absolve people from feeling bad about her mother's death, but now the comments washed over her. People didn't mean to be crass, they were simply observing the proprieties. If there was a problem it was with Zu, not them. They were behaving normally, it was Zu who had no idea what normal was. Deepika had certainly been no role model and Tony had been too absorbed in Deepika and the boys to be of any use either. She cleared her throat.

'Dad might have had the odd fling, but nothing serious. Nothing he's told us about anyway. He's been too busy bringing up my brothers.'

'Brothers?'

'Yes, twins,' Zu said proudly. 'They're eighteen now. One's off to uni in October and the other's having a gap year, so Dad has a bit more time on his hands.'

'Good! No children at home is another plus point. I would never have married Gary if he'd had children.' She scribbled something in a notebook. 'Yes, I think he sounds ideal. Right age and, more importantly, a *man*.'

'As far as I know,' Zu said jokingly.

'All agencies have this problem.' Masha was unimpressed by Zu's levity. 'Women outnumber men by about four to one, especially in the thirty-six-plus bracket. So your father is ideal. Forties – so not too old. Widowed – I mean, that is about a billion bonus points.'

'Why?'

'No one divorced him! No pesky ex-wife in the background stalking new girlfriends and snaffling cash. Kids have left home. Women will be falling over themselves to look after him.'

'Right,' Zu said slowly. 'So what do we do now?'

'You take home our brochure and think. Then if you are interested, ask your father to fill in this form and come in for a chat – probably with Gary, not me. He has better understanding for male clients. My rapport is with the women, I know how we suffer. He has to make a video as well, but don't worry. Is for our eyes only, just so we can all check him out and maybe discuss any help he needs with grooming or body language.'

'Dad's grooming's fine!'

Masha smiled and handed over a white vellum folder, emblazoned with the Temperley logo. 'Like we say, ten minutes to fall in love. Ten minutes to create best possible impression. Go home, have a look and call me soon. But I know it's going to work out, Zulekha.'

'Please, call me Zu.' She paused. 'Do you really think you have the right woman for my father?'

'I'm pretty sure I know who she is already. Just sign the forms and I'll put them in touch.'

6

In the middle of the day the Tube back to Edgware was blissfully empty, bar a handful of German tourists in a tizz about needing to change on to the Piccadilly Line. Zu sorted them out and then, enjoying the rare luxury of a seat, switched her iPod to Fauré's *Requiem* and started studying the Temperley form.

Obviously she couldn't submit it on Tony's behalf, but nothing was to stop her having a practice run and working out how to present him to his best advantage. She pulled out the fancy biro that Leela had given her for her birthday – astounding she hadn't yet lost it, it had been four whole months – and studied the form.

Name:

'Tony Forbes,' Zu wrote confidently. Then she doubted herself. Perhaps Anthony would be better, or Antonio to give him an edge? There was that guy on *Strictly Come Dancing*, which Anjali had forced her to watch a couple of times, who called himself Anton du Beke when he was apparently Tony Beke from Petts Wood. Tony was such a daddish name. Zu chewed on a cuticle. No, she had to tell the truth, Dad was always Tony to everyone, except Grandma Forbes when she wanted to sound posh. If she wasn't truthful then there was no point to any of this. But then she saw

Height:

Bugger. Everyone in the family was a titch. Deepika had been five foot two, the boys were five foot seven and Tony was . . . Tony was generously 'Five foot eight inches'. Well, if he wore stacked heels like Tom Cruise on a movie set, he might just get away with it.

Date of birth:

Easy, '11 July 1968.'

~~Single / Separated / Divorced / Divorcing /~~ Widowed / ~~Have co-habited~~

Easy. Zu felt better now.

What kind of work have you done in your life? What do you do now? Do you enjoy your work?

Zu didn't know all that much about Tony's life before he met Deepika. She knew he'd travelled for a year or two after uni, that he'd played in an orchestra and busked occasionally (Zu found this wildly improbable in the same way that she and Anjali used to cry with laughter at the idea their parents must have 'done it' respectively twice and three times to produce their broods), and he had moonlighted in various bands.

Before the twins were born, Zu dimly remembered a bohemian figure. Her father didn't work in an office like the other dads and was his own boss, so he'd been able to attend school plays and assemblies, often more than Deepika, who'd worked in a mortgage brokers back then. When Zu was in the Infants she'd loved seeing him in the audiences; as she grew older it made her uncomfortable. Kids are square: they like meals at regular hours consisting of fish and chips and ketchup, and 'real' dads who wear ties and suits and do things like wash the car at weekends. Dads who attended school events, were somehow weird, Zu thought, this was Mummy territory.

Then the twins were born and after a year or so it became clear Deepika was in no state to go back to work. So Tony had knuckled down and opened the repair shop and had become just like the rest of the fathers. So Zu was briefly happy, but only, of course, until Mum started drinking and the spectre of the kids at school finding out about her was so much greater than anything else. By then she couldn't have cared if Shrek on a unicycle had turned up to cheer her on, she just wanted someone there who wouldn't slur her words or swear loudly or slump over sideways like Mum had once done at the carol concert (they'd blamed it on antibiotics, but it was at that point the other kids had begun to whisper and giggle, and Zu had begun mastering the art of walking past, head held high).

Never mind. Sticks and stones. It had all made Zu stronger. Other people had it much worse. Back to the questionnaire.

'Was violinist. Now run own instrument repair business. Yes, I enjoy my work.' Or did he? Business had been tough the past couple of years. Tony had never said it, but he surely must miss his old life on the road with the orchestra — a different capital every night, rather than being stuck in a tatty workshop with Barry and Beth all day long. Even if he'd been having a passionate affair with Beth, it was still a depressingly narrow circle.

How do you see your future plans?

'I'd like to start playing in orchestras again,' Zu wrote, but immediately crossed it out, wondering what was the truth. Really, she should ask Dad, but that would be a deep and meaningful question and deep and meaningful was banned. Dad had so often tried to talk to her, both before and after Mum died, but Zu had always rebuffed him. It was a rubbish situation, it had ended horribly, but it was over and they just needed to move on.

What is your nationality and ethnic background? Is it important to you and would you like to say why?

'White British.' Was it important to Tony? He obviously wasn't racist — he'd married Mum. At the same time, he was undeniably an Englishman: he drank PG Tips and turned scarlet at the faintest ray of sunshine.

What papers and magazines do you take?

'Take' amused Zu, it made Dad sound like a provincial

rector subscribing to *Beekeeping Monthly*. 'The *Guardian* and occasionally *Private Eye*,' she wrote.

Mention some books that you have read and enjoyed recently.

Zu wasn't sure Dad had had time to finish a book since the twins were born. There was a pile by his bed, one about Churchill. *The Gathering Storm* – that was it! She'd put that down, it made him sound clever; although maybe women would like something more touchy-feely like that book Anjali loved – what was it called? – *The Source*. No, no lying, she'd go for the macho approach. What was that memoir of a Spitfire pilot he'd loved? He and Raman had had a very animated conversation about it . . . '*First Light*,' Zu wrote triumphantly.

Have you been to the cinema or theatre recently?

'No.' Or not that Zu was aware of, he never mentioned anything he'd seen. How depressing.

What sort of films and plays do you like?

War films, but in general he tended to watch whatever was on, often falling asleep halfway through. As for plays, Zu could only think of the boys' school shows, in which both had notably failed to shine. 'Shakespeare,' she tried. It didn't mention telly, which was just as well as Dad was a big *Top Gear* man, though he also loved box sets, which were very hip right now. Oh well, Temperley's loss. You didn't ask, you didn't find out.

Describe your educational background.

'Sandown High School, Isle of Wight. Royal College of Music,' Zu wrote. Not Eton and Cambridge, but it would do.

Do you enjoy travelling and have you ever lived abroad? What are your favourite countries?

Well, yes, he did, and no, he'd never lived abroad, but he'd been all over the place touring. Where were his favourites? Zu had no idea. Before the twins, they'd had a few holidays in Greece. Zu remembered white beaches, splashing in the surf, sitting under a carob tree in the heat of the afternoon, her head on Mum's lap, watching a lizard scuttle across a pathway.

They'd been to France once when the boys were about four. That was the time Deepika had stormed off for no apparent reason; hours later, Zu had opened the door to a gendarme. Mum was half standing, half leaning on his arm, her unfocused eyes still indignant as she yelled, 'Zu, tell this man, I just had to go to the shops for some milk.'

'To bed,' the French policeman had said with a sly wink that made Zu want to punch him. Mum had buckled into him and he'd had to heave her up. Dad had come rushing out of the kitchen just as she collapsed on the floor and Zu had never felt more soiled.

Deepika had stayed in bed for two days and when she finally came down she had no memory of the incident. Unsurprisingly, there were no more family holidays until after she died, when Tony took them to stay with Grandma and Grandpa Forbes on the Isle of Wight for a week of rain. No wonder she and her brothers were desperate to fly as far away as possible.

Didn't Tony feel the same? Didn't he yearn to backpack around Peru or canoe down the Mekong? Occasionally Zu had made vague noises about him visiting her in Grozny, but he always refused: it was too dangerous and he couldn't risk the boys losing another parent. She was relieved. Tony visiting would have meant her colleagues might start to become interested in her family, and the fewer details revealed on that score, the better.

But surely he must long to escape too, even if just for a few days? Whatever happened, Zu resolved she'd persuade him to take a long weekend break. She could even volunteer to go with him, she supposed.

What sports/exercise do you take regularly?

He cycled to work. Would that count? Have to.

What are your favourite foods? Do you enjoy cooking?

'Curries.' Dad used to joke – unfunnily – that he'd only married Mum because the Thali King had stopped giving him credit. He loved roasts too and he'd got pretty good at them. But it wasn't a question of enjoyment; he'd had to put a meal on the table every night, whether he liked it or not. The thought made Zu shudder. She'd done her best to help him at the time, the result being that she'd vowed never ever to be tied down like that again.

He didn't smoke. (Just writing that made Zu yearn for a Marlboro Light – imagine, apparently when her parents were teenagers you could actually smoke on the Tube and in the cinema!) He drank socially, Zu decided would be the best description. How would she describe her own habits? Luckily, no one was asking.

He had no pets, his kind of music was anything pre-historic, stuff before 1990, plus, tragically, Coldplay. Politically, he was a Leftie, much to Leela's confusion.

His favourite activities? Sleeping, Dad always said, but Zu didn't want him coming across as lazy. 'Listening to music,' she wrote dubiously.

What would you choose to be in a different life?

Christ only knew. 'A rock star,' she tried, but immediately scratched it out. Stop being facetious. She had to take Temperley seriously, it was the quickest route to solving the problem.

Now describe your soulmate.

Zu's mind went as blank as if the plug had been pulled. Soulmate. There was no such thing. Mum used to witter on about how she'd married Dad because they were destined to be together – well, look how that had turned out. What a stupid question. Much better to put 'What kind of person are you hoping to meet?' Something blander, less likely to get the hopes up of all the deluded romantics out there.

Her pen hovered, but nothing came to mind. She'd leave this one blank she decided, as the train came roaring out of the tunnel at Golders Green. It was over to Tony now, assuming he was interested – but with a little persuasion, Zu was sure he would be.

7

It was nearly three in the morning and Gillian Eversholt was lying in bed, watching the lights of passing cars flashing through her thin bedroom curtains. She'd been in the middle of a wonderful dream involving herself and Jon Hamm when her nearly sixteen-year-old daughter Holly had stuck her head round her door.

'Mum, we're back now! Just thought you'd like to know.'

'Thanks, darling,' Gillian replied groggily.

Since then, every time Gillian had been on the verge of dropping off again she'd been woken by a shriek of laughter or music that kept being turned to the max and then switched right down again.

It had been like this every night of the summer holidays. Gillian's mental health was only still intact because for the first three weeks Holly had been staying with her dad in Australia, meeting her newborn baby sister. But since her return, it had been unbridled hedonism.

She and her gang of hulking youths and Amazonian girls moved in a pack from house to house, systematically eating their way through the contents of carefully stocked larders and fridges, like an army of giant mutant locusts.

They kept night-shift hours, at their liveliest between about eleven p.m. and four a.m., though once Gillian had come downstairs at six in the morning to find them all mesmerized by a DVD. They never rose before noon.

They blocked toilets with tampons, they left cigarette butts on the patio.

Occasionally, Holly dropped a terrifying snippet of information about where they'd been and what they'd done: 'So then the police arrived and kicked us all out'; 'Freya decided to walk home alone but on the way this old pervert drew up beside her and said: "Hello, gorgeous," and offered her fifty pounds for a blow job!'; 'And so everyone ran to the exit and Jarmon got knocked down and, like, broke his ankle.'

They were teenagers, Gillian told herself, this was how they were supposed to spend their time. All right, she had spent her adolescence obsessing about ponies and practising the violin, but everyone told her Holly was entirely normal and there was no point getting worked up about it.

Until she was twelve, Holly had been an adorable child. She'd worn sparkly hairclips and her most treasured possession was her Sylvanian Families castle. When friends came over they consumed a biscuit and a beaker of juice, not three weeks' worth of Tesco shops.

She and Gillian used to spend hours arranging the rooms in the castle, inventing stories for the bunny rabbit families. The pair of them couldn't have been closer: they could spend hours lying on the bed together, just staring into each other's eyes, smothering each other in kisses. They liked watching trashy reality shows, huddled together under a blanket on the sofa, and reading all the books Gillian enjoyed as a child, from *The Little Princess* to *Ballet Shoes*. Gillian's sister, Alicia, had voiced the occasional warning that they were possibly too close, that perhaps

Billy, Gillian's husband, felt excluded from their tight duo, but what could Gillian do? Her daughter was the love of her life.

But shortly after turning thirteen, Holly had started to change. She began rimming her wide green eyes with kohl, the bunches disappeared and instead her hair was worn straight round her face. Her most treasured possession was no longer her Sylvanian Families castle but her phone, which beeped constantly like a life-support machine.

Sometimes she spent hours lying on the sofa, yawning hugely as if she'd just stepped off a transatlantic flight, but on other occasions she was feverishly cheerful, her eyes bright, her cheeks scarlet. Conversations with her were like sticking your hand in the waste disposal, the most innocuous questions met with snarling fury.

She stayed out past her curfew and then lied and said so-and-so's dad's car had broken down and they'd tried to call but there was no signal and Gillian would say she was going to check up on this but then didn't. Because the thought of not trusting her child was unbearable. Once, she came home obviously drunk, so Gillian grounded her and told her she couldn't go to her friend Tilly's party, but then Holly wept so pitiably and swore she'd never do it again and Gillian, of course, relented. Normally she'd have beaten herself up for her inconsistency, but things weren't normal because her husband Billy had just told her he'd met the love of *his* life. A love who wasn't Gillian but a twenty-one-year-old Australian barmaid called Perdita, and the two of them were going to live in Perth together.

Holly hadn't taken the news well. Neither had Gillian but, as always since she'd become a mother, her own shock and grief were overshadowed by her worries about how her child was suffering.

There was only one area where she'd prioritized her needs over her daughter's. Gillian had decided to sell their house in Hastings and move back to London. She'd never wanted to move to the seaside in the first place, leaving behind her sister and the friends she'd accumulated over years in various offices, followed by NCT and baby groups.

In Hastings, she'd been working so hard setting up her own business that she hadn't ever made proper 'mum' friends and now she needed all the support going. She would have stayed if Holly had really protested, but she'd taken the suggestion well. 'My school's a shithole,' she'd said, news to Gillian who'd spent all her savings on making sure they were in the right catchment area. 'The sooner I leave, the better.'

So they'd packed up just over a year ago now and to Gillian's relief Holly had settled quickly into Alison Feure Academy and had made all these friends who were now snoring downstairs.

With hindsight, Gillian wasn't so sure that north London was the best place to relocate to with a teenager. Holly appeared to spend most evenings loitering around Camden Tube, surrounded by vomiting drunks, angry bag ladies and the hungry homeless. Gillian felt faint every time she thought of her little baby there, but Holly loved her outings, rushing out of the front door confident and happy, shouting (Gillian was sure) lies over her shoulder about where she was going, then returning, eyes bright, gabbling: 'And then the man waved a bottle in Jarmon's face and said he'd swing for him but we just laughed . . .'

Gillian drifted off only to be woken what seemed like minutes later by the alarm shrilling. Eight a.m., time to take out Waffle, the Labradoodle. Oh well, she thought blearily, not daring even to glance at her crumpled face in the mirror. They did say any sleep you had before midnight was the most beneficial and she'd been in bed at nine, sad old lady that she was. Looking on the bright side, she still wasn't on top of last week's workload, and now, with the house quiet, would be an ideal time to catch up.

She opened the door of the living room, which doubled as her office. The air was thick with teenage hormones and the stench of cheap perfume, cigarettes and alcohol. Pubs used to smell like that before smoking was banned. Holly, as a child, had pointed at smokers, yelling: 'What's he *doing*? He's killing himself!' But now, just as the rest of the world was outlawing nicotine, her lungs were furred with tar, she wheezed incessantly and oxygen was the enemy.

Two people of indeterminate sex were asleep on the sofa and one was on the floor. In the kitchen she found that all the cereal and all the milk, as well as half the contents of the fridge, had vanished. There were dirty plates everywhere, with a couple of burnt pans in the sink. Gillian had been looking forward to her weekly treat of a croissant, but naturally the bread bin was empty too.

She opened the giant packet of prunes in which she hid her Bendicks Bittermints. Phew. Still there. Life wasn't worth living if someone had snaffled your last Bittermint. Billy used to do it all the time – even on their first romantic weekend away together she'd come out of the shower to see him shoving the chocolate on her pillow into his mouth. If only she'd spotted the signs, she would have been out of there like a greyhound from the traps. But if she had there would have been no Holly and that thought was unbearable.

'Come on, Waffle,' she said. 'We're going to the shops.'

In the deli on the corner, she decided to treat herself to a loaf of Pain Poilâne, some of the succulent-looking pâté and a chunk of overripe French cheese.

The sulky French assistant, who was always cross despite having a flattering pixie cut that would suit only one woman in eight thousand and a knack for jauntily knotting scarves around her neck, rang up the bill. Nine pounds seventy-eight, she'd been suckered again. Feeling cross with her extravagance, Gillian opened her purse and frowned. Last night she'd gone to the cashpoint and taken out two hundred pounds. But now there was – nothing.

Perhaps she'd not put the money in the purse but in her pocket. She felt in her jeans, in her jacket. She must have left it at home somewhere.

'Sorry, but I'm going to have to pay by card,' she said brightly. The assistant scowled and pointed at a sign.

'No cards for less than ten pounds.'

'Oh! Well.' Gillian looked around wildly. A box of fancy biscuits. She'd hide them in the prunes as well. 'OK now?'

'I suppose,' the assistant agreed sourly.

All the way home, Gillian wondered where the money could have gone. She must have shoved it in the bottom of her other handbag, though why she would have done that, she couldn't imagine. Had it fallen out of her pocket? Unlikely. Back home, she looked for it as much as it was possible to look for anything without disturbing the rancid, slumbering bodies.

Eventually she gave up and toasted the bread, lathering pâté on one slice and cheese on the other. She tried to ignore the urge to start hunting again and browsed through the Saturday supplements, as usual feeling guilty and cross because her house bore no relation to the ones featured there, her wardrobe was utterly inadequate and her social circle didn't even begin to compare with the superwomen featured.

Hating herself, yet unable to stop, she began reading about Philomena Cross, a model who'd just launched a successful range of gloves and scarves, despite recently splitting from her millionaire partner and father of her two sons.

'I think divorce has put me in the best possible place,' she says. 'Every morning the boys and I just jump up and down on the bed singing because life is so fantastic. Being a single mother is just so cool.'

Gillian flung down the paper in irritation. Of course. Being a single mum was *so* cool. No loneliness, no back-breaking slog. Just jumping up and down on the bed singing. Of course, Philomena no doubt had teams of nannies, which would make life somewhat easier, but still . . . did she really relish fighting to get the kids to bed, before watching a solitary DVD and climbing under her Hungarian goose-down duvet alone? Were you in the best possible place lying awake alone until two a.m., when your child crashed in, obviously drunk and reeking of cigarettes? What was so cool about having no one to share your worries with when your child's teacher said she was lagging in maths, when all the other mums were boasting about how their child was doing GCSE two years early?

'Yeah, right, Philomena,' she sneered.

'You all right, Gillian?' said a sly voice at the door. 'Talking to yourself?'

She looked up. Holly's best friend, Freya, was smiling pleasantly at her, all honeyed limbs and golden locks. Gillian tried to like Freya but sometimes she found it hard. Freya had been cast as Dorothy in the school production of *The Wizard of Oz* and was predicted perfect GCSEs. But it didn't do to go down that road or you'd end up like Mrs Prior, mother of Gillian's arch enemy at school, Arabella, who had joined Friends Reunited as if she'd been in their year, clearly to check that Arabella was still outshining her schoolmates, twenty-five years on.

'I was talking to Waffle,' Gillian said with as much dignity as she could muster.

'If you say so.' Freya opened a cupboard. 'Shit. There's nothing here. And I'm starving.'

Holly stuck her head round the door, her red-gold curls bouncing round her face, making her look like a Botticelli angel. Had there ever been a more beautiful child?

'Hiya, Mum.'

'There's no food,' said Freya.

'What will we do?' Holly asked, as if a tsunami was advancing on their two-bedroomed cottage.

'You ate it all last night.' Gillian's voice was neutral. Again she wondered where her money could have gone. *Could . . .? But no.*

'Shall we go out?' Holly asked. 'Go to the caff for breakfast? What do you think, guys?'

'Yeah,' said a couple of male voices behind her. Gillian recognized Damian and Jarmon, both pupils at the local private boys' school where mothers sold their kidneys to gain their child a place. She wasn't thrilled that boys were staying the night, but at least those two seemed good, upstanding, cricket- and rugby-playing types who wouldn't lead her daughter off the straight and narrow.

Stop worrying about Holly, Gillian told herself as the gang crashed out. *Think about yourself for a change*. If she had someone to go out with on a Saturday night, perhaps she wouldn't be clinging needily to the dream of the two of them staying in together, curled up in front of *Strictly*, sharing a tub of ice cream, like in ye golden days of yore.

Gillian had dabbled in online dating, always with disastrous consequences. All the men fell into definite categories. There were the ones who went on about wanting a relationship but then, when they eventually met, rapidly informed her there was no spark but said they would happily engage in casual sex with her. There were the ones who talked to her for months and months, but never asked her out, or the ones when the first date went brilliantly, then you never heard from them again. The ones who were witty and delightful on screen and handsome in person, who then announced in a solemn voice that they were the reincarnation of Guy Fawkes. Her friends had had even worse experiences – take June, who'd actually been introduced to one guy's mother, asked to sign her joint birthday card with him, only to be dumped the very next day. By text.

Now, however, for the first time in months, she felt her attitude towards men softening. She couldn't watch her daughter turn into a woman while she became a shrivelled, sexless husk. But how to change things? Perhaps she needed to try the arranged approach again, but this time throw more money at it? She was a freelance PR so her income varied wildly, but last year had been surprisingly successful.

She opened her laptop and Googled 'dating agencies exclusive'. Biting her lip, she leant forward to study the results. She'd just have to remember to delete her history before Holly logged on for her hourly Facebook session. If her daughter discovered what she was up to, she'd be mincemeat.

8

A week had passed and Monday morning rolled round again. Tony yawned, turned over and saw the sun already high in the sky through the gap in the curtains. It was going to be another scorcher, he thought, glancing at his antique clock radio.

Just gone six. For years this had been the boys' natural waking hour.

Deepi used to groan in despair at their wake-up chirrup of 'Morning time!' followed by an almighty thud as they threw themselves over their cot bars, and the pad-pad as they teetered across the landing into their parents' bed. How adorable, most people would have thought, they were babies, they just wanted to be with their mummy and daddy. They didn't know that grown-ups needed their sleep. But to Deepi, the boys had simply represented exhaustion and misery.

Shortly after she died, of course, everything had changed and his sons had morphed into adolescents, who never wanted to get up at all. Every morning Tony had had to bang on their door, yelling 'School! Get up! Now!' like Sergeant Foley in *An Officer and a Gentleman*, while they groaned and protested.

And now the day he'd once longed for had arrived when, with no one to chivvy, Tony could sleep until the decadent hour of half past eight and all day at weekends.

But, of course, he'd long gone native. Hardly surprising, given that most nights he was in bed by ten and by dawn had almost always slept enough – though whether he wanted to get out of bed was another matter. They did say you needed less sleep as you got older. Which reminded him. It was his birthday. Forty-eight today.

'Shit,' Tony said.

Deepi once had made a big deal out of birthdays: decorating the house, huge cake, an elaborate dinner, piles of presents. After she'd lost interest, Tony had done his best to keep up appearances for the boys' sake. But now they'd gone and the pretence was over. The house was unbedizened, the fridge contained nothing but a pint of semi-skimmed milk and some cranberry juice. The only indication that today was any different to any other was the small stack of cards on the bedside table. No parcels, not even from Zu. At around ten the previous night she'd handed him an envelope. 'This is a bit of a punt, but let me know what you think,' she'd said. Tickets, Tony had decided, possibly for Bruce Springsteen or maybe Elvis Costello, he was touring soon. Either would be great. He'd ask Beth to come with him, he hadn't seen much of her lately outside work. To his surprise, she'd declined the annual barbecue invitation, saying she had other plans, and Tony had wondered if it was her way of hinting that she felt taken for granted. Either way, with the boys gone, he should up his game with her.

His phone began ringing. Probably his parents, calling from the bungalow in Shanklin, though it was early for them. Early for anyone. Surely not bad news? Tony's insides shrivelled when the phone rang at strange hours; it had been one in the morning when the police had come to the door about Deepi.

'Hello?' he blurted in terror.

'Dad!' said a croaky young man's voice.

Tony sat up. 'Kieran! Are you OK?'

'Happy birthday, Dad!'

Tony's throat tightened. He'd last seen Kieran four days ago, when he'd waved him off at Heathrow. Since then he had emailed a couple of times, saying he'd arrived safely and settled in and, all importantly, was online. But hearing his voice was another thing altogether. Tony still couldn't believe that his youngest-by-ten-minutes son's voice had even broken, let alone that he was capable of travelling alone to Africa to teach orphans.

'How's it going?'

'Great. The others are nice, there's this guy Felix who's cool and a girl called Linny who makes us all laugh, she's like "God, the people here are really poor" and she's like "The shower isn't always hot and the toilet sometimes gets blocked." The kids are cute and the staff are great, they're like "Why don't you go to Lake Malawi for the weekend?"'

'Be careful, won't you, Kier? Don't swim. There's Bilharzia in that water.'

'Er, like you are the first person to tell me that.' Tony knew Kieran would be rolling his eyes. Despite everything they'd experienced, the boys still considered themselves immortal.

'Take your malaria pills.'

'I will. I am. Promise.'

'Have you heard from Ro?'

'A couple of emails. Sounds like he's having fun.'

'Good.' Tony hadn't heard a word. Which was hardly surprising. Ro had nagged and nagged for a mobile since he was seven but when he finally received one for his thirteenth birthday he seemed to have immediately programmed it to ignore all Tony's calls and texts – especially those that came in after midnight, demanding to know his whereabouts.

Tony was doing his best not to worry, reassuring himself that thousands of kids went off to Thailand every day of the week and came to no harm. Hell, he'd done it himself. But you just never knew. It was bad enough having Zu in Chechnya, without her brothers both following her. Tony always told himself that lightning never struck twice, that their family had already had its share of grief and woe. But life didn't work like that. Tragedies weren't like infectious diseases, dreadful at the time but immunizing you from future harm. Another bad thing could happen anywhere, anytime.

'Listen, Dad,' Kieran said. 'I've got to go, the bell's ringing for classes to start. But have a great day, yeah? What's the plan?'

'Three wild guesses! Giovanni's, of course.'

'What? You're cutting out on me.'

'I said, we're going –'

'I can't hear you, Dad! But I love you. Talk soon, OK. Bye!'

'Bye.' Tony stared at his phone as if it were a rare and precious treasure. He couldn't brood about the boys. He turned instead to his cards.

First he opened his parents'. A painting of a pond with

ducks on it. *Happy Birthday, Tony. With love from Mum and Dad x.* A cheque fluttered out. A thousand pounds. Thank Christ. Tony had been relying on that to get the rotting sash windows in the living room replaced. He'd call them later to thank them. Mum hadn't exactly stepped up to the plate after Deepi had died, she could never come and help with the boys because 'How would Dad manage on his own?' Tony never retorted that his dad could easily operate a microwave. What was the point? His parents had been generous financially and for that he was grateful.

Leela's next. A Jiffy bag containing a card and a Ralph Lauren tie wrapped in blue and gold paper. Tony grinned. Typical of his mother-in-law, she knew he never wore ties – why would he, in his line of work? But it was the thought that counted. Leela hadn't even known when his birthday was, much less acknowledged it, before Deepi died.

Finally he picked up Zu's sky-blue envelope. He ripped it open and a card bearing a photo of Joe Strummer fell out. But no tickets.

Dear Dad

Happy Birthday. I've got a bit of a weird one for you this time ... It's trial membership of an 'introductions agency' for a month. I know, I know. Don't be insulted. But what have you got to lose? They're called Temperley, I've been in to see them and they're totally reputable. I've emailed you so you can Google the link.

Love,

Zu x

Tony's hands grew cold. It was as if someone had opened a cupboard door and seen all his laundry, lying higgledy-piggledy where he'd chucked it. He'd done his very best to conceal his loneliness but it must be laughably visible to all – like a dodgy comb-over.

Zu thought he needed a girlfriend. He'd wondered if she wondered about his love life, but of course they'd never talked about it. He showered, dressed and had a slice of toast, expecting Zu to appear, keeping his face fixed in a 'What a great idea, but hey! No need!' expression, but she didn't come down and in the end he had to leave for work.

As he cycled, he thought back to the first couple of weeks after Deepi died, weeks that blurred, like the spokes of a turning wheel. The doorbell never stopped ringing, people kept arriving to help out with the boys. Leela turned up with so many meals that they had to buy an extra freezer to accommodate them all, though Tony could barely eat a mouthful. He preferred whisky. He was so torn up, he never felt drunk and no one ever said anything, but looking back he must have reeked and slurred, just like his dear, late wife.

Everywhere there were these reminders of Deepi he couldn't bear to get rid of. Her book, spine bent open on the bedside table with its cover image of a woman in a long white dress holding high heels as she walked along a beach. Her knickers and T-shirts were in the washing basket. (Leela had been the one to launder them in the end and then do God knows what with them.) Her hairbrush was filled with strands of her black hair, the bathroom cabinets overflowed with her clutter. Her stash of whisky and gin bottles was hidden in the base of the grandfather clock.

Again, Leela had been the one to sort it all out, to dispose of the evidence, he had no idea how or where. Tony resented the way she'd come from nowhere to being their linchpin almost overnight, but he knew he could never have made it through that time without her. In the end, Leela had been the one to have a word with him, to impress on him that – for the children's sake – he needed to start living in the present, absorbing his suffering rather than trying to ignore it.

He returned to work after three weeks, fugged up with tranquillizers. Despite them, tears ran down his face as he cycled in but he quickly realized it was good to be back in some kind of routine, to deal with clients who were pissed off because he had to send away for a part and who had absolutely no interest in Tony's personal life – or, actually, scrub that, probably would have been fascinated had he chosen to share the details with them – but who would never know why the genial cello-repair chap had suddenly become so taciturn.

Occasionally someone would ask tactlessly if, in some way, Deepi's death hadn't come as a relief. Tony knew where they were coming from, but it wasn't like that at all. Yes, their life together in recent years had mainly been hell, but as long as Deepi had been alive, even when the hospital called in the middle of the night saying she'd been admitted covered in cuts and bruises, there'd always been hope they could make her better.

After all, when she had been sober – and that had been the majority of the time they'd been together – no one had been more fun, more engaging. And there was always a reason for the drinking: it had been raining for days, she had a headache, she was upset about the rift with Leela, the children were stressing her out, Tony wasn't earning enough. Perhaps if they'd worked harder at tackling those issues (obviously they couldn't have done anything about the rain), the drinking would have stopped. Tony still tortured himself, wondering how he could have done it better.

Gradually, outside support started to die away. Leela visited less frequently. Picking the boys up from school, going in for parent-teacher meetings, watching concerts, he felt so isolated, one father amongst the dozens of mothers, most of whom fell silent as he passed or pretended to be furiously absorbed in a notice on the PTA board. But he preferred them to the ones who had made their interest in a newly single man loud and clear. He'd kept them at bay, but at the same time as he started weaning himself off the pills and his sex drive resurfaced he'd started to keep a vague eye open for women to sleep with.

He'd indulged in some mild crushes on some of the twins' friends' mums, though the ones he fancied always turned out to have husbands with names like Dirk who ran boxing clubs and had tattooed knuckles.

Naturally he'd gone online and browsed various dating sites, always meticulously deleting his history afterwards. He'd even emailed a few who sounded interesting and who – no coincidence, obviously – also bore a striking resemblance to Deepi. But the exchanges had always fizzled out before he actually met anyone. She'd reveal that she owned a Gareth Gates album or say something like 'You know it wasn't Al-Qaeda who brought down the Twin Towers?', and Tony would lose interest.

In the end, about eighteen months after Deepi died, he'd slept with Pauline, a cellist who'd come to him with some broken strings. He used to cycle round to her house in his lunch break. After the first time, secretly – and pathetically – he'd cried with relief and guilt. It had continued for another six months before she'd moved to Norwich and neither made any effort to continue things.

After that there'd been a couple more flings, one with Mairead, who was a single mum at Zu's school, and one with Cecilia, another divorcee, who'd brought in her son's viola to have its strings tightened, *fnaar, fnaar*. But there was nothing Tony had felt confident enough about to tell the boys. He just couldn't face shattering what pathetic equilibrium they had achieved by bringing a new woman on to the scene. Not until he was absolutely sure things with that woman were going to work out.

And they never quite did. Mairead insisted they always ate in Pizza Hut because she had a load of two-for-one vouchers. Cecilia, he suspected, hadn't wanted a date at all, but someone to endlessly mull over the pitfalls of the eleven plus with and to reassure her that yes, indeed, the system was unfairly weighted to rich people who could afford tutors.

He'd gently informed them both it was going to have to stop because he wasn't over Deepi. As excuses went, it was practically cast iron and the women retreated gracefully.

The therapist he saw once a month, who was called

Morna and served tea with far too much milk, told him he had to allow himself to love again. Tony told her he would. When the time was right, he added to himself.

Which he guessed was now, he thought, slogging up the hill to the workshop. But *he* should have taken the initiative, not Zu.

Anyway, for the past three years he hadn't thought about it that much – partly because he'd been so busy with the boys and work, but also because of Beth, who'd joined the business repairing brass instruments. Beth was completely different to Deepi: big-boned when his wife had been what shops referred to as petite, mousy-haired rather than raven black, and robust – in her clothes and behaviour – when Deepi had been so perfumed and soft and feminine.

They'd got it together one night after the pub, when he'd had a couple of pints more than usual and, under her skilful questioning, confided in her about how hard it was to bring up two teenage boys and keep an eye on an angry twenty-something daughter, whose idea of a good time seemed to be heading for godforsaken corners of the earth that everyone else was fleeing.

He'd walked her to the bus stop and bent to peck her cheek and suddenly they were having a surprisingly passionate kiss. They'd ended up taking a minicab back to her minuscule, book- and CD-cluttered flat in Enfield and had energetic and uninhibited sex, after which he'd had a cup of tea and taken a minicab home.

It didn't feel like a betrayal being with her and, even better, she seemed comfortable with the arrangement: not asking if she could stay the night or be 'introduced' to the kids (of course, she'd met them loads of times in passing). She seemed quite happy with their mid-afternoon trysts in the back room of Forbes Musical Instrument Repairs, when Barry was out seeing to a keyboard. She took the relationship for what it was – stuck in a continuous present of decent sex, silly jokes, a mutual hatred for anything connected to Simon Cowell and a shared passion for *Flight of the Conchords*.

But, recently, things had gone rather quiet. It had been nearly a month since they'd had a night out, at the end of which they'd snogged but then she'd said she was tired, so he hadn't gone back to hers. Tony resolved to take her out to dinner. Not with him and Zu tonight, that would be too full-on, but later in the week. He'd take her somewhere really nice: not the Chinese Garden round the corner which was their regular haunt, but somewhere in the West End. The Ivy, if he could get a table. Tony had never been to The Ivy in his life and had no idea what kind of restaurant it was, but he had a feeling it was the place you took a woman if you really meant business.

He pushed open the workshop's black door, excited by his plan.

Beth was standing at her bench. Radio Three gurgled in the background.

'All right,' she said, barely glancing up from her euphonium. 'Guess who owns this? A nine-year-old. Her mum told me she'd bought it because it would help her secure her daughter's place at a grammar school. "Anything that helps her stand out from the crowd," she said. Can you believe? I'm almost tempted to sabotage it.'

'Well, please don't,' Tony said, heading to the kettle.

Didn't she know it was his birthday, he thought, pathetically. Last year, he seemed to recall a quick fumble in the kitchenette but she'd probably not marked the date in her calendar in red pen. 'Where's Barry?'

'Repairing that organ in Haywards Heath.'

'Of course.'

'So what's the news?' Beth still seemed strangely absorbed in her work. 'Good weekend?'

'Yeah. Quiet. How about you?'

She shrugged. 'Not a lot. We . . . I went to see a movie.'

We? 'Oh yeah? Anything good?'

'Mmm. *Cries from the Heart.*'

'Oh.' Tony had been hoping to see that. Maybe Zu would accompany him instead. He swallowed. 'And?'

'I really enjoyed it.' She kept her eyes on the instrument. Tony picked up the violin with loose strings off his bench.

'It's my birthday,' he tried desperately.

'Really?' Beth looked up and smiled. She had a small gap between her front teeth which Tony had always found oddly alluring. 'Congratulations. Sorry I forgot.'

'We're going out for dinner tonight to celebrate,' he continued. 'I was wondering . . .'

Beth was still smiling. Not an overjoyed 'I thought you'd never ask' kind of smile but more an 'Oh shit, how do I get out of this' grin. Tony's lower abdomen performed a handstand.

'How about dinner in the week?' he tried hastily. 'Just you and me. I thought –'

'Tony,' she began as her phone started ringing in her back pocket. She looked at the Caller ID and her normally pale face suddenly turned a rather becoming shade of rose. 'Hello?' Her voice was far softer than normal, as if it had been drenched in Lenor. 'Hi. Mmm. Hang on a second.' She put her hand over the mouthpiece. 'I'll just take this outside,' she said, her hand already on the door.

A hot, squirmy feeling shot along Tony's body, through his legs, up his torso and into his neck and head. Beth had a new boyfriend. Here he'd been, smugly assuming he was in the driving seat, when all along she'd been seeing someone else and obviously dreading telling him in case she lost her job. What must she think of him? Probably that he was a sad, elderly pervert preying on young female members of staff when no doubt her boyfriend was thirty and owned a Learjet.

He had to move on. Fast. Take Zu up on her offer. Find a woman who was really suitable for him. Take control of the oars, before life carried him off downstream and over the weir.

Beth came back into the room looking nervous. He forced himself to make eye contact with her.

'Well, so if you fancied a pizza or whatever later in the week to mark my being even older than I already was, then . . .' He shrugged.

Beth's relief was palpable. 'A pizza would be *great*,' she squeaked, bending back over the euphonium. 'Maybe make it a lunch, then Barry can come too.' She looked up briefly, but bent her head again before making eye contact. 'Better get on! The mad mum's coming to collect this at five.'

9

Zu opened her eyes and grabbed her phone from the bedside table, squinting to check the time. 'Shit!' It had gone eight. She'd really meant to have breakfast with Dad, to say happy birthday, to see what he made of her present. But then she'd gone on to Skype last night and ended up chatting to Monika from Hungary who was now in Dushanbe but with whom she'd shared a room in Grozny for two months. Then she'd been all wound up and needed to read for ages before she was remotely sleepy and now . . .

She ran downstairs to hear the door shutting. She opened it just in time to see Tony's bicycle disappearing round the corner.

'Shit.'

She stomped into the kitchen. On the counter was a note:

Meet me at Giovanni's at seven. X

No mention of the card.

Did he like his gift? It didn't sound like it. Zu would have been furious if Dad had tried to pair her off, but then Zu and Tony were fire and ice, Congolese jungle and Siberian tundra. Maybe he wanted to thank her in person.

'Bollocks,' Zu told herself. She didn't do delusion. Tony hated her present and — worse — by giving it to him, she had given him the green light for a meaningful *talk*. Why hadn't she gone for a pair of socks?

Fed up, she went back to bed for a couple of hours and then spent most of the day on the phone, following up various job leads and getting nowhere. Tony still hadn't texted her when she left for Giovanni's at six forty-five.

Back in the day, they'd always gone there whenever Mum declared she'd had enough of curries and poppadoms. The owners, Paolo and Susanna (no one had a clue who Giovanni was), still made a huge fuss of them and put extra olives on their pizzas. Zu knew it was out of pity. There'd been that night when Mum had got very noisy after insisting on ordering a second bottle (she'd been boozing at home all afternoon already) and then she'd fallen flat on her face on the way out and a sort of white foam had dribbled from her mouth. Zu thought she'd die of shame but Paolo had made some excuse about a slippery floor and ever since had been even kinder to them.

The food wasn't gourmet but the portions were enormous and the garlic bread was world class. Zu occasionally suggested going elsewhere, but Tony would put his foot down. Family traditions were to be maintained at all costs.

Tony was waiting at their usual corner table, Paolo's faded 'Happy Birthday' banner hanging limply above his head. At the sight of Zu, he stood up, looking strained. Her last hope died.

'Sweetheart.' He hugged her, as she pulled off her headphones. 'Sit down. How's your day been?'

'Good, really good.' If Zu had been run over by a truck while simultaneously attacked by a lion she would have said the same.

'You look pretty.'

Zu snorted. Time to cut to the chase: 'So. I take it you opened your card?'

'I did.'

'And . . .?'

The pause seemed to go on forever, like when they were announcing the results in one of the reality TV shows Anjali was addicted to, but eventually Tony said, 'I thought it was a great idea!'

'Really?'

His expression was unreadable. 'Yeah. I mean, at first I was a bit surprised, but then I could see no reason why not. You're right. I have been in a bit of a rut and I do need to get out there and meet more people.'

'So will you get in touch with them?' Zu grinned, relieved.

'Absolutely! Tomorrow!'

She considered reaching for his hand, but rejected the thought as far too soppy. Instead, she swallowed and said, 'Dad. I don't want you to think I'm trying to replace Mum.' Though God knows, there were enough times when she would have happily swapped her for anyone who didn't cry in their bedroom with the blinds down, the telly yapping to itself from its stand on the wall and clothes and snotty tissues balled up everywhere.

'I don't think that.'

'But we have to move on?' she tried.

'We have to move on,' he agreed, after a second.

Zu clenched her fists. Why was he like this? Why was he stuck in the past? He knew Mum had been a night-mare, so why couldn't he escape her? She looked around. 'Shall we order some drinks?'

'Good idea.' Tony waved ineffectually for Paolo, but the owner was busy flirting with two middle-aged ladies. He sat back in his chair and reached for a breadstick instead.

'So?' he asked. 'What news on the job front?'

Ah, good. Safe subject, if an annoying one. 'Nothing,' Zu said. 'All quiet. No one hiring. I've been looking outside Russian-speaking countries but they're quiet too.'

'You don't have to go away again,' Tony said. 'There must be plenty of jobs here you could do.'

'Or something in Russia that's not aid-related,' Zu said.

'You really don't want to stay in England?'

Oh, God. 'I'm young. I want to see the world.'

'I understand.'

Zu's efforts to keep a lid on things failed. 'Dad, don't look so sorry for yourself.'

'I'm not looking sorry for myself.' Tony reached for another breadstick. He looked like Fiona Bruce interviewing Prince Philip. 'I just worry about you. Any parent would. People are kidnapped where you work. People are executed.'

'People *have been*. Past tense. Not any more. We have plenty of protection.' Zu thought of Vladimir, one of their bodyguards. They'd had a brief and physically incredible relationship until Vlad had asked her to meet his family and she'd had to end it. Amazing body, though. Those arms . . .

'I still worry,' Tony said.

'You never worried when I first went away,' Zu snapped. 'Why all the fretting now?'

'I did worry. I've always worried.'

77

'*I* didn't notice.' Zu knew she was being childish, but she couldn't help it.

Tony sighed. 'Zu, you've been amazing for years. I know it can't have been easy with so much attention on Mum, and then the boys. But I've never for a second stopped looking out for you. I didn't stop you going to Chechnya . . .'

'You couldn't have.'

'Well, I didn't share my reservations. I let you go. But I'm telling you now. It's great to have you back and I'm not relishing you leaving again. That's all I'm saying.'

'Fine.' Zu looked around. Thank God. Paolo was advancing. She needed a drink fast. Why did Dad always do this to her, make sure she felt guilty for leaving him, when he must know why she didn't want to stay? She wished the boys were here; they'd always managed to hog the limelight with their chatter and teasing. With them gone, she felt horribly exposed – like in one of her dreams when she was walking stark naked through the streets of Grozny.

'Zu! How are you?' exclaimed Paolo.

'Never better.' Zu smiled as brightly as she could. 'Now, seeing as we have a birthday to celebrate, how about a bottle of Prosecco?'

*

Temperley Bureau Questionnaire – Strictly Private and Confidential

Name: *Tony Forbes*

Height: ~~*Five foot eight in.*~~ *Five foot six ½ inches*

Date of birth: *11 July ~~1968~~1963*

~~Single~~ / ~~Separated~~ / ~~Divorced~~ / ~~Divorcing~~/Widowed / ~~Have co-habited~~

What kind of work have you done in your life? What do you do now? Do you enjoy your work?
Used to be session violinist. Now run own instrument repair shop. I enjoy it ~~but work's a bit thin on the ground right now and I miss playing the violin.~~

How do you see your future plans?
Until I've paid off the mortgage and seen my sons through uni, no big plans.

What is your nationality and ethnic background? Is it important to you and would you like to say why?
White British. ~~Hardly, otherwise I wouldn't have married a Hindu girl, I'd have married a girl from the Isle of Wight, which would mean my wife would probably not have had severe post-natal depression and would still be alive.~~ No, it's not.

What papers and magazines do you take?
Read the Guardian *and* Observer. *Enjoy* Private Eye.

Mention some books that you have read and enjoyed recently:
First Light *by Geoffrey Wellum,* The Race of a Lifetime: How Obama Won the White House, *currently reading* War and Peace ~~*(again) but find I fall asleep most nights before I manage more than a page.*~~

Have you been to the cinema or theatre recently?
Not ~~for about twenty years~~ recently, but I'd like to go more often.

What sort of films and plays do you like?
Favourite films are ~~The Great Escape, Phil & Ted's Excellent Adventure, The Dam Busters, Bridge over the River Kwai, Groundhog Day~~ La Grande Illusion, Battleship Potemkin, Three Colours: Blue.

Describe your educational background:
A levels, degree in music, postgraduate studies at Royal College of Music.

Do you enjoy travelling and have you ever lived abroad? What are your favourite countries?
~~Used to love travelling before domestic obligations took over and ran out of money.~~ Keen traveller, love France, Italy, Turkey, would love to go further afield to Far East and South America.

What sports/exercise do you take regularly?
Cycling.

What are your favourite foods? Do you enjoy cooking?
Love most foods, especially Thai and Indian. Would love to learn to cook better.

Do you smoke?
No.

Do you drink?
Socially.

Do you have any pets?
No.

What kind of music do you like?
Classical, especially Mozart, Bach, Handel. The Clash, The Damned,

The Only Ones, Elvis Costello, Joe Jackson, Talking Heads, Ramones, Amy Winehouse, Coldplay. ~~Andrew Lloyd Webber~~

What is your political point of view?
Disillusioned Leftie.

What are your favourite activities?
Cycling, attending classical concerts (would like to do more of this), reading, long walks.

What would you choose to be in a different life?
A concert violinist.

Now describe your soulmate:
~~I was married to her. She became ill. It wasn't her fault, it was~~ ~~chemicals in her body set off by having a baby. But she wasn't easy.~~ ~~So, thank you, I don't believe in soulmates any more.~~ *Just looking for someone I can have a laugh with, relax with, eat with, watch films with, ideally grow old with.*

Having only just managed to salvage the birthday dinner, Zu resisted pestering Tony about when he was going to contact the agency. After all, there were plenty of other things to worry about. Her job-hunting efforts were getting her nowhere and because she hated being at home she was going out as often as possible and her meagre savings were dwindling fast. Her feet weren't just itchy, they were burning with the desire to escape.

When her phone rang on the Thursday displaying a new number, she grabbed it, praying it was Oxfam, who, word had it, might be recruiting for their Moscow office.

'Zulekha?' Bollocks. Not Oxfam, though it was an eastern-European accent.

'Masha. How are you?'

'Fine. Sick of this hot weather. My skin is too pale for it. We install air-con in house, I can't wait. But enough of me. What of you? Or, more importantly, your father? Why haven't we heard from him? Our ladies clamour to meet him.'

Zu envisaged hundreds of love-struck women in floaty, flowery dresses and, for some reason, jaunty berets; women who were creative, who went to wine-tasting events, who collected pebbles to make bad collages and went on walking holidays in Tuscany. She didn't want to give them false hope.

'He said he'd do it, but if he hasn't called he hasn't called. He was probably just trying to shut me up. We may have to let this go.'

'No need to be defeatist,' Masha said briskly.

But Zu was emboldened. 'Look, he said he'd do it, but he must have changed his mind. And, anyway, I've got no money. I can't find a job and my savings are running out. I can't afford the membership, even with your discount. Sorry to have wasted your time.'

'Don't be silly. There is no way I'm letting jewel like your father out of our grasp. He's having complimentary lifetime membership as of now.'

This put Zu off her stride. She tried to get back on track. 'No, no, really –'

'I insist!' Masha paused, then said, 'And, Zulekha, you said you were looking for job?'

'Yes, but nothing's about at the moment.'

'Not true!' Masha crowed triumphantly. 'We need an assistant. And you would be perfect. Beautiful, clearly intelligent. And you speak Russian.'

'Me?' It was ludicrous. In a dating agency? Zulekha was about as romantic as a tube of thrush cream.

'I know this is out of blue but my instincts never lie. What are you?'

'What do you mean?'

'I'm Gemini,' Masha said. 'And you are . . .?'

'I'm Taurus,' Zu said warily. People who went on about star signs were one of her many pet hates. So one in twelve people in the world were all meant to have exactly the same personality just because of their birthdays? Hitler was a Taurus, incidentally. She decided not to tell Masha that.

'The bull. I love it! Tenacious and focused. Just what we need. My husband, Gary, is Aquarius and can be so *vague*. He still can't decide about kitchen worktop.' She paused, then, 'Zulekha. Help us out. It'd only be for a few weeks until we find someone permanent.' Another pause before the killer hook. 'Maybe then I can help you find other job back in Russia.'

Zu's heart began to beat faster. 'What would you pay me?'

'We must discuss this,' Masha said smoothly. 'A fair amount.' There was a tiny pause and then she added, 'So how about you come in at ten tomorrow?'

For a second, Zu hesitated, but then she said: 'Ten's fine.' After all, why not? It would only be for a couple of weeks until something decent came up and she could keep her Russian ticking over. She'd be earning some cash, seeing life, having an unexpected experience – and Zu liked unexpected experiences. There'd be loads of funny stories to entertain Anj with and if she kept in with Masha she was sure she'd help her find another job.

'And will you please persuade your father to get in touch?'

'I'll ask him. Er, I'll see you in the morning then.'

'I look forward to it,' said Masha, her tone making it clear that she was the kind of woman who was rarely crossed.

Gillian was sitting in the lobby of Leela Enterprises Inc., a four-roomed Portakabin on an industrial estate in Stone-bridge Park, having arrived punctually for her second meeting with her latest client. Gillian was pleased to have won the Leela gig. It was a decent-sized brand but it could definitely do with a push. It was weird, she thought, how the more she was convinced she'd failed as a mother, the more her work prospered. No doubt the cake-baking, stay-at-home mothers whose houses she collected Holly from muttered about how she'd given so much to her business she had no energy left for her own daughter.

Gillian shrugged. If she didn't have the business, she had nothing. And for now she had all sorts of ideas about how to reposition the Leela brand and a folder under her arm to show Leela herself.

Leela's PA, who was a frightened-looking woman in her forties wearing unfortunate jeggings, said Leela was run-ning half an hour late. Gillian jabbed at her iPhone – she'd become shamefully obsessed with her Gina the Giraffe app; she had to feed, water and play with Gina regularly to keep her alive, no doubt as some sort of Holly substitute – when it started ringing.

'Hello, you,' she said to her sister, Alicia.

'Happy birthday to you, squashed tomatoes and stew. You look like a monkey and you live in the zoo.'

Gillian laughed. 'At least you're not singing: "How old are you now?"'

'That's because I already know. And have festooned your house in banners just in case any of your neighbours are ignorant of the fact. Forty-three today. Hip hip hooray.'

'Ha ha ha.'

'I'll always be younger than you. When you're one hundred and five, I'll be one hundred and three. I'll give you my present when I see you. You're going to love it.'

'I hope so.' Despite her advanced age, Gillian's heart fluttered venally. Alicia always gave her great presents – quite right too, given that she was married to a banker and lived in an enormous house with a tennis court in Balham, and even though she didn't work had a live-in nanny for her three privately educated children, and – even worse – was nice and funny. She could bloody well share some of her good fortune.

'What did Holly give you?'

'A lovely bracelet. And she's going to take me out to dinner tonight.'

'Really? Has she had a personality transplant?' Alicia was unimpressed by her niece's journey into adolescence.

'Holly's big on birthdays. Every one takes her closer to being grown up and having fun.'

'With no idea that is, in fact, an oxymoron.' Alicia laughed.

'Well, for me, birthdays are just a brutal reminder of my decay.'

'Another year's worth of aching joints and failing eyesight, as we hobble one step closer to the grave.'

'All the more reason for me to expect a fabulous present.' They giggled. The door opened and Leela's PA stood there, twisting her hands.

'Gillian? Leela will see you now.'

'Great. Got to go.' Gillian shoved her iPhone into her Mulberry bag (Christmas present from Alicia) and followed the PA into the inner sanctum. Leela stood up behind her desk, immaculate as ever in a grey pinstriped trouser suit, as she held out her arms.

'Gillian! So good to see you again.' Kiss kiss. The musky pong of Leela perfume. 'How is everything?'

'Great,' Gillian lied, trying not to think about the row last night when Holly announced she wasn't going to uni because it was 'posh' and instead had set her heart on fashion college. 'Fantastic. And you?'

'Very good, very good, although, my goodness, my family can be a burden sometimes. I mean, it is a wonderful thing to have four children but the problems they bring.' Leela shook her head. 'You have just the one, I think?'

'That's right.' Gillian smiled tightly. She was sick of the phrase 'just the one'. It was always said in pitying tones, implying *Poor, infertile you*. Or, if the person she was speaking to knew she worked, there'd be overtones of *Careerist bitch, putting your desire for shoes and personal fulfilment above the dream of a large family*. Always, always was the unspoken (or sometimes voiced) accusation: *You don't know what problems are when you have only one child*. These thoughts were clearly running through Leela's head, but all she said was: 'Girl, boy? I can't remember.'

'A girl. She's fifteen.'

'Ah. The difficult age. I had a daughter too. She is dead now.'

Gillian knew this, it was in the press cuttings. In fact, horrible as it was to admit, one of the things she was hoping to persuade Leela to do was give an emotional interview to *Grazia* about her heartbreak at losing her daughter. But now she had to act surprised.

'I'm so sorry!'

'You didn't know this?' Leela looked annoyed. 'It was in the press cuttings.'

'I did, I did, yes!' Damn. A trap. 'But I'm still very sorry. You never said, how did she die? If you don't mind me asking?' she added as an afterthought.

'A car crash. Very tragic. And before you ask, because they all do, no, I will not give an interview to discuss it. I'm not that Katie Price.'

'Of course not,' Gillian said hurriedly. 'I wouldn't have dreamt of asking.'

Leela nodded. 'She was a difficult girl, my daughter. Harder work than all my sons put together. Much harder. I wish you better luck with yours.'

'Mine's pretty hard work at the moment,' Gillian admitted.

'You mustn't let it trouble your conscience. I could not have been a better mother. But some children are just bad apples.'

Holly's not a bad apple! And I'm not a completely terrible mother. Though more and more, Gillian did wonder. 'Indeed,' she smiled. She leant forward, brandishing her folder. Orla Kiely. Gillian still hadn't got over her schoolgirl obsession with fancy stationery and the underlying conviction that a pretty pencil case could set all wrongs to right.

'If you need any advice, you can always come to me,' Leela said graciously. Gillian wondered if she should genuflect. Leela was looking at her closely. 'You do look tired. When you leave we'll make sure you have plenty of my eye gel. It will do you wonders.'

'Thank you.' Bad mother. Ugly. What else could her new client throw at her? 'So. I –'

'So what ideas have you for me? We haven't all day. As you know, I'm an incredibly busy woman.'

'Quite.' Gillian smiled and cleared her throat.

It was eight on Monday morning and Zu was standing in front of her wardrobe, dithering in a most un-Zu-like manner about what to wear. Since leaving school she'd worn jeans virtually every day, much to the disgust of her Russian friends. But even she, with her total lack of fashion sense, could see they weren't suitable for the first day in her new job.

Eventually, she'd plumped for the only pair of trousers she possessed, which were grey, and matched them with an anthracite T-shirt. She'd applied and reapplied make-up but it made her look so alien that in the end she'd just washed it all off and simply put a blob of Leela multi-purpose balm on her lips before setting off to the Tube.

She still wasn't at all sure this was a good idea. Yes, it was a job, but one that was in no way suited to her personality. All right, she could use her Russian, but everyone knew what Russians in London were like – gangsters, dripping with bling and wanting a supermodel PhD astrophysicist girlfriend at the click of a finger. There was no way she'd be able to keep her temper dealing with such people, day in day out.

But what was the alternative? She had almost no money – her previous job had paid a pittance. She could hang around Farthingdale Road for the next few weeks, growing skinter and skinter until eventually she had to find a job as a waitress or working in a shop, which she'd hate even more. At Temperley, at least she could continue her job hunt while earning money, and she could also keep an eye out for a potential new girlfriend for Tony. Tony, who had merely raised an eyebrow when she'd told him about the new job, unlike Anj, who'd almost had a hernia laughing. Since the birthday dinner she and her father had been tiptoeing around each other and sticking to platitudes. When she'd asked him if he was going to get a move on and actually fill in the Temperley form, he'd said yes, yes, he'd said he would, hadn't he, and he just needed a bit of time to think what to write.

To the strains of Elgar, she walked from Baker Street to Temperley, trying to imagine this becoming her new daily routine. She buzzed the buzzer.

'It's Zulekha.'

'Darling! Come in!'

At the top of the stairs, Masha greeted her with two kisses. Sweet perfume invaded Zu's nostrils, making her eyes itch. Zu didn't like scent; Deepika used to wear something that smelt of lily of the valley and, as a result, sweet sticky smells made her jumpy.

'I was worrying you'd change mind overnight,' Masha said. She stepped back, looked Zu up and down, shook her head, bit her lip and then turned to open the door to the office. 'Gary! Zulekha's here, thenk God!'

A tall man with grey hair and saggy, age-spotted skin, that told of countless long lunches and holidays in Bermuda, appeared. In his sixties perhaps, wearing a well-cut pinstripe suit that strained across his belly, a blue shirt and a tie.

'Welcome on board,' he said in a gravelly voice. He held out a large nicotine-stained hand. 'I'm Gary Temperley. Captain of the ship. Masha is going to be interviewing clients this morning, so I am the lucky one who's going to be showing you the ropes.'

He led Zu into a small backroom office. A large cupboard ran along one wall. There were three desks with terminals, a grey carpet and sash windows with views out over the London rooftops. There was a cork-board covered in photos, clippings, postcards and invitations. Zu's eyes fell on a bride and groom – her in white draped taffeta, him in his monkey suit, both grin-ning manically.

'Cheesy, isn't it?' said Gary, seeing her expression. 'But it's what the clients all want. That's Nicola and Graeme. She called us about a year ago, thirty, working in the City. She'd bought a gîte in the French countryside last year and done it up, she'd run a marathon and this year's project was going to be finding a husband. She signs up with us, three dates and bingo! On the fourth, she and Graeme hit it off, six months later they're engaged. Great publicity for us. Everyone happy.'

He dusted his hands together. Surprised, Zu laughed. Gary grinned. He looked her up and down. 'How about you? Can we find you a husband? Perk of the job. Old Lyuba's sitting on a yacht on the Caribbean as we speak. Or perhaps you already have someone.'

'I'm single,' Zu said tersely.

'Best way to be. Wish I'd learnt to keep it that way. Masha's my third and last wife. More trouble than it's worth, this whole marriage business. But don't tell the clients that or we'll be in big trouble. They're all chasing the happy ending.' He emitted a Vincent Price cackle. 'Wa ha ha. Little do they know it's the miserable beginning.'

'Masha was your interpreter, right?'

'Yup. Old ugly man marries much younger gorgeous Ukrainian. Clichéd or what?'

'Oh!' He'd said just what Zu was thinking. Gary laughed.

'Don't worry. I know everyone thinks that and it's true. I'm a man, I'm predictable. Nearly everyone's predictable. Makes our job easier – and harder. Now, let me show you the database.'

This consisted of eight filing cabinets stuffed with questionnaires. 'It'll be your job to transfer the info to the computer as it comes in,' Gary explained.

Zu flicked through the photos of the clients. Some were smiling, some looked serious, most looked like serial killers on day release. Zu couldn't decide if she pitied them for their loneliness or despised them for being so needy. Either way, there had to be someone for Tony among them.

'The clients never see each other's pictures,' Gary warned. 'We used to let people inspect them before they went on dates but without fail the same ten people always got chosen. The guys picked the sexy blondes, the girls went for the men with full heads of hair. As I said, predictable. The other fourteen hundred and ninety people on the books didn't get a look in. So now we decide who goes with who.'

There were about fifteen hundred clients on the books in total; twelve hundred women and three hundred men.

'It's the problem all the agencies have,' said Gary. 'Far, far more ladies than gentlemen.'

'Why?'

'Haven't you noticed? There are always far more gorgeous, single women than single men. Women are screwed on every front – over thirty-two, no one's interested so they need us, while age makes no difference to a bloke, thank Christ! In any case, even desperate guys don't usually use agencies. They find the face-to-face stuff too embarrassing. They'd rather go online. Plus it's cheaper and most men are tightwads. Anyway. The odd man comes to us and we headhunt some.'

'Headhunt?'

'Yeah, it's a huge part of the job, finding good men for the agency. Younger women too – we need them. The clients can't get enough of them. They're dreadful golddiggers, the rare under-thirties we see, but that's the client's problem, not ours. We offer them reduced rates or free membership, like your dad. Who, as Masha told you, is practically our holy grail. Though no one's yet told me how tall he is.'

'He's quite short,' Zu confessed.

'We'll see what he says. If he puts five eight on the form, he's really five six. See those markers on the wall there?' He pointed towards some faint dashes on the cupboard door. 'It's a height indicator. Everyone lies about how tall they are. That tells the truth.'

'Really?'

'Go and stand by it.'

Zu obeyed. Gary donned tortoiseshell reading glasses and peered. 'You're five one and a half, I reckon.'

'I'm five two!' That extra half inch was very important.

Gary laughed, but kindly. 'Anyway, height issues apart, your dad'll be just fine. Unless he's a lardarse – but, looking at you, that seems unlikely. Or he smokes. Nobody wants to know smokers. Filthy, cancer-ridden creatures.' He patted his jacket pocket. 'Pack of Stuyvesant in here, must nip out for one in a minute.'

Zu grinned. So Gary would be fine with her taking regular Marlboro Light breaks. This was turning out better than she could have hoped. 'So why do you need a Russian speaker?' she asked.

Gary was bent over the computer monitor, reading an email. 'Mmm. Sorry?'

'I said, why do you need a Russian speaker?'

He didn't turn but his shoulders stiffened. 'Didn't Masha tell you?' He tried and failed to sound casual.

'She said lots of the clients were Russian.'

'Well, yes, that's part of it.' He hesitated and then said, 'And there is the other side to the business.'

'The other side?'

'The Russian and Ukrainian side.' He cleared his throat. 'Temperley isn't our only business. It's our British one. But we also have Close Encounters, which is our eastern-European operation. We run a website for British men to correspond with Ukrainian women. We individually matchmake the men who pay a premium to us and we organize four tours a year to Ukraine for the men to meet potential wives.'

'Right,' Zu said slowly.

'She didn't explain that?'

'No.'

'Oh, well.' Gary turned, smiling. 'She probably just forgot.'

'So what is my part in that?' Zu asked.

'Not much. I've told you. You just do the normal office stuff – answering the phones, keeping files updated. But your Russian may just come in handy if one of the guys needs an email translated, or if one of the girls calls up freaking out about sorting a visa, but not more than that. Then there's things like some of the guys may want to send the girls chocolates and flowers – you can help with that.'

'You charge them to send emails, don't you?' Stuff Zu had heard in Chechnya was coming back to her.

'We charge them to sign up to the agency, then it's fifty pence to send one of the girls an email and fifty pence to receive one. It's hardly going to bankrupt them. More, if the emails need translating. I mean, fair enough, how else would they get in contact? I mean, they could meet on Facebook, but then they could be anyone. Through us it's safe. Masha's absolutely brutal about vetting the men. Any dodginess in their past, she sniffs it out instantly. These girls are her sisters. She's not going to let them down.' The buzzer rang. 'Oh, hang on a sec.' He went to the entry-phone. 'Hello? Oh yes, hello, Alastair! Come on up.' He pressed the button. 'Al Wyatt,' he said, turning to Zu. 'Bless him. He lives round the corner and he's always popping in. Been on the books nearly a year now and still no luck . . . you'll see why.'

Zu couldn't wait. Was Al a hunchback? Did his breath reek? Instead, a perfectly ordinary-looking, if somewhat Hoorayish man in his mid-fifties appeared, panting, at the top of the stairs. Pink shirt, brown cords, full head of hair, damn him. Zu eyed him up and down. So this was the competition. Well, Dad could hold his own here, even if he was about six inches shorter and far balder.

'Al!' Gary held out his hand.

'How are you, Gary?'

'Very well. Let me introduce our new assistant, the gorgeous Zulekha.'

'As in Zuleika Dobson?'

'No, it's an Indian name,' Zu said.

'Do you know who Zuleika Dobson was? A heart-breaker. Broke all the boys' hearts at the varsity. Oxford,' he added. 'My old alma mater.'

Zu began to get an idea why Al might not be having any luck. 'Yes, I do know who Zuleika Dobson was,' she said politely.

'So how did it go with Emily last night?' Gary asked.

'Wonderfully. That was what I thought I'd pop in to tell you. She couldn't have been more charming and I'm going to invite her to meet Mother this weekend.'

Gary's expression didn't change.

'Now, Al. We have talked about this. Don't you think it's a little soon? Perhaps wait at least a couple more dates?'

Al's lips set stubbornly. 'When you know, you know. Ten minutes and all that . . .'

'Usually ten minutes,' Gary sighed. 'Look, you thought you knew with Amanda. And Nazish. Honestly, mate, sometimes it's best to treat 'em a bit mean and keep 'em keen.'

Masha stuck her head round the door. 'How are you getting on? Oh, Al! What a lovely surprise.'

'Al's been telling me all about how well it went with Emily,' Gary said cheerfully.

Masha's eyes didn't flicker. 'Oh, yes? Why don't you sit with me for a moment, Al? Have a coffee. Tell me more. Zu, darling, can you make two coffees? Mine always espresso. Al – now don't tell me! You like it white, no sugar.'

'You're incredible, Masha.'

Masha ushered Al into the interview room.

'Right,' Gary said to Zu. 'You take in two glasses of water as well and a plate of biscuits. If you can make a decent espresso for my wife, you've a job here for life.'

13

Zu had arranged to meet Anjali in Soho after work. Accompanied by Duruflé's *Requiem*, she walked there, down bustling Marylebone High Street, then left into Wigmore Street, noting the Wigmore Hall. At lunchtimes she'd be able to nip in and enjoy a concert. She carried on down a nightmarish chunk of Oxford Street then passed into Soho. It wasn't yet dark but the market in Berwick Street was shutting for the day.

Crowds of thirsty media types stood outside every pub, yelling into phones and smoking. A transvestite pushed past her in a short pink dress, wobbly on stacked heels, Adam's apple bobbing. Tourists gawped at the flashing lights of the strip bars. A man mopped the doorstep of his delicatessen, with its window display of blue and yellow pasta packets and cans of exotic-looking beans.

For the first time since she'd left Chechnya, Zu felt content. She didn't actually know central London that well, she realized, she was far better acquainted with downtown Grozny. But if she had to stay a while, then it needn't be all bad. She just had to spend as much time as possible at the heart of things and as little as possible in Farthingdale Road, Edgware.

But what about the agency? She'd enjoyed the day more than she could have anticipated. She liked Gary, the work was clearly going to be easy and – she had to admit it – gossiping about the likes of Al was fun. But the Close Encounters stuff had freaked her out. Zu knew about mail-order brides – you'd have to be blind and deaf to live in Russia and not come across them. From the hookers that descended on the hotels every night to the delightful young women who worked in AidInt's office, it seemed that virtually all Russian women had one goal – to marry a foreigner.

The European and American men Zu had known out there hadn't been able to believe their luck, the way these gorgeous creatures threw themselves at them. Zu had always found them pathetic for not seeming to realize that their draw wasn't their good looks or their hilarious personalities but merely their passports.

Did she really want to be part of something that helped these men? But, at the same time, it was helping the women. Zu knew that as soon as they arrived in Europe or America, most of them planned to dump their husbands and run. And who could blame them for wanting to escape?

All right, Zu loved Russia, but she knew she wasn't like normal people; that normal people didn't want a life that involved waiting an hour for a packed bus every night in sub-zero temperatures in winter and a mosquito-laden fug in summer, then walking half a mile from the bus stop to their high-rise with shopping they'd had to queue for, only to find the electricity had been cut off again and the lifts weren't working. It was a tough life and the women seemed to bear the brunt of it all. Ukraine would be the same, probably worse. So why not assist them? If she'd had no way out of Farthingdale Road but marrying an ugly old man, who knew, maybe she'd have done the same.

Anj was sitting at a corner table of the French House, which had been their favourite London pub since they were sixteen, a bottle of white wine cooling in a bucket.

'Good girl,' Zu said, kissing her. 'How was your day?'

'Fantastic. I got the script of a new horror. It's got a woman burned alive and a scene where someone gets savaged by wild beasts.'

'Eyeballs?' Zu knew Anj loved a good prosthetic eyeball.

'No eyeballs. But otherwise it's the goriest I've read in ages. I hope I get it.' She filled Zu's glass. 'But, more importantly, what about you? How was it?'

'Do you know, I quite enjoyed it.'

'You in a dating agency.' Her cousin shook her head.

'Yeah, yeah.' The joke had worn thin. 'It's only going to be for a couple of weeks. Hey, I've got a new joke,' she said to move things on. 'What does an accountant use for birth control? His personality.'

'Raman'll piss his pants when he hears that,' Anjali retorted sarcastically. 'Hey, maybe you could find Bosey a girlfriend.'

Bosey was Raman's best friend, who always wore baggy pants and a beanie as if he were a gangsta rapper in the hood rather than the son of a stockbroker from Berkhamsted.

'I'm working in a dating agency, not a home for the criminally insane.'

'True.' Anjali laughed. 'Perhaps matchmaking is your destiny. I mean, it's in the blood, isn't it?'

'You mean because we're Indian?' Zu spoke in her best

mock-Punjabi accent. 'Like, we're all mystical and can read people's auras as well as cook a mean curry.'

'That'll be it.'

Zu sipped her wine. Teeth-strippingly dry, just how she liked it. 'No, work was OK,' she continued. 'Masha's tough as old boots, but I like that, and Gary, her husband, is fun. There's just one thing.'

'Oh, yes?' Anj raised a beautifully threaded eyebrow. She was always trying to attack Zu's caterpillars but Zu refused to let her anywhere near them.

Zu told her about Close Encounters. Anj listened without comment. It was one of the many things Zu loved about her, the way she never interrupted and only rarely passed judgement.

'Interesting,' she said when her cousin had finally finished.

'So what do you think? Is it too dodgy? I mean, is this the sex trade we're talking about?'

'I don't think so,' Anj said. 'No one's forcing these women to do anything, are they?'

'Poverty's forcing them.'

'Yes, but we're not talking starving to death poverty, are we? Just, they don't have as much as we have. If they want a better life, and this is the best way of pursuing it, then why not?'

'Russian men are useless,' Zu said, almost talking to herself. 'Even the ones who don't beat up their wives just sit on their arses like kings expecting their wives, who usually have full-time jobs, to wait on them hand and foot.'

'Sounds like Raman's dad.'

'They all die of alcoholism when they're about forty,'

Zu said, then added bitterly, 'unlike here, where the mothers do.'

'Just one mother,' Anj said quietly. But Zu didn't hear her, captivated as she was by her new line of argument. It was hell living with an alcoholic and a good proportion of Russian women had to do that. Another plus point for agencies like Close Encounters.

'Remember, Naani came over here as practically a mail-order bride. She wasn't too miserable. And I was fixed up with Raman.'

'But you knew him. You agreed to your parents' choice.'

'These women meet the guys before they marry them, don't they? I repeat, no one's forcing them. What I'm saying is just because they're not wildly in love with them doesn't mean it won't work out. After all . . .'

'After all, Mum and Dad married for crazy love and look what happened to them.' Ten minutes to fall in love. Dad always said it had been love at first sight. Ha!

Anj shrugged. For the first time it occurred to Zu that Anj's aunt's sad story might have played some part in her cousin deciding to go down the arranged route.

'Look, if you want to do the job, do it. Don't let the morality of it scare you off. You said that Masha's vetting the guys, making sure there are no psychos among them. And, as you keep pointing out, it'll only be for a few weeks.'

'OK, then,' Zu said after a pause.

'So we're all happy?' Anj asked briskly.

'Well. Satisfied. For the time being. The only downer is the commute.'

Anjali looked at Zu as if she'd announced she was

the Duchess of Runcorn. 'Don't be ridiculous. Move in with us.'

'What?'

'Move in with us. We have a spare room. You know Raman's never there. He's always at work or taking his clients to lap-dancing clubs. He says he only watches, that he finds it boring, but whatever. And when he is home he's usually accompanied by Bosey. Or Digger. Or both. I feel like I'm at some kind of repressed homosexual orgy. It'd be great to have some female company.'

Anjali and Raman lived in a dinky mews house off Regent's Park, a house which, Zu suspected, had contributed significantly to Anj's decision to marry Ram. Zu was tempted by it too. If she lived there, she could walk to work. She could walk home from Soho in the evenings. But much as she wanted to be shot of home, could she really abandon Tony?

'Problem?' Anjali asked.

'Dad.'

'You're only going a few stops down the Northern Line, not to a recent war zone where aid workers are routinely kidnapped and murdered. He should be delighted. Well, not delighted – but relieved. Anyway, if you're serious about fixing him up, he'll need a bit more space to entertain the ladies.'

'Well . . .' But Zu couldn't. It would be a betrayal of her father. She'd be able to walk to work but she'd feel too guilty to enjoy it.

'It ain't happening?' Anj was watching her expression. Zu shook her head, just as a voice above them said, 'Forbes?'

Zu looked up. 'Henchie? What on earth are you doing here?'

'I could ask the same of you,' Jack Henchie replied.

Zu shook her head. 'I thought you were in Belarus.'

'I thought you were in Chechnya.' Instead of his uniform of crumpled T-shirt and jeans, Henchie was in a white shirt, red tie and pinstriped suit. His dark hair, which used to curl on the nape of his neck, was cropped and his trademark three-day stubble had vanished. But he still had that windswept look about him as if he'd just walked in from the desert.

He turned and smiled at Anj. 'Sorry, sorry. I didn't mean to interrupt.'

'Not a problem.' Anj beamed.

So he hadn't changed. Jack Henchie was always intent on seducing everybody: women, men, children. Zu was the only one who refused to succumb.

'So what are you doing here? Latrines to be dug?' Henchie always called aid workers 'latrine diggers'.

'Of course. Can't you smell the sewage? No, I'm working in London for now.' Zu had no desire to go into the details. 'What about you? Oil dried up?'

'Nope, still there. But I've been relocated. I'm working in the London office, just up the road, off Marylebone High Street.'

'Zu's off Marylebone High Street too!' Anj exclaimed. Zu shot her a look.

'You said you'd never come back,' she said to Henchie.

'You too.'

'I was made redundant. I'm looking for something permanent and in the meantime . . .'

'Jack! What are you having?' called a skinny woman in a red skirt suit, who was standing in a rowdy group at the bar.

'Don't let me keep you,' Zu said hastily. Skinny had short curly fair hair and was watching Jack with a pouty expression. Well, the ladies had always had a soft spot for Henchie.

'They can wait. Here, let me buy you two a drink. What are you having?'

'We're going,' Zu said, just as Anj said, 'A large glass of white would be great.'

'You're not disturbing anything,' Henchie said. 'I'm just here out of duty with some work people. I'd far rather talk to you.'

'We're going,' Zu repeated.

Jack Henchie grinned. 'Well, if you're working near me, we should have a drink soon. What's your number?'

'Facebook me.'

'I'm not on Facebook. Juvenile rubbish.'

'Oh yeah, I forgot how old you are. You don't know how these new-fangled computers work. Call me, then. I'm working at the Temperley Bureau.' She stood up and, reluctantly, so did Anj. Henchie bent over and kissed Zu on both cheeks.

'I'll be in touch,' he said and headed back to the bar. Within seconds, he was surrounded by women.

'Who's he?' Anj hissed.

'Just a guy I used to bump into sometimes in Chechnya. He works in oil.'

'He's gorgeous.'

'All women say that,' Zu sighed.

'But he *is*.'

'And he knows it,' Zu said briskly.

'I hope you're going to have a drink with him. He clearly has the hots for you.'

'Nonsense.'

Anj shook her head. 'And you're working in a dating agency. You can't see when a guy fancies the pants off you.'

'That's just the way he is with everyone,' Zu said, stepping out into the warm night air. 'Come on. Let's go for a pizza.'

14

Zu and Tony sat watching television together. This almost never happened any more: most of the time Zu was online and Tony was reading. But tonight she'd decided to humour him and watch an episode of *Top Gear*.

'I don't get it, Dad,' she sighed, after Clarkson had made another joke about poor people. 'Why is this so funny?'

'It's not really,' Tony said wearily. 'It just appeals to my puerile side.'

They sat in silence. Zu itched to check her phone. She itched to be living with Anjali – though there the telly was tuned permanently to *America's Next Top Model*. 'His face is so long. People must always be asking: "Why the long face?"'

'Clarkson's a prat,' Tony conceded. 'But he's funny and the cars are amazing.'

'You could use a clump of his hair if you ran out of Brillo pads. All right, all right, I'll stop now.'

'Go on Facebook. I don't mind.'

'No. No. It's good to spend time together.'

'Leela called me this afternoon,' Tony said. 'She said Anj asked you to move in with her, but you said no.'

Zu flinched. 'Well, yeah. I . . .'

'I don't mind, you know,' Tony said. 'Great central location and no *Top Gear* blasting in the background.'

'I'm sure Raman watches it all the time.'

'You'd have much more fun living with Anjali than boring old me.'

'Don't be like that,' Zu sighed.

'Like what?' Tony was indignant.

'So self-pitying.'

'I wasn't being self-pitying. I was twenty-six once too, you know. I wouldn't have wanted to be living at home either.'

'I'm happy to be here. It's only . . .' The memories were everywhere: in the dent in the wall where Deepika had once hurled a vase, in the stain on the carpet where she'd once been sick. Maybe Zu should suggest Tony should move, but where could he go? 'It's fine, Dad.' She changed tack. 'The only way I might change my mind is if you take up my offer to join Temperley. Start bringing the ladies home.'

Tony looked coy. 'Maybe,' he said after a second. 'If you find me someone suitable.'

'You mean you will?' Zu wasn't given to girlie shrieking, but she clasped her hands together in excitement.

'I'll give it a go, yeah.' Tony's eyes were now fixed on the hobbit-like one of the *Top Gear* trio. '*If* you find –'

'I will, Dad. Don't worry about that.' Zu stood up. 'I'm just going to do a couple of things,' she said, before hurrying up to her bedroom to log on remotely and start properly inspecting the Temperley database.

15

First thing on Monday morning, Zu broke the news that Tony was ready.

'Excellent,' said Masha.

'About bloody time too,' said Gary. 'And what good timing,' he continued. 'Because guess who Uncle Gary has coming in at ten o'clock? A woman who will be perfect for him.'

'You haven't even met Dad yet. How do you know who's perfect for him?'

Gary shrugged. 'You've told me enough about him for me to have a pretty good idea what will work. When you've been doing this as long as I have your instincts are finely tuned. Why don't you sit in on the meeting and see what you think?'

'I can't do that!'

'Nonsense.'

'Is it professional?'

'Don't see why not. Your pa's said he'll go on our books, you work here. If they're not right for each other you say so straight away, save us all wasting our time.'

'All right.' Zu was unconvinced by his argument but she wasn't going to turn down the chance to vet a potential stepmother.

The phone rang. 'Hello, Temperley,' Gary boomed. 'Ah, Megan! How did it go?' He nodded eagerly. 'Excellent. So did he kiss you? He did! Ha! Tongues, were there tongues? Yes, I know, my dear, but you have to humour an old pervert.'

Zu stared at her screen, desperately trying not to laugh.

'Of course you don't have to divulge the gory details,' he continued. 'Though if you don't it means you definitely had a tongue sandwich . . . Yes, I know, I'm gross . . . Well done, darling. Bye.' He hung up. 'Megan and Chester did it.'

'She said snog, not shag,' Masha corrected, frowning as she clicked on a flooring website. In her accent it came out as *sheg*.

'Snog means shag, everyone knows that.'

'She'd have told us.' Masha turned to Zu. 'Funnily enough, it's the girls, not the guys, who're all gagging for it.' *Gegging for it.*

'Why's that?' Zu asked politely, though she thought *Why not?* Why shouldn't girls enjoy sex too? She certainly did; much preferred it to lovey-dovey holding hands and phone calls ending with 'I love you', which was so many men's style.

'The men spend too much time wenking in front of Internet. Nothing left for real thing.'

'I would have put it a bit more delicately, my dear,' Gary said. He shook his head ruefully. 'Sorry, Zu, dear. You can take the girl out of Odessa but you can't take Odessa out of the girl. It's that bawdy port culture – very crude.'

'I've never been to Odessa,' Zu said. 'Always wanted to. The clubs are supposed to be amazing.'

Masha and Gary exchanged a look that Zu couldn't quite interpret but, just as she was about to ask what it was, the phones all started ringing. Before she knew it, it was ten and Tony's future wife was buzzing at the door. Zu's heart pirouetted as she heard her climbing the stairs. She wasn't audibly wheezing or stopping for a breather, so she must be fit at least. Zu smoothed down the front of her T-shirt, took a deep breath and stepped out on to the landing.

'Hello, I'm Zulekha. Nice to meet you.'

An attractive, dark-haired woman with a pale face, long nose and a wide mouth, like in a Modigliani painting, smiled, holding out her hand. She was wearing a red jersey sundress with a black bra strap peeking out under the spaghetti strap and her blue sandals were scuffed. Zu instantly approved. People with polished shoes were some of her pet hates, along with people who had matching underwear. She'd once had to share a room in Chechnya with a Canadian called Mona, whose bras and knickers were all paired off – like ideal Temperley clients. Once she'd picked up one of Zu's saggy black M&S cotton numbers from the laundry pile and said, not joking, 'Do you think someone used these for cleaning the bathroom?'

Zu ushered Gillian into the meeting room, where Masha was waiting to greet her, then disappeared to make coffees. When she returned, the pair of them were laughing away like old friends.

'I hate to ask, but have to know: how old are you, Gillian?' Masha asked, pen poised over her Smythson notebook.

'I'm forty-three, as of two days ago, so totally over the hill in man-attracting terms, though you know I use sun protection and drink lots of water, so possibly by candlelight I could pass for – ooh – forty-six?'

'Don't be ridiculous. You look at least decade younger.' Masha scribbled something, then leant forward encouragingly. 'And what is your job?'

'I have my own PR and marketing business.'

'And you're single? Separated?'

'Divorced and I have a teenage daughter. It's hard to meet men after the age of twenty-five, I've found, so finally I'm humiliating myself and admitting I need help.'

Zu liked her, she decided. There was a wryness to the cast of her mouth, an intelligence in her eyes. She was dark, she was attractive, but she didn't look remotely like Deepika – that would have been creepy.

'Who would be your soulmate?' Masha asked.

'I'd like him to be into orgies with goats and camels, to look like Rufus Sewell, be as funny as Michael McIntyre and as rich as Bill Gates.' Gillian was poker-faced.

'Oh.' Masha frowned, running mentally through potential candidates. Then she got it. 'Oh! Ha ha. Is joke!'

Gillian smiled. 'Well, it's more interesting than the truth. I'd just like him to be kind, really. It sounds boring, but someone who'd enjoy watching *Mad Men* and cooking with me, who'd help round the house, not like . . . never mind. Oh, and he has to love my daughter. That might be a tall order at the moment but she's lovely deep down. Yes, that's the most important thing: my soulmate must understand that my daughter's the most important thing in my world.'

As soon as she was out of the door, Masha turned, jubilant.

'They're perfect for each other! She'd enjoy riding on back of a motorbike and going to funky bars in Brick Lane.'

'Dad doesn't ride a motorbike, he thinks they're death traps. And he's never been to Brick Lane in his life.'

Masha ignored her. 'I think she is very promising. Gary, Gary!'

'What?' Gary stuck his head round the door.

'Zu thinks Gillian is perfect for her father! I predict Christmas wedding.'

'Fantastic. I love winter weddings, so romantic in the snow. She could wear a white fur hat, completely Anna Karenina.'

'Anna Karenina committed suicide,' Masha pointed out.

'So she did. Oh well. One of my weddings was at Christmas.'

'What, to Amanda? But that was on beach in Barbados.' Masha shook her head in despair at her husband's idiocy. 'What *do* you think of Gillian, Zu?'

Next wife was pushing it; nonetheless, Zu had a good feeling about this. Gillian was attractive, funny, sensible. The only thing that jangled was the daughter bit. Of course any normal mother would want her boyfriend to like her children, it would be weird if she didn't – but the thought of Tony being a surrogate father to a teenage girl was very unpleasant.

Dad was never around for me. *But he'll have loads of time for* her.

Zu stifled that little voice. What a selfish cow she was. Not to mention the fact that she was jumping the gun. Dad might not even want to meet Gillian, so why the unwelcome visions of him and some random teenage girl going bowling, cooking Sunday lunch together, curling up in front of a DVD? She didn't want Dad to be lonely and perhaps her wish was about to be granted even sooner than she'd hoped.

'It could definitely work. I'll call Dad and let him know.'

'Marvellous!' Gary offered her his blobby hand in a high five. Zu smacked it even though she thought high-fiving was the most evil American import since McDonald's and end-of-term proms. But she was pleased and she had to show it somehow. Matchmaking was continuing to prove far less painful than she'd feared. In fact, though she could barely admit it to herself, she was beginning to enjoy it.

16

A week had passed. Tony had been into the office to meet Gary, and made a video that Masha and Gary pronounced themselves delighted with, and that Zu found cringeworthy, but agreed would do. August continued wet, grey and windy and on a Thursday morning Zu was crossing Baker Street, en-route to work, wearing an orange cagoule and immersed in the sounds of Haydn's *Little Organ Mass* when she felt her phone vibrating in her pocket.

'Hello? Naani? Aaargh!' A cyclist had had to swerve to avoid her; now he was riding off, glancing over his shoulder, swearing and shaking his fist. Zu stuck a finger up at him. Another pet hate: urban cyclists – all that silly Lycra and self-importance. 'How was India?' she continued from the safety of the pavement.

'Marvellous! Though I was mainly in Bangladesh, actually. I sourced some new factories that will be able to do the job for half what I'm paying now, plus I found some new essential oils that are just too gorgeous and that people have been using for centuries to treat insomnia or whatever. I'm so excited. And before I left I found the perfect woman for Tony.'

'Oh, really?'

'She's doing my PR, very nice lady, divorced, teenage

daughter. I don't know, there's something about her I just know makes her right for him. Shall I tell him?'

'Well, maybe. But, actually, I think I may have found someone too.'

'Oh yes?'

'Mmm. She has a teenage daughter as well. They're going to go on a date at the weekend. So maybe see how that goes before we start bombarding him with possible girlfriends.'

'All right,' Naani said sulkily. 'But I tell you, this one is perfect.'

'If she's perfect she won't mind waiting a week for Dad to meet her.'

Leela snorted. 'So how are things otherwise, Zu? Found a job yet?'

'Well. Sort of.'

'What does "sort of" mean?' The steeliness which was the key to the Leela brand's success crept into her voice.

Zu told a sanitized version of the story, as she continued towards the agency. Leela listened.

'So you are working for a marriage bureau?'

'Just for the time being.'

'Are you sure it is reputable? Not some knocking shop? And you say you think you've already found someone for Tony?'

'Well, possibly. She's forty-three, divorced —'

'That's not good!'

'It would be worse if she wasn't divorced at this age. Then she'd be like one of those simpleton daughters who still lives with her parents and wears "Hello Kitty" T-shirts.'

Leela ignored this. 'Nothing wrong with living with your parents. That is what dutiful daughters do.'

Zu was used to such digs. 'Anyway, I thought you said the lady you had in mind was divorced too? She has a teenage daughter, so she won't be nagging Dad to have any more children . . .'

'I should hope not at his age! Not to mention hers. Ach, these old mothers you see everywhere, always pushing double prams, I notice. IVF, you see. It's not what was intended for women. After all, it's not like you can't have children *and* a career. Not that I'm boasting, you understand. The Gita says pride does not lead to Nirvana. Still.'

Zu ploughed on. 'She does have a career, her own business in fact. She's very funny and bright, seems kind.'

'Beautiful?' Naani was suspicious.

'Just . . . attractive.'

'Well, let's see how it goes.' Leela sounded mollified. She clearly liked the idea of her daughter's legendary beauty not being eclipsed by another woman.

'You should meet my bosses some time, Naani,' said Zu, eager to change the subject. 'You'd like them. There's Masha, she reminds me of you a bit, very entrepreneurial . . .'

'Is she worth millions? Does she have four children? Does she come from a culture with no history of women working?' Advantage Naani. Without pausing, Leela continued, 'And your brothers? How are they?'

'Really well. Rohan will be back soon, actually, for the beginning of term, but he's found Thailand incredibly culturally enriching.' That was one way of describing the non-stop party he was revelling in. Bless him. Zu's heart expanded as it did every time she talked about the boys. 'And Kieran is having a wonderful time too.'

Naani snorted. 'So long as he isn't catching Aids from those children he's looking after. They all have it, you know.'

Oh, Naani. Once, Zu would have argued with her, but she'd learnt not to waste her energy. 'I've got to go, Naani. I've just arrived at the office. But I'll call later and tell you what's happening with Dad.'

Gary was out wooing clients in the City and Masha was on the phone to the builders. 'No, I told you, we want a wet room. No! With shower screen this will not be achievable. I want it to be like boutique hotel Gary and I visit in Costa Rica . . . Yes, you can, Fred . . . Look on website. Hang on minute.' She grabbed another phone before Zu could lunge for it. 'Peter? Yes. Hello. Yes, I am very happy. Have ideal woman for you. I will give you details and you arrange a meeting. I just know she's perfect —' A third line started ringing. 'Zu, darling . . .'

Zu was already answering. 'Hello, Temperley.'

'Oh, hello,' said a man's voice. Relaxed. Somehow familiar. 'I'm a single man looking for someone to have a drink with tonight and I was wondering if you could help me. Ideally she'd be young, never wear skirts and swear quite a lot and smoke too much and have lived in Chechnya and I was wondering if you knew of anyone who fitted the bill.'

'Fuck off, Henchie.' Zu smiled. She'd wondered a couple of times if he'd call, then forgotten about it.

'Charming. Is this how you treat all your clients? May I

suggest your skills would be put to much better use dig-
ging latrines.'

'I said –'

'I heard you. So how about it? What are you doing
tonight?'

'Nothing.'

'Good girl. Do you like cheese?'

'Yes.'

'I knew you would,' Henchie said happily. 'I'll see you at
La Fromagerie. Motcomb Street, just off Marylebone
High Street. Half six any good?'

'Fine,' Zu said.

'Excellent.'

The rest of the day passed quickly. Zu filed forms and
answered the phones, and at four Masha deemed her suitable
to help conduct an interview with a new client called Sarah.
She was in her mid-thirties, tall, flat-chested, in an ankle-
length tweed skirt and a string of pearls round her neck.

'So what kind of men are you interested in, Sarah?' Zu
asked nervously.

'Well.' Sarah twisted the pearls. 'He has to be big and
very blond; Nordic-looking, basically.'

'Like Boris Johnson?' Masha suggested.

'Right,' Sarah nodded. 'And I'd like him posh, if that's
not too politically incorrect.'

'Like Boris?' said Zu.

'Mmm hmm. And slightly bumbling.'

'You basically want to go out with Boris Johnson,' said
Masha.

'Well, everyone else has,' pointed out Zu.

It took a while to persuade Sarah that she might at least dabble with some of the other men on the database. 'Is biggest problem we have,' Masha sighed after she left. 'These people have fixed idea of who is right for them. Is why they're still single, they reject anyone who doesn't fit the blueprint. They need to widen their horizons. Take me. Gary was not my ideal man, or I thought he wasn't. But then I meet him, he take me out for dinner, he make me laugh, I think . . . hmmm. And look at us now.' She glanced almost slyly at Zu. 'Is what I tell girls in Odessa. Yes, he is older than you. Yes, he is not George Clooney. But does he drink every night? Will he beat you? Or will he send you flowers –'

'And give you an unlimited decorating account,' Gary pitched in cheerily.

'My life in Odessa was hard,' Masha continued, still looking at Zu. 'My mother worked in factory for thirty years. She spends the Eighties queuing for every item of food. She goes on street with everything she owns – her ugly ornaments, her iron, her spoons – she displays them on tea towel hoping someone will buy them. She fed me and my brother and she went hungry. Now I can take her on shopping trips to Harrods.'

'I may not have looked like the handsome prince, but I delivered,' Gary boomed.

'You understand this, don't you, Zu?'

It was a test. Masha wanted to be clear that Zu had no problems with Close Encounters.

'I understand.'

'Good.' Masha glanced up at the clock. 'Gary, theatre starts in half an hour. We must go. Zu, you will lock up?'

'Of course.'

17

La Fromagerie was a deli selling things like rosewater for five pounds a bottle or a glossy chunk of fennel for two pounds eighty-six. There was a little cheese room off to one side that you could peer at through a glass door. Zu pushed it open and was assaulted by the odour of rancid socks and rotten eggs, candle wax and seaweed. She inhaled deeply. Despite the prices, she liked this place.

When she came out, she saw Henchie sitting at one of the low wooden tables that were scattered around. His back was towards her, so Zu watched him for a second. She really didn't know Henchie that well – they'd met maybe a dozen times, always in a crowd of expats, and their conversation had always consisted of banter. She'd guess he was about thirty-five and . . . she remembered now . . . although there was always a girl on his arm, he also had a son who lived in London. She dimly remembered him drunkenly showing her photos once and her telling him to stop trying to make her feel sorry for him, that she knew his game, and him laughing and buying her another drink.

If there was a genetic lottery then Henchie was certainly a winner. He actually looked better with his hair shorter, she decided now. He was wearing some fancy watch and a green shirt with the sleeves rolled up; the hairs on his arms golden in the dim light. But Zu could resist him. All right, she was a sucker for a pretty face, but she'd never fall for someone so obviously good-looking – if she did, then she'd be in the same category as those girls who liked Katie Price and who screamed at the sight of a chocolate bar.

'Hello,' she said, tapping him on the shoulder. He whirled round.

'Zu!' Kiss kiss. That smell again, slightly bitter.

'Why have you brought me to a cheese shop?'

'Because I love cheese,' he said cheerily. 'What do you think?'

She looked around the dimly lit room. 'Bring it on. The stinkier the better.'

'You like rancid cheese?' he asked with a grin.

She nodded.

'Good girl,' he said.

'Ahem.'

'What?'

'Am I a girl?'

'Sorry, *woman*,' he half laughed, half sighed. 'I'd forgotten what you're like. We'll order a selection of their finest.'

So they did, as well as a bottle of red wine.

'Cheers,' Henchie said, clinking his glass against hers.

'I know we're in a cheese shop but do we have to be quite so . . .' she giggled. 'Cheesy?'

He put his glass down. 'Still the same soft, romantic Forbes, I see.'

'Still the same shy, retiring, un-lecherous Henchie.'

'Do you know something about cheese? It contains more pheny– pheny– anyway, something chemical which works like a love drug. Eat enough of it and you'll feel all smoochy and romantic.'

'Really?' Zu did her eyebrow-raising trick.

'So what's happened?' Henchie asked, grinning. 'What are you doing here scoffing Bleu d'Auvergne? Why aren't you in some dive in Grozny, eating sheep's brains and doing karaoke to Whitesnake?'

'And you? Why aren't you in a former Soviet republic with a blonde on each knee and a Mafia boss plying you with brandies?'

'You first.'

'I told you. I lost my job. I'm looking for another. If you know of anything . . .'

'Yes, but in the meantime I've discovered that you're working at a dating agency. What the hell is that about?'

'They offered me a job. I needed to do something.' Attack was the best form of defence. 'What about you? What's your excuse for wearing a suit?'

She expected he'd cite an enormous salary and then she'd tease him a bit about this but, instead, he looked at his hands and said softly, 'Remember I have a kid?'

'A boy.'

'Xander.' That pleased, proud expression that Zu knew from when she talked about her brothers. 'He was living with his mum in Richmond – you know, Sara and I had never been an item, it was just a one-night-stand accident. But I saw Xander whenever I was in town. Called him as often as I could. Then one day Sara fell down dead in the street.'

'Oh.' *Was she drunk?* It was a natural assumption. Deepika had fallen down in the street – and everywhere else – all the time, but Zu knew better than to voice it.

'Brain aneurysm,' Jack continued.

'Oh,' Zu repeated. She always hated the way people gasped in horror when she told them about Mum. Apart from anything else, it churned up her guilt that, actually, her mother's death had not been altogether unwelcome. Quietly, she said, 'That's sad.'

'It is.' Jack gulped his drink. 'Anyway, Xander went to live with her parents, but of course I wanted him to live with me. They pointed out I was never here, so I quit the jet-setting and found something in London. Stable, boring, everything they could require. But they're still being arses. Making a fuss about my bad-boy past because once upon a time I used to drink a bit and did some coke.' He saw Zu's expression. 'All right, not that long ago, but I've sorted all that now. I've made a massive effort. But I'm still only allowed to see Xander once a week, every other weekend and for two weeks of the summer holidays.'

'Poor kid,' said Zu.

'Yeah.' Jack looked sad for a second, then brightened. 'But he's great. Want to see a picture?' He'd already thrust his iPhone under her nose.

Zu decided not to remind him they'd been here before. 'He's gorgeous,' she said dutifully but, looking closer, saw that he really was, with a black mophead and enormous hazel eyes. He reminded her of her brothers at that age – their desolate faces when the shouting got too loud Zu used to pull one of them on to each knee and start singing to them loudly, to distract them.

'He's hilarious. Do you know what he said the other day? We were in his grandparents' garden and I said, "Now don't pick that flower or it won't grow." As soon as

I turned my head, he'd picked the flower. He said: "But, Daddy, it wasn't growing, it was just standing there."'

'Right,' said Zu, staring into her glass and trying not to smile. Parents, they were all the same – well, most of them anyway. She couldn't imagine Mum being touched by such childish wit. She'd have yelled: 'Don't pick the fucking flower, OK?'

Time for a change of subject. 'So how do you like living in London?'

'It has its moments. I mean, I miss Russia. There's nowhere like it.' For a second he was lost in reverie, no doubt reminiscing about some Wild-West-type saloon in a hick town. 'But London's the greatest city on earth. I just haven't seen as much of it as I'd like yet. The people I know are working too hard to ever enjoy themselves – or they've moved to Hertfordshire for the schools and are moaning about the price of babysitters.'

'Poor you, Henchie,' Zu teased.

'I know.' He rolled his eyes in mock pity. Then he said, 'Maybe we should try and improve things for me. Create the Make London Fun club.'

'Meaning what?'

'Meaning we make London fun.' He spoke as if to a small child. 'I'll go first. I'll come up with something special that you can only do in London and we'll do it.'

'All right,' Zu said, not believing anything would actually come of it. She took a bite of creamy Roquefort. Yum. There was certainly a better selection of cheese in London than in Grozny. 'So have you seen any of the old crowd recently?'

'I saw old Daniel from Conoco the other day – he was

passing through and we had a few beers. Just a few,' he stressed, raising his hands in a show of mock innocence. 'And Michelle, the French woman, who was doing the PhD, she was in town . . .'

'Michelle? Oh yeah, the one with the large – You two had a thing, didn't you?'

'Hardly that. A couple of drunken encounters. Not that you'd recall, you were too busy copping off with that South-African mercenary. Christ, he was dodgy.'

'Yes, yes, Henchie.' Zu blushed. The South African had been gorgeous, though then he'd got over-keen and, as usual, she'd had to dump him and he'd kept coming round to cry – literally – on her flatmates' shoulders.

'Hey, Jack!' said a voice behind them. 'Fancy seeing you here.'

It was one of the girls from the bar the other night – golden-blonde hair in tight curls, a green dress that crossed over her body – and another, all in black with brown hair piled on top of her head. Henchie turned.

'Oh, hi, girls. Are you stalking me? Zu, this is Melissa and Cathy from my office. Melissa, Cathy – Zu. Want to join us?'

'OK,' they giggled. Zu felt herself tense up. She didn't want to spend an evening with Melissa and Cathy. No offence, girls, but she could see they'd have nothing in common, that they were already looking at her cagoule on the bench beside her, at her worn navy jumper, and wondering who on earth she was. Most of the time Zu didn't care about stuff like that, but there were occasions when the Melissas and Cathys of this world, women her age, just stirred up too many memories. Memories of school, of other girls whispering about her and her differences. Abruptly, she stood up.

'I should get going. I've a long way to go.'

'Really?' Henchie's eyebrows shot up.

'Back to Edgware. And I have to be up early in the morning.'

'Oh, don't go,' said Melissa. Cathy just giggled.

'Are you sure?' Henchie looked annoyed. Well, he wasn't used to women running out on him. But why should he care when there were new members of his harem sitting right there?

'Sure.' She fumbled in her tattered brown satchel for her purse. 'Here,' she said, handing him a twenty-pound note. 'Do you think that'll cover it?'

'Don't be silly, Zu,' said Henchie. This time Melissa giggled.

'You're not buying me dinner, Henchie. We'll split it.'

He looked as if he were about to argue, but then he said, 'OK,' and took the money.

'If it's too much, I'll pay you back next time I see you,' he said. 'I'll be in touch soon.'

'Great,' she said and then, awkwardly, 'Thank you.'

'You're welcome,' Henchie said wryly, as Cathy said: 'Shall we get another bottle of red?'

Gillian and Holly were in Debenhams in Oxford Street. What could go wrong? Gillian had thought. After all, shopping was her daughter's favourite pastime. She was trying to restore the peace after the most epic row to date when she'd banned Holly from an all-night rave in Wiltshire.

For days the house had vibrated with loathing. Doors were slammed so violently that Gillian feared the ceiling would collapse. Holly's voice had dropped an octave from the yelling and, after being housetrained for five years, Waffle had suddenly begun leaving little puddles on the kitchen rug.

Now the rave was over and Holly, having been informed by her friends that it hadn't been 'all that', was slowly calming down. To hasten harmony, Gillian had decided to treat them both to a new outfit. Now, however, standing in a changing room, twisting this way and that in skinny jeans which had looked great on a picture of Elle Macpherson but made Gillian's thighs look like the last two sausages in the packet, she wondered what on earth had possessed her.

'I like this one,' Holly announced, pulling back the curtain. 'Oh, sorry!' she exclaimed cheerily as her mother was revealed wearing nothing but an ill-fitting flesh-coloured bra and the jeans. 'What do you think?'

'Put the curtain back,' Gillian hissed. She looked at the black, ripped faux-leather dress. She hated this bit. If she pointed out any flaws then Holly would set her heart upon it.

'I prefer the pink,' she tried.

'Mum! The pink's lame. So girly! I *knew* you'd like that one best.'

'You asked for my opinion.'

'You said I could choose. I can buy what I like.'

'I know.'

'So why are you criticizing me?'

'I'm not. I said I preferred the pink one. If you like that dress, get it. Only . . .'

'Only what?'

The assistant's head turned. What a hopeless mother, she was clearly thinking. From behind her, Gillian heard a girl about Holly's age exclaim, 'You should try it in blue, Mum, you always look great in blue.'

'I'm getting it *and* I'm going to try on the other black dress you were pulling a face at.'

The curtain closed again. Gillian pulled a top over her head that she was hoping would make her look carefree and boho. The mirror revealed a crazed librarian. She was about to take it off when her phone rang. Good. Finally the vet's assistant calling back about Waffle's de-worming. Or would it be another Temperley suitor? They'd sent her on two dates so far, both unsuccessful, but third time lucky.

'Hello?'

'Oh, Gillian. Hi. It's, um, Tony Forbes. Temperley gave me your number.'

Gillian was jolted. 'Oh, hello, Tony. How are you?'

'Fine thanks.' Quite a deep voice. Classless. No regional accent to help place him. All Masha at the agency had said was that they were perfect for each other and Gillian had to trust her. 'So, I was wondering if you fancied a drink some time?'

Holly pulled back the curtain again. 'Who are you talking to, Mum?'

'Just a minute. Um. Yes. A drink would be lovely. Soon. Can I get back to you?'

'Are you talking to a *man*?' Holly's jaw dropped. Gillian hung up. Damn. She'd managed the dates so far without Holly twigging, but her clear run couldn't have continued forever.

'Was that your boyfriend?' Holly continued.

'No, it wasn't.' Gillian shoved the phone back in her bag.

'I bet it was. Mum, do you have a boyfriend?'

'Don't be silly.' They both giggled. Holly struck an attitude in another black faux-leather dress. She looked undeniably beautiful, but she also looked like she was applying for a job in an establishment where grown men wore nappies and had dummies shoved in their mouths.

'Muuum! Do not tell me you still like the pink best.'

'The decision is yours, darling.'

'Whatever. Like, why did I bring you with me, anyway? Like, what you know about fashion could fit on my little finger.' Holly's eyes turned to the skinny jeans. 'Oh my God. What's that? Look at your love handles creeping over.' She reached out and grabbed the top firmly so it settled over Gillian's bust, once splendid but long ravaged from a year's breastfeeding. Why had she bothered?

'It's no good. It just doesn't fit you. I hope you're not going to pay all that money for something that doesn't fit. What was all that about not increasing my allowance this month? You've got plenty to spend on clothes for yourself, haven't you?'

'I work very hard, so I can occasionally buy myself an outfit.'

'Why do you need one? Is it for the boyfriend?'

Gillian swatted her gently on the shoulder. 'Don't be ridiculous.'

They laughed, friends once more, even if Gillian was deflated. Holly was right, she was mutton dressed as lamb. She wouldn't buy the jeans, she'd settle for the silk scarf. Accessorizing – a sure sign of middle age, kidding herself that a piece of wispy blue silk near the face might somehow help her lose ten years.

'Come on,' she said to Holly. 'Change back and I'll pay.'

'For the dress?' Holly said hopefully.

'Just this once. If you promise you will do some holiday work this afternoon.'

Holly shrieked. 'Oh, thank you! You're the best mum in the world.' She flung her arms round her and kissed her. If it hadn't been for the fact that she reeked of tobacco, Gillian would have notched this up as one of their good moments.

19

All the way to meet Gillian, Tony's stomach was performing handstands. What was he doing? he asked himself, as the Northern Line carried him to Hampstead. It had been bad enough going into the agency and answering Gary's questions – decent bloke though he seemed to be – and then making that dreadful video. But having to actually go on a date was Guantanamo-level torture.

What was he doing? Actually, he knew the answer to this: he was trying to make Zu happy. She wanted him paired off so he'd do his best to oblige. She was right. He'd been a hermit too long and it was time to move on. Zu insisted Gillian was perfect for him and she had at least sounded sane on the phone . . .

Gillian had suggested a bar in one of the Dickensian, postcard-perfect streets off the High Street. It had dark red walls, candles burning in nooks, a wooden floor covered in a selection of bright woven rugs, little cane tables tucked away in corners and according to the pretty waitress – Colombian? Guatemalan? – that was Gillian, waiting at one of them.

He took a deep breath and approached.

'Gillian?'

'Hi, Tony!' She stood up, smiling, and held out a hand. Long, dark hair, big eyes, a turned-up mouth. She wore a pale blue silk shirt under a soft black jacket. She was attractive, definitely, but was she his kind of attractive? At least she wasn't going to try to kiss him; Tony found people who kissed you on first meeting deeply unnerving. Did they think they were French?

'So, is it to be wine?' he asked, sitting down. 'Or are you driving?'

'Vodka and tonic for me,' she said, smiling. 'I've learnt that the only way to fuel these sessions is with hard stuff.'

Tony smiled back. 'How long have you been doing it?'

'Just a couple of weeks. You're only my third. You?'

'This is my first. You're a veteran of the trenches in comparison. So how has it been for you? So far?'

'Well, my first date was with a man who asked: "If you were starving to death on a desert island, which body part would you eat first?" And then I had coffee with a guy who complained that his mother hadn't ironed the shirt he'd wanted to wear. He must have been about fifty.'

They both laughed a little too long, then she said, 'The agency told me you're a widower. You seem young for that.'

'My wife died in a car crash,' Tony explained. 'She was just about to turn forty.'

'I'm sorry.'

No gasps. No screams. Good. 'And you? I mean . . . are you a widow?'

'Divorced. My ex has just had a baby with a twenty-two-year-old.' She shrugged and raised an eyebrow. 'Good luck to them both. Do you have children?'

He told her about the boys and Zu, whom Gillian had met.

'I was a bit surprised when they said they wanted me to go on a date with her father,' Gillian said. 'But then I thought: "Why not?" I mean, she's beautiful and very polite. But whatever brought her from Chechnya to a dating agency in central London? Quite a change.'

'Who knows? Zu doesn't like being questioned. Once or twice I've tried to put it to her that it worries me stupid having her working in all these danger zones and she's –'

'Flown off the handle?' Gillian smiled knowingly. 'That's what Holly would do.'

Tony shook his head. 'Flying off the handle isn't Zu's style. She more . . . retreats into herself. She doesn't argue but you know she's going to nod politely and then just go off and do whatever she wants to do. It does worry me, what's going on underneath that brisk surface. I beat myself up wondering how I could have paid her more attention after my wife died. I was so wrapped up in the boys, you see . . .' He stopped, aware he might be revealing too much. 'Anyway, what she does is very noble. The world's a better place thanks to people like her. But I have to confess I'm glad there's a global recession and she's working behind a desk just a few miles from me, even if her job's not one I would have predicted.'

'Maybe she wants to help you?' Gillian suggested.

Tony shook his head. 'Oh, no. She's just trying to earn some money.' He realized he might have inadvertently insulted Gillian by suggesting that meeting her hadn't helped him at all. 'Er, so . . . what about your daughter? What's she like?'

Gillian told him a bit about Holly.

'Hard work,' Tony said sympathetically.

'I'm sure nothing like as hard as it's been for you. With three of them.'

'Most single mothers can't stand the sight of me,' Tony confided. 'They hate the way I get showered in praise when I just do the same as them.'

'I can see that. But then you probably didn't have the same support network as a single mum would have. No doubt you wouldn't have had a clue as to where to turn to for advice a lot of the time. Or did your mum help out?'

'Not really, she's always been too busy going on cruises with my dad. Spending my inheritance.'

They smiled at each other, then both took a too-big gulp of their drinks. 'Did your children ever smoke dope?' Gillian asked.

'I think they all had their moments,' Tony said, wondering if she was going to invite him back to hers for a smoke. 'I tried to be strict with them, told them we had a zero-tolerance policy on drugs. It was tricky because, of course, all around them their friends' parents were doing it, but I think the message got through. It never turned into a problem, or at least one that I knew of.' *Anyway, my children were never that attracted by drugs because they'd seen their mother in such a state.* But they weren't anywhere near having that conversation yet.

'I've never caught her in the act, but Holly reeks of it more and more. She says it's people around her and, anyway, it's harmless, but I don't know.'

'It's just a phase,' Tony said comfortingly.

'Yes, maybe. I hope so.' Gillian glanced at her watch. Tony glanced at his. The hour was up. Temperley was very clear that no one should spend more than an hour on a first date and discouraged them from going for meals at this early stage.

'Well, thanks,' she said as they stood on the pavement, hugging themselves against the evening chill. 'I enjoyed that. Perhaps we could do it again in a couple of weeks.'

Tony felt a rush of inexplicable terror. 'Yeah, maybe,' he said vaguely. 'That could be good.'

'Great. Well. See you then.' She looked down at the ground, then up at him, smiling shyly. 'I won't kiss you, though.'

'That's fine.'

They walked to the Tube together, where she went south and he went north. Cycling home from Edgware station, he tried to concentrate on the road, but his thoughts were skidding all over the place. He *liked* Gillian, definitely. But he just didn't want to sleep with her. Or rather if she offered herself to him, nude, he'd say yes, but he had no overwhelming desire to rip her clothes off.

Ten minutes to fall in love. Tony thought it was a daft slogan, but that was how it had worked with Deepi.

He'd fallen for her because of her gorgeous eyes and slender waist. But that had turned out to be no foundation for family life. When they were screaming at each other after the twins were born, when Deepi refused to let him anywhere near her sore, leaking, Caesarean-wearied body, he'd secretly wondered if Leela was right about arranged marriages. If it was better to see marriage as a contract, rather than a romantic endeavour. He'd wondered again when they'd been arguing about who'd changed the most nappies in this tiny semi in Edgware, when Deepi was telling him how if she hadn't met him she'd have probably been paired off with a Bangalore billionaire and be living in a palace waited on hand and foot. Yes, all that grief because he'd been instantly smitten by pert breasts and a dazzling smile. There had been more to it than that though. In the early days they'd sit up talking all night and have such fun and if he was away from her just for the day his heart would ache with longing.

Later, of course, everything had changed. He'd sit watching TV with his heart thudding, phone in hand, waiting for the call to come summoning him to bars where she'd got into fights with strangers, from parks where she'd be sitting barefoot and shivering on a bench, robbed of her bag. It was the selfishness he found hardest, the fact that when she was drinking she genuinely didn't seem to give a monkey's about him or the children, that nothing mattered except the booze. She'd go to any lengths and risk losing everything just for a few drops of liquor.

And the lies, the way she'd swear that everything was OK and then he'd find the cooking sherry was gone and when he searched the wardrobes there were empty vodka bottles stuffed inside suitcases, in the arms of coats, inside pillowcases in the linen cupboard. It was like she was having an affair, but with the bottle.

'Go to a support group,' Renu, his sister-in-law – and one of the very few people who knew what was going on – urged him. But he couldn't: sharing his experiences would be too shameful, and besides, he was afraid to leave the children alone in the house at night in case Deepi drank too much and attacked them – that had never happened but you never knew.

'Let her take responsibility for her actions. Let her

realize the consequences,' said Renu. Eventually, he'd listened to that bit and stopped calling in for her to work saying Deepi was sick again, so she'd lost her job, but then she'd been furious and she'd drunk even more.

'Kick her out,' urged Renu. 'She has to reach rock bottom before she can turn around.' But that was so much easier said than done. Every time he'd braced himself to do it, she seemed to sense it and would pull herself together. She'd go to AA and vow it was all over.

Just before she died she'd been in one of her sober phases, but then they'd argued about the boys and what school they might go to next, of all stupid things, and she'd stormed off in the car to the supermarket and hadn't returned, and a couple of hours later the policeman had knocked on the door.

As always, when he replayed the scene, Tony smacked his forehead and his bike swerved wildly for a second. 'You fucking idiot.' If only he'd prevented her leaving, hidden the car keys, taken away all her money, stopped her bank account so she couldn't pay for the booze. But he'd tried all that at one time or another and somehow she'd always outwitted him.

He didn't deserve another woman. He'd as good as killed the one he had, no matter what the therapists all said. In the morning he'd break it to Zu that Gillian was lovely, thank you, but not for him and, thank you, but enough was enough.

20

Zu had gone out on Sunday night with some old friends from uni, who were passing through London. She didn't get in until midnight, by which time Tony was long asleep. No note saying how it had gone but that didn't mean anything either way, she decided as she drunkenly brushed her teeth. She'd accost him in the morning.

But the next day, as ever, he'd left the house before she woke up and when she called, the phone went straight to voicemail. Oh well. She left a message, asking him to call her, then headed to work.

'Any news?' Gary bellowed as soon as she walked into the room.

Zu shook her head. 'I've left him a message.'

'Well, why don't I call Gillian now?' He picked up the phone and bashed the speaker. Zu's heart flopped as Gillian picked up.

'Oh hi, Gary.' She sounded wary. Zu knew.

'Just wanted to see how it went?'

'Oh, Gary. Listen. I'm really sorry. I liked Tony. He's definitely the best of the lot. But the spark just wasn't there.'

'What?' Masha mouthed indignantly.

'Gillian,' Gary cooed. 'Are you sure? You know, one of our Temperley mottos is "Leave your comfort zone". If you like someone, then the fancying bit may grow. You know that guy you used to work with? At first you thought he was a bit fat but then you got to know him and he made you laugh and –'

'That never happened to me, Gary. Anyway, I thought it was ten minutes to fall in love?'

'Sometimes. But sometimes love is more organic. Like muesli.' Gary chortled. 'C'mon. What do you say? Give Tony another shot.'

'I'm sorry, Gary. It's just not going to happen.'

'Think it over,' Gary urged. 'But look, if it really isn't going to happen, of course we won't force it. I hope you're going to come to our party next Thursday.'

'I can't, I have a work do that night. Sorry.' Her tone changed. 'I have to go, one of my clients is on the other line and she's very demanding. Sorry!' *Click*. Dial tone.

'Bugger,' said Gary.

''S'OK. Plenty more to choose from.' Zu shrugged, suppressing the urge to kill Gillian. Didn't she know a good thing when she saw it?

'Absolutely,' Masha chimed in. 'Always I had my doubts about this match.'

'Will you break it to your father?' Gary asked. 'Or shall I?'

'I'll do it,' Zu sighed.

'Well, now he can come to the party seeing as that ungrateful woman will not be there,' humphed Masha. The party was taking place the following week, at an art gallery in Clerkenwell belonging to a former client they'd successfully matched.

'I don't know if he'll want to. But I'll ask.' For the rest of the day, Zu was put out over Gillian's rejection. She hadn't been that pretty anyway. Her face was a bit horsey. Her shoes were stupid. She dreaded breaking the news to Tony and – as the day went by and he didn't call – she realized she'd have to do it in person. Not that night, though, because she was meeting Henchie again. To her mild surprise, he'd called the day after their trip to La Fromagerie and asked if she could make the inaugural outing of the Make London Fun club on Monday night.

'I'll meet you at Eros. Seven thirty.'

'Eros? That's where tourists meet.'

'Exactly. We're tourists in our own city. See you there, missy.' The last was said in an atrocious Dick Van Dyke Cockney accent. Zu groaned and laughed as she hung up. *Why not?* she'd thought. And now here she was, standing beneath the swirling neon signs of Piccadilly Circus. Groups of French, Italian, Spanish and Brazilian tourists were yabbering away, poring over maps and flirting with each other, the carved fountain towering above them dominated by Eros's winged statue. Zu had never really looked at it before. Before the flashing hoardings were erected with just a donkey and cart trotting past, it must actually have been a splendid sight.

Jack was wearing faded jeans and a T-shirt and looked far more like his old self than he had in La Fromagerie.

'Aha.' He stood up and kissed her briskly. 'Glad you're here. Did you know the statue isn't actually of Eros, it's of his twin brother, Anteros?'

'I didn't know that. *Dix points* to team Henchie.'

He nodded in mock smugness. 'Do you know who Anteros is? He's the God who punishes those who scorn love and the advances of others.'

'Really?'

'Just sayin'.' He grinned. Zu stuck her tongue out. 'Apparently if you stand under him at the stroke of midnight you'll be lucky in love forever.' Before she could make a sarcastic comment, he continued: 'Commissioned to commemorate the great philanthropist Lord Shaftesbury who stopped little children going down coal mines. Which seemed very appropriate for you as well.'

'I've never stopped a child going down a mine – all for keeping them busy, myself.'

'Ah, don't downplay your do-gooding, Forbes. Everyone knows you're the angel of Grozny.'

She faked a yawn. 'So what touristy stuff do you have in mind?'

'If it's good enough for them, it's good enough for us.' He turned and started dodging through the crowds, then stopped abruptly. 'For example, have you ever been here?'

'To the Trocadero?' Zu was aghast. 'Of course not!'

Jack gestured to the doors.

'We can't go in there. It's horrible.'

'How do you know? You've never been.'

They walked into a cacophonous, neon maze. Everywhere were booths selling fluorescent candy, Chinese lanterns, postcards of Beefeaters, 'I Heart London' T-shirts and Japanese manga.

Confused tourists directed there by their guidebook's description of 'London's premier dining and entertainment area' scratched their heads. Jack and Zu walked down some steps and suddenly found themselves in an open space with dozens of teenagers in tracksuits break-dancing to the sound of silence. In a room to the side, more kids were playing pool.

'It's like a youth club on acid.'

'Enjoy it for what it is,' Jack said, as they headed towards the escalators. 'Come on.'

Two hours later they had played on most of the arcade games, gunning down aliens and zombies. Satisfyingly, Zu had beaten Jack at least seventy-five per cent of the time. They'd lost a lot of money, then won it, then lost it again on the two-penny falls. They'd chased each other round on the dodgems. They'd played air hockey. They'd been in the casino, where they'd won one hundred and fifty pounds on roulette the first time they played and lost it all the second time.

'Enough now,' Zu said. 'Time for a drink.'

'Plenty of bars here.'

She raised an eyebrow. 'Do you mind? The joke's running its course.'

'All right then, we need to find an olde worlde London pub. Preferably one with wenches in mob caps pulling pints.'

'Yup, that sounds like your kinda place, Henchie.'

'All right, we'll find one filled with Chippendale stud-muffins for you, Forbes.' He paused. 'Or we could get a bite.'

'I guess,' Zu said. As ever, she had given no thought to eating. Food was fuel to her, no more. 'Where will we go?'

'Well, it really has to be an Angus Steakhouse. Don't you think? Have you ever been to one?'

She shook her head.

'Well then. Isn't that the point?'

They walked across Leicester Square. Zu pulled her cigarettes out of her satchel and offered one to Henchie. He shook his head.

'Filthy habit.'

'You used to smoke about a hundred a day.'

'Used to, yes. I gave up. Xander asked me to. You should follow my example. How long have you smoked for?'

'Since I was a teenager. My mum smoked quite a lot. I used to pick up her butts from the ashtray. And I used to pick up her wine glasses at parties and swallow what was left.'

'Trying to be grown up,' Henchie said fondly. Zu smiled and nodded. It hadn't really been like that, it was that she'd seen Mum lured away from her by the booze and she'd wanted to understand what exactly was so appealing about it. But she'd already told Henchie more than she normally told anyone. There'd be no more revelations for now.

They made their way down a side street lined with cafés selling cappuccinos to bewildered tourists and on to Charing Cross Road. The Steakhouse's windows were filled with couples staring miserably past each other's shoulders, jaws moving rhythmically.

'Is this really a good idea?' This time Jack asked and Zu seized the initiative.

'Course it is. They serve alcohol, don't they?'

She realized as she sat down that so far she'd actually enjoyed the evening without a drink. Strange for her, as she usually liked to be well-lubricated. Every now and then she wondered if she should curb her fondness for alcohol – but she wasn't like her mother, she wouldn't let it get out of hand.

Jack was looking at the menu intently. 'It's got to be prawn cocktail, then two sirloins well done.'

The Trocadero was one thing, but this was too much. 'I can't! I can't eat steak well done. That's not a food choice, it's a crime.'

'Really? Most girls can't stand bloody meat.'

'I am *not* a girl.'

'Sorry, sorry, Millie Tant. Most *women* don't like rare meat.'

'Most women can't drive or do maths, they say.' She shrugged. 'But remember who got the jeep out of the mud that time we were driving back down from the mountains? *And* I got an A in my maths A level.'

Henchie held up his hands in surrender. '*And* you like stinky cheese. Do you like offal?'

'Love it.'

He shook his head. 'Wonders will never cease. All this time I've known you and I never knew I could have been sharing a plate of tripe with you.'

Zu laughed. 'I'm sure we often ate much worse than tripe in Grozny.'

'Just as well I love dog and cat meat.'

'How's Xander?' she tried after they'd ordered (two prawn cocktails, two sirloins rare) and embarked on a bottle of vinegary red.

Jack smiled. 'Cute as hell. Want to see a picture I took at the weekend?'

'Sure.' The iPhone was passed over. The first picture that came up wasn't a little boy though, it was a woman with a golden sheet of hair blowing behind her, wrinkling her nose at the camera in an 'aren't I cute' way. Very beautiful. But Jack's women always were.

'Oh, sorry. Not that one.'

'Who's that?'

'Just someone,' Jack shrugged, snatching the phone off her and scrolling on. Zu glimpsed several more pictures. Poor woman, she was probably sitting in her bedroom right now, working out how to word a text to him. Zu had seen Anj do plenty of that over the years. 'Here. This one.'

Xander was holding a fishing net and beaming into the lens.

'Lovely,' Zu said. He was.

'His grandparents are still being twats. I want to take him skiing in February and they're going all tight-lipped about it. Anyone would think I was a convicted drug dealer, instead of a reformed caner.' He gazed mournfully into his wine glass then, looking up, asked, 'So what about your family? What's going on there?'

'My family?' Zu was startled. 'Not a lot.'

'Your mum's dead, isn't she?'

'How did you know that?'

'I just did. You mentioned it once when you were pissed, I think. Sorry. Do you mind me asking?'

'No, not at all.' *Yes!*

'Where was she from, your mum? And your dad?'

'Dad's English. Mum's British Indian.'

'Which makes you . . .?'

'English, of course, Henchie.'

'But do you feel at all Indian? Have you ever been there?'

'I've never been. Mum's ashes are scattered in the Ganges, but . . .'

'You didn't scatter them?'

'No. My grandmother did. One day I'd like to go there . . .' She trailed away. What about you, where are you from?'

'Well, I was born in Scotland, lived in Norwich for the first years of my life, went to boarding school in Surrey, uni in America, worked all over the world. Don't really feel I belong anywhere.' He finished his glass and refilled both. 'And how did you end up in Chechnya?'

'I did Russian at school – I loved it because it was so different from everything else. Different alphabet, different grammar.'

'Fucking impossible grammar – two forms of every verb.'

'I like that.' Zu smiled. 'And I liked the literature, all those massive themes. Everything seemed on such a huge scale compared to Edgware – that's where I grew up.' She didn't add that the scale helped her put her own troubles in perspective. 'And then I went to St Petersburg for part of my uni course and I just loved it – the history everyone was living through, the way everyone wants to wear Gucci but at the same time they've all read *War and Peace*.'

'Have you read it?'

Zu nodded smugly. 'In the original, of course. And then in the holidays two friends and I travelled round Uzbekistan, Kyrgyzstan and Kazakhstan and we just had such an adventure . . . we lived off one jar of chocolate spread. We were always bribing people, we were always dirty – it was brilliant.'

'Ah, you young people,' Henchie said teasingly.

'Yes, Grandpa. How old are you?'

'Thirty-six.' He smiled. 'Actually, I do remember enjoying all that before I joined the oil business and sold out to The Man.' An almost dreamy look passed over his face, then he and said: 'Look, don't answer if you don't want to, but how do you think losing your mother affected you? Because I worry about Xander, what it's going to be like for him growing up without a mum. I mean, mine was fairly useless, she bunged me off to boarding school when I was seven, but at least I knew she was out there somewhere.'

He gazed mournfully into space. Zu knew this was her cue to reach out her hand to him, to tell him her heart bled for the poor little abandoned boy. She'd seen many other women do the same, only to have it thrown back in their faces. *It's not going to work on me, Henchie.*

'So do you think Xander will be OK?' he repeated.

'Sure. He's very young.' Reluctantly, because they were talking about a little boy whom she obviously felt sorry for and wanted to help, she continued, 'It was easier for my brothers than for me, I think.'

'Brothers?'

'Yeah, I've got two. Twins.' Her pride must have been audible because Jack's expression changed somehow. Zu cleared her throat. 'They're eighteen now but they were only ten when Mum died.' Zu remembered one Sunday morning when they'd been going to visit someone, probably Anjali's family – by that stage they tended to avoid most social interaction. They'd all been in the car waiting for Mum. When she eventually emerged for some reason she flung herself over the bonnet and was taunting Tony to run her over. She'd snapped off the aerial and started banging the windows with it. The boys had been screaming hysterically; Zu, who was about fourteen, had her arm round both of them. Everyone in Farthingdale Road must have heard. It was ten in the morning for Christ's sake. How had the boys processed that?

'Are you OK?' Jack asked.

'Yes, yes, it's just hot in here.' She pulled herself together and took a bite of the prawn cocktail, but the prawns tasted of old sponge and she pushed the dish away.

'Xander will be OK,' she said. 'He won't really remember his mum. Even my brothers don't remember that much.' At least that was what Zu hoped. Was it worse that their mother had never really been available to kiss their bruised knees, help with their homework, hug them when one of the kids at school said nasty things – or was it worse to be like Zu and remember a time when Deepika had done all those things and then to witness the change?

'And what about you? How old were you?'

'Eighteen.'

'That's tough. Someone told me that the worst thing about losing your mum is that you no longer believe in happy endings. You're not innocent any more. You know that the worst thing can happen. I hate thinking that might be the case for Xander.'

'I knew that before my mother died,' Zu said.

'Did you?' Henchie was surprised.

'She'd been ill for a long time,' Zu said hastily.

'And how does it feel when you hear people moaning about their mothers: that they're always nagging them to come and stay for the weekend, or whatever? Do you think "ungrateful sods"?'

'I'm always moaning about my father, so no. Doesn't mean I want him dead. Parents are meant to be annoying.'

Henchie laughed. 'I hope I'll be able to live up to that gold standard.'

Mercifully, the conversation moved on. They talked about Chechnya, what had happened to friends there, how Putin was pouring money into the region in the hopes of appeasing the terrorists. It was good to talk to someone who understood what it was like out there: most people hadn't got a clue and if you tried to tell them they'd start yawning and glancing at their watches.

'So do you want to go back?' she asked as she munched on the last chip. The steaks had arrived semi-cremated and they'd quickly abandoned them.

Henchie shrugged. 'I'd like to be somewhere in the old Soviet Union. It's what I know. It speaks to me. It seems so much more alive than here. But it's not going to happen now. Not until Xander's old enough to come with me, at any rate, and I can't see that ever going down too well with the in-laws. What about you?'

'Desperate to.' She laughed. 'Though at the moment there seems to be about as much chance of getting there as to the moon.'

'Now that's one place I've always wanted to go.'

'When I was a kid I so wanted to be an astronaut.' Zu had forgotten all about that until now.

'You'd be brilliant. Floating around in space mending portaloos.'

'Astronauts actually wear nappies most of the time,' Zu

told him. 'I've always wanted to share that nugget with someone.'

Jack laughed. 'Well, all the oligarchs are working on it. Won't be long before we'll be able to go on holiday to the moon. In nappies.'

'But if it's a holiday destination I wouldn't want to go there. There'd be a moon Trocadero and a moon Angus Steakhouse. It's the silence that appeals to me. The solitude. Earth being a tiny green and blue ball far away that I could look down on.'

'A party animal like you? You'd be lonely.'

'I'm not really a party animal,' she said softly.

'That's not how I remember you. What about that night in the Royal Bar? You and that German photographer with the BO.'

'What German photographer?'

'Better that you've forgotten all about him. Phwoar, did he need deodorant.' The waitress reappeared with the dessert menu. Henchie shook his head. 'The bill, please.' He smiled winningly at Zu. 'You don't have a cigarette, do you?'

'I thought you'd cleaned up your act.'

'Fags smoked at night don't count. Everyone knows that.' The bill was plonked in front of him on a plastic tray. 'I'll get it.'

'Don't be macho, Henchie. We'll share it.'

'I'm earning a lot more money than you.'

'That's not the point.' She slapped down some cash. 'Dutch.'

He laughed. 'Dutch it is, Millie Tant.'

They stepped outside. After the Steakhouse's sweaty

interior, it was bone-bitingly chilly, autumn suddenly in the air. Zu, in a T-shirt and trousers, wrapped her arms tightly round herself. She'd always felt the cold horribly. The winters in Chechnya were freezing, of course, but the summers were hot and sticky, unlike here where there always seemed to be a breeze.

'Look,' Jack said, gesturing upwards. In the clear night sky the moon glowed, almost full. Almost perfect. 'That's where you'd like to be.'

'One day,' Zu said. She ground out her cigarette under the heel of her trainer. A wispy violet cloud passed over the moon then disappeared into the blackness. She thought of Farthingdale Road and her father. She didn't want to go back there until she knew he'd be fast asleep; didn't want to break the news about Gillian. 'Shall we find a pub? Let's have another drink.'

21

Another whole day had passed before she and Tony sat down together, over pasta with grated courgettes, crème fraîche and mint. A Jamie recipe, Tony told her proudly. *As if I care*, Zu thought, taking a large gulp of wine and saying, 'Very nice. So, are you going to tell me? How did it go with Gillian?'

'Fine. Hmm, I think it could have done with a touch more salt.'

'Only fine?' Zu's relief that she wasn't going to have to break his heart mingled with offence that he wasn't more enthusiastic about the woman selected for him.

Tony sighed. 'Don't take this badly. Gillian was very nice. But I don't want to go on another date with her. Or with anyone. I just don't think I'm ready for all this.'

'How can you not be ready?' Zu cried, exasperated. 'It's been eight years.'

'I know. Not not-ready like that, more just . . . I need to do it myself. Not be set up by anyone else. I just can't face all the getting-to-know-you stuff. I don't believe that's how love works. It shouldn't be like a job interview. It should be more like Cupid's dart hitting. A bolt from the blue.'

Oh, please! 'OK,' Zu said testily.

'Do you understand?' Tony asked imploringly.

'You had bolts from the blue with Mum.'

'That was different. Mum's problems had nothing to do with how we felt about each other, how we fell in love. There was . . . It was . . . One day you'll understand.'

'How patronizing are you!' And wrong. She'd never understand, she didn't want to.

'Sorry,' Tony said humbly.

She shrugged. 'It's up to you, Dad. I was only trying to help.'

'I know. I appreciate it.'

At least she wasn't going to have to break the news that Gillian didn't fancy him. She cleared her throat. 'Look, Dad, why don't you give it just one more try. The agency's having a drinks party on Thursday for a few clients at an art gallery in Clerkenwell. You could come along, meet a few people? Then if it doesn't work out, it doesn't work out. We'll say no more about it.'

A pause.

'What do you think?'

'In an art gallery?'

'Yeah. So at the very worst, there'll be paintings to look at.'

Tony sighed. 'OK. I'll come.'

The party was in a quiet backstreet of graceful Georgian terraced houses just off St John's Street. As Zu approached, she saw Tony, in jeans and stripy blue shirt, standing at the top of the entrance steps, with an expression on his face as if he was about to dive into a pit of fire.

'You made it!' she exclaimed.

'Of course. Traffic was actually pretty good. I've just avoided paying the congestion charge.'

'Well done.' Normally Zu would have drenched this Daddism in sarcasm but she hadn't been sure he'd really come and here he was. Her heart filled like a sponge with one of its unexpected bursts of love for him. She squeezed his hand. 'Thank you.'

Tony smiled. 'Thank you for inviting me. I can drive you home now.'

'Thanks.' God, this was turning into a gratitude festival.

Zu rang on the big black door. It was opened by a woman of about her age. She wore skinny jeans with a tight pale-orange jumper, and her red, curly hair was held on top of her head with what looked like a sparkly pencil. She had a heart-shaped face and a long, straight nose that tilted at the end. She was undoubtedly pretty, but there was also something slightly grubby about her, like a used handkerchief.

'Hiyaaa.' She had a weird accent that was half American, half Kate Middleton and entirely annoying. 'Come in. You are?'

'Zu. From Temperley.'

'Tony.' Tony looked bewildered. 'Are you Masha?'

The woman creased with laughter. 'Me? God, no. I'm Josie, Elin's sister. Elin, the artist,' she explained, as he continued to look blank.

'Oh, right!'

'Come in, come in. There's already a few of you here.'

They followed Josie into the gallery. The walls were lined with huge canvases daubed with smears of orange paint, blobs that could be hearts, childish houses with smoke coming out of the chimneys, blobby flowers, stick people. In the middle of the room, a woman who had to be Elin – petite, long hair with silver streaks, dressed in leggings, leather gladiator sandals and a voluminous blue smock – held court.

'Are those paintings meant to be good?' Tony whispered to Zu.

'I don't know. I never know with art. If they're on the wall, then they must be.'

'It looks like the kind of thing Rohan did after Casey Trander dumped him and he drank nine pints of snakebite.'

'Philistine.'

They tried to stifle giggles. Zu's heart bubbled again at one of their rare moments of togetherness.

About thirty men and women were standing around holding glasses of wine and conversing. The volume was low; body language was awkward. It was very obvious that none of them had met before and that everyone was on their best behaviour. Zu looked at them appraisingly. Average age probably late forties. Women, smartly dressed in heels and dresses, hair carefully blow-dried, skin just starting to go leathery but carefully made-up, skinny arms and legs. Men – on the whole – in suits that just revealed the curve of their gut, their cheeks fat, red and veined. Oh God. Tony wasn't going to be pleased to be counted within their numbers.

There were only two lively corners of the room – one where Gary was booming with laughter, and the other where Masha, in a white jumpsuit, was entertaining a group with anecdotes about builders.

Josie, who'd come up behind them, turned to Tony. 'So I know Zu works for Temperley, but what's your connection to all this?'

'Me? I'm Zu's dad.'

She pushed him gently. 'Get awaaaay! How can that be possible?'

Tony actually blushed. *For God's sake*, Zu thought. 'Dad married young,' she said crisply.

'You must have done. Bloody hell.' Josie looked him up and down. Tony blushed even deeper. *Yuck.*

'Where's your mum?'

'She's not here. She's dead,' Zu said briskly.

'Oh my God.' Scarlet, chipped nails flew to Josie's painted mouth. 'But that's awful! How . . . I mean, did she . . . I mean, don't talk about it if you don't want to.'

''S'OK,' Tony said. 'She was killed in a car crash.'

Masha rushed up. 'Darling,' she said to Zu, 'come and meet some of the clients. They need help to start mingling. Once you know a few names you can start introducing them to one another. Come.'

So Zu was whisked off and within minutes was talking to Matt Billen, who'd just joined Temperley two months ago. He was in his forties but he wore brightly coloured trainers and a purple velour hoodie. His brown hair was just slightly too long for his beaky face.

'I enjoyed filling in the agency's form,' Matt said. 'It's so rare you have an opportunity to analyse yourself like that. It made me think about all sorts of things. Am I creative? Well, I think we know the answer to that. Am I intellectual? Well, not in a poncey Oxbridge way but if you could study emotional intelligence I'm pretty sure I'd have the PhD. Am I religious? Absolutely . . .'

Zu smiled politely. They talked a bit more. Matt told her he was only interested in women under thirty. 'Which writes virtually all of this lot off,' he said with a dismissive wave at the room.

'Temperley isn't really for the under-thirties,' Zu explained. 'If that's what your heart's set on, then maybe you should try online.'

Matt shook his head.

'I've been there, done that. The Internet's full of con artists. Nobody posts an accurate picture and they all lie about their ages. At least you guys are telling the truth. I want to meet a woman who's young, like me.'

'You're forty-two.'

'That's young! For a man.' Matt downed his glass and looked about for a waiter to refill it. 'Your service is meant to be exclusive. It's bloody expensive. If you can't find me a woman who's twenty-seven or twenty-eight then I don't know what I'm paying for.'

Zu looked wildly around the room. She spotted Tony in a corner talking to Masha. He looked tense. She wanted to be looking after him, not this spoilt loser. She grabbed the first available passing woman.

'Hi, I don't think we've met. I'm Zu. I've just started at Temperley. And you are?'

'Hi. I'm Antonia,' said the woman. She was very tall with a magnificent bosom displayed to best advantage by her blue and white dress. She had black curly hair, huge baggy eyes and a square chin that gave her the unfortunate look of an inbred minor European royal. She also had, despite the sexy outfit, an oddly sexless air to her.

Matt regarded her with barely disguised contempt. Zu felt a flare of pity. She'd been meaning to introduce them but, instead, she pointedly turned her back on Matt and asked Antonia, 'So how long have you been with Temperley?'

'Four months,' Antonia said, blinking hard. 'And it took at least another four months to pluck up the courage to join. I'd just come out of a long relationship.'

'Oh, right.' Zu smiled politely.

'Mmm. I'd been with Jeremy for nine years. I really thought that was it, you know. I mean, we were married in everything but name; we'd been trying to have a baby for the last nine months we were together. And then one day I wake up and he tells me he's in love with a twenty-nine-year-old and the next thing I know he's packed his bags and he's gone. I mean, I even had the prescription in my bag for his piles medicine. I went round and put it through their letterbox.'

'Right,' Zu said faintly.

More talk, more introductions, more drinks, more sad stories. Suddenly it was eleven and the party was over. Tony approached her through the diminishing crowd.

'Shall we make a move? Or do you need to stay on?'

Zu glanced at Masha. 'I need to stay and tidy up.'

Masha gave a regal wave. 'No, off you go. You live practically in countryside. We can tidy up, don't worry about us.'

'Thank you, Masha,' Zu said. Suddenly Josie was standing between her and her father.

'You couldn't give me a lift too, could you? You're in Edgware, aren't you? I'm in Hatch End.'

'Hatch End's nowhere near us,' Zu said as Tony replied, 'Sure!'

Josie gasped. '*Would* you? Thank you!'

'It's a pleasure,' said Tony, his neck flushing, as voices shouted in Zu's head: *Uh oh.*

She had to graciously vacate the front seat of the car, although she hated the back, where she always felt nauseous, not least after a few drinks. Josie's cloying perfume was choking her, so she wound down the window, letting in a chilly wind.

'It's so sweet of you to give me a lift,' Josie was saying. 'Taxis are so expensive here. I've just come back from living in Nashville and there everything's so much cheaper. London's come as a shock.'

'What were you doing there?' Zu asked. She was jealous. She'd been to loads of places but never Nashville, despite her secret passion for Dolly Parton. Very few people knew about that.

'This and that,' Josie sighed in answer to Zu's question. 'Right now I'm mainly working in a beauty salon, doing massages and the like. It's not exactly a classy place, it's called Gor-Jus.' She spelt it out, laughing. 'Trying to get a singing career off the ground, along with forty-six million other people. Waitressing. Some other jobs. Elin said I could serve drinks at this thing tonight but we don't really get on – I thought her last husband was a prick and she didn't appreciate me saying so, even though I was right as it turned out, but she got lucky with your agency so all's well that ends well, eh?'

'Why did you come back from Nashville?' Tony asked as they sped past King's Cross, all light and bustle, confused tourists, junkies and drunken office workers heading for the last train home.

'I split up with a boyfriend.'

They continued along the Marylebone Road, then up the Edgware Road. Groups were sitting outside restaurants smoking shisha pipes, enjoying the cool evening air. Normally Zu would have loved the tour of London by night but now she just wanted to get Josie out of the car.

'Makes sense for me to drop you off first,' Tony said, twisting his head round towards Zu when they stopped at the lights in Swiss Cottage. (Why was there actually a Swiss chalet straight out of a ski resort, sitting in the middle of the traffic? She must find out, it was the kind of thing Henchie would like to know too.) 'I'll go on to Hatch End,' Tony added.

'I don't mind coming with you,' Zu protested.

'That's daft. It's late. You've got work in the morning. Get off to bed. I'll be back soon.'

'But . . .'

'Yeah, grab your beauty sleep,' Josie said, as they approached Edgware and its rows of slumbering, suburban houses with lock-up garages and Wendy houses in back gardens. Why was she being so petty, Zu thought, as the car pulled up on Farthingdale Road. If Dad wanted to go back to Josie's, that was his business.

'Lovely to meet you,' Josie said. 'See you again soon, yeah?'

'Sure.' Zu thought of that old cartoon: *Yeah, like never. Is never good for you?* She blew a kiss at Tony. 'See you later, Dad.'

'Take care, darling.'

'I will.' The car revved off into the night and Zu opened the front door of the empty house.

22

As they drove on, Tony was very aware of Josie's perfume. It was flowery, light and sweet, not dissimilar to the one Deepi used to wear (usually to disguise the stink of gin). Feminine. Beth didn't do perfume. He'd missed it, he suddenly realized.

They chatted nonsensically but companionably: about whether that was Venus they could see shining brightly up there, or was it a satellite; about Elin and her ex-husband, who at fifty-six had announced he was in love with a nineteen-year-old Trinidadian and moved out that same night; about the other guests at the party. Tony had spoken to a couple of them but he'd found their obvious neediness terrifying and had hastily backed off. Josie, twenty years younger, just found them all hilarious.

'They were such losers. I don't know what *you* were doing amongst them.'

'Just doing Zu a favour,' he shrugged, vowing to curtail any dealings with Temperley forthwith.

Josie lived on a road of 1930s semis that had seen better days. As they drew up, she turned and smiled and said, 'Do you fancy a coffee?'

'Why not?'

Even then, he wasn't completely sure what she was suggesting. He'd gone out of his way to drive her home. Probably she just wanted to thank him in some way, revive him with caffeine before the drive back to Edgware. He followed her up the shabby staircase and into the studio flat on the first floor. Clothes were drying on the back of radiators, with knickers posted all over the small book-case. A book called *Meditation and the Art of You* lay splayed open on the floor. A dirty mug containing some yellowing liquid sat by the door.

Josie had fiddled with her iPod (what was wrong with CDs, for heaven's sake, he wondered, then reminded himself his father would have asked 'Why not the gramophone?') and some trancey music that was definitely more the boys' vintage than Tony's began playing as she moved into the kitchenette to make him coffee in a chipped Winnie the Pooh mug.

Handing him the coffee, she picked a couple of celebrity magazines off the sofa and chucked them on the floor, then sat down and drew her legs up into herself. Tony noticed her little brass toe ring. She patted the space beside her.

'Tell me about your wife.'

So he told her an edited version. The alcoholism bit he missed out: too grubby. Her eyes, which were like deep, black caves, had welled up with sympathy and then she'd put her beautiful hand on his arm.

'You poor, poor man,' she said. 'And poor Zu. How did she cope?'

'Well, obviously she was broken-hearted. But . . .' He wasn't going to go into it. How Zu had already put up with years of her mother becoming more and more sad, growing more and more distant from her, behaving more and more erratically. How her way of coping had been to leave home as soon as possible. How they'd never talked about Deepi's disintegration, just soldiered on side by side to get the boys ready for school in the mornings and in bed at night, trying to hash out some pretence of a normal life.

'And what about the music? You used to play in orchestras, right?'

'Mmm hmm. Second violinist. Hoping for a promotion to first but then when the babies were born the touring didn't go down too well with my wife. The repair shop was a better idea.'

'But you still play?'

He shook his head.

'Why not?'

'I haven't had time.' He shrugged feebly, knowing that recently there'd been plenty of time, but the thought of making music again just didn't appeal.

'Play for me some time? Please? I love music. Well, obviously I do, or I wouldn't be doing the singing. I don't know much about classical but I'm willing to learn.'

'OK,' he said, as Josie leant forward and brushed her warm, soft hand across his cheek. Suddenly, they were kissing wildly, tugging at each other's clothes. Both hastily began undressing themselves. She had perfect breasts and her bottom was a peach, Tony thought, pulling impatiently at his jeans and wiggling out of his T-shirt.

He continued covering every inch of her in kisses – her legs, her back, her nipples – then he was inside her on the stained blue rug. She was thrusting at him and he felt intense heat and then his body grew gloriously light.

He fell on her so hard that she gasped. She stroked his

back gently. Neither spoke, but as Tony's breath slowed down, his thoughts came into focus. He rolled off Josie and lay awkwardly beside her on the sofa. She reached up and snatched the knobbly grey fleece throw from the sofa and draped it over them.

'That was . . .'

'Amazing,' she said and they both laughed. They lay silently for a moment. Tony's heart pounded in his ribcage. As ever, his thoughts returned to Deepika. The last time they'd done it had been at about 10.45 p.m., after he'd watched the news and come to join her in bed. She'd been on the wagon at the time and things looked very promising; she'd put down her book, grumbling a bit but eventually she'd responded to his touches and even seemed to enjoy herself, although at some point she might have muttered 'Oh, hurry up.'

He needed to communicate this unexpected happiness to Josie. He cleared his throat: 'I don't have much of a way with words but right now the *Hallelujah Chorus* is playing in my head.'

'I've got Kool and the Gang singing "Celebration",' Josie whispered and his heart swelled as if it were a glass being filled with wine.

Without saying anything, he followed her into her dark bedroom. There was a mattress on the floor; the duvet was on the other side of the room. She picked it up and they snuggled beneath it. Normally, Tony couldn't sleep in a strange bed but they were both out in minutes.

A couple of hours later, he'd woken, desperate for a pee, not knowing for a second where he was. Then he'd seen her sleeping beside him. For a moment his breathing stopped. He was spending the night with a gorgeous, perfect woman. He thought of Zu back in Farthingdale Road. Should he text her to let her know where he was? But no, he was too embarrassed. It was illogical – Zu was an adult, she'd wanted this for him, but he couldn't bring himself to. If she was worried, she'd have called him in any case.

He stumbled to the bathroom, then he went back to sleep, but before he knew it he was opening his eyes to behold the sight of Josie, hair damp, alluringly dressed in a towel and saying she had to run or she'd be late for work and could he let himself out, and he'd said no, he'd come with her.

He'd pulled on last night's clothes and minutes later they were out on the pavement. The skies were so grey that the idea of them ever being blue again, let alone spotting the sun, seemed an impossible dream. He kissed Josie on the cheek, aware of his stubbly chin against her soft skin which even in this dull light still seemed to glow.

'So, I'll call you,' he said.

'OK. Great. I'd better run.'

'What's your number?'

She told him hastily and he jabbed it into his phone. Then she pecked him on the cheek again. 'You're really sweet, Tony,' she said. 'See you.'

'See you.'

He stood watching her, feeling like Gene Kelly, wanting to run down the street jumping in the air and clicking his heels together. He was a jar of honey, a pot of gold discovered in a dusty chest. For the first time in years, he was purely happy.

23

Tony drove to work, happily aware of his stubbly face, of the fact he was wearing the previous day's clothes. What would he say if Beth or Barry commented? What about Zu, what would he tell her? He checked his phone but she hadn't texted or called.

Inside the workshop everything was – jarringly – the same as ever. Radio Two blared hits from the Eighties and the smell of resin mingled with the earthy fug of Barry's camomile tea.

'Where's Beth?'

'Looking at a trombone in Sudbury.' Barry grinned at him companionably. There were flakes of his breakfast toast stuck in his grey beard. 'Big night, then?'

'Eh?' How did he know? 'Oh! Yes. Went to a sort of party in an art gallery.'

'Oh yeah? Poncey?'

'A bit, yeah . . .' He teetered on the brink of telling him what had happened but then shyly retreated. 'So . . . how are your holiday plans coming along?'

'Elinor and I were thinking October. If that's OK with you. Cyprus again.'

'Fine by me.' Maybe he and Josie could go away some-where soon? She liked travel. It was years since he'd done anything adventurous. Morocco in November. It could be perfect. Or maybe Rome. He'd never been there, but as a boy he'd been obsessed with gladiators. The Forum in autumn. Strolling past the Trevi fountain, feeding each other mouthfuls of ice cream. It was a delightful thought.

He wanted to call her all day but he knew better so he forced himself to wait, while fantasizing about their long and happy future. The last woman he'd jumped into bed with on the first night had been Deepi and despite all the pain and misery he'd always known that she was the only woman in the world for him. The Beths, the others, they'd been lovely, but he'd known all along that they weren't the answer. Perhaps with Josie he'd have a chance to do it all again but this time be spared the unhappiness, the addiction, the pain. He knew he shouldn't hope but he couldn't help himself.

Barry left just after five to tune a piano, leaving Tony finally alone to pick up the phone.

Dum. Di. Dah. Dum. Di. Dah.

He tried again. Same cold, electronic tune. Shit. In his befuddled state he must have entered her number wrongly. But that was OK, he could always ask Elin for the number, or actually . . . he remembered the name of the beauty parlour she worked at. *Gor-Jus.*

A quick Google and he had it. He dialled instantly then as he heard the phone ring was seized with sudden terror. His instinct was to hang up but then he remembered the phone would still register his number and he'd look an idiot. Dating was so much more complicated since his day when answerphones were considered the height of sophistication, along with avocado-coloured bidets and video-cassette recorders.

'Hellloo, Gor-Jus,' bleated an African-sounding woman's voice.

169

'Uh. Hi, may I speak to Josie please?'

There was a pause and then, 'Whom may I say is calling?'

'It's – uh – Tony.'

There was another long, long pause. More indistinct voices. The roar of a hairdryer and then –

'Hello?' said Josie, sounding dull and flat.

'Hi, Josie, it's me! Tony!'

'Hi, Tony,' she said abruptly.

'I . . . listen, sorry to call you at work but I wrote your number down wrong.'

'Did you?'

'Listen, I was wondering . . . you're probably busy tonight but do you fancy a drink some time soon? Or dinner perhaps?'

Josie sighed. 'Look. Tony. There's no easy way of saying this, so I'll just say it. You're a sweet guy. Last night was fun. *Really* fun. But I'm not really into having a relationship right now. With anyone. I just want to concentrate on finding myself for the moment.'

'Oh. Right.'

'Sorry. It's nothing personal. Like I said, you're sweet, but . . . I've got to go. A client's waiting.'

He said nothing.

'Don't be like that, Tony!'

'Like what?'

'Making me feel bad.' She sighed again. 'It's nothing personal. I'll see you around. Bye.'

He'd parked a good ten-minute walk from the workshop. As he made his way to the car, he shivered in his thin clothes. A gust of wind shook raindrops on to his arms and cheeks and the sky darkened to a plummy black.

Lightning cracked and suddenly rain began falling on the pavement like tiny bombs. People were running for shelter but Tony kept the same pace. The drops multiplied until the rain was coming down like a sheet. Tony's shoes squelched, his hair dripped, but he kept walking. It was almost as if he felt he deserved this drenching, as if it might purify him.

By the time he reached the car, he was shivering uncontrollably. At home he headed straight for the shower and then, wrapped in a towel, turned on his computer. Two emails waiting. One from Kieran, one from Ro. He poured himself a glass of whisky and sat down to read, reliant on them to cheer him up.

Hey Dad,

How are things? The orphanage is really great! I'm learning so much about myself as a person!! The children are cute but – wow – the poverty is indescribable. If u want 2 know more, follow my tweets.

Tony wanted to bash his head against the wall. Was it too much to have hoped to bring up children who were vaguely literate? Time to read Rohan's.

Hi Dad,

Wish you'd get a life and post your status on Facebook. Even better, tweet! All good here. Very hot, though rained a bit yesterday. Love to the Zooster.

R x

Tony went over to the mantelpiece and picked up the one picture of Deepi he allowed himself to display. It was taken three years before she died. She was wearing a grey stripy T-shirt and was smiling into the camera, mouth slightly open, eyes turned to the left – probably distracted by Rohan sweeping all the ornaments off the mantelpiece or Kieran scribbling on the walls in purple marker pen.

That had been during one of the good times, like a patch of blue sky peeking through the clouds, when Deepi was on the wagon and Tony was just beginning to hope they could rebuild their life again.

A week later they'd had the neighbours over for tea and Kieran had come running out of the kitchen and pulled at his arm. Tony had gone in there to find Deepi slumped on the floor making a strange moaning sound, a faraway look in her eyes. Tony had instantly swept her up in a fireman's lift and carried her to the bedroom.

'What's wrong with Mummy?' Kieran asked.

'Nothing, she just has a tummy bug,' Tony had said, wondering if his heart might be about to give out. Then he'd returned to the living room and told everyone Deepi was feeling faint and had had to go to bed. He'd fooled nobody. All evening he'd had to laugh at jokes and refill teacups, all the time knowing that Deepi must have smuggled bottles into the house.

There'd been two more years of misery, then another good patch. No pictures existed from that time, though. Deepi wasn't a terribly pretty sight by then: haggard, a tooth missing where she'd knocked it out – who knew where or how.

If she hadn't crashed the car that evening, what would

have happened? Probably more misery. But it would have been nice to have found out either way. That was one of the worst things about losing Deepika, the narrative cut short, like not being able to watch the last episode of *The Wire*. Which, incidentally, Deepi would have loved, assuming she'd been sober enough to follow it.

Tony couldn't help it. He reached for the photo album in the bookcase – the album that started off so neatly: pictures of the two of them grinning at each other like loons on their wedding day, her in that white Bianca Jagger trouser suit. Joy and energy radiated from her smile; she looked like a woman who loved life.

Next came pictures of her nine months later, awkwardly holding baby Zu, who had one arm sticking out from under her blanket and one leg in the air in a 'don't drop me' pose. Deepi was under a tree, squinting into sunlight, and half her face was in shadow like a harlequin: a precursor of the good Deepi/bad Deepi that was to come. There were pages of Zu crawling, Zu walking – she'd been such a jolly baby. Zu's first day at school in her maroon uniform. Zu grinning with a gap where a tooth should have been. Deepi pregnant and looking a little nauseous, her arm on Zu's shoulder in the Isle of Wight.

At which point the pages stopped being neatly laid out. Instead, a jumble of loose photos slipped out on to the floor. Zu cradling one of the twins, apprehensive but proud. Tony holding up another twin. Absolutely none of Deepi: she'd been in bed refusing to come downstairs except in dire necessity. Ah, here was one now – taken when the twins were about seven. She was horribly skinny, her complexion sallow, and she was unsmiling. Her once clear brown eyes appeared milky and dull. Her heart was still beating but she looked like a woman who had long, long ago stopped living.

Tony shook his head. 'I miss you,' he told the photo.

For the first time in more than a year, he felt his body dissolving into great, heaving, undignified sobs.

24

Gillian sat at the kitchen table drinking tea and watching Richard, the father of the family who lived opposite, on the side of the road where the houses had south-facing gardens and cost a hundred grand more. He was standing on his doorstep, arm round his tousle-haired son; they were off to play football together. The mother, Vanessa, stood in the doorway smiling, wishing them luck. They were a proper family – you saw them all returning from Tesco, bringing in the bags, setting off in their Audi for a weekend in a family-friendly hotel in the West Country.

Had she and Billy ever looked like that to outsiders? No, they'd have been arguing about whether they should bring spare plastic carrier bags to the supermarket (her, yes, eco; him, no, dreary and they'd probably break) and – before his escape to Australia – he'd hated holidays.

She yawned and scratched Waffle's ears. It had been another bad night. Holly had crashed in at about three. Gillian had listened to her moving around downstairs, then the hum of the television as she settled down in front of *Sex and the City*. Would she remember to turn the gas off after she made herself slice after slice of cheese on toast under the grill? Would she leave the front door open, allowing anyone to walk into the house? Would she have smuggled in one of her friends? Now she looked at the clock. Eleven thirty. Having been desperate for her daughter to sleep, now she'd have to wake her. Bracing herself, Gillian tapped on her bedroom door. Silence. She pushed it open. Holly lay on her back, her curls framing her face, chest rising slowly up and down. She looked so beautiful asleep. She was such a sweet, loving girl in essence but it was only at moments like this that Gillian could still see it.

'Holly!' she said tenderly.

Holly rolled on to her side and groaned. 'Fuck off, Mum. I feel like shit.'

'That's because you only went to bed a few hours ago,' Gillian snapped, all gentleness vanished.

'It wasn't that late. I've probably got a virus. There are all sorts going round.'

Gillian marched towards the curtains and pulled them open to reveal a sea of old coffee cups and ketchup-smeared plates. She'd announced several months ago that she would no longer clean Holly's bedroom, sure the squalor would eventually crack her. Evidently not.

'Get up!'

'Aargh, Mum, it's too bright.'

'You're not a vampire.'

'Just five minutes more. I'm tired.'

'You need to reset your body clock. You go to bed at dawn and then you want to sleep all day. School is starting next week, what's going to happen then?'

'But I *have* to stay out late! You've said I can't come home alone, even though everyone else is allowed to. No one wants to leave until three so what am I supposed to do? I'm the only one with such a pathetic set of rules.'

Gillian had long learnt to distrust Holly's 'everyone

else', this mythical set who didn't have to do homework, and had their tongues pierced at twelve. It usually translated into around two kids in a year group of one hundred and fifty, two who dropped out of school, pregnant, at fifteen.

'You could stay in,' she suggested. 'Anyway, it's not true that everyone else has no curfew. I bumped into Joanna Crimms in Sainsbury's the other day and she said Sylvie always has to be in at midnight, sometimes two on a special occasion in the holidays.'

'She's lying,' Holly shrugged.

Living with her daughter was like being a citizen of a cruel dictatorship, Gillian thought, with evidence that didn't fit simply rejected out of hand.

'Like Joanna has any idea anyway what her precious Sylvie gets up to,' Holly added. Her expression made it clear that Gillian and Joanna Crimms were pathetic dupes, with no idea of the depravity their daughters wallowed in as soon as they let them out of their sight.

Irritated but pretending to be playful, Gillian yanked at the duvet. It pulled back to reveal Holly's lanky body, dressed in a T-shirt, and a little plastic bag containing what looked like dried herbs. The centre of Gillian's stomach turned icy.

'What's this?' she said, knowing full well.

Holly sat up and squinted. A pause. Then she replied defiantly: 'What does it look like?'

'Holly, this is dope.'

'I know. I'm looking after it for Freya.'

'You expect me to believe that?'

'Believe what you like.' Holly pulled her best 'you're

177

such a loser' expression. 'I wouldn't have thought it was *that* unreasonable to believe something your only daughter tells you.'

'Holly, get up, right now. I want you ready to leave in ten minutes. And I'm flushing this down the toilet.'

'Don't do that!' Holly screamed. 'Freya will kill me.'

'*If* Freya gave these to you, then Freya is breaking the law. If you bring up her name again I will contact her *and* her mother and tell them both that. Now hurry up. And for looking after illegal drugs you're grounded for a month and I'm stopping your allowance.'

'Mum!'

'You heard me. Out. Of. Bed. Now.'

At the wheel of her Citroën, with Holly sitting beside her, eyes closed, iPod headphones clamped on, Gillian wondered if she'd overreacted. It was only cannabis, after all. Everyone smoked it. God, even she'd had the odd puff in her time (it had made her feel nauseous) and Gillian was so law-abiding that if she was in the loo in an aeroplane and the seatbelt sign came on she nearly had a panic attack, convinced the flight attendant would start kicking the door in and calling the air marshalls.

But dope was illegal. Or, then again, perhaps it wasn't? Hadn't the government downgraded it recently? But then maybe they'd graded it back up again. She'd check when they got home.

Alicia lived in a large, detached house in Balham, similar to the house they'd grown up in before their parents had decided to downsize and move to Turkey. Gillian had always taken for granted that she'd live in something similar one day, never dreaming that house prices would be so absurd and her marriage so disastrous that instead she'd end up in a cottage next door to a housing estate, with just one child instead of the four whose names she'd already chosen (Holly, Juanita, Asa and Cosmo – actually, thank God she'd only had one child in the end, as those others would have been laughing stocks their entire lives).

The Citroën turned through the high white gateposts and crunched up the drive, parking between the two four by fours. The Porsche was missing: Alicia's husband, George, was working, as ever. According to Alicia, both sisters were single mothers – 'Well, I might as well be for all I see my husband' – but she also admitted that life for her, with millions in the bank and the full-time nanny and no job, was somewhat cushier.

Alicia was in the kitchen – all distressed units and Quookers and steam-assisted ovens. There were basil plants and borlotti beans in labelled jars and retro tins full of obscure French biscuits. She was putting the finishing touches to an elaborate salad to accompany the roast. A pale pink cashmere jumper and bootcut jeans were just visible under her Cath Kidston apron. From the garden came the sound of her three sons rampaging, like boys should.

'Holly!' She kissed her catatonic niece on both cheeks. 'Come and help me do the potatoes.' She patted Gillian on the wrist. 'You must be exhausted. Go and have a drink and read the papers in the conservatory.'

'Er, why is she exhausted and not me?' Holly protested.

'Because she is a single working mother and you are a schoolgirl.'

'Why aren't your schoolboys helping out?'

'Oh, believe me, they've done their dues. Licked the paving stones clean with their tongues this morning.'

'You go into the garden,' Gillian said hastily. 'I'll chat to Alicia.'

Holly rolled her eyes. 'And, like, what am I going to do in the garden?'

'Go and watch TV, then,' Alicia said brusquely. 'Or there's a pile of magazines in the conservatory if you prefer.'

Holly snorted and ambled off. Alicia watched her.

'If I catch her smoking in the house she's in big trouble. How's she being?'

Gillian didn't want to talk about it. That was one of the worst things about the Holly problem, she couldn't discuss it with anyone. She'd bump into other mums in the street and they'd moan about how hard it was to get their children to do their homework and Gillian would nod and agree, thinking she'd given up on homework ages ago. The state of their rooms! Yes, awful. But did they hide bags of dope in there? Were they screaming like sirens, saying they hated you, that you'd ruined their lives? Gillian couldn't confess to any of it because she knew the judgements that would be made: well, her husband left her, she works, she doesn't do anything for the PTA. Easier to grab a knife and begin slicing up an avocado and say: 'She's fine. What's up with you, Ali?'

'Beep, beep, beep, beep, beep, beep and it's time for . . . bourgeois news! And headlining tonight is worries about Jonny. His teachers say he's so clever he should definitely go for the Eton scholarship, but I don't think I could cope with my darling at boarding school.'

Boarding school. Now that was an idea. 'And the second headline?'

'Thousands dying of famine somewhere far away. But meanwhile, back at home, the ironing lady scorched my cashmere socks.'

'Oh my God!' Gillian flung her hands in the air in mock horror. Ali always made her smile.

'I know. I was devastated, darling. Staff! Anyway, how about you? Thrill me with a dispatch from the gritty world of single motherhood.'

'A few more dates.'

'With the bald dwarf?'

'You mean Tony? No, I've told them that's not going anywhere. Since him there's been Julian, who was charming and self-deprecating on the phone.'

'I remember, you forwarded me his text. I was excited about him. So?'

'So, in person, he was startlingly handsome – a bit professorial. Tweed jacket, messy hair.'

'Oh, how sexy! He'd take you over his desk.'

'Steady. But, yes, I did have to do my utmost not to collapse with nerves at actually being in the company of someone who was halfway presentable and try not to jump ahead to when he met Holly.'

'So?'

Gillian put down her knife. 'So then he asked if I was "properly English". I assured him I was and he said: "Good. You just don't know any more. All those eastern Europeans, look like us, but they're diluting our blood, our traditions, taking our jobs. Not that I'm racist or anything."'

'Oh, lovely!'

'I know. Then there was a guy who, for some reason, took his shoes off when he entered the pub.'

'He what? Was it a Japanese pub?'

'He was so nervous he just didn't know what to do with himself.'

'Cute,' Alicia tried.

'Not cute. Ridiculous. And then the next one spent all evening pouring his heart out about how wonderful his ex was and how he'd never get over her.'

'Touching that he felt he could confide in you.'

'Do you know what I was thinking? "It'll be over in an hour and then I can tell Alicia about it."'

'Oh God, yes! I love hearing about your adventures.'

'All my married friends do. It makes you feel better about your dreary lives.' Gillian gestured ironically around the cathedral-like space.

Alicia stuck her tongue out. 'I'm sure there's someone I could fix you up with. I mean, there's Enrico I used to work with, but actually, no, he has that subscription to . . . Never mind. I think you could do better than him. Now let me put my mind to it.'

'What the hell else have you been doing all this time? Anyway – drum roll – I have another date tonight, so let's see how that goes.'

'Who with?'

'He's called Kevin. And he sounded quite sweet on the phone. Sort of shy. Polite. A gent.'

'Wear your pencil skirt!' Alicia was already making wedding plans, Gillian could tell. 'You look fantastic in that. It was one of the great upsides of your divorce, you losing all that weight. I must get round to consulting the lawyers myself, I hate this muffin top. All those yummy-mummy Pilates classes and still it won't go. So where are you meeting him?'

Holly coughed in the doorway. 'Are you going out tonight? I thought you were staying in with me.'

'No, I'm going out.'

'But I'm grounded!'

'That's your fault, not mine.'

Holly sighed. 'I know, you'd rather be out with a man than at home with your daughter. I mean, fair enough. Don't let my feelings come into it.'

Gillian's heart was a dishcloth being wrung out over the sink. 'Come on, honey. I'll only be gone a couple of hours. You've been out every Friday and Saturday night for as long as I can remember.'

'She is forty-three, you are fifteen,' Alicia interjected.

'Very nearly sixteen.'

'Very nearly sixteen. And when you grow up in spirit as well as in years and earn money and pay taxes and understand an iota of what it means to be a mother, let alone an adult, you can go out whenever you want. But if you're grounded I'm sure it's for a good reason. Anyway, you've school tomorrow. You should have an early night.'

As Holly reeled, Alicia opened the French doors and bellowed, 'Lunch, everybody.'

25

It was the usual fun-packed Monday morning. Gillian had to drag Holly from her bed, almost dress her herself and push her out of the door to make sure she made it to school in time for the first day of term. At the end of the day she'd had a call from the deputy head. Back at school just seven hours, Holly had already sworn at a teacher and been disruptive in lessons.

'Only the first day. It's unacceptable. Also, she smelt strongly of cannabis.'

'I'll talk to her,' Gillian promised, knowing how that would go.

Her mood wasn't improved by the events of the previous evening. She had met Kevin Armstrong at E&O in Notting Hill. It was very busy, very noisy (she'd kept having to cock her head and ask him to repeat himself, to the point where she feared it was time for a hearing aid). Kevin had been pleasant enough for the first twenty minutes but then he'd peered at her closely in the dim light and said, 'You do look very good for your age, I must say. Have you had plastic surgery?'

She needed to call Alicia. Once she'd turned the experience into a funny story she'd feel so much better. But where was her mobile? After a brief, fruitless search – under the Ikea sofa cushions, behind the framed pictures of cute Holly on the mantelpiece, her coat pockets, her four handbags – Gillian picked up the landline to locate it. She expected it to be under a pile of paper in the kitchen that she kept meaning to sort, but instead the sound of her phone warbling 'Hand in Glove' by The Smiths came from upstairs. From Holly's bedroom.

What was it doing there? Maybe it had fallen out of her pocket when she'd been wrestling with her daughter that morning.

She returned to the bedroom, flinging open the window to let some fresh air into the slum. Reluctantly, she collected an armful of dirty clothes, uncovering an overflowing ashtray full of what were quite obviously roaches.

'For Christ's sake!'

This was getting ridiculous. None of Holly's friends had been over last night, she must have been smoking alone. No wonder she'd been unable to get out of bed this morning. A fluffy pink pony still stood on the chest of drawers. In the bookcase, there were all the Harry Potters and Holly's once-beloved compendium of fairy tales. How could things have moved on so fast?

It was a second before Gillian remembered what she'd come in for. She redialled her mobile. Soft ringing emanated from the pink-and-white-painted chest of drawers. She opened Holly's underwear drawer and began rifling among the knickers and tangled tights.

'Aha.'

The mobile was there. Next to it was a string of pearls that Gillian recognized because they were one of her sister's most prized possessions. Next to that sat a sheaf of used banknotes. Pulse thudding, blood vessels straining, Gillian counted. Nearly three hundred pounds. Where had this come from?

Gillian remembered that morning, a few weeks ago, when she'd run out of cash in the deli. She'd sort of wondered then, but dismissed it. This time there could be little doubt. Holly must have stolen the cash – probably from her purse. Or – God! – maybe from Alicia's.

She grabbed her phone and called her sister, this time with quite a different story to tell.

'What are these?' Gillian was having to stop her voice shaking with rage as she held up the necklace and the cash in front of Holly's face. The mobile sat on the table in front of her.

For a second, Holly registered fear, but only a second. Then she cleared her throat.

'OK. That's Alicia's.' Her voice was high and breathless. 'I tried it on yesterday and I must have put it in my pocket and forgotten to give it back. And that's money which Granny Parkin gave me because she felt sorry for me because I wanted those trainers and you wouldn't buy me them. And that's your phone. Which you must have dropped in my room and I probably put it away to keep it safe. By the way, Mother, nice to know you've been rifling through my drawers.'

'Granny Parkin gave you the money?' *Billy's bloody mother. Of course.*

Holly shrugged. 'Call her and ask her. Now, if you don't mind, I have homework to do. GCSEs this year, Mother.'

Within a couple of minutes, a thudding bass beat floated

from under her door. Gillian could hear her daughter shrieking into her phone: 'So did she pull him?' She felt almost paralysed with pain. She picked up a photo from the mantelpiece: Holly aged three, grinning into the camera so widely her cheeks could have split. She had been such an adorable toddler, running around on those chubby legs that Gillian had always had to fight the urge to bite.

Gillian could remember her sweet hot breath on her cheeks as she held her up to watch Santa Claus going past in the annual Christmas parade. Remembered her dancing naked on the lawn, shouting 'Me name is Bumpy!' She'd been a little bundle of infuriating, all-consuming love. And Gillian hadn't truly appreciated it because she'd been so bamboozled with exhaustion, so frazzled trying to earn money, sort out childcare, run the house and feebly – and uselessly as it turned out – trying to keep her marriage on track. She had failed to appreciate the glory of those years, had wished they'd go faster. If only she could spoon-feed her daughter Weetabix again, make cupcakes together, snuggle up reading *Charlie and Lola*. On and on, for as long as she wanted.

She hadn't appreciated Holly's innocence; now she was being punished. She called Audrey Parkin, her former mother-in-law.

'Audrey, have you been giving money to Holly?'

'You are being very hard on her, you know, Gillian. She has to survive and her allowance is very limited. I know clothes aren't everything but being a teenager is tough. I remember when I was seventeen, all I wanted was a green mini dress like Twiggy wore in *Vogue*. I saved to buy a copy from British Home Stores, it was –'

'She's been using the money to buy cannabis, Audrey.'

'You're being over-dramatic. Everyone smokes cannabis. My friend Moira, remember her, uses it to help her MS. Now when can Holly next visit me? I can't do next weekend because it's the choir's annual trip and the following weekend Moira's coming. Her son is a mountaineer now, perhaps he'd make a good boyfriend for you, anyway . . . So maybe October some time?'

Gillian hung up, light-headed with anxiety. The doorbell rang. Who the hell was this at nearly ten on a week-night? Bloody Jehovah's Witnesses, they had no shame.

'I'll get it,' shrieked Holly, racing past her down the stairs. Gillian followed her. The door opened to reveal Freya, looking terrified. Next to her stood a tall woman, expensive blonde hair tied back in a ponytail, jeggings tucked into Uggs (bad look, Gillian observed, relieved that even in times of high stress her fashion radar was still working), tight baby-blue cashmere sweater. Rhiannon Browning, Freya's mum.

'Hi, Rhiannon,' said Gillian, determined to breeze this one out. Maybe she was recruiting helpers for the school jumble sale, she was that type.

'Hello, Gillian. Hello, Holly. I was just wondering if you could shed any light on what has happened to my son's iPhone.'

'Sorry?' Holly pushed a strand of hair out of her eyes. 'I don't know what you're talking about.'

'Of course you don't,' Rhiannon snorted. 'This is the second time this has happened, Holly. Don't think I didn't notice when my Gucci watch went missing a few weeks ago. Well, listen. I don't realistically expect you to rush off and find that for me, nice as it would be. But my son wants his phone back. I really don't think that's too much to ask.'

'What the hell are you talking about?' said Holly.

'Come on, Holls,' said Freya wearily. 'It went missing after the last time you were at our house.'

'And? What are you accusing me of?'

Freya stared miserably at the floor.

'I hate doing this,' said Rhiannon. 'But I have to tell you, Holly, you are not welcome at our house. Ever again. And I don't want Freya coming here either.'

'Like I give a shit!'

'Holly!' Gillian gasped.

Freya turned to Gillian. 'She's changing,' she said earnestly. 'She was my best friend, but since she started to get so friendly with Jarmon all she cares about is smoking weed . . .'

'Come on, Freya.' Rhiannon turned to face her. 'I'm really sorry,' she said. There were tears in her eyes.

They walked away and Gillian shut the door.

'Stupid cow.' Holly shrugged, squatting down and burying her face in Waffle's neck. 'She's always been a liar. I don't care. She's got really boring recently. And I've got other friends now.' She turned to Gillian, her face a picture of innocence. 'I'm starving. Can we have chow mein for supper? I really fancy a chow mein.'

Daughter on drugs and stealing! Help!

Kentishfailure 21:19

Hi, this is my first posting on these boards so I hope I've got the etiquette right. Basically my daughter's 15, in year 11. Recently she's been staying out late and hanging out with a dodgy crowd, I've found cannabis in her bed though she says she's only looking after it for a friend and worst of all I found my sister's necklace in her room and a friend came round and accused her of stealing a phone to sell it for drugs. I'm at my wit's end! Has anyone been through a similar experience and how did they deal with it? Any advice would be so gratefully welcome. I'm a single mum and feel I have no one to turn to. Thank you.

Underthesea 21:21
Welcome to the boards, Kentishfailure, great to have you with us. Can't offer any useful advice but sure someone will be along in a minute to help. Love and big hugs, hun.

Deardiary 21:23
You'd need to tell us a bit more about yourself before we can really help but the single parent bit stands out a mile. Do you work? If so, no wonder your daughter is turning to drugs. I had a high-flying career in advertising but I gave it all up when ds1 was born. Nothing is more important than being at home with your children, instilling the right values in them. I hear this story all the time and it's always the same old thing – I had to work because we wanted exotic holidays, a second car, designer clothes. Well, none of that matters – if you hadn't been working and concentrated more on your husband and your child then none of this would have happened.

Kentishfailure 21:23
I don't know what to say to that, deardiary. Maybe if I'd been less strict when she was a toddler she'd be less inclined to push the boundaries now. Maybe none of this would have

happened if I'd breastfed my daughter for two years instead of only one. Maybe it's because I had a couple of drinks a week when I was pregnant. What does ds1 mean by the way? And thanks for your kind welcome, underthesea, though I see it's not generally shared.

NewYorker 21:29
Aw, Kentish, don't let diary put you off. She's a regular right-wing nutter who stalks these boards bullying everyone with her neo-con rhetoric. You were just unlucky to meet her on your first visit. Now fwiw I think you need to just relax. Smoking doobie is what teenagers do, hun. It doesn't really hurt. No more than junk food or vaccinations, anyway – please look at this link to see what the MMR is doing for our children and then sign this petition to stop it. Good luck, honey, it will pass like all phases and you and your beautiful dd will be just fine.

Leosmama 21:36
Agree about ignoring diary. My heart went out to you when I read your post. My ds1 was also a dope fiend and I'm afraid I have no happy ending for you. He graduated from cannabis to LSD to heroin and is now in prison serving a six-month sentence for robbery. My advice is to stop it short – if she's stealing already there is big trouble ahead. Ground her, stop any kind of allowance and make it clear that if this carries on you are kicking her OUT. Kids on drugs need the short, sharp, shock treatment and I only wish I'd learnt that many years ago.

NewYorker 21:39
Now, Leo, I know you and I have discussed this before but really, kicking a teenager out on the streets???

Leosmama 21:39

NewYorker, just stop the hippy shit and start making bagels or whatever it is you guys are famous for.

Deardiary 21:40

That's the first sensible things Leosmama has said in years. Threaten to kick her out. Today's children have no idea how easy their lives are. Send her to do voluntary work in the third world for a year.

NewYorker 21:41

Diary, third world is a very outdated term. We say developing world now.

Leosmama 21:46

Like that'll stop Diary, NY, you know it will only encourage her. It's like the way she says coloured instead of black. Btw do you think we scared Kentish off? Please come back. I can help you.

NewYorker 23:48

Been busy on the eco-living boards but Kentish hasn't returned. I think we scared her off. :(

Leosmama 23:55

Think you're right. :((((

26

A fortnight had gone by, September was crisp and bright, and with every day that passed Zu began to feel more and more settled in her new existence. After the Temperley party, she'd felt utterly bleak, convinced Tony had got it together with Josie. But then Dad had apologized for not coming home, said the car had broken down and he hadn't wanted to call and wake her, so he'd kipped on Josie's sofa.

Zu hadn't believed him at first, but Josie had never been mentioned again, the phone didn't ring and Dad still spent every evening in front of the Dave channel. It was true! She'd been wrong! Nothing had happened between him and Josie – or maybe something had, but Dad had seen through her and stopped it there. The relief was breathtaking. At the same time, Tony said he wasn't going on any more Temperley dates, which was frustrating, but fine. She'd give him some time, see who signed up, then work on him again.

Now she was sitting with Masha, who was interviewing a potential new client. Bing was a burly Scotsman, forties, cable-knit jumper, cords and a thick head of brown hair, who worked in the oil business.

'So what kind of woman are you looking for, Bing?'

'She's got to have curly hair.' He spoke in firm, Aberdonian tones.

Masha's pen hovered over the page. 'Got to have?'

'Aye.' He nodded vigorously.

Masha cleared her throat. 'Bing, the whole point about Temperley is that we like to take our clients a bit out of their comfort zone. I know you tried online dating and it didn't really work for you. Well, that's because you were always going for the same type. A woman with straight hair might also be a woman who sets your world on fire.'

Bing thought. 'I suppose I'd settle for just a wee bit of a wave,' he said finally.

Zu tried not to catch Masha's eyes but she felt her shoulders shake with suppressed giggles.

'God, these fusspots!' Masha exclaimed, as they watched Bing walk out into the street. 'They all have some fixed idea that they must fall in love at first sight, when Cupid's arrow strikes. They don't understand. Love is not like this. Is something which evolves over time. When I meet Gary I not think: "This is man of my dreams." But look at us now. Love develops once you sit by someone in an office day by day – you see they have bald head, perhaps, but they also make you laugh. Is a process.'

'I'll say,' Gary agreed. 'It was my delightful personality that won her!'

'What about "ten minutes to fall in love"?' Zu asked.

'To fall in lust. Is just nice slogan.'

'Well, not always –' Gary began, but a phone rang. 'Hello, Temperley? Peter!'

Masha clasped her hands together. 'He was going on the date with Jeanie. This must be success. The pair of them had so much in common it was spooky.'

194

They turned their heads expectantly to Gary. He was grinning and shaking his head. 'Oh dear. Yes, well Masha is an even more brilliant matchmaker than we gave her credit for. How funny. I am so sorry, Peter. But as she said, you did have loads in common. All right, my friend, courage!'

He hung up. 'Darling, you did a brilliant job putting Peter with Jeanie.'

'I know.' Masha was complacent.

Gary paused a second before his punchline. 'You did so brilliantly – it turns out they've already both been married. To each other. For twenty-six years.'

'No!' Masha gasped. '*Chyort voz'mi*!'

'Luckily, he thinks it's funny. Apparently, she does too.'

Gary couldn't stop laughing. Zu joined in and, after a second, so did Masha. During her time at Temperley Zu had laughed more than she had in years. It was a good feeling to have your sides ache, to feel tears run down your face. It took her back to school, Year Eight, before things with Mum had got really bad and she was still one of the gang. She remembered Mr Brownhill yanking at the whiteboard and it falling on his head. She'd thought she'd die giggling. She was still looking for other jobs all the time, but – though she wouldn't admit it to anyone – she was enjoying Temperley far more than she could ever have imagined.

'Remember that time you introduced Emma C to Colin?' Gary gasped.

'Oh my God!' They laughed even more.

'Classic,' Masha explained. 'When they met, Eemma said, "But I've been out with you already!"'

'Turned out she'd been out with his identical twin for three years.'

They chortled more, as Zu's phone rang. 'Hello, Temperley?'

'Forbes. What's so funny?'

'Not you again, Henchie.' She grinned. She'd seen Henchie twice more since the night at the Trocadero, both at lunchtime. Once they'd wandered around the Wallace Collection, another time they'd gone to a lunch-break concert at the Wigmore Hall. Tonight, however, he had another Make London Fun evening planned.

'Meet me at Bond Street Tube at five,' he said. 'We're going to Greenwich.'

'I've never been here before,' she said as, at around six, they emerged at Cutty Sark station.

'Nor me. Shameful, isn't it?' They headed past twee boutiques and cafés, towards the vast park, and began climbing the hill.

'This is worse than the Temperley stairs,' Zu panted.

'You shouldn't smoke so much.'

Both gasping, they stood on the line marking the meridian and looked back down across the park and the river to the dome of the O2 and the towers of Canary Wharf, blinking in the evening light.

'What did it look like before all that was built?' Henchie wondered. 'Was it meadows with sheep grazing?'

'Or slum tenements,' Zu said, fumbling in her satchel for her cigarettes. 'I know that Henchie is ignorant of such worlds.'

Henchie smiled. 'Henchie is now going to take you on a journey into worlds you never knew existed.'

Zu found herself blushing at the suggestiveness of his words. She was about to tell him to fuck off, when he said, 'Come on. We're going to the Observatory.'

It turned out Jack had booked a special stargazing evening at the Royal Observatory. First, about twenty visitors sat in the planetarium and watched a film about the Russians' and Americans' race to have the first man on the moon. Seeing footage of Gagarin in his capsule orbiting high around the earth, of Armstrong and Aldrin bouncing across the moon's surface, Zu was seized with envy.

'That's what I want to be,' she said to Jack, as they were herded from the planetarium to the Observatory itself. 'The first person on the moon. But I can't. I've been beaten to it.'

'You could be the first woman.'

'True.' She thought. 'It would be amazing. In space the differences between men and women must disappear. Without gravity, no one's stronger.'

'Why do you care who's stronger?' Jack said. 'We're in the twenty-first century. You don't need to have big muscles to do what you want to do.'

'It's not just that . . . it's just . . .' How to explain without talking about Mum? 'It's not just about physical strength. Women have a tougher deal than men. When babies come, they're stuck at home. For men, nothing changes.'

'Not necessarily. Sara still did whatever she wanted to do, she just left Xander with her parents.'

Zu twisted her hands. How to explain Mum raging that

life had become nothing but feeds and nap schedules and trips to the playground? Mum slipping a bottle of vodka into her coat pocket to help her cope. Obviously most mothers didn't feel like that – and the ones that did, like Sara, were still talking to their own mums and able to dump their kids on them. But not Deepika. And Zu knew that she'd be the same, that children or any kind of family life would be too much for her, and of course she'd have no mother to dump her children on either. But that was fine: she'd been forewarned, she'd never go there.

But all she said was: 'Anyway, they're not planning any more space expeditions. Plus I'm not good enough at science.'

'You told me you got an A in maths A level.'

'I think you need more than an A level.' She considered for a moment. 'Maybe I should get a job with Richard Branson. Taking rich people into space.'

'Why not? I'm sure there'll be loads of Russians going.'

'Loads of Temperley clients. On the hunt for a Martian bride, because no one else will have them.'

They were climbing the steep wrought-iron steps up to the Observatory. They stood under the fibreglass dome and listened to a talk about its history and then one of the children in the audience was allowed to press the buttons that opened it to the skies. ('Control yourself, Henchie, I know you wanted to do it,' Zu whispered.) Then they took turns at looking through the twenty-eight-inch lens.

'Where would you like to look?' the guide asked Zu when her turn finally came. 'Planets or moon?'

'The moon, please.'

He helped her push round the huge telescope until it

was fixed on the moon. She bent to look into the mirror which reflected the eyepiece. Right in front of her was a grey surface with a huge circle in the middle and a spot in the middle of that. It was so clear, so close, Zu's spine tingled.

'That's Tycho,' said the guide. 'It's an asteroid crater. We think it's from the same asteroid family that was responsible for the extinction of the dinosaurs.'

'Tycho Brahe,' Henchie said behind them. 'He was at a royal banquet and he was too embarrassed to leave the table for a wee and eventually his bladder exploded and he died.' He chortled. The guide gave him a school-masterly look. Zu rolled her eyes.

'No way!' exclaimed an American tourist in white polo neck and size 50 jeans, who was waiting her turn. 'Now you mention it, where is the bathroom?'

Zu continued staring at the moon. She should be able to touch it. She remembered reading there was no weather on the moon, because it had no atmosphere. 'Is this the hot side or the cold side?' she asked the guide, while Henchie entertained more tourists with the tale of Tycho Brahe.

'The hot side.'

Finally, she had to relinquish the lens to the fat American.

Afterwards, they sat at a communal table in a Greenwich noodle house and slurped at bowls of duck soup and drank beer.

'So how's work?' Jack asked.

Zu pulled a face. 'I've become weirdly fond of Gary and Masha. But still . . . I need to move on soon. Living with my dad's not ideal for a start.'

'I wish I saw more of my parents,' he said. 'My dad's in Singapore.'

'Is he? I didn't know that. What does he do there?'

'Business,' Jack said vaguely. 'And Mum's in Mallorca. They divorced when I was eleven. I went to boarding school.'

'Hence the posh accent.'

'I'm not posh! You're just common.'

'I'm not common,' Zu protested. 'I am solidly middle class.'

'I don't quite know what you are,' Jack said softly. Zu's stomach lurched oddly. It was a date moment and they were not on a date. Because Henchie was not her type – too obvious – and anyway, he was quite clearly with the woman on his iPhone. Well, maybe not with with – he'd break her heart next week or in a couple of months, and leave it trampled underfoot like an unwanted cardigan on the first day of the sales. Whatever. Zu wasn't going to waste energy feeling sorry for all these women, she was just glad she wasn't one of them.

She swigged from her beer bottle.

'Anyway,' she said hastily. 'At the weekend I'm escaping briefly. Hen weekend.'

'Aye, aye. You didn't tell me you were getting married.'

Zu ignored this idiocy. 'Polly, who was on my uni course. I've been getting emails for weeks. They all have headers saying things like "Sooooo excited".'

Jack grinned. 'Magaluf? Ibiza?'

'Guildford. We're leaving there on a canal barge Friday night, then returning Sunday morning after a trip to Godalming, where we'll have dinner on Saturday night.'

'Godalming? That's where my school was. Wow. Amazing night life there. Not.'

'It'll be adequate for our needs, I'm sure.'

'Well, I know you, Forbes. As long as you have a karaoke mic you'll be happy. And a few jellied penises. And L-plates. And a T-shirt that says "Girls on Tour".'

'And plenty of vibrators and veils,' Zu agreed. Although her tone didn't waver, she was distracted by her stomach doing another pancake flip. It was the way Henchie had said 'I know you.' It was ridiculous. He had that girlfriend, didn't he? What was going on?

Just as she thought it, his phone rang. He looked at the caller ID, frowned and rejected it, but immediately it rang again.

'Sorry, I'd better get this.'

'Sure.' Zu shrugged.

'Hello,' he said curtly. 'Yeah. What? Oh shit, OK. Really? Well, turn the water off and call a plumber. It's in the cupboard in the hall at the back ... No, you know. Come on! Oh shit! All right, I'm on my way.'

He hung up, looking very cross. 'There's an emergency at home. I have to go. Some leak. My – um – my flatmate can't fix it.'

'I didn't know you had a flatmate,' Zu said innocently.

'They're just staying for a bit before going back to Russia.'

'Oh? They're Russian?'

Jack ignored her teasing tone. 'I'm really sorry. I'm going to have to get a cab. Can I drop you anywhere on the way? Angel Tube maybe?'

Zu shook her head. 'I'll be fine. I'll take the Light Railway from Cutty Sark. Watch the moon from the train.'

'Are you sure? I'm really sorry about this.'

Zu started to feel annoyed. 'Do you want your ceiling collapsing? Just go!'

'OK.' He bent and kissed her. A brush of stubble against her cheek. 'See you soon. OK?'

'OK,' she said. Once he'd gone, paying the bill at the counter, she followed him out on to the pavement and smoked a cigarette. She watched the moon for a long time before she made her way back to the station.

27

'So, a little bird tells me that something might be going on in your love life,' said Leela.

Tony almost jumped out of his skin. It was a grey Thursday morning, he was in the workshop and the rain which had been falling since Sunday was still throwing itself in huge handfuls at the window panes, making it clear that autumn had arrived. The last thing he was prepared for was a conversation with Leela about his dating failures.

'Er . . .'

'Zulekha is working at a dating agency. She has set you up with some of its clients.'

'Just one, Leela. And it didn't work out, unfortunately.'

'Tttch. One is not enough to judge the whole experience by. I think it's a marvellous idea. Everyone is using these agencies these days. My assistant, Alison, she met her husband on match.com. And Giuliana, who I play bridge with, she married a chap she met through the personal ads. It turned out he was a psychopath and they got divorced about six months after they had their second child and now he's being so obstreperous about alimony, but you know . . .'

'Yes, Leela. It's all the rage, I know, but –'

'Zu is trying so hard to help you, Tony. You must promise to give it another go. Or if you don't want to, I met a lady recently who I think could be just up your street. She'll be at my Diwali party – by the way, you do have that in the diary, don't you? October twenty-sixth. Must be off, Delhi on the other line. You do promise, don't you? Deepi wouldn't have liked you lonely for so long.'

'Speak soon, Leela. Great to hear from you.' His phone beeped. Someone trying to get through. No doubt a client wanting their piano tuned.

'Promise?' Leela repeated.

'I promise,' Tony said with his fingers crossed. Beth watched him curiously as he hung up, swearing softly under his breath. One missed call. A number he didn't recognize. He dialled his voicemail.

'Hi, Tony.' It was a breathy female voice, posh with a transatlantic inflection. He'd have known who it was any-where. 'It's Josie. Remember? Listen, I'm sorry I was so rude on the phone. I was under a lot of stress. But if you'll forgive me I'd really like to see you again.'

Having been humiliated once, Tony restrained himself from returning Josie's call for thirty hours. When, on Fri-day afternoon, he finally allowed himself to call, he felt as if he were back in the sixth form summoning the courage to ask Vanessa Torrance on a date (her sister had picked up and told him, giggling, that Vanessa didn't talk to dweebs and that was the end of that).

Now Tony's hands actually shook as he called up the number. Josie's phone rang twice and he wanted to hang up but then he heard that voice that reminded him of a large Drambuie and a Cubanos.

'Tony! How are you?'

'I'm well. Um. How are you?'

'I feel so bad about what happened between us. I was having a rough day, my boss was being a bitch, and when I heard your voice I just panicked at how I don't deserve you.'

'Right . . .'

'Yeah, but I couldn't stop thinking about you. So. If you'd like to see me again that would be great. I mean, I should be so lucky, but you never know and –'

'How about tonight?' Tony interrupted.

Josie had a tattoo at the base of her spine in the shape of a dolphin. Tony traced it dreamily with his forefinger.

'When did you have that done?'

'A couple of years ago. In Nashville.'

'What's it like there? I've always wanted to go. All those musicians, it must be a riot.'

'It's a dump,' she said abruptly, rolling on to her back. 'Really, I wouldn't bother. Half the place is populated by fundamentalist hicks and the other half by wannabes working in Walmart and kidding themselves they're going to be the next Shania Twain. In which number I include myself. Tragic, really. Except I couldn't even work in Walmart without a green card.'

'What took you out there in the first place?'

'What do you think?'

Tony looked as blank as if someone had pulled out a cloth and wiped off his expression.

'Isn't it always a man?' Josie sounded just a touch impatient. 'I was very much in love. I followed my heart. And . . . my heart led me into all kinds of adventures.' A tiny shiver. 'But I'm back now. Safe. And hungry after all that good lovin'.'

The lovin' had, indeed, been even more sensational than the first time. Josie had turned out to be the kind of girl who knew tricks, who used toys, who talked dirty in bed. Occasionally Tony had felt out of his depth, but he loved it.

It was Sunday lunchtime. With Zu on her hen weekend, Josie had been able to stay Friday and Saturday night. They'd spent the whole of Saturday in bed, having sex, snoozing, watching telly and eating takeaway. They'd fallen asleep around three and had just woken up. Tony couldn't remember when he'd last behaved so decadently.

After they'd had sex for the second time on the Friday he'd summoned the courage to ask about why she'd backed out on him. 'I just got scared,' she'd said. 'Sorry, Tony. You were so lovely, I thought you were too good for me.' As excuses went, Tony was happy to buy it. After all, he knew about chickening out, about feeling he was unworthy of love.

'I'm hungry too,' he said now. 'Do you fancy a fry-up?' At the back of his mind the thought lurked that Zu would be home in a couple of hours and really he ought to have Josie out of there and the place vaguely tidy in good time. Not that he was ashamed of Josie or anything, just that he'd rather tell Zu about her when the time was right.

'A fry-up would be fabulous. You are such a nice man.'

Tony blushed. 'Well, I try.'

She nuzzled in close to him.

'You don't mind if I stay the night tonight? Or maybe a few nights? If it's OK? You see, my landlord's evicted me. Stupid man. There was some problem with a payment I thought I'd made online not going through and he lost his rag and gave me two hours to pack up and leave.'

A worm shifted in Tony's stomach. 'Well . . . It might be tricky tonight. Zu will be back soon.'

'Oh, great! I can't wait to see her.' She stroked his back, light, tickly strokes. 'Don't worry, I'm not asking to move in or anything! Just if I can stay for a couple of nights until I sort something out. Would that be OK?'

'Absolutely.' Why not?

'So few people have been nice to me,' she said, rubbing her hands absently up and down his spine. 'You know, Mum and Dad split up when I was six and Dad got custody because Mum married this new guy and moved to South Africa and then they sent me to these horrible boarding schools where I was useless because I was dyslexic. They always preferred Elin to me, she was better at lessons, netball, an all-round good egg. I've always had to look out for myself. It's been so lonely, you know.'

'I'll look after you,' Tony promised. He was deeply moved.

'You are a darling, darling man.' She knelt up and kissed his balding head. 'Why aren't you married?' she added.

'Sorry?'

'A guy as lovely as you. You just should be. I can't work out why nobody's pinned you down yet. I mean, your wife died a while ago, so you're allowed to have met someone else.'

'I know,' he sighed. 'I guess I just haven't had the energy until recently.'

'Why?'

Josie was so young, she had no idea. 'Well, bringing up

the boys took it out of me. They were quite hard work, that and my job. I just didn't particularly feel like socializing and . . .'

'It was more than that, though, wasn't it? You felt guilty about replacing your wife.'

Tony was startled. 'How did you know?'

'You don't exactly have to be Sigmund Freud to work it out. But why, Tony? She'd have wanted you to be happy, wouldn't she?'

Tears pricked unbidden at Tony's eyes. He blinked them back. 'Of course she would.'

'Then why?'

'Maybe because . . .'

Before he could articulate it, Josie hugged him. 'You poor, poor man. I feel so sorry for you.'

'Aren't you going to say it's useless to try to rewrite the past? To say: "What if?"'

'No, everyone does it. Of course you beat yourself up about her dying. You'd be weird if you didn't. Shit, I've done my share of things I'm not proud of . . .' He thought she was about to illuminate this statement, but she carried on: 'Anyway, your wife's with the angels now.'

He shook his head. 'I don't believe that. Don't believe in God.'

'Really?' Josie sat up and gestured around the room. 'So what do you think this is all about then?' When he said nothing, she continued, 'But there must be a plan. Someone has to be in charge. I mean, don't get me wrong, I'm not a God-botherer or anything, but what do you think happened to your wife?'

'I believe she's vanished. She's dust. Her family's Hindu,'

he said. 'So my mother-in-law's convinced she's been reincarnated as a princess or a butterfly or something.'

'Wow, yeah! Maybe a magnificent panther prowling through the jungle! How cool would that be?'

Tony felt his first flicker of doubt. He was enjoying talking about Deepi but Josie clearly didn't appreciate what it was to lose someone. Why should she, though? She was so young. And Deepi had been so unhappy, probably she would have preferred roaming silently through the jungle to life in their cramped terraced house.

'Or an eagle,' Josie was continuing dreamily. 'I'd love to come back as —'

Downstairs, the front door slammed. They looked at each other, confused.

'Fuck,' said Josie, sitting up and covering her breasts. 'It'd better not be Carl.'

'Who's Carl?'

'An ex of mine. He has a habit of finding me and, you know, giving me a bit of grief. Breaking in once or twice.' She frowned, calculating. 'He can't have worked out I'm here.'

'The ex you followed to Nashville?'

'Oh no, another one.'

A voice in the hallway called out. 'Hey! Dad! It's me! I'm back early.'

'Is that Zu?' Josie grinned. 'Ah, bless.'

Tony winced.

'It is,' he said.

28

Zu's day had begun at six, crammed into a bottom bunk designed for a child of three, woken by the noise of Sophie, the maid of honour, having rampant sex with Lee, whom she'd picked up three hours previously at Tru nightclub in Camberley.

She shut her eyes again and tried to remember what had brought her here. Everything about the weekend had been entirely predictable. The canal boat's loo had blocked four times and Zu had had to fix it. One of the hens was heavily pregnant and monopolized every conversation with talk of birth plans. Another had just had a baby and spent the entire time sitting on her bunk pumping milk from her swollen breasts. Another had just been dumped and kept bursting into tears, and everyone had to reassure her men weren't worth it.

Polly kept crying too and saying how ecstatic she was to have them all around her. Zu had performed a magnificent version of 'Bette Davis Eyes' on the portable karaoke machine before they hit the town. No one had slept more than two hours.

And now Polly was standing above her in a vest and boxer shorts, hands on hips, glitter from the make-up session the night before still all over her face.

'Sophie! Sophie!' she was hissing. 'What the fuck do you think you're doing? What about Jeremy?'

The moaning intensified.

'Sophie!' Polly stamped her foot. 'Jeremy is Tobias's best friend. What am I going to say to him about this? Are you expecting me to lie to my future husband about what went on this weekend?'

'Chill, Polly, it's a hen weekend,' said a sleepy voice from one of the other bunks. Claire, who'd scored several grammes of coke last night down a Camberley back alley-way. 'What else did you expect?'

'I didn't want any of this in the first place,' Polly hissed. 'I wanted a quiet meal in a local restaurant but you made me do this, Soph, and now I know why. It's so you could shag any passing bit of trade.'

'I ain't trade,' Lee barked indignantly.

Polly and Sophie had had a screaming fight and Polly had then ordered them all – apart from her sister, Jemima – to get off the boat right now and told them they were no longer invited to the wedding. Hence Zu had found herself on a morning train to Waterloo, surrounded by women who kept running to the loo to vomit up last night's Pinot Grigios. All in all, a pretty good time, she thought, with the bonus of not having to clean up the boat before they returned it to the hire place. And now she'd be back early. In her munificent mood, brought on by the karaoke (she'd done a fantastic 'Heart of Glass' too, she remembered), Zu had decided she'd take her father out to lunch. They'd share a bottle of wine and she'd put forward some names of women on the database whom she thought might be suitable and get him back in the dating saddle. Then she'd have a long nap.

She unlocked the front door. The house seemed oddly quiet and dark for midday.

'Hey! Dad! It's me! I'm back early.'

From upstairs came the sound of anxious scurrying. Zu's heart tom-tommed. Burglars! They'd murdered Dad and were now ransacking the place. 'Hello?' she bellowed, eyeing the ugly vase on the console table that Grandma Forbes had given her parents for a wedding present. She'd attack them with that – that would show them.

'Hello!' said a slinky voice from the first-floor landing. Zu looked up to see Josie leaning over the balustrade, dressed in nothing but Tony's London Philharmonic T-shirt.

'Nice to see you again,' she said with a smile.

'And you,' Zu replied robotically.

Tony appeared behind Josie, hair askew as if he'd been rolling about. Zu's mouth felt as dry as autumn leaves.

'What are you doing here?' he asked.

'I live here.'

'But the hen weekend?'

'Ended early.' Zu couldn't believe it. Dad had obviously been carrying on with Josie all this time and hadn't told her.

'Do you fancy a cup of tea?' Tony began descending the stairs. He was wearing jeans and what looked like a burgundy pyjama top. Nothing on his feet.

'A vodka I'd have thought was more your style,' Josie chuckled.

'I thought we could go out for lunch.' Zu was just going to have to take this in her stride. Dad was an adult, he could consort with whomever he chose. Only he must have been lying to her.

'Lunch would be fun,' Josie said. She nudged Tony and giggled. 'We haven't even had breakfast yet.'

'We could try the new gastropub near the park,' Tony said. 'It's meant to be really good.'

'Lovely,' Josie exclaimed.

At least the rain had stopped, so they sat outside. Yes! Zu could smoke. But as soon as she lit up, Josie started coughing ostentatiously.

'I'm sorry,' she croaked. 'But I'm asthmatic. So please could you not do that?'

Zu stubbed out the cigarette. She watched through narrowed eyes as Josie ordered virtually everything on the menu. She was sexy, in a cheap sort of way obviously, but what else did she have going for her? Gillian had been a million times classier. Men. Zu despaired.

'So how long has this been going on?' she hissed, when Josie disappeared to the loo.

'Just since Friday. Nothing happened after the party,' he added hastily. 'Well . . . something did but . . . Anyway, it's just since Friday.'

'Right.'

'Zu! Don't be like that.'

'Be like what?' Zu retorted disingenuously.

'So angry.'

Zu hated showing anger. It was the emotion that had consumed so much of her life, lying in bed waiting for Mum to crash in, when just the night before Deepika had been on the wagon, having promised another fresh start. Hopes rose like a wave, then were dashed as they hit a rock, again and again and again. She'd never forgive her mother for putting them through that rollercoaster ride, but she'd decided early on to keep her fury to herself. After all, Tony had enough to deal with. So now, she felt humiliated, as if she'd totally lost control. If only she could have a cigarette. She breathed deeply. Tony continued:

'This is my life. I can do what I like with it.'

Zu shrugged. Be glad for Dad, she told herself firmly; but her dislike of Josie was like a huge zit the night before a party, throbbing and unshiftable.

'I've got to go,' she said, standing up.

'Already? Don't you want pudding? A coffee?'

'I'm tired. I need to get back, have a nap.'

'You've hardly touched your food.'

'I know. It was quite a night and I'm just not very hungry. See you, Dad.' She bent and kissed him quickly. 'Say bye to Josie, will you? I'll see you back at home.'

'Can't you wait to say goodbye yourself? Though, actually, don't worry, you'll see her anyway. She's going to stay a few days as she's between flats right now.'

'Right.' Zu backed away, nearly stepping on a child pushing a toy car around on the ground. 'Fine.'

'It may not last,' she repeated to herself, all the way home. But she'd seen the way Tony had looked at Josie, admiration mingling with protectiveness. This was a man in love. It wouldn't last, but for now he'd listen to no reasoning.

Anyway, she and Tony couldn't question each other's choices. She hated it when he nagged her about her job, so she couldn't nag him about his girlfriend. She was just going to hope things fizzled out of their own accord. She opened the front door, went straight upstairs and climbed into bed. She'd hardly slept; things would seem better after a nap. But sleep wouldn't come and instead she lay and listened to her father and Josie crashing in, moving around downstairs, listening to loud telly and then shutting the door of his bedroom. After which there was no sound, just endless, unsettling silence.

29

Zu lasted two more days sharing the house with Josie. Then, on Wednesday morning, she called Tony at the workshop. 'Dad, it's me. Listen, don't take this the wrong way but I'm going to move in with Anj. Tonight.'

'Oh.' Tony felt as if he were shrinking, somehow withdrawing from the room. 'Why? I mean, sorry, I know why you –'

'Like you always said, it's so much handier for the commute,' Zu said firmly.

'Yes. Indeed. I do see that. And you'll have so much more fun living with Anj and Raman than with boring old me and –'

'Dad, it's nothing to do with you.' She didn't mention Josie, though it was quite obvious that this was what it was all about. 'It's just the commute. Temperley's got a few evening events coming up and it's such a pain coming back to Edgware late at night and I can't drive because you can't park in central London and, anyway, there's the congestion charge and you need the car and . . .'

'I understand, sweetheart. I understand.'

'So could I borrow the car tonight? To move my stuff?'

'I'll drive you.'

'No need.'

'Don't be silly. What would you do? Drive over to Anj's

and then drive back to Edgware and then get the Tube back? Ridiculous.'

'But I . . .'

'It would give us a chance to say goodbye,' he said firmly, desperate for her to just grant him this time together.

'Yes, OK,' she said eventually. 'You can give me a lift.'

Josie fluttered around as they loaded the car.

'Wow. Is that all you have? I came back from Nashville with ten suitcases. Had to pay more in excess baggage than I did for the flight. It cleaned me out.'

'I always travel light,' Zu said. Normally Tony admired his daughter for leaving home for a year with just a wheelie bag but now he felt annoyed. Josie was just trying to make conversation.

'I'll miss you, Zu,' she said.

Tony could see Zu struggling to stay polite. That was better. 'Yes, well,' she managed. 'Like I said, I need to be nearer work.'

'Shit, yeah. It's been the only bad thing for me about moving in here, having to get the bus to Hatch End every day. But otherwise –' she stroked Tony's arm – 'otherwise, it's fantastic.'

'Ready?' Zu asked him.

'Sure.'

'Bye, Zu. Take care. Come back and see us soon, yeah?' Josie was hugging her. Tony couldn't see his daughter's expression, but he could imagine it. He climbed into the driver's seat.

'Right then. Off we go.'

*

After an unseasonably hot spell, the weather was turning colder again, the nights growing shorter. Tony's phone rang as he was sitting at his workbench tightening the strings on a Stradivarius. When he saw Josie's name superimposed over his badly lit and out-of-focus photo of his three children, he felt as if angels were creeping up and down his spine.

It had been a fortnight since Zu moved out and, although he obviously missed his daughter, things between him and his new girlfriend just grew better and better. He wanted to travel the world with her and at the same time stay in with her, to introduce her to everyone he knew but simultaneously keep her close and all to himself.

A couple of days after Zu left, a burly man with a bald head, a goatee and a green tattoo on his arm that said 'Liverpool' had dropped off Josie's ten suitcases. She'd unpacked four; the other six sat opened and overflowing in the bedroom. There'd been no more talk about her finding somewhere else to live and a week ago she'd said she'd had enough of the bus journey to Hatch End and had packed in her job at Gor-Jus. She'd look for something else soon, she said, after she'd chilled for a couple of weeks.

'Hi, Josie,' he said now. The radio was loudly blaring out Will Young. Nonetheless, he spoke softly, not wanting Barry or Beth to hear.

'Heeey! How's it going?'

'Good! How about you? The audition?' She'd gone off that morning to try for a part high-kicking and warbling in the background of a new talent show on Channel 5.

'Next,' she said cheerfully.

'Sorry?'

'That's what they told me: "Next." Then: "We'll let you know." Which means they'll let me know if I'm successful; so I'll be staring at the phone for three weeks until I finally give up hope and kill myself.'

'Don't do that!' Tony exclaimed.

'As if. Not now I have something to live for. Now, listen, darling, I just have a teeny-tiny confession.'

Tony was up, then down. She had something to live for, but she also had something to tell him. She must be leaving him. Going back to America and/or to her ex, Carl, who stalked her wherever she went. Of course, he'd known it was too perfect to be true.

'I've turned your dinner orange.'

'Sorry?'

'Like, traffic light, nuclear orange.'

'Sorry, what dinner?'

'I was making you curry because I know that's what Deepika used to cook you. But the corner shop didn't have any turmeric, so I decided to use yellow food colouring and now everything's sort of . . . irradiated.'

Tony laughed so loudly that the other two looked up, startled.

'Are you angry with me?' she said in a soft, pleading voice.

'Angry with you? Of course not! I'll be home as soon as I can.'

'To eat Chernobyl curry.'

'To eat Chernobyl curry.' He lowered his voice. 'And then to take you to bed.'

He couldn't remember the last time he'd felt so happy.

30

Billy's phone in Perth was ringing. Gillian clutched her handset so tightly it risked cracking. She hated calling her ex and virtually always communicated with him by email.

But after nearly a whole night online, clicking from site to site, finding herself alternatively berated for her pathetic parenting or supported with an unconditionality she found unnerving (Did these people know her? No – so why were they so sure she was a brilliant mother and it would all turn out right in the wash?), she knew she must speak to someone real or lose what little was left of her mind.

'Hello?'

Billy. Who she'd once made love to in a pile of newly mown grass at the back of a cricket pitch; with whom she'd gone on a drunken pub crawl through Soho, ending up at four a.m. in a transvestite called Emerald's flat in the tower block above the supermarket in Brewer Street, dancing to 'Hold on Tight' by ELO. She'd listened to him complain about his irritable bowel. Once, when he'd refused to take the rubbish out, she'd thrown a jar of expensive face cream at his head and it had flown out of the window and smashed on the pavement below. Now he was just a voice on a phone, over eight thousand miles away.

A baby was crying in the background. Good. Gillian hoped it kept him up all night and that when he changed its nappy it did a projectile poo all over his head. Was she bitter? Hell, yes!

Gillian told him what she'd learnt.

'You're totally overreacting,' Billy said when she finally finished. 'It's only spliff. It's what teenagers do. Frankly, I'd be more worried if Holly wasn't into something like that.'

'I told you, it's not spliff like it used to be,' Gillian said. 'It's called skunk now and it's specially grown in greenhouses and it's way stronger than it was in our day. Users are forty per cent more likely to become psychotic than non-users and there's all sorts of evidence that it damages teenage brains.'

'Sounds like scaremongering to me.'

'It's true. I'll send you the links.'

'Never did me any harm.'

'I beg to differ.' Gillian couldn't help herself.

'Please don't make this personal.' Billy sighed.

'Billy, just educate yourself a bit and then let's talk again. Have a read.'

'When I find a minute I'll have a look. We're pretty busy here, you know! Babies are hard work.'

'No messing, Morse!'

'Surely there are things you can do?' Billy continued over Gillian's splutters. 'Ground her. Cut off her allowance.'

'I've done that. But she has to go to school. Oh, and that's another thing: the teachers have asked me to come in for a meeting because her work's terrible and she's always late.'

'That's not good.' Billy could relate to schoolwork issues; that was solid yes/no, tick-the-box stuff.

'And your mum gave her some money, which didn't help.'

'I'll tell her not to do that again.'

'It's this Jarmon she's been hanging out with. I think he's selling it to her.'

'She told me about Jarmon. His father's a QC. He's not going to be a drug dealer.'

'I disagree.'

'Well, have you spoken to his parents?'

'A couple of times. His mother told me there wasn't a problem; implied I was some sort of square to deny my child drugs.'

Billy sighed. 'OK. I'll look into it all but, in the meantime, just take a chill pill. It's normal teenage stuff. She was great when she was over here, really helpful with Perdita and the baby. She'll get through it and so will you.'

'Just fuck off to the beach then,' Gillian said, but he'd hung up.

The meeting was in a small windowless room behind Holly's school's chemistry labs. Gillian was seated opposite Holly's year tutor and the school counsellor. Neither of them looked old enough to hold a driving licence, let alone to be in charge of one thousand teenagers.

Be that as it might, however, they were the bosses today.

Gillian's skin was dehydrated, her arms were tingling with tension and her mouth tasted of metal from the sleeping pill she'd taken at three to give her a few hours' oblivion.

'Holly's attendance is getting worse and worse,' said Miss Lefever.

'She's always making up excuses for not doing her

work,' said the year tutor, Miss Twain. 'More and more elaborate ones that make no sense. Of course, we were hoping that Holly was going to attend this meeting.'

Miss Lefever was hopeful. 'She was in school today, she must have forgotten.'

'Yes, of course,' Gillian said sarcastically, just as her phone started to ring. Madonna singing 'Like A Prayer'. Shit. Her Leela ringtone. She'd had to designate a special one for her because Leela was like Madonna: she did not take at all kindly to being ignored. 'Sorry,' she said. 'Sorry, I just have to get this. Hello, Leela.'

'Hello, Gillian. How are you?'

Oh God. She had that 'I've got all day to chat' tone. 'I'm fine, Leela. However, could I call you back later? I have a meeting now. *Regarding my daughter.*'

'Oh no! Is she in trouble?'

'Mmm hmm.'

'You must tell me all about it later. You know this is something I really can help with.'

'I'd love to,' Gillian said, grinning apologetically at the teachers. What must they make of her? No wonder Holly was going off the rails if her mother couldn't bear to switch off her phone for just five minutes. 'Thank you, Leela.'

'Just reminding you about the Diwali party on Friday. You are coming, aren't you?'

'Of course, looking forward to it.' *Sorry. Sorry.* The two women's mouths were cats' bottoms of disapproval. 'See you then, Leela. Goodbye, goodbye.' She turned off the phone. 'So sorry, that was my most important client.'

'Back to Holly.' Miss Twain fingered a large turquoise pendant.

'Oh yes, absolutely.'

'We know things are hard for her. She's been under a lot of pressure, starting at a new school, her father moving abroad. We want to be as supportive as possible.'

'Actually,' Gillian said, 'I'd rather you weren't supportive. I'd rather you told her that rules are rules. That you frightened her. Made her realize she's throwing her life away.'

The teachers exchanged unsubtle glances. *Stupid old bat*, their expressions said. *No understanding of the ishoos our young people face.*

'Look,' said Miss Twain, 'I know her behaviour can be . . . challenging. But she's a fifteen-year-old girl. It's not unusual. I've seen lots of fifteen-year-old girls in this situation before and, believe me, they nearly all come through it.'

'*Nearly* all?'

'Virtually all.'

'She's smoking cannabis,' Gillian said. 'Did you know that? A lot of it. And I think she's stealing to support the habit.'

'Right. Cannabis smoking is very common in young people, you know, Gillian.'

Gillian exploded. 'I know you think I'm some fusty, middle-aged, middle-class mum who knows nothing about the world we live in, but it's not true! I lived in Colombia for six months. I shared a house with two gay men. I once met Boy George in a squat my friend Jane was living in. I've stayed up all night dancing. Often! I've lived. I don't want to stop my daughter living, I just don't want her to die.'

There was a long, awkward silence.

'We hear you,' said Miss Twain gravely.

Gillian was off again. 'I've tried to be a good mother. I mean, I know I'm single but my husband was a skirt-chaser, what could I do? Possibly I went back to work a bit too early after Holly was born, but I had a fantastic nanny who treated her like her own. And I know I did controlled crying but I was desperate, honestly, I'd have lost my mind if I didn't get more sleep and it worked brilliantly, I wish I'd done it months earlier. And you know I tried not to let her watch too much telly, only it's hard when all your friends are watching *Doctor Who* and you don't want your child to be the only one in the class who isn't allowed to. And likewise when she was invited to parties, I mean, was I going to be the one who made her stay home alone, doing her homework?'

This time Miss Twain and Miss Lefever couldn't help but exchange smirks.

'So what are you going to do about her?' Gillian almost yelled.

'I think it's time to bring in the drug counsellors.' Miss Lefever smiled broadly, as if all was well with the world.

31

Another fortnight passed, it grew colder, then weirdly hot again, and bulbs began to flower early as the leaves on the trees turned red. Rohan returned home for a night, long-haired and with a bag of filthy laundry, and the next morning Tony drove him to Salford. He'd hoped his son would meet Josie but she was clubbing with a friend in Walthamstow and stayed the night there. It was always the way with Josie. Tony had the sensation of living life as if he were permanently wearing rollerskates. At times, he glided along, cushioned from bad things by fat, pink hearts. But then came a giddy feeling of losing control, of never knowing quite when he was going to fall over.

Now was one of those evenings. He was just finishing off work on a cello, when his phone rang.

'Tony!'

'Hi. I'll be home in about half an hour. Everything OK?'

'Yeah, it's just . . .'

'Just what?' His tone made Beth look up.

'You know my ex, Carl? He just was here?'

'What? The stalker? Outside?'

'No, I let him in.'

'Why?'

'It was raining and he looked cold and I thought, "This

is silly, what can he do? Maybe if we talk nicely we can put all this behind us." So he came in and had a cup of tea and actually we had a nice catch-up. But then we had a bit of a row and it all got sort of nasty.'

'Nasty?'

'Don't worry, it's all cool now. I love the way you're so protective. I just threw a cushion at him. And he threw one at me and then he left. So everything's OK. But, you know, it'd be good if you came home soon because I'm a bit shaken up.'

'I'll come home right now. Have you double-locked the door?'

'Yeah, of course I have. See you soon. Would you pick up *Grazia* for me?'

'Everything OK?' asked Beth as Tony finished the call.

'I hope so.' Tony didn't want to go into details. 'Josie's just a bit shook up about something.'

'I hope I get to meet her soon.'

'Yeah, we should all do a dinner. Listen, I'd better dash. See you tomorrow.'

He cycled home, heart pounding. Why had Josie let that psychopath in the house? She hadn't mentioned him much, just every now and then said that he was a little bit 'obsessive'. He could have done anything to her: raped her, attacked her. Why did every woman who came into Tony's life fall into danger?

He burst through the door. It was another icy night, but indoors his house was like the hothouse at Kew. Josie, as usual, was lounging on the sofa in a vest and tracksuit bottoms, peering at her phone, but when she saw him she threw it to the ground and bounded up and on to him, wrapping her legs around him like a monkey, smacking kisses all round his face.

'Heey, my best boy! I've been looking forward to you coming home all day.'

'Are you all right?'

'Me? Of course.'

'But . . . Carl. Josie, you must never let men into the house. He could have . . .'

'Bless you. Carl's harmless, really. As I say, he just threw a cushion at me, silly boy. It's fine.'

'It must have been frightening.'

Josie flexed non-existent muscles. 'I'm a big girl. I can look after myself.'

'But . . . You won't let him in if he comes back?'

'Of course not. It could have been worse, it could have been Kevin.'

'Kevin?'

'Did I never tell you about him? Yeah, I did, my old landlord, the one who kicked me out because I'd messed up the electronic banking. Complete nutter, so unreasonable, it was just a mix up with sort codes and whatever and I've told him he'll get the cash as soon as I find a decent job.' Her phone bleeped. 'Oh, look. Jake's just sent me an email and a picture of his dog. Look, isn't he gorgeous? Maybe we should get a dog?'

'I don't think so,' Tony said. He cleared his throat. 'Shall I put on some pizza?'

'Don't worry,' she said cheerily. 'I'm actually going out tonight, so don't worry about me.'

'Oh. Where are you going?'

'I'm meeting Jakey and Maxim.'

'Maxim?'

'Yeah. Max. *You* know. The Czech bodybuilder I shared that squat with.'

'I don't know.' Images of a twenty-stone Schwarzenegger, hung like a donkey, assailed him.

'We're going to have a reunion, go out clubbing together.'

'On a Monday night?'

She laughed. 'Yes, old man. Monday's always been the best night of the week. It's when the hard core come out. I'm really excited, it's like old times.'

'Right.'

'You're not jealous, are you? I'm just having a night off, to let my hair down.'

A night off from what exactly? They had only had a month together, hardly a life sentence. Tony had to be mature here, he thought. Josie was of an age where she wanted to go to nightclubs. It would be petty and jealous to be paranoid about what she might get up to.

'Tony? You're jealous, aren't you? It's so sweet.'

'I'm not jealous,' he lied. 'But . . . maybe I should come too.'

She laughed. 'Don't be daft. You'd hate it. You stay in and get an early one. Don't wait up for me. Love you, gorgeous man.'

'Love you too,' Tony said after a second.

32

Zu was on the phone to Matt Billen, the annoying client from the Temperley party who'd wanted only young women. Dutifully, Zu had scoured the database and although none of the women she'd found were teenagers, they were as young as Temperley went. They were all beautiful too *and* they had good jobs. All right, they'd also be insane if they fell for Matt but, as Zu was learning, there was no accounting for taste.

'How did it go with Deanna?' she asked him now.

'Deanna was nice, she was fine,' he said. 'But . . . I'm sorry, Zulekha, just not right for me.'

'Could you be more specific?'

'Yes, she was *old*, and you know my opinions on that.'

'She's thirty-five.'

'Exactly. Ovaries withering. Desperate. You know I'm only interested in women under thirty. And I am paying enough for your services so it's the least you can do for me.'

'I understand,' Zu said. Hanging up, she reported the conversation back to Masha, who'd been busy studying her bathroom mood board on her iPad.

'Ageists!' she bellowed. 'I am sick of them. As soon as woman reaches twenty-nine, she's no longer viable. Even when that idiot is collecting his pension he'll still think he has more in common with a twenty-year-old than a sixty-year-old. Bloody *men*. You excepted, darling.'

'Naturally.' Gary smiled from his desk.

'We don't have anyone on our books younger than thirty,' Zu said.

'We can only keep sending him ones who tick boxes in every other respect and finally he'll see light. Or he'll leave.' Masha returned her attention to the mood board. 'You know, I still love mosaic tiles but then is problem when grouting gets dirty. So maybe slate – but will it be too dark . . .?'

Zu glanced at the clock. Only another half an hour to go and then she was meeting Henchie. His turn to choose. She'd been looking forward to this. Moving out of Farthingdale Road had left her disorientated and in need of every friend she could muster. Polly used to be a good one but the couple of evenings they'd spent together post-hen had disintegrated into attacks on Sophie, followed by long diatribes about how her mother-in-law-to-be was hijacking the wedding arrangements.

Of course, she had Anj to come home to, but Anj was knackered most evenings and wanted to relax in front of *The Only Way is Essex* reruns, while Zu wanted to go out, to enjoy London, to distract herself in every possible way from dwelling on what was going on back at Farthingdale Road; how her father had disregarded all her advice and ended up not with lovely Gillian but with a dim failed singer/masseuse. Sometimes Zu wondered if she was being a snob, but she knew her father – and he deserved better than this. Still, he would have to learn that for himself.

It did annoy her that Henchie was so obviously living with some woman and wouldn't 'fess up to her, but that was Henchie's way. His girlfriends had always been in the background – his friends were the people he actually had fun with. Zu was the same really; she'd had plenty of flings but the men she'd slept with weren't usually the ones she chose to have conversations with. So long as he didn't try it on with her, who cared if he was shagging someone else?

Henchie had planned a blinder. They met at Canary Wharf, where – along with a crowd of oddly dressed people – they boarded a coach with blacked-out windows. As they drove, men in grey uniforms started running up and down the aisles, looking under seats. 'No runaways here,' they shouted.

After ten minutes they'd disembarked in what looked like a wasteland and, surrounded by tramps pulling at their sleeves, trying to sell them DVD players and car parts, made their way into a warehouse full of neon signs showing twenty-foot-high go-go dancers. Stalls sold sushi; a man approached Zu and out of nowhere asked her: 'At a dinner party, your host serves raw blowfish – what do you do?'

'This is *Blade Runner*,' she said, confused.

'Ding ding, jackpot!' Henchie laughed. 'I thought you'd never get there.'

It was something called Secret Cinema, which recreated the mood of famous films before screening them.

'And this is my favourite film of all time.'

'Thought it might be,' Henchie said smugly.

They'd watched the film in a neighbouring warehouse. The audience whooped and cheered as two actors, in *Blade Runner* costumes, were suspended in fixed positions at the top of the wall, recreating in real life the happenings on the screen. Zu had tried hard not to cry at Batty's dying speech about seeing things you wouldn't believe. Afterwards, there was a party with shimmying pole dancers and women in cheong sams who offered them albino pythons. Stalls sold LA newspapers and fake scorpions in jars and occasionally actors dressed as Rachael, Batty or Pris ran through the crowd. Zu was in heaven and on her fourth beer, trying to resist growing unwise yearnings to hit the dance floor in one of the booths, when she felt her phone ring in her pocket. She pulled it out.

'Hello, Naani,' she bellowed above the noise.

'Zulekha, where are you?'

'Just a minute.' With an apologetic wave at Henchie, she hurried outside.

'Zulekha? How are you? You are living with Anjali and Raman. Why does no one tell me this?'

'I meant to, Naani, it's just work's been busy and –'

Leela snorted at the oldest excuse in the book. 'How is work?'

'Great, thanks. But it's Diwali tomorrow, so I'll tell you . . .'

'Hmm. It's kept you out of mischief. I suppose that's better than nothing. Any news on a proper job? Ashok Kumar, you remember, who has a very successful gold import business, said he might be looking for someone to assist him.'

'Great, Naani, that's good to know.'

'Shall I tell him you'd like to meet?'

'Um. Wait until I have my diary and I can tell you when would be a good time.'

'Why don't you have your diary?'

'I just . . . left it at home. I'll bring it tomorrow.'

Naani *tttched*. 'When will you learn to be more organized, Zulekha? Anyway, on the subject of Diwali, I called Tony and he asks if he can bring his girlfriend. Who is this woman? Why did you not tell me about her? Is this why you moved in with Anjali?'

Zu's heart crumbled like a derelict building. 'I don't know much about her, Naani,' she said stiffly.

'This is not the nice lady with the teenager you told me about?'

'Um, no. This one doesn't have a teenager.'

'Is she a nice lady?'

'Honestly, Naani, I don't know. I've only met her a couple of times. Dad met her at a Temperley party, but she's not a Temperley member, just someone's sister and . . . Is she coming to Diwali then?'

'Of course. Do you think I wouldn't welcome her into the bosom of the family? Now what about you?' she continued, as Zu tried to take it all in. 'I've heard that Rahul Mehta's son is on the market and he is very eligible. A doctor, soon to be consultant, lovely house in Sunbury. Shall we see what we can do?'

'Naani! You know I don't want matchmaking.'

'Better go, darling, New York's on the other line. See you tomorrow. Look nice, please.'

'Yes,' said Zu. She hung up. She fumbled for her cigarettes. Naani had invited Josie to Diwali. She shook her head as she inhaled. Be logical, she instructed herself. If Josie was Dad's girlfriend, then it was very generous of Naani to invite her. But Josie was just so . . .

'What are you doing?' Jack asked beside her. 'I thought you'd run away.'

'No. I just had to take a call.'

'Are you OK?'

'Fine. Just a work problem.' She ground out her cigarette butt under her trainer. 'Let's go back in.'

33

They'd ended up staying until midnight and then going on to a karaoke bar somewhere in the West End where she drank three cocktails and performed a vigorous version of 'It Must Have Been Love'. When they were finally kicked out around two, Jack had insisted Zu took a taxi.

'Doan be silly. I can walk. 'S a beautiful night.' She gestured up at the sky. 'Look at the moon! Bright and clear again!'

'You're in no state to walk,' Jack insisted. 'It's too far and you'll be mugged.'

'I can look after myself.'

'I'm putting you in a cab.'

She remembered serenading the driver with 'It Must Have Been Love', then asking urgently if he'd open the window and him telling her if she puked in his taxi he'd kill her and her telling him to fuck off. At which point the taxi had pulled up abruptly and she'd had to walk the last half mile home, stopping just once to upchuck neatly in a bin. Neatly because there wasn't any food to vomit, just pure alcohol, diluted only by a tiny bit of juice.

No one had mugged her. As if! Zu was always putting herself in dicey situations: Chechen policemen had held rifles to her throat, FSB men had waved their fists in her face. But they always backed down. Sometimes she almost wished something bad would happen, because she deserved a punishment – for what, she didn't quite know. But it never did.

The alarm on her phone woke her at eight. She was ravenous. Zu never got hangovers, she didn't understand all the moaning about headaches and paint-stripper mouths. She ate six slices of toast and Marmite, only switching on fully when she spotted Anjali's note on the breakfast bar.

You raver, you! See you at Diwali x

Diwali. She'd been so shaken by Naani's news, but the drink had made her forget completely. Diwali tonight, when Josie would be introduced into the family fold as Dad's official partner.

She eyed a half-eaten slice of toast, her appetite suddenly diminished. But then she looked out of the window. It was a sunny day; the air outside looked as crisp as an apple. A cloudless night for the fireworks. Who cared if Dad's girlfriend wasn't ideal?

There'd be three hundred people at Diwali, she wouldn't have to talk to her. She'd been overreacting and she was going to Get Over It. After all, she'd got over worse. When Mum died a lot of well-meaning, know-nothing people had told her to take what was good about Mum forward with her in life. Ha! As if. But even if Mum had been Mother Teresa, the truth was, losing someone was never positive. The scars stayed with you forever and changed you irrevocably. Sometimes the past's hold was much stronger than the lure of the future.

'Enough!'

Zu pulled on her scarf and headed out the door to work.

*

From halfway up the stairs, she could hear Gary booming down the phone.

'Well, she's only thirty-two, Matt . . . All right, I hear you . . . Yes, we'll keep looking for someone younger. All right, mate. Ciao. Arsehole.'

'Did you hang up before you said that?' Zu grinned.

'Huh? Oh yeah, I'm sure I did.' For a second Gary looked worried but then he continued, 'I'm going to persuade Matt to try some of the Close Encounters women. It's the only way he's going to find what he wants – a twenty-year-old who's desperate to marry him. I'm going to persuade him to go on the next Odessa tour. Talking of which . . .' He grinned at Zu. 'We've been meaning to ask you for a while. Will you go too? I have to stay here to mind the shop but we could really do with the extra pair of hands – Masha likes to bugger off visiting friends and family, and Nadia in the Odessa office can't cope on her own. It means a free trip to Ukraine for you. So what do you say? We leave on December twenty-eighth so we can have New Year there and we're going to start booking soon.'

'I'll think about it,' Zu said. A free trip to Ukraine was hugely tempting, but a free trip with the likes of Matt Billen was another prospect entirely.

'You do that, love. Now, hold the fort, will you? Meeting Masha at Alfie's Antique Market to check out some curios.'

Before she knew it, it was nearly six. She wondered if she could get away with going to Naani's party in the cords and striped jumper she was wearing or if she ought to nip out to Marylebone High Street and buy a dress, because one of the millions of Diwali traditions was that you had to wear something new. Reluctantly, she was reaching the conclusion that she really ought to buy something when the door opened and there was Gary, redder in the face than usual, followed by Masha, also looking distinctly flushed.

'Hello, darling! Just bagged a fabulous nineteen-thirties cabinet.' He rubbed his hands together. 'Money, money, money,' he sang in a bad imitation of Agnetha from Abba. Clearly, they'd stopped off at a pub on the way back. 'Going down the drain. La di da da. So where are you off to tonight?'

'My grandmother's having a party.'

'A party? Good stuff. All the family will be there?'

'Most of them.'

'Including the dom?'

'Sorry?'

'Gary,' Masha said warningly.

'The dom. You know, Elin's sister, whatsername. Your Dad's squeeze. The one with the *past*.'

'What past?'

Gary looked amused. 'You didn't know?'

'Didn't know what?'

Masha tugged at his arm. 'Gary, you've drunk too much.'

'What's this about Josie's past?' Zu asked.

'I think I've put my foot in it,' Gary said, looking like an overgrown schoolboy.

'What is it?' Zu was a dog with a bone. 'Masha! Why do you call her "the dom"?'

Masha couldn't make eye contact. 'Well, it's just that

Josie . . . You know, she's been a bit all over the place. And for about a week, not longer, I mean no time at all really, she was working as a dominatrix.'

'A what?' But Zu knew. She felt as if she were shrinking, removing herself from this and going somewhere else where it was not happening. Josie was one of those women who advertised in the back of the *Standard*. Miss Slapper. All black leather and chains and whips. Men on their knees, begging for mercy. Was this what Tony was into? Zu considered herself very broadminded. In her time, she'd dealt with every kind of person, including many, many prostitutes. But that was in Chechnya, recovering from a horrible civil war, with people on the breadline. This was London. And, whatever the circumstances, she didn't want her father going out with a prostitute.

Masha looked appalled. 'I'm so sorry.'

''S'OK.' Zu pretended to be absorbed in an email. 'Oh no, Antonia's going to cancel her date with Brian because her ex is sick and she needs to go round and feed him chicken soup. That woman is infuriating.'

'Honestly, Zu, it was only for about a day. Elin mentioned it when we were buying the painting, said she hoped things didn't go any further with your father because . . .' Zu had never seen Masha so uneasy. 'And you know these women aren't hookers. They don't have sex with the clients, they just . . .'

'Whip them. Make them beg for mercy,' Gary sniggered. Masha glared at him.

'You're a bad boy,' she said frostily, oblivious to the irony of using such a term. 'I think we should be off now.'

'Sorry, Zu. Have fun tonight.' Gary stuffed his hands in

the pocket of his cashmere overcoat. He was just the messenger, but Zu hated him. Not as much as she hated Josie though. Her father was living with a prostitute. Zu suspected he was in love with her. She'd be seeing them both in a couple of hours at Naani's. Oh God. Suppose Naani found out.

'Zu? Are you OK?' Masha asked at the door, her face still ashen under the layers of bronzer. 'I'm so sorry.'

'I told you. I'm fine.'

34

Josie was uncharacteristically nervous. She tweaked her hoop earrings and put a hand on Tony's arm to stop herself wobbling on her platform wedges as they made their way from the Tube down Leela's quiet, suburban street.

'So who's going to be at this do?' she asked.

'Pretty much everyone,' Tony said.

He was anxious too, unsure if he'd done the right thing accepting Leela's invitation. He'd debated going on his own but a strange new side of him, a side that was sick of the silence around his private life, told him just to get Josie out in the open. Asking Leela if he could bring 'a friend' had turned his bowels to water, but she'd simply said, 'Of course, I'd love to meet her,' and genuinely sounded as if she meant it.

'Like who?'

'Well, the family will have all got there first for the religious stuff – you know, they get it out of the way, like church at Christmas before the presents and telly. So there'll be Leela, my ex-mother-in-law, and Arun, Deepi's brother, who's a bigshot doctor, and his wife, Priyanka, who has only one topic and that's schools – she'll be asking in five minutes where you went and sussing you out from your reply.'

'Well, she'll love Roedean.'

'Unfortunately, Deepi's other brother, Mahesh, and

Renu, his wife, won't be there. They're lovely but they're visiting family in India.' Secretly, Tony was a little relieved about this. Renu and Mahesh were the only ones from Deepi's family they'd had any contact with when times got tough. Renu, in particular, had been amazingly support-ive. Tony knew she'd want him to be happy, but he suspected she might not consider Josie the most suitable candidate for that. He continued: 'Darshan, their son, who's a bigwig accountant, will be there and Anjali, who Zu's staying with. Sweet girl. And Zu, of course.'

'Ah, it'll be lovely to see her,' Josie said warmly.

Tony felt sad. Josie wanted so much to be liked. Why did his daughter have to be so rigid?

Leela's high iron gates were wide open, the driveway full of cars and lit with torches. Josie regarded the house appraisingly. Tony saw it through her eyes: as wide as five buses, two storeys high, elephant grey – a far cry from red-brick, terraced Farthingdale Road.

'You weren't lying when you called it a mansion.'

'She's done well for herself,' agreed Tony, as Glenda the Filipina maid, who seemed never to sleep or take a day off, opened the opaque-glass-panelled front door and ushered them into the marble-tiled hall, decorated everywhere with candles for the festival. A Hindu guru glared down at them from the wall.

'Tony, this room is the size of your entire house,' Josie hissed. He shrugged. 'Why doesn't Leela give you any money?'

Tony felt uneasy. 'She would if I asked, but I don't want her to.'

'Right.' Josie had moved on to the mahogany-panelled

drawing room with its pitched roof and enormous fireplace surrounded by carved gargoyles. Tony's heart leapt as if at the sight of a long-lost lover as he spotted Zu in the crowd of brightly dressed people – the women mainly in saris, the men in suits. His daughter was wearing her usual trousers and a stripy top, but still looked different in a significant but impossible-to-pin-down way. He watched her holding a glass of champagne and chatting to Priyanka, nodding and laughing, a model guest. She hadn't spotted him. He started approaching, when –

'Tony!' It was Leela, in her best scarlet salwar kameez, embroidered with silver threads, her arms dripping with gold bangles. 'And you must be Josie. How do you do, dear? I'm Leela Sangar.'

'Leela!' Josie tried to hug her. Leela stepped back sharply. Tony's guts twisted.

'Thank you so much for coming,' his ex-mother-in-law said.

'Wouldn't have missed it for the world. What an amazing house!'

Leela bowed her head in faux modesty. What was she really thinking? Did she approve of Josie? Was she shocked at how young she was, how tight her trousers were? 'I'm very lucky.'

'You deserve it all. Your business is amazing. I've been buying your stuff for years. I never dreamt I might meet you.'

'Oh, really?' Leela purred. 'What is your favourite product?'

'How do I choose? I love the body balm and the eyebrow gel and the lipstick. You've been an inspiration for me to start my own business one day.'

To Tony's amazement, Leela cooed, 'Well, what's stopping you? Any help you want, I'm more than happy to be your mentor. Please call me whenever. And I'll make sure you receive a goodie bag of our latest products. I'd love your opinions on them.'

'Oh my God! Have I died? Am I in heaven?' Josie pinched herself and cackled with infectious laughter.

Leela was positively glowing. She looked over her shoulder and beckoned imperiously. 'Zuzu! Have you said hello to Josie yet? We've just been introduced.'

Zu turned round, a look of pure hatred on her face.

'Hello,' she said frostily, then turned back to Priyanka.

'Zu!' Josie rushed over and kissed her. Zu looked as if she'd smelt something bad.

'How are you? Great to see you. You look *amazing*.'

Zu turned on her heel and walked away. Josie stood, open-mouthed.

'What was all that about?'

'Don't know,' said Tony, as Arun tapped him on the shoulder. He was obviously Deepi's brother with those strong Punjabi features: aquiline nose, liquid eyes, thick hair – the bastard. As ever, he reeked of expensive aftershave and was in a designer suit. Tony was very aware of his Marks & Spencer's number.

'Tony, old boy. What's up? How's the little business?'

'Doing very well, Arun. The recession's helped. People aren't chucking their instruments away, they're having them mended.'

'Good stuff, good stuff.' Arun stifled a yawn as he took a mini chicken tikka from a platter.

'And you?' Tony felt duty-bound to ask.

'Exhausted,' Arun sighed. 'Work's . . .'

Anjali appeared behind him in an orange Punjabi suit, covered in sequins. 'Hiya, Uncle Amit.' She leant forward and kissed Tony. 'How are you, Uncle Tones?'

'Fine, thank you. Where's Raman?'

'Still in the office,' Anjali shrugged, as Leela once again appeared.

'That husband of yours works so hard,' she said approvingly. 'Surely it can't be long before he's made partner.'

'Here's hoping,' said Anjali with a smile.

'You two are so marvellous. Real success stories.' She glanced at her Rolex and clapped her hands. 'Firework time! Everyone outside.'

The garden was illuminated by hundreds of tiny flickering oil lamps. Lanterns hung in the trees that lined the stone paths. There was a whee and a bang and flicks of blue skidded across the sky like paint from a brush.

'Ooh!' exclaimed Josie, reappearing at Tony's side. Golden sparks, then red ones fizzled. She clapped her hands like a little girl. 'I love fireworks. Is this like Guy Fawkes for Indians?'

'No,' said Tony, 'it's just a coincidence that Diwali often falls close to Bonfire Night.' Then, seeing Zu on the edge of the crowd, he made a decision. 'Just going to the loo. Back in a sec.'

'Mmm.' Josie's head was tilted towards the sky, now filled with silver drizzle.

In the dark, Zu didn't see him approaching. 'What is it?

What's wrong?' he said sternly in her ear, making her jump, but then she turned to face him, eyes blank.

'Nothing.' A Roman candle flashed, illuminating her breath like a dragon's in the cold night air.

'Why are you being so hostile to Josie?'

'I'm just not sure about her, that's all.' The earth beneath him shook as a purple and gold explosion whammed. Orange and silvery stars followed.

'Can't you give her a chance?' he said as the crowd 'Aahed' at a Catherine wheel.

'I'd rather just let you get on with it.'

Tony's throat tightened. 'I've been very lonely.' He took a deep breath. 'And now I'm not any more. So, please, let me try to make a go of things here.'

'It just all happened so quickly, her moving in and everything.' Zu stared at him, eyes wounded.

Well, too bad, he thought. *I have to start living life for me now.*

'What's going to happen at Christmas?'

'I was hoping you'd come to me. And the boys. That was the plan.'

'Will *she* be there?'

'I don't know, I hadn't thought about it. I guess, I mean, she doesn't get on with her mother . . .' Again, the sky brightened, fully illuminating Zu's sceptical expression, then grew dark again. 'She might want to go to Elin's but they're not great mates either.' She remained silent, so he stumbled on. 'You'll come, won't you, Zu? Even if Josie's there? It wouldn't be Christmas without you.'

The fireworks embarked on their grand finale. It was as if a child had been let loose in the shop as everything started exploding together. The ground shook beneath their feet.

'Zulekha!' It was Neelam. 'We haven't spoken all evening. I need to hear all your news.'

Zu shot Tony a look as she turned her back on him. The crowd started applauding. The fireworks were over. Tony couldn't see Josie and he didn't know where to turn, everyone seemed deep in conversation, so he headed back into the house and, although he really didn't need to pee, towards the loo. He washed his hands and splashed water on his face, hoping that might make him look less tired. Stepping out into the tiled hall, he took a deep breath, bracing himself to rejoin the fray now thronging around the buffet.

On the wall hung a framed black and white picture of Deepi, garlanded with orange flowers, next to one of her father. Tony stopped and looked at it. It was her graduation portrait; a robe was draped round her shoulders, a mortar board was on her head and she was beaming at the camera. Despite the daft outfit, she looked beautiful: young and carefree, like the kind of woman who'd dance on tables, who'd spend hours on her hands and knees pretending to be a tiger to entertain a child, who'd leap on her husband at the end of a long day and ravish him. The woman she'd been until something took over. Yearning for her tugged at Tony's heart, like the anchor of a boat.

'Hello,' a voice said. He turned, rearranging his features. It took a moment to place her. Gillian, whom he'd gone on his one Temperley date with.

'What are *you* doing here?'

She laughed. 'I might well ask you the same question.'

'Leela's my mother-in-law. My ex-mother-in-law.'

Amusement lit up Gillian's face. 'Gosh. That must be –' she paused – 'interesting. She's my client. I do her PR.'

'Oh. That must be . . . interesting too.'

They smiled at each other. 'She keeps me on my toes,' Gillian said. 'But I'm enjoying this party. Amazing food. That *rajma* – Leela said it was made with kidney beans. Delicious. I'll have to get the recipe.'

'Ask Leela for the recipe and you'll have a client for life.'

'So . . . how are you? I'm sorry I –'

'I enjoyed our date,' Tony interrupted. 'But I think perhaps we were looking for different things.'

'Yes,' she agreed hastily. 'So any luck since?'

'Well, not with the agency. You?'

She shook her head. 'No joy. I'm actually having a break from it for now.'

'Gillian, Tony!' Leela exclaimed. 'Two of my favourite people. I'd been meaning to introduce you for quite some time. And now you've met all by yourselves. Shame that Tony . . .'

'What?' Tony said.

'Oh, nothing.' She smiled at Gillian. 'So you are enjoying the party, I hope.'

'Very much so.'

'There you are!' Josie exclaimed, yanking at Tony's arm. 'I've been looking for you everywhere. You've got to come and eat, there's this incredible sort of aubergine mash thing.'

'Oh yes, that's good,' Gillian agreed.

'Hiya.' Josie held out a hand. 'I'm Josie!'

'Gillian.' Tony couldn't help but notice her expression change. She thought he was a sad fool, running around with someone the same age as his daughter. He wrapped his arms round himself protectively.

'You look gorgeous, Gillian,' Josie gushed. 'I love that dress – it must be designer.'

'Topshop.'

'No! Really? How clever are you!' She put her hand on Gillian's arm. 'Coming to play cards? Apparently it's a Diwali tradition.'

'Really?' Gillian's face lit up. 'I might just do that. I used to be a bit of a demon poker player.'

'The women don't usually behave like demons at these events,' Tony warned. 'They giggle a lot and maybe bet a pound.'

'Well, you show them how it's done then, Gillian!' Josie urged.

'I might just. I didn't think Hindus were into gambling.'

Leela laughed. 'It's like everyone is surprised to see us drinking. But we Punjabis are party people. They say if you don't gamble on Diwali you'll be born a donkey in your next life. It's a free pass for us to indulge our vice for one night of the year without feeling guilty.'

'Well, let me get stuck in,' Gillian said. Her phone rang and she pulled it out of her bag. 'Excuse me, I have to take it, it might be a client. Hello?' Her face changed. 'Yes? Yes . . . Right . . . Are they OK? I see. All right. If you text me the address, I'll be right over.'

She hung up, her previously smiling face suddenly ashen.

'Everything OK?' Leela asked.

'I need to go and pick up Holly.'

'Ach! Is the girl in trouble again?'

'No, no.' Gillian was quite obviously lying. 'No trouble,

but she needs me.' She smiled brightly, but not with her eyes. 'Thank you so much, Leela, it's been wonderful.'

'Sure you can't stay a bit longer? Or take some food with you?' Leela looked around. 'Glenda? Where is Glenda? She can put some into doggie bags for you.'

'No, no, really, Leela, but thank you. Nice to see you, Tony. And you, Josie.'

'You too.'

She hurried towards the door. Tony watched sympathetically but Josie yanked his arm. 'Now, come on. It's time for cards.'

35

Gillian drove across north London, hands clammy on the steering wheel, heart thudding sickeningly, other cars honking as she lurched perilously into their lanes. What was going on? What had Holly done now?

The deal had been that Holly would stay in and do homework and Gillian would be back by ten and then they'd watch a DVD together. But she'd just had a woman who called herself Camille's mother on the phone, sounding close to hysterics. She hadn't said exactly what the problem was, just that Holly was at her house and Gillian needed to take her home *now*, or she was calling the police.

'What the hell did she do?' Gillian exclaimed.

She was exhausted. What would she do now? Yell at Holly? Ground her? She was grounded already. It clearly hadn't worked.

Camille lived in a mansion block near Regent's Park. The traffic was heavy and it took Gillian nearly an hour to arrive and find a parking space. She ran across the street and up the front steps. The door was black gloss, flanked by two bay trees in urns. She hammered the brass knocker shaped like a lion's head. A woman of about her age appeared, very skinny, jeans and red cashmere jumper, heavy bags below her eyes.

'Camille's mum? I'm Holly's mum.' *Things no one told you about being a mother, part 956. You will never be called by your real name, ever again. You are just an appendage to your child.* 'Is everything OK? Where are they?'

'Watching television. You're the last mother to arrive,' Camille's mother added accusingly.

'I'm so sorry. I was right the other side of London. I didn't know she was here.'

'Mmm.' Camille's mother folded her arms. 'Holly said you had a very busy social life.'

Gillian congratulated herself on resisting the temptation to bash her in the chops. 'So what happened?' she asked tightly.

'They were all here to watch the fireworks from our balcony. There's a huge display in the communal gardens. But I found four of them in the bathroom, doing cocaine.'

'What shall I do?' Gillian asked Alicia from her bed two hours later. Music thud-thudded from under Holly's door. 'The dope was one thing, but now it's Class As.'

'Just remember, everyone takes cocaine. Well, not everyone, but you know what I mean. Half George's office are on it – how else would they stay up seventy-two hours straight doing those deals? So don't freak completely. Just stop her allowance and ground her.'

'I did both of those, ages ago. She just laughs at me. And how can I ground her properly? She needs to go to school.'

'After school, straight home.'

'But I have to go out myself – I have to go to the shops, walk Waffle, see clients. How can I stop her escaping? I guess I won't go out at night any more,' Gillian concluded.

'You are *not* letting Holly stand in the way of you having

a social life.' Alicia sounded furious. 'No, no, no, no. Not on. You are human too.'

'OK.' Gillian was unsure. Perhaps she should confine herself henceforth to the kitchen, making Holly nutritious meals, hovering over her when she did her homework, limiting Waffle to a run around the garden. But that was what Camille's mother did, judging by her enormous kitchen with spreadsheets on the wall showing each of her four children's movements that week and the Post-Its on the fridge saying DON'T FORGET CUPCAKES FOR BAKE SALE. And, according to Holly, it was Camille who'd scored the coke from her 'friends on the estate'. Whichever path you chose, you were doomed.

36

Zu's November wasn't much fun. She wasn't speaking to Tony and, while Anj and she were as close as ever, she knew her cousin was baffled by her reaction to Josie. The morning after Diwali she'd berated her for leaving early and refused to buy Zu's excuse that she felt ill.

'You're never ill. It was Josie, wasn't it?'

'Josie's well, well fit,' Raman had chortled, looking up from his copy of the *Financial Times*. 'Lucky old Tony.'

'I know she's a bit brash,' Anjali continued, 'but she's very sweet. She told me about this new hairdryer that has a rotating brush so you can do a practically salon blow-dry at home. I couldn't believe it! I hadn't heard of it – and me, a make-up artist.'

Zu said nothing.

'Zu, it's your father's life. You have to let him make his own choices.'

'I know,' Zu said crossly. She couldn't bring herself to tell Anj about the dominatrix stuff. Even if Ram hadn't been there, she couldn't completely trust her not to tell him and the phwoaring that would ensue would be unbearable. But if she didn't tell Anj, how could she be expected to understand? They were all just going to have to think her an intolerant cow. Which she was, of course, but there was so much more to it than that.

They didn't talk about it again. Instead, Anj turned her attentions to another subject.

'So what's going on with you and that gorgeous Henchie guy?'

'Nothing! You know that.'

'You see a lot of him.'

'No, I don't. Maybe once a week.'

'Sometimes twice.'

'Sometimes. But nothing is going on. We're just mates. He has a girlfriend.'

'How do you know?'

'I've seen pictures of her. She called once because they had a problem with the boiler. She's Russian.'

'What does she think of the two of you hanging out together?'

'I have no idea.' Zu did wonder if 'They', as Henchie had referred to the mystery woman, knew anything about her. Russians didn't go a bundle on platonic friendships, they didn't understand them. You had your girlfriends and your man. But whatever was going on at Henchie's house, nothing was going on between her and Henchie and that was all that mattered.

The weeks passed, the Christmas lights were turned on in Marylebone High Street. It rained all the time. It grew dark while Zu was eating lunch. At work they were continuing their preparations for the Odessa trip. Zu was making a list of the men coming, booking them in to the Hotel Odessa where they had a special reduced rate.

Matt Billen had continued to reject the half-dozen women they'd suggested for him, but now – finally – on date seven, with Edda, who was a beautiful, gentle Irish-woman with flaming red hair and green eyes and aged just thirty-one, he seemed happy.

'The date went brilliantly,' he was telling Zu now. 'I really, really like her. So much so that –'

'You're going on hold,' Zu gasped.

'No, I was going to say we did the deed. But, yeah, now you mention it, I would like to go on hold. For now at least.'

Zu hung up and broke the news.

'Splendid!' Gary exclaimed. 'And have we heard back from the luscious Edda?'

'Not yet. I just emailed her, but when she's working she can't make calls.'

'I'm sure she'll be in touch soon. Oh yes! We'll have Matt off our hands by Easter. Thank God.'

A phone started ringing. 'Hello, Temperley,' cooed Zu.

'Hello,' said a soft Irish voice. 'Zulekha? It's Edda here, Edda Mulroney.'

'Edda, hi! We were hoping you'd get back to us. How did it go with Matt?'

'I'm fucking going to kill him.'

'Oh?' Edda hadn't come across as a four-letter girl at the interview.

'The fuckhead. He's given me crabs.'

After work, Zu headed out to meet Henchie. They'd started a new game, which was eating their way alphabetically round the world. So far they had tried Albanian food in West Hampstead, Burmese at the grotty end of the Edgware Road, Cambodian in Camden ('Alliteration!

Double points,' Jack had exclaimed) and Dutch – not in Denmark Hill as Jack had hoped – but in Bloomsbury.

She was just heading out of the door for Egyptian night when her phone rang in her pocket. She was trying to set the burglar alarm and answered without thinking.

'Temperley.'

'Zulekha?'

'Oh, hi, Naani.' She'd called and left a message the morning after Diwali, thanking her grandmother for the lovely party, but since then, dreading the post mortem, she'd managed to spend six whole weeks playing phone tag and not being caught. 'Ha ha, I've been answering the phone at work all day, I forgot this was my mobile.'

'Zulekha, why have you been so silent? I've left you so many messages.'

'Sorry, Naani. Every time I call you back I get voicemail and it doesn't seem worth leaving a message.'

A snort. 'So am I going to see you? I'm off to Haryana on Saturday, you know, and it's been ages. Any chance you could pop over after work one evening? I'd love a catch-up.'

'It's tricky, Naani. I'm really busy this week . . .'

'Hmm. Well, as soon as I'm back in the New Year I'll pin you down to a lunch. You and Anjali. Just girls. But tell me, then, what is your thinking on Josie?'

'I think she's fine,' Zu said abruptly.

'Good. I'm glad. I must say I have my doubts. She's a little . . . brazen, shall we say. But she was very friendly and charming. She knew a lot about Leela Limited, she's a big fan of all the products – I sent her some and she sent me a very sweet email back. And she seems so bubbly, which has to be good for Tony, he's been such a misery guts for so long.'

'Absolutely.'

'You don't think so?'

'I do, Naani. I said: "Absolutely".'

'You sounded unsure.'

'I'm just in the office now, Naani. It's hard to talk. But I'll come round as soon as you're back. How lovely — scorching Haryana instead of freezing England.'

'What is it you don't like about her, Zulekha?'

'I've told you. Nothing. I just don't know her very well.'

'You have no idea how lonely it is being a widow or widower. Even when the room is packed you feel so isolated. You know at the end of the day you will get into bed by yourself, that there will be no one to share those little gripes with. So, please, don't be too rough on your father. Let him seize happiness where he can.'

Zu was astonished. She'd never heard Naani speak like this, ever. Naani seemed about as lonely as Simon Cowell was lacking in confidence. Of course Leela had been sad when Naana had died but she'd been so busy organizing the funeral and the wake, it had never occurred to Zu that she might be concealing her suffering. Suddenly she saw Naani's calls demanding she come over in a different light. Perhaps Naani wasn't trying to control them all. Perhaps she just wanted company.

'Look, I'm sure I could find time to visit tomorrow,' she tried.

'No, no, it's *Red* magazine beauty awards tomorrow. Don't worry, Jaan. I will see you in the New Year. Have a lovely Christmas.'

'I –' Zu began. But Leela had gone.

She and Jack met at Meya Meya, just off the Edgware Road, and sat at a formica table in the basement. They ordered *fateer*, which was a kind of Egyptian pizza, and *koshury*, a mixture of rice, pasta, tomato and vegetables, and drank a bottle of Shiraz, which Henchie had brought with him since there was no licence.

'Glad you made it,' he said as he filled her glass. 'I thought you might be a bit embarrassed after last time.'

'What would I be embarrassed about?' Zu was going to brazen this out, since she remembered virtually nothing about the second half of the night except they'd visited a Soho karaoke bar.

'Um, the limbo dancing with the group of Korean businessmen? The short one wanted to marry you.'

'They were all short.'

'One was particularly teeny-weeny. And particularly interested in yo-ou.'

Zu ignored this. 'So what's the plan for tonight? More karaoke?'

Henchie shifted in his chair. 'Maybe a bit later. I was wondering if we could do a bit of shopping first.'

'*Shopping?*'

He laughed at her disgusted expression. 'Aren't you a girl?'

'Oh, yes, I forgot, and we *girls* love nothing more than retail therapy.'

'Listen. It's Thursday, it's late-night shopping and there's less than three weeks until Christmas. And there's a few people I need to buy for and I want you to help me choose.

I don't want to leave it until the last minute like I did last year because that doesn't go down at all well with the grandparents.'

'Have you heard of a marvellous new invention called the Internet?' asked Zu, opening her eyes wide. 'You go on to something I believe is called "Google" and you type "present for boy aged —" How old is he again?'

'Nearly five,' Jack said proudly.

'Nearly five. And, lo, on the glowing screen before you a list of suggestions of suitable presents for your son will appear, and you choose one and enter your credit-card details and it will arrive in the post a couple of days later. Meanwhile on cold winter evenings you can sit in a pub, rather than schlepping round Oxford Street.'

'You're such a miserable git. Where's your sense of fun? Going shopping is a great London experience.'

'If you love jammed pavements and boiling-hot shops and you're a masochist.'

'Don't you have Christmas shopping to do? We'll blitz it tonight and then on Christmas Eve, when we'd normally be tearing around like maniacs, we'll be sitting here eating *shwarma*. How about it?'

'I don't know.' Zu emptied her glass, then filled it up again. She found herself saying, 'I still don't know what I'm doing for Christmas. So buying presents seems slightly premature.'

'Why don't you know what you're doing?'

Zu shrugged. She'd been thinking about this, ever since Diwali. There was nowhere else to go but to Dad's. Anjali and Raman were going to his parents' place in Nottingham. Leela would be in the Punjab. All her friends would be with their families. She could buy a ticket for somewhere hot and spend the week alone there, but Kieran and Rohan would be coming home. If she ran off, she'd miss yet another Christmas with them and she wasn't sure her conscience could take it. She was going to have to go back to Dad's. And if she did, she might as well arrive laden down with gifts. It would be a peace offering, like the Germans and the British singing 'Silent Night' together in no-man's land.

'If you're thinking about not going home, don't do it,' Jack said softly. 'It's really not worth perpetuating feuds.'

'It's not a feud,' Zu lied.

'Then go.'

Zu shrugged. 'Whatever happens, I won't stay long. I'm going to Odessa on the twenty-eighth.'

'Oh, so you decided to join the saddos.'

'I wanted to see Odessa.'

'It's great.' Jack smiled at a fond memory. 'The girls . . . well, you know what Paul McCartney said.'

'Something about the Ukrainian girls being knockouts?' replied Zu with a yawn. Gary was always quoting that line from the Beatles. 'I'm more interested in the architecture, personally.'

'Yeah, yeah. The opera house, the stately boulevards. Because Ukrainian men, sadly for you, are well unfit. Pock-marked, scrawny, look fifty when they're thirty.'

'Stop describing yourself, Henchie.' Zu bit into a fala-fel. 'Will you be seeing your family?'

'Only Xander. My dad's in Singapore with his third wife and Mum's in Mallorca with her second husband. That's why I know a bit about feuds.'

'You don't like either step-parent?' Zu was interested.

'I like my stepmother but she won't last long, they never do. Dad's a nightmare. And, no, my stepfather is not my favourite man. But if I could do it all again, I'd have swallowed my tongue a bit more in the old days, rather than flying off the handle every time he opened his mouth.'

'Right.' Zu pondered this, then stood. 'OK, let's go shopping. So long as there's a drink at the end of it.'

'There'll be a drink.'

Regent Street glowed a phosphorous orange under the street lights and there was still slush on the streets from the snow that had briefly fallen at lunchtime before melting in bright white sun. Shoppers bustled, a Salvation Army band played. Lights, meshed intricately like a spider's web, glowed overhead. Despite her 'bah, humbug' mindset, Zu was infused with cheerfulness as Jack held open the door of Hamleys for her.

'Enter, Madam.'

'So what are we looking for?' she asked. Trains chuffed, baby dolls ga-gahed, battery-powered dogs yapped. Carols were blasting through the speakers and it was very, very hot.

'Some ludicrously extravagant toy to show what a devoted father I am. Preferably one I'll enjoy playing with even more than Xander. And when we've done that I need to nip into Liberty to procure a bribe for his grandparents. An item of clothing for his granny – you can help me with that.'

'I know nothing about clothes.'

'I know that,' he teased. Zu glanced down at her jeans and black V-neck jumper and shrugged and grinned.

'It's one of the best things about you that you don't care about stuff like that,' he said.

'Is that a compliment or an insult?'

'A compliment. But you can still help me,' he continued.

Zu's stomach buckled unexpectedly. 'Surely you have an idea what the ladies like by now?' she countered.

Jack ignored her. 'Who do you have to buy for?' He picked up a glove puppet and put it down again. 'Your dad, your brothers . . .'

'My grandmother. She's a nightmare because she has everything.' Zu smiled at a memory as they stepped on to the escalators. 'One year my brothers bought her a goat for an African village but she didn't like that *at all*. Charity begins at home as far as she's concerned.'

'I'm sure the African villagers don't like being given smelly goats either. They'd much rather have Xboxes. Who else then?'

'Anjali, my cousin that I live with. Raman, her husband. I suppose I should buy Masha and Gary something small. And Josie.'

'Josie?'

'My dad's girlfriend.'

'You didn't tell me he had a girlfriend.'

'It hasn't been going very long.' Zu picked up a train set. 'Can't go wrong with one of these, can you?'

'Aha. So there *is* a feud. I knew it. Now what did Uncle Jack tell you? Go home and be nice to her.'

'There's no feud. I just don't really know her. That's why I'm here shopping, making an effort.'

'Perfume,' Jack said. 'Go for perfume. Or bubble bath, that's what you lot all like, don't you?'

She shrugged.

'You should meet Xander some time,' he said suddenly. 'Come out with us for a day.'

'Me?' Zu was startled.

'Why not?'

'I don't think I'm very good with children.'

'What about your job? Those poor, lickle-ickle street children.'

'That's different, then I'm in work mode.' In truth, she adored looking after children, but she wasn't sure she wanted to get too close to just one. She remembered the boys suddenly, silently eating their supper, their faces frozen, while Mum was pulling on her coat and heading out of the door, intent on another bender. The thought of spending time with any other boy that age was more than she could bear. It would bring back too many other memories.

Oblivious to her thoughts, Jack scoffed at her. 'I've seen you in action, you're brilliant. I could do with some tips from you.'

'Maybe,' Zu said dubiously. How many women would have collapsed with joy at his request? She shook her head faintly. 'OK. Let's get shopping.'

They chose a ridiculously expensive mini-car for Xander, which the staff promised they'd have gift-wrapped and sent to Jack's address a week before Christmas. 'Giving me a whole week to play with it by myself,' he crowed.

Then they moved just up the road to Liberty, where they decided to buy silk scarves for Xander's granny and for Leela. 'Can't go wrong with a scarf,' Jack said knowledgeably.

'You're like that guy with the silly glasses that Anjali's obsessed with. Wok Garn or whatever he's called.'

'Gok Wan. This girl I was seeing for a while was into him too. One of the reasons the relationship didn't last.'

'There's always an excuse, isn't there, Henchie?'

'Yes, Mrs Long-term Relationship. What's been your longest? Two nights?'

Zu stuck up two fingers as they walked through the jewellery department and into the noise and bustle and headache-inducing smells of the perfumery department. Zu picked up a random bottle of scent and examined it cautiously.

'Who's that for, your cousin?'

'Maybe Dad's girlfriend? Do you think she'd like it?'

'Versace. Quite tarty. Is she tarty?'

'Um. Yes.'

Jack raised an eyebrow. 'Sounds interesting.'

'I'll buy it then.'

'Are you close to your dad?' Jack asked as they fought their way towards the cash desk.

'I was,' Zu said.

'Past tense?'

'Enough of the questions, Henchie.'

'Look, don't buy her Versace. Go for that.' He nodded at a pile of fancily wrapped gift boxes. 'Molton Brown. Much safer. Bland yet lavish. She'll like you for it much more than if you give her a perfume worn by Italian strumpet junkies with faces like biltong.'

Despite herself, Zu laughed. 'OK.'

They visited the Useless Objects department, as Jack christened it, which was full of old, roughed-up Underground signs that cost nine-hundred pounds and expensive teapots. She bought Kieran and Rohan prints for their rooms at college to make them look sophisticated, and a fancy cushion for Tony.

'I hate to say it, Henchie, but you were right. I've broken a record. Nearly all shopped and with seventeen days still to go.'

'Henchie is always right. Write it one hundred times before our next drink.'

'Anything you still need to buy before I do that?' she asked.

'I thought we'd make a trip up to ladies' clothing.'

'Oh yes? Purchasing fripperies for our fancy woman, are we?'

'Let's see. You could get something for your cousin there.'

They climbed the wide wooden staircase to contemporary fashion. Satin, cotton, velvet, fake fur, merino, denim and cashmere; periwinkles, shamrocks, vermilions, icterines, heliotropes, amaranths and papayas; coats, dresses, skirts and flimsy tops. Standing there, Zu finally understood why people got so excited about clothes. She wanted to reach out and stroke the materials, hold the colours up to her face. Quickly she found a lacy blue T-shirt that she knew Anjali would love.

'Just your lady to buy for now,' she said.

'Mmm,' Jack said, holding up a dress. It was silk and a sort of reddish colour that reminded her of the colour of the dusk sky in Siberia. It had a floaty skirt and a nipped-in waist.

'What do you think?'

'It's nice,' Zu agreed.

'What size are you?'

'Me?'

'She's roughly your shape.'

'What, she's a midget?' Jack said nothing. 'I'm an eight. I think.'

Jack started leafing through the rails for an eight. 'It's four hundred and sixty-five pounds,' Zu felt obliged to warn him.

'Mmm hmm.' There was a strange, unreadable expression on his face. Zu was uneasy. Where did he find the energy to keep on moving from woman to woman to woman? What was he looking for? Would he ever really find it?

'Growing up at last, Henchie?'

He ignored her as he held the dress by its hanger. 'Right, shall we pay and then we're outta here? Time for a drink in an Ecuadorean bar.'

37

Gillian had just got home from a meeting with Leela. She shut the front door behind her and knelt down as Waffle bounded into her arms. After a moment's love-in she got up and headed up the stairs to her bedroom, Waffle following. She knelt down, lifted up her rug, yanked at the loose floorboards beneath and hauled out a safe.

She punched in a code and the heavy door swung open. Gillian looked for a moment at her jewellery sitting there – the diamond ring that had belonged to her grandmother, her sapphire engagement ring, her gold necklace, her turquoise earrings. All right, so it wasn't up there with Elizabeth Taylor, but they were still her jewels. There was also her chequebook and her iPod. Gillian added her handbag and retrieved her laptop. She couldn't keep her phone in there, she needed it for work, but she slept with it under her pillow now.

The house was quiet. With luck, Holly was at school. The rules were she was allowed out of the house to go to school and come home again, though short of appearing every day at the school gates and bundling her daughter into the car, Gillian had no idea how to enforce this. There were no punishments left. She wasn't giving Holly any money, so what could she take away next? Food? Deny her access to the bathroom? She had no idea.

She jumped as the landline started ringing. No one called

the landline any more, even her parents Skyped. It would be a telemarketing call from India, she told herself, trying to quash the bad feeling in her stomach. She picked up.

'Mrs Eversholt, hello. It's Richard Vine, I'm the head teacher at Alison Feure Academy.' He spoke slowly and cheerily, like a children's party entertainer.

'I know who you are,' Gillian said. Waffle, who'd been snoozing in her basket by the radiator, suddenly looked up, eyes wide with anxiety.

'I'm sorry to be making this call, Mrs Eversholt.' His tone changed from jolly to grave. 'There's been an incident. Holly was caught today selling marijuana to some of the younger pupils. As a result, we have felt compelled to exclude her for five days. A letter will reach you tomorrow outlining our decision and giving details of the various disciplinary committees you may appeal to.'

Selling marijuana. Well, of course, that was how she'd kept funding the habit. Gillian almost felt relieved to have made the connection.

'Mrs Eversholt?'

'Yes, I'm here.'

'Holly is on her way home now. I'm sorry, Mrs Eversholt, but this was a grave breach of the disciplinary code and we had no choice.'

'I understand.'

She hung up. Probably he'd expected some effing and blinding and 'What do you mean, my little princess has been excluded?' Excluded. What a stupid expression. Suspended, they'd said in Gillian's day. Next step up, expelled, although at Gillian's grammar school no one had ever merited such a punishment; the very idea was scandalous.

Her brain was wrapped in a damp gauze cloth, everything seemed fuzzy. Eventually she roused herself to call Alicia. 'I'll come over right away,' her sister said.

She was there within the hour. Holly was still not back. Gillian had called her mobile several times, but wasn't surprised to get no answer.

'Now, please try not to freak out when you do speak,' Alicia said.

'You wouldn't say that if it were one of your boys. You gave up a career as a barrister to devote more time to their science projects.'

'I know, but this isn't one of my boys. I'm giving you perspective. Other people always see your situation more clearly than you.'

Gillian sniffed. 'I'll remember that next time one of your boys only gets nine out of ten in his spelling.'

'Don't! Now that *would* be the end of the world.'

Despite herself, Gillian laughed. She loved her sister. What did people do without them? Holly, of course, was an only child because Billy had been insistent they could only afford the one. Hah!

'Lots of people get expelled, you know,' Alicia consoled. 'Winston Churchill. Richard Branson, I think. They've done OK.'

'I can't quite see Holly hunched over a microphone telling the nation that this is our finest hour.'

'Yes, but what's to stop her setting up an airline?'

'Maybe . . .' Gillian was unconvinced.

'Jonny did say that a lot of kids fuel their habit by dealing on the side,' Alicia continued.

'Your Jonny! How the hell does he know?' Gillian

thought of her apple-cheeked nephew, barely pubescent, reciting Latin poetry for fun. Why hadn't she sent Holly to a school like his? She should have gone without clothes, holidays, haircuts, a car, to keep her in a bubble.

The door slammed. Waffle jumped up, barking, and ran into the hall. They heard Holly speak to him, then go upstairs to her room.

'She's been suspended and she hasn't even bothered to tell me!' Gillian headed to the door and up the stairs. She opened Holly's bedroom door without knocking. She was lying on her bed, lighting a spliff.

'Put that bloody thing out immediately.'

Holly took another drag.

'I'm sixteen. I can do what I like.'

'You've been suspended from school!'

Holly shrugged. Gillian couldn't help herself. 'Do you want to ruin your life?' she screamed.

'Don't be such a drama queen. You did a degree. Look where it got you. Living in this shithole, no man, tapping away on your computer all day. Now that's a ruined life.'

A huge tear rolled down Gillian's face.

'Look at you, crying. Pathetic!'

Gillian slammed her daughter's door, ran to her own room and flung herself on her bed. She felt Alicia's hand patting her on the back. She could only cry more.

'I wish I could kill that little cow,' Alicia said.

But when Holly finally came downstairs the following morning around eleven, she was – to Gillian's surprise – abject.

'I can see what a mess I am, Mum,' she said, sitting on the kitchen countertop, the expression on her face the same as when she was nine and Livvy had told her she didn't want to be best friends any more. 'I'm going to take this week easy, detox, and when it's over I'll go back to school and take my GCSEs. We'll start from scratch.'

Gillian held out her arms. Holly fell into them. She felt as if she were watching them both in a TV documentary. 'Look at Gillian,' said the voiceover by someone like Fearne Cotton. 'She thought she and Holly were at the end of the road, but Holly wants a second chance.' Cue music – Take That and that song about a little patience, which was one of her embarrassing secret favourites, then the credits rolled.

'You know why this has all happened?' Holly sobbed into her mother's shoulder. 'It's because you and Dad split up. I miss him so much, Mum.'

'I know, darling,' Gillian soothed. All those women in the chatrooms were right, she'd known it really. She'd been so selfish to break up with Billy, except he had broken up with her. She should have done more to persuade him to stay, swallowed the betrayal and humiliation. But he still would have left. He didn't want to be with her any more. She'd failed as a wife and she'd failed as a mother.

Never mind. The important thing was that for the first time Holly was repentant. 'As it happens,' she said cautiously, 'tomorrow is the day we have the appointment with the drug counsellor anyway. So shall we go and see what she has to say?'

'OK.' Holly nodded meekly.

Fearne Cotton said: 'Aaah.'

Gillian slept better that night than she had in a long time.

The appointment was at noon the following day. At eleven Holly had only just got up. She took her time showering and dressing, then she asked – batting her eyelashes – for a full cooked breakfast.

Afterwards she went into the garden and started playing with Waffle as if they had all the time in the world.

'We need to leave, darling,' Gillian called from the patio doors. Her voice was steady but inside she was a kettle boiling over, her insides scalded, steam escaping from her ears and mouth.

'I've changed my mind.' Holly shrugged. 'Mum, let's just leave it. I don't want to see some stupid counsellor. I'll stop smoking skunk. I'll go back to school.'

'Holly . . . !'

'I need to go for a walk. Clear my head. I'll take Waffle. Just let me have twenty pounds, Mum. For a snack.'

'Twenty quid for a snack? Don't be ridiculous.'

'Just twenty quid, Mum. God, you'd pay a dog walker. Why do you begrudge me?'

'I wouldn't pay a dog walker. I walk Waffle myself.'

'You're such a tight-fisted cow.'

'For God's sake!' Gillian stormed back into the house.

Holly followed. 'If you'd been nicer to Dad he wouldn't have left,' she taunted.

Gillian saw a china figurine on the shelf beside the cooker. A porcelain shepherdess with a frothy white skirt, a crook, a yellow apron and matching bow in her hair. Holly had won it in a tombola at a school fair aged seven and adored it. It was hideover, but it was a fixed point in the kitchen landscape.

Gillian snatched it and hurled it to the ground.

'I can't believe you did that!' Holly grabbed a china spaniel, an equally ugly, equally beloved ornament, and threw it hard at Gillian. It just missed her and shattered on the floor.

'Get out. Get out right now.'

'No problem,' Holly said, heading for the door.

Help 16 yo dd now kicked out of school for selling drugs – won't go for help. WWYD?

Kentishfailure 23:00

We've agreed with the school that she'll return after Christmas but who knows what will happen? I know I'm a bad mother so please no repetition on that score but how can I change things? People say kick her out but how can I do that? Where would she live? I can't have my child homeless or in a hostel. She won't see a counsellor. I'm sure she'll end up dead like Amy Winehouse.

NewYorker 23:03

Oh, Kentish, I was hoping we'd see you back here. Welcome back hun, lots of *hugs* from your friends here. Now, listen. You've done your best. Patience and understanding will work in the end. This is a bad time but it doesn't mean your dd will end up a junkie.

Grandanse 23:05

Maybe she needs a hobby. Are there Rangers nearby she could join? Maybe judo??

Kentishfailure 23:09

Thanks everyone and thanks for not telling me I'm a bad working single parent.

Sadly, she is not the hobby type, her hobby seems to have always been giggling with her girlfriends (except she's lost them all now) and watching TV, which she does plenty of when she's vaguely alert.

Leosmama 23:16

Sorry to see you back again, Kf. My advice to you again is kick her out. You've tried everything else. She is an adult now and she has to reach rock bottom before she will come back up again. That may mean she'll be homeless for a while, it may mean she ends up in prison, either way the lesson will be learned. Good luck. I'm so sorry another mum is suffering like I did.

Grandanse 23:22

You didn't mention you're a single, working mother but obviously that's where the problem lies. Why do people have kids just to leave them in the care of others? No wonder our society's such a mess.

38

As the weeks passed an unspoken pact seemed to have developed between Josie and Tony that, although they spent the bulk of the week together, at weekends and sometimes on a Monday she went out with her old muckers to clubs with names like Envy, where they . . . Well, Tony actually had no idea what they did; the clubbing part of his life was far behind him and he'd never wanted to know.

It was a reasonable situation. Couples were allowed separate lives. It wasn't healthy to live in each other's pockets. But why, Tony wondered, did all the fun in Josie's life seem to happen with her friends, while time with him seemed to be reserved for bottles of wine on the sofa, shared curries, DVDs and early nights?

Tony would suggest the cinema.

'Ah, do you mind if we just stay in? I'm bushed.'

Another time he suggested a drink with Barry and Elinor.

'Oh, do we have to? They're . . . Don't take this the wrong way, baby, but they're so old. And dull.'

'I'm old too.'

'Yeah, but you're different. You're my rock.' She climbed off his lap and padded into the kitchen, randomly opening cupboards and inspecting the contents, looking put out that a cake or crisps hadn't magically materialized. 'I was wondering about a holiday. Somewhere hot over Christmas. I thought how about a week in Dubai?'

'Could be good.' Tony kept his voice neutral.

'There are some deals at five-star hotels I've checked out. It would be about four grand for the two of us.'

'Four grand? I haven't got that kind of money, you know that.'

Josie pouted. 'You said business was going well.'

He sighed. 'Josie, I have three kids to support.'

'Kids!' Josie snorted. 'They're adults now.'

'The boys have got years of uni ahead of them. They need financial support.'

'Can't they get loans like everyone else? Oh, Tony, please. You must have a bit of spare cash.'

'Not four grand I don't, no.'

'Fine,' she said tightly. 'I'll make some pasta and pesto, shall I? Seeing as how broke we are.'

'Josie, don't be like that.'

'I'm not being like anything. It just makes me sad that we can't have special time together. Time when you're not working and we can really chill . . .'

Time like the weekends, when you're never here. 'Anyway, we can't go away over Christmas. The boys will be back. And Zu,' he added, though he wasn't sure about this at all and it was breaking his heart. 'They'd have nowhere to go.'

'Couldn't they go to Leela's?'

'She doesn't celebrate Christmas, she always goes to India.'

'I never spent Christmas with my mum. And I was lucky if Elin would have me.' Her expression changed. 'I

278

did ask Elin if she'd have me for Christmas but she's hiking the Inca trail.'

'Why did you ask Elin? You know we want you here.'

'Zu doesn't.' Josie pouted.

Tony scratched his head. 'Zu is upset about her mother dying. She'll come round.'

'Her mother died eight years ago!' A moment's tense silence and then Josie said, 'I'm sorry, angel. I didn't mean to sound so harsh, but shouldn't you all be getting over this?'

'We certainly should,' Tony agreed, wondering why it was still proving so bloody difficult.

The following evening, cycling home down Farthingdale Road, Tony spotted Josie standing outside on the street, talking to Marta from three doors down. Josie was bouncing Marta's four-month-old baby, Arthur, on her hip. They were an attractive picture: Josie's red-gold hair shining in the pasty light of the ecobulb, the baby gurgling and smiling as if he'd been snatched from a Pampers advert and Marta just looking glad of a second's break.

'Isn't he gorgeous?' Josie cooed. 'Baba. Woodgie, woodgie, angel boy. Look, Tony!'

'Very cute,' said Tony dutifully. Babies actually did nothing for him. He'd loved his own, of course – in the sense that he'd have killed for them – but in a slightly abstract sort of way. It was only when they'd started responding that he'd really felt a connection and only maybe around the time they started to babble and walk that he'd actually truly fallen passionately for them.

'Adorable,' Josie sighed.

'Bloody hard work,' Marta said.

'I'm with you on that,' Tony agreed.

'How you survived twins, I will never know. Well, of course your wife didn't.' Even as she was saying it, a look of horror passed over Marta's features. 'Oh, sorry! That was a joke. It came out all wrong. Sleep deprivation is a terrible thing.' She tapped Josie on the shoulder. 'Which is something to think about before having a baby. Look, I have to go but good to see you, Tony. I am sorry. I really am. I am a total idiot.'

Over supper of noodles in sesame oil and defrosted prawns they were both uncharacteristically silent. Eventually, Tony said, 'Do *you* want a baby?'

Josie wrinkled her nose. 'Well, they are cute. Those chubby legs and big eyes. When I smile at Arthur he goes "Ah, gah". It's adorable.'

This had to be nipped in the bud. 'I couldn't go through all that again,' Tony said.

'I'd do all the work,' Josie countered in her most winning voice. 'Change all the nappies, get up in the night. I mean, how bad can it be?'

'You love your lie-ins. You never get up before noon.' This was increasingly becoming an issue as Tony found himself sitting around on weekend mornings waiting for her to stir.

'I'd change. I'd do it all, Tony, honestly I would.'

He smiled back, knowing full well she wouldn't. 'It's not like that. It's a job you have to share.'

'But there are single mums all over the place. They cope.'

Tony thought of Gillian. He'd been thinking about her a lot since Diwali. There was nothing tougher than being a single parent and worrying about a child. He could have called her but he was worried she'd think he was a weirdo stalker, so he'd had to let it be.

'Single mums cope, but that's usually just about it. It's not like being Liz Hurley with armies of retainers. Anyway,' he continued, clearing his throat, recognizing that this conversation would be a watershed, 'it's not just about division of labour. Even if you did all the nappy changing and all the getting up in the night, I'd still love our baby. I'd still worry about it. And, to be honest, I don't think I have the energy to worry about another child. I've got Zu probably about to go off to Chechnya again where she might get kidnapped or beheaded, the boys away now too. I'm all spent.'

'Exactly! You *are* all spent! Well, almost all,' she added hastily. 'Having another baby would bring you back to life again.'

He looked at Josie, sitting there in her denim shorts over thick black tights and his green Paul Smith jumper, which Leela had given him and which was probably the most expensive item in his wardrobe. Despite Marta's constant complaining about how hard her life was, Josie still had no idea that babies were more than cuddly things in patterned babygros – that they were disruptive, noisy, covered you in vomit and shit, tore at your heart, took away all your money, left you ashen and exhausted. Another baby might possibly bring him back to life; more probably it would destroy him.

'Let's not talk about it now,' Josie said sweetly, squeezing his hand. 'It's early days. We'll come back to it in a little while.'

'Right,' Tony said. But later unease whined at the back of his mind like a mosquito, preventing him from falling asleep. A woman who wanted his babies but couldn't see why he wanted his children home for Christmas? Before he could examine the issue too closely, his phone buzzed with a text. He picked it up curiously.

Dad. Will come home for
Xmas. See you 24 Dec.

'Who is it?' Josie asked idly.

'It's Zu,' he said. His heart beat faster, pumping with determination that he would make this Christmas the best ever, to show Zu that he loved her more deeply than she understood, to make her and Josie – not love – but like each other too. To achieve, for the first time in nearly twenty years, some semblance of a happy family Christmas.

39

Usually Zu enjoyed the build-up to Christmas. Even in the drabbest corners of Chechnya, in towns of hopeless high-rises built by Stalin, where everyone died of drink at the age of forty, you sensed a new, silly, giggly air once the countdown began.

Urgent matters became trivial compared to the plans for the aid-workers' Christmas party. Zu would outline potential problems with the new homeless hostel they were opening to her boss, to be told: 'All right, we'll deal with it after Christmas.'

It was the same at Temperley. Instead of throwing tantrums and demanding their money back when a date didn't work out, even the most high-maintenance clients merely shrugged and said things like 'C'est la vie.'

Their minds were on last-minute presents and primping themselves for 'you never know this might be the night I meet the one' parties – because wouldn't it just be ironic that having shelled out to join an agency you'd bump into the person of your dreams by complete chance?

Zu tried to look forward to returning to Farthingdale Road. Henchie forcing her to do her shopping meant she was uniquely well prepared and that made her more confident. It would be fine. OK, Josie was dodgy and Dad was a besotted fool, but they were all adults. They could work it out. All the same, it was hard to feel completely positive – not least when on the sixteenth Kieran emailed her saying he'd decided to stay in Malawi for Christmas, 'because I'm having such an amazing time!!' She was pleased for him, but her own heart broke still further. She didn't blame him, she'd done the same herself many times, but it gave her for the first time an inkling of Tony's feelings in the past when she'd decided not to come home, preferring to attend a party in Minsk or St Petersburg. If Rohan hadn't been coming she'd have bailed out, but he still was – she checked – so she resolved just to get on with it.

On the evening of the twenty-third, they turned off the computers and Masha produced a bottle of champagne.

'We need to toast our break,' she said, handing the bottle to Gary with a flutter of her eyelashes. 'Not that it's going to be long. Because on twenty-eighth we go to Odessa.'

'Yes. I haven't forgotten.' In the end Zu had decided to go because – well, why not? She'd never seen Odessa and more importantly, she'd have an excuse to leave Farthingdale Road after just a couple of days.

As if reading her mind, Gary said, 'Are you going to your father's?'

'Mmm hmm.'

'With Josie?' Masha was sympathetic.

'Mmm hmm.'

'As a professional matchmaker, she is not the woman I would have wished on your father.' Masha shrugged. 'But the heart has its reasons of which reason knows nothing. Pascal,' she added after a moment's silence.

Gary squeezed Zu's arm sympathetically. 'At least you don't have Masha's mother arriving tomorrow night at Heathrow.'

'No, you don't. Truly, it could be much worse.' Masha raised her glass. 'Well, whatever Christmas holds, let's try to enjoy it. Here's to getting through it.'

'To getting through it.' Zu was heartfelt.

'To getting through it!' Gary echoed. 'Merry Christmas, gang.' Glasses clinked and they swallowed the fragrant, fizzy liquid in one.

Henchie had called her. They were going out that night, her turn to choose. 'So what are you going to treat me to?' he asked.

Zu had been thinking about this for a while. She took a deep breath.

'I want to go to a carol service at Southwark Cathedral.'

'All riiight.'

'It's not about God,' she explained hastily. 'It's about the music. There's just something about hearing carols at Christmas time. The past couple of years I've been away and I've missed it.'

'I'm up for that. What time?'

'Six.'

'I'll see you there.'

The cathedral was packed. Zu looked up at the soaring Gothic arches, the gaudy stained glass over the altar, the massed stone statues of saints below it. The air was thick with centuries of carols. She wasn't remotely religious but she always appreciated a good Christmas sing-song.

'Takes me back to school,' Jack said. 'Standing in chapel.'

'Your school had a *chapel*?'

He shrugged. 'Sure did. So why Southwark Cathedral? As opposed to St Paul's. Or Westminster Abbey.'

'We used to come here when I was a kid.'

'I see.' Jack nodded, inspected the order of service and then said, 'With your mum?'

'She was brought up a Hindu but she always liked to stick two fingers up at her upbringing.'

'I like the sound of your mum. She was clearly quite a character.'

'That's one way of putting it,' Zu said as the organist fell silent. The congregation's whispers died. A phone rang and was hastily silenced. People coughed. Then a high, clear voice sounded behind them.

> The holly and the ivy,
> When they are both full grown . . .

The notes soared, like swallows, up to the pillars and arches.

> Of all the trees that are in the wood
> The holly bears the crown.

The congregation joined in:

> O, the rising of the sun
> The running of the deer . . .

Hairs crisped on Zu's scalp and – oh no, oh fuck! – she felt the first tear plop on to her cheek. Carols always made her cry, but usually she was alone, a bit drunk in her room in a shared flat in Grozny, listening to a CD of King's College choir, and she'd tick herself off for being maudlin and homesick.

But now, back in the cathedral where Mum had taken them every year – until the time when she'd had a bottle of vodka in each coat pocket and swigged at one throughout the service and someone had tapped her furiously on the shoulder and ordered her to leave – Zu could suddenly no longer stand it.

Another tear slithered down her cheek. She rubbed it away furiously with her gloved hand. She didn't believe in a word of the mumbo jumbo, but it still conveyed so many memories of easier, safer times. Times when she'd tried to stay awake all night on Christmas Eve to catch a glimpse of Santa, almost sick with excitement at the prospect of the new toys in the morning. When Deepika had kissed Tony under the mistletoe and when they'd pulled crackers, rather than when they'd had to carry Mum, comatose, out of the room and lay her out on her bed.

'Are you OK?' Jack asked in her ear as a female cleric read a lesson.

'Fine,' she hissed. 'Something in my eye.'

There were prayers, a carol from the choir, another lesson, then the organ thundered into the introduction of 'O Little Town of Bethlehem'. The tears stung again. Zu stared fixedly at the stained glass and started to sing. There was something so comforting about the words: 'deep and dreamless sleep', 'everlasting light', 'the hopes and fears of all the years'.

She blinked and carried on singing as loudly as she could manage until the trembling in her voice ceased. Jack sang too. He had a fine, strong tenor voice, not bass – she remembered that now from karaoke night, she'd been surprised by it then. He wasn't embarrassed and that surprised her not at all.

At the end of the carol, they sat. A choir boy, probably about the age the boys were when Mum . . . *Stop, Zu!* . . . came up to the lectern and began to read the sixth lesson.

'The people that walked in darkness have seen a great light . . .'

She spent the rest of the service fighting the tears. It was a relief when finally the organ blasted out the first bars of 'Hark! The Herald Angels Sing'.

'Ready for the descant?' Jack whispered as they came to the last verse.

'Hail the heav'n born prince of peeeeeace. Hail the son of righteousness. Light and life to all he briiiings . . .' His voice teetered and cracked as he hit the top note and now they both started to giggle. Cross heads turned and a woman looked at them pointedly, but it just made the giggling worse. Zu had to stuff her hand in her mouth to stop noises coming out, but her body shook and a different kind of tears poured down her face.

'Shame on you,' she chided Jack as the congregation slowly shuffled out.

'Sorry! I wanted to cheer you up. I know you're not going to tell me what's wrong,' he continued, 'but it can't hurt to make you laugh a bit. So where are we eating tonight?'

'What are *you* doing for Christmas?' Zu asked as, an hour later, they sat in Nordic, a Scandinavian restaurant in Soho (it was the nearest they'd found to Finnish, having decided French was too boring and Fijian possibly not one of the world's greatest cuisines). They were eating reindeer with berry chutney – nicer than it sounded – and drinking vodka. All around them statuesque blondes in tasteful knitwear were toasting each other and laughing loudly.

'Going to my sister's in Sussex for Christmas lunch, then back to London to see Xander first thing on Boxing Day. I'll give him his present in the morning, then take him ice skating in the afternoon.' He sighed. 'It doesn't seem right not to be with your child when he's opening his stocking. My sister's fine but she's militantly child-free, as she calls it, and everything about her house is so grown up.'

'White sofas?'

'Yup, and cushions everywhere you daren't rearrange. There's this stainless-steel kitchen which is a complete misnomer as if you touch any surface it leaves a grimy mark. She's got this bossy sign on the kitchen wall that says EAT and there's another in the living room that says LOVE. I keep wanting to put one up in the loo that says DEFECATE.'

Zu rolled her eyes at the schoolboy humour. 'Were you with Xander last year?' It came out sounding more pointed than she had intended. Jack smiled wryly.

'*Touché*. I was in St Petersburg with a twenty-five-year-old Kazakhstani. But, you know, now Xander's mum has gone it's my responsibility to make the memories. At least, that's what I'm trying to do but Sara's parents won't let me.' He paused. 'Any more thoughts about spending a day with us some time soon?'

Zu thought of the dress Jack had bought in Liberty. Who was it meant for? 'I'm sure tons of candidates would be in the queue ahead of me for that.'

'Not interested?' Jack sounded teasing.

'Not interested' sounded so blunt. Not that Zu usually had a problem with bluntness, but it wasn't that she wasn't interested. She was scared, although of what she didn't quite know. 'Yeah, maybe some time. I'm just not sure . . .'

'In the New Year. After you get back from Odessa. I think he'd like you.'

She raised an eyebrow and popped a forkful of chutney in her mouth.

Jack sat back in his chair.

'So I know you won't talk about it but was the service bringing back old memories?'

'Henchie. Stop trying to be my shrink.' She sighed. 'Yes, it was. But guess what? You're right, I don't want to talk about it.' She looked into her glass and eventually said, 'In Russia there are so many people who are so much worse off than me. Five of them in a one-bedroom flat, electricity for a couple of hours a day; they have to walk miles every day to work in some shitty, backbreaking job for ten dollars a day, they eat meat twice a year, their sister has Aids. You know . . . What happened to my mum is peanuts in comparison. Shall we nip out for a cigarette?'

'It's not a competition,' Jack said gently. 'Just because other people are suffering, it doesn't make your feelings irrelevant. So many aid workers are like that. They've seen the "horrors of war" – ' he said this in a portentous Hollywood-trailer voice – 'so everything else is insignificant.'

'It's why I don't think I can last much longer at the bureau. All these clients with their daft worries. "Am I too fat? Am I going bald? Will I ever get married?" They need some perspective.'

Jack was silent for a moment, then said, 'It's not that daft. Everyone just wants to be loved. And to love in return.'

'I should be getting back,' she said.

'So early?' Jack looked disappointed.

'I said I'd be at Dad's early in the morning.' She hadn't, and she wouldn't be, but the sudden underlying crackle in the air had made her uneasy.

'All right then. Well.' He raised his glass. 'Merry Christmas.'

'Merry Christmas.' *Clink, clink.*

40

Zu stood on the doorstep at Farthingdale Road, surrounded by plastic bags of presents. She pulled off her
headphones as Josie answered the door. Her hair was in a
topknot, she had no make-up on and she was wearing a
pink vest and purple leggings. She looked less vibrant
than Zu remembered, as if she'd faded in the wash. Nonetheless, she flung her arms round Zu.

'Zu! Great to see you, baby. Merry Christmas.'

'Same to you.' Zu tried her best not to recoil.

'Shame Leela couldn't come. She's gone back to India.
She always goes at this time of year for a couple of
months.'

'I know that,' Zu said acidly, then tried to change her
expression to a sweet smile that probably made her look
constipated.

'Well, of course you do. God, what I would have done
for a granny like that. Mine hated me because I went on
anti-hunt marches. Leela's been saying that maybe I should
retrain as a beautician. She knows she could find me work.'

'Really?' *Been saying?* Were they talking regularly? Zu
tried to smile serenely.

'Don't stand out there in the cold! Come in, come in.'

'Thank you.' It was useless being sarcastic, Josie simply
didn't get it. She plonked her bags down in the hallway as
a voice behind her cried: 'Zuzu!'

'Ro!' She span round. There was her baby brother, looking skinnier than ever (though sadly no taller) in a black T-shirt, dirty jeans and khaki donkey jacket.

'Good to see you,' Zu said gruffly. Bloody tears were there again.

'And you.'

'You could have kept in touch more.'

'You're one to talk! All those months in places with no Internet connection.'

'You're never off your iPhone – would it really have been that tricky to send your sister the odd text?'

'I've been studying very hard,' he said piously and then they hugged.

Josie cleared her throat: 'Hi! I'm Josie, your dad's new girlfriend.'

Did she have no sense of what was appropriate? Rohan stepped back. Zu saw his knowing expression. So Dad had prepared him, warned him of their falling-out. She had said nothing to the boys, mainly because she found broaching the subject too painful.

Ro held out a hand. 'Good to meet you.'

Tony appeared at the door. 'Ro! Zu! My two favourite people in the world. Apart from Kieran obviously. Bugger that he's not coming, isn't it?'

'Dad!' Ro hugged his father. Tony's eyes swivelled to an enormous sack on the ground. 'What's that?'

'My washing. Good to be back.' He ruffled his dad's hair playfully. Zu felt one of those occasional stabs of envy brought on by watching her brothers with their father. Their relationship was so easy compared to hers. Maybe it was because they'd only known Tony in head-down, coping mode, while Zu remembered him differently as someone happy, carefree, confident: father-like.

'Well, I'm off to the shops,' Josie said loudly as the embrace resumed for what she clearly considered too long. 'I'll see you guys later.'

'See you,' they chorused and turned to go inside, a unit.

Having left their bags in their rooms, they convened in the kitchen for a cup of tea. The surfaces were sticky, the sink speckled with food particles and the floor clearly hadn't seen a mop in months. Zu was shocked. Her home would never feature in a Domestos advert but it had always been vaguely clean and tidy. She realized she'd drawn comfort from that because it indicated that Dad was fundamentally fine.

'So what shall we all do tonight?' she asked, certain of the answer.

'I thought a DVD,' said Tony.

'But what about Midnight Mass?' Ro looked pained, still the little boy, despite the long hair and earring, who hated any tradition to be out of place. 'We always go to Midnight Mass.'

'I thought we'd moved on from there,' Tony said gently.

'You mean *you've* moved on,' Zu heard herself snap. 'Now Josie's in your life.'

She shouldn't have, but it was too late. Tony rolled up the sleeves of his jumper as if he were preparing for a fight.

'We never took Midnight Mass seriously, did we? It was always a bit of a joke.'

'It's one of the things we *do*,' Rohan protested. He looked around the room. 'Everything's different this year! Look, the tree's tiny.'

294

It was indeed, a dwarf compared to their usual tower-ing giant. Rohan continued: 'You haven't put up the lights and what's that angel doing on the top? We always have a star.'

'Come on, Ro,' Tony tried.

'There should be tinsel on the pictures. And why are the cards on the fridge? They should be in the living room.'

'We can fix all that,' Zu said hastily. 'We'll do it this afternoon. Drink some mulled wine, listen to Slade on the radio. It'll be fun.'

Tony looked at her gratefully. 'Sure we can.'

'Or maybe we should do what you say,' Rohan said dubiously. 'I mean, life moves on.'

'No, no,' Tony said, searching in the cupboard for three clean mugs. 'We'll go to Midnight Mass.'

'No,' Zu said firmly. 'We'll watch a DVD. Life has to move on.' Bending forward, so he couldn't see her expres-sion, she started fumbling around in the cupboard under the sink for the Cif.

On Christmas morning, Zu woke about seven. It was still dark outside, but as she squinted in the darkness there was a stocking at the end of her bed. Yes! she thought, child-ishly delighted for a second. Dad hadn't forgotten after all. The thought of him creeping in after she was asleep made her throat tingle. She was going to make a huge effort to forget the dominatrix stuff, she resolved, just as someone knocked on the door.

'Yes?' Zu had a fearful vision of Josie in a cute Santa outfit come to serenade her with 'Rockin' Around the Christmas Tree'.

"S' me.'

Rohan shuffled in clutching his stocking, hair askew, wearing a long baggy T-shirt and boxers.

'Santa visited you too?'

He smiled. 'Look, I don't want to sound like a perv, but can I get in with you? It's freezing. The temperature's dropped overnight.'

'Of course.' Zu pulled back the duvet and he climbed in beside her. Just like when they were children, they took it in turns to empty their stockings. A paperback for Ro, some bubble bath for Zu. A set of biros for Ro, a hairband for Zu. Underpants for Ro, some tights in extra large, which would need to be exchanged, for Zu. Lots of chocolate for both and half bottles of champagne.

'There's even a satsuma at the bottom,' said Ro, grinning, as he neatly assembled all his booty at the end of the bed.

'When Dad was growing up, satsumas were a wild luxury. I mean, those were the days when you used to get orange juice as a starter in posh restaurants.'

'I wonder what Josie's got in her Christmas stocking.'

'Ro!'

'Well, you've got to agree, she's well fit.'

'You *are* a pervert. Get out of my bed.'

'Do you think Dad's happy with her?' Ro's tone was more serious now. 'He told me you weren't getting on.'

Zu's soul zipped up like a purse. 'It's been a while and she's living here, so I guess so. And what I think is irrelevant.'

'He doesn't seem happy,' Ro continued. 'I thought he would be, but last night I was watching him and he looked so tired.'

'He's just getting old.' Zu couldn't bear to discuss it.

'I guess.'

'I need to get up,' said Zu. 'It's time to put on the goose.'

When Josie eventually descended around eleven, Zu was bright pink in the face. She had a bandage on her thumb where she'd gouged out a section putting hatches in the sprouts and a burn on her wrist from the oven. Tony had tried to help, but she'd insisted she'd do Christmas dinner. A mistake, obviously, but she had a stupid urge to prove this was her territory. The windows had steamed up from the heat and a weird, horribly acrid, sweet smell was coming from somewhere Zu couldn't identify. It took her back to the time when she'd had to do an awful lot of this sort of stuff. She wasn't enjoying doing it again.

She had to look for the crackers. She went into the so-called dining room aka the repository for the boys' punchbags, Space Hoppers, old scooters and all the other junk they couldn't bear to throw away. She knelt down and opened the ugly rosewood trunk in the corner inherited from Great Uncle Phil. Inside was a pile of bank statements. She didn't think about the morality, she just pulled them out and looked at them.

They were recent and they were all printed in red.

She pushed her hair back from her face. She took out the cracker boxes and dumped them on the table. She returned to the kitchen. Just behind her came Josie in a tiny pink camisole that just covered her bottom.

'Oh, yuck,' she said, spying the sprouts now neatly piled in a pan. 'I hate Brussels.'

'And a Merry Christmas to you too,' snapped Zu.

'Sorry. Merry Christmas.' She kissed Zu on both cheeks. 'Everything else looks delicious. So what's for breakfast?'

'Look in the bread bin,' Zu said shortly.

'OK,' Josie retorted equally curtly. She took out two slices of Hovis and put them in the toaster. 'God, Christmas is boring,' she said with a little yawn. 'What do you do on a day when the shops are shut and you're forced to stay indoors?'

'We actually usually go for a walk once the meal's on,' Zu said. She rubbed the windowpane with her sleeve. It was sleeting briskly. 'Maybe not today, though.'

'Let's see what's on telly,' said Josie, opening the fridge and taking a slurp directly from the orange-juice carton. 'There's bound to be a lovely old musical to cheer us up.'

'I'm quite happy already,' Zu said. She didn't know what had got into her, she felt like a wind-up toy whose setting had been switched to 'tetchy'.

'Oh, will you just loosen up?' Josie suddenly exploded. 'I'm trying to be nice but you just keep on treating me like dirt.'

'Hardly! I let you into our house for Christmas Day. I get up at dawn and slave my arse off cooking lunch for you. You roll down at noon and complain about being bored.' Zu knew she was exaggerating but the chance for a fight was just too tempting.

Josie's face fell. 'Don't be so nasty to me. All I've done is make your dad happy. It's not like I have anywhere else to go. My mum —'

'At least you still have a mum!' Zu roared and Josie dashed, crying, from the room.

*

'Zu, please. Josie is trying, really she is. I don't know why you can't make a little bit of an effort too.'

Zu reached in her pocket and pulled out a bank statement.

'What's that?' Tony asked disingenuously.

'Dad, you're nearly two thousand pounds overdrawn. How did it happen?'

He shook his head, unable to meet her eye.

'Just . . . stuff.'

'You were so careful. Never going on holidays abroad, not painting the outside of the house. Scrimping so we could all go to uni. And now all the money's gone.'

'Zu, I know it looks stupid. Sometimes I have been a bit stupid. But I've been lonely. It's been so nice having someone to treat.'

Zu crossed her arms over her chest. She remembered what Leela had said about loneliness. Tony was right, it was his money, but still . . .

'Look, I've made mistakes,' Tony said. 'I have spent too much and I've told Josie that has to stop. I haven't been as sensitive to you as I should have been. But, please, for everyone's sake, can we all just be friends for one day?'

Zu tried to laugh. 'We're not in a Michael Jackson video, Dad.'

Relieved, Tony laughed too, then he tried: 'Now, listen. Josie's been crying.'

Somehow that was the spark that made it all explode. 'Josie's been crying? Why is it all about Josie now? Have you forgotten who was here first?'

Tony's face turned very white. 'Have you forgotten,' he

retorted quietly, 'that you've hardly been here for years? So coming back and suddenly acting like you're Lady of the Manor is not fooling anyone.'

'Have you forgotten that for years I was here but nobody paid a blind bit of notice?' Zu replied icily. 'That it was all about Mum and then about the boys?'

'I noticed, of course I did!' Tony reached out for her, his face appalled, but Zu stepped back. She'd never ever voiced this feeling before, even to herself, and already she was furious with herself for having let it slip out. It was self-indulgent, it would help no one, but all the same . . . All those years of just keeping her head down and at the end of it all to find herself obliged to spend every Christmas for the rest of time with Josie . . .

'Do you blame me for running off? Can't you see that in these other places people need me? I can help them. I can't help you. I've tried and it's never worked.'

'Zu.' Tony was crying now. She hated herself. Who made their own father cry? She pushed past him to the door. 'I'm going back to the kitchen,' she mumbled. 'I need to baste the goose. Can you just give me some time in there alone, please?'

Tony knocked on the door about half an hour later. Mariah Carey was bellowing out of the radio. Slowly Zu had pulled herself together. She was mortified by her outburst and she just wanted to be alone, to lick her wounds. But first she had to get through Christmas dinner.

'Josie wants to say sorry,' Tony said. 'Will you accept her apology?'

'Of course I will.' Zu smiled weakly, then squared herself. Josie stood behind him, grimacing in what she supposed was an apologetic smile.

'Sorry, Zu, you'd been working really hard. You must have thought I had a nerve, moaning.'

'Not to worry. I was just stressed putting the meal on.' Josie patted Zu on the back.

Zu nodded, then cleared her throat. 'Lunch is almost ready.'

They could have been in the Reading Room at the British Library. The only sounds, save the odd bland comment from Ro, were forks scraping and glasses being emptied. The food wasn't great: the goose was too dry, the potatoes soggy, the veg *al dente* to put it politely, but everyone knew better than to comment. They'd be eating leftovers for months, Zu thought, as she cleared away the half-touched plates.

They pulled crackers and laughed listlessly at the jokes. They opened their presents and exchanged polite 'Oohs' and 'Aahs' and 'Thank yous'. Zu studied her pile: a fancy corkscrew from Rohan which he'd obviously snatched off a garage shelf at the last minute and from Tony a bottle of Clarins bubble bath and hand cream. A flowery skirt she'd never wear from Naani, a couple of books she'd already read from Anj. Josie had actually done best of all with a nifty Swiss army knife. Zu had one already, of course, but at least it showed some understanding of what Zu was about.

'Thank you, that's great,' Zu said as politely as she could.

'Shall we Skype Kieran?' Tony asked.

So they did and saw their brother moving awkwardly and jerkily five thousand miles away in a place where the sky was a fierce blue and the orange earth parched. Zu ached to join him there.

In silence, they watched the Queen followed by *Back to the Future*. They had goose sandwiches. They watched *The Great Escape*. They went to bed, but Zu didn't sleep: she'd left her pills at Anjali's and tonight, without them, there was no chance of oblivion. Instead she lay rigid, listening to squeaks and snuffles from her father's room beneath her, and counted off the minutes until morning.

41

Gillian was determined to make Christmas perfect so she had bought a tree so tall that its top bent sideways, squashed by the ceiling. She'd asked Holly to help her decorate it but she'd refused, so, alone, she'd buried it in fairy lights and weighed it down with decorations.

'Happy Christmas,' she'd whispered in Waffle's ear.

She prepared Holly a small stocking packed with sweets, magazines, tights, knickers, make-up. Nothing she could sell or barter for drugs. She'd bought her a new coat – again – hoping she wouldn't flog this one. She bought a duck, perfect Christmas dinner for two people.

Usually they went to Alicia's for Christmas but this year she was having her in-laws over, and the sisters agreed that Holly's presence was too risky. Gillian rang her parents in Bodrum and exchanged pleasantries, lying about Holly, saying she was doing brilliantly, all was good, she was looking forward to visiting them – maybe at Easter. Then she hung up and cried and cried and cried, but silently so Holly wouldn't hear her, the sides of her mouth sagging like a tragedy mask.

She spent Christmas Eve watching *A Night at the Opera* with Waffle snoring on her lap. Holly was in her room, headphones clamped on, glued to Facebook, but better she was there than out God knows where scoring skunk. Perhaps the next day would pass, if not happily, then at least peacefully. Perhaps it would signal some kind of fresh start.

'Don't hope for anything,' Gillian told herself as she drifted off to sleep.

On Christmas morning, Gillian took Waffle for a long walk and when she returned she prepared lunch. Holly still hadn't emerged from her room. Gillian decorated the table carefully with china Santas that had belonged to her grandmother. She put on a CD of the King's College choir singing carols.

She had a feeling that it was the calm before the storm. Sure enough, one o'clock came and the duck was ready. Normally she was happy to let Holly sleep all day if it kept the peace, but she wasn't going to eat Christmas lunch alone.

The doorbell rang. Gillian jumped. Waffle started barking. Who on earth could it be? Surely not Jehovah's Witnesses? She ran to the door. On the porch stood Holly with Jarmon beside her. Both were dressed in stained sweatshirts and baggy jeans. There were dark circles under Holly's eyes and her hair was greasy, even if she was smiling radiantly.

'Hiya, Mum.'

'I thought you were in bed.'

Holly smiled lazily and pushed her hair out of her eyes. 'I went out last night. Sorry, I should have left a note. I forgot.'

'But you're grounded,' Gillian said automatically.

'Oh, and a Merry Christmas to you too! Look, I'm back now, aren't I?'

'Hiya,' Jarmon mumbled, holding up a hairy and dirty hand.

'Merry Christmas, Jarmon.' Gillian was too flabbergasted to respond more rationally. She tried desperately to keep her temper. Holly was here. She'd sneaked out. She'd returned. When Jarmon had gone there'd have to be another horrible row. The thought made her want to climb into bed and never emerge again.

'Sorry I don't have any presents,' Holly said and then giggled. 'I did get you something but I left it somewhere.'

'Never mind, darling, it's just lovely to see you. Lunch is ready.'

'Great, I'm starving,' Holly said, following her into the kitchen with Jarmon hot on her heels. 'Hey, look, Jarms, crackers!'

'Let's pull one.'

'Shall we eat?' Gillian asked.

'What? Maybe later.' Jarmon yawned.

'Well, I'm hungry, so do you mind if I start?'

Jarmon surveyed the beautifully laid table and shrugged. 'Feel free,' he said graciously, picking up a plastic whistle that had dropped from the cracker and blowing it so hard that Waffle ram, hawling, from the room.

The lunch – so carefully prepared – now tasted like soggy bath mat to Gillian. Having said she was starving, Holly barely touched it, while Jarmon ate heartily. Afterwards, they disappeared up to Holly's room. Gillian was sure they were smoking in there but she didn't have the energy to investigate. She'd leave it till the morning, she decided, and for now she'd try to relax in front of a Hitchcock film. She sat on the sofa, tears streaming down her face.

Around seven, she decided it was time for a cup of tea. She turned on the kettle, she went to the fridge. The milk carton sat in there, empty.

'Fuck, shit, bollocks.' They'd somehow managed to sneak in there and use it all up. Thank God for the corner shop that never closed. A pint of milk on Christmas Day would probably cost a tenner but it would be worth it. Her heart sank as she remembered her wallet locked in the safe in her bedroom. What a hassle. But then she remembered she'd left a twenty-pound note in her pocket when she'd returned from a last-minute trip to the deli on Christmas Eve.

She pulled on her coat, hat, gloves and scarf, and called for Waffle, who bounded over eagerly. 'We're just going to the shops, darling.'

They returned five minutes later. Gillian was white-faced and furious. Without removing her coat, she stormed up the stairs to Holly's room. Holly and Jarmon both lay flat on their backs, side by side on the bed, staring at the ceiling.

'Money is missing from my coat.'

'What?'

'There was twenty pounds in my coat pocket yesterday. You sneak out and it's all gone.'

'It wasn't me.'

'Who was it then?'

'It wasn't me, Mum! Now will you just put a lid on it.'

'If it wasn't you, it was Jarmon.'

Holly sat up. 'How dare you accuse my friend!'

'Well, if it wasn't you and it wasn't Jarmon then the

fairies must have hidden it. I'm going to have to search the house, including your room.'

'Mum! What about my human rights?'

Something behind Gillian's eyes turned white, then red, then black, then spots danced. She felt her body tilting as if she were an old sea dog just returned to dry land. She couldn't take it any more. She had tried so hard to suck it up, to be understanding, to be patient, to turn the other cheek. Why? What for? Holly was vile. She didn't care what happened to her any more.

'What about my human rights? It's like living with an abuser. If you were my husband everyone would be telling me to kick you out. Everyone tells me to kick you out anyway. Try surviving by yourself, then you might stop being so nasty.'

'All right,' Holly said laconically, standing up. 'I'll go.'

She was dressed within five minutes and five minutes after that the door slammed.

42

Zu and Tony sat at the breakfast table eating toast and peanut butter (her), and Bran Flakes (him). Outside, frost covered the lawn and the sky was a brittle blue.

'Did you sleep well?' Tony asked. It was the first thing either of them had said to each other that morning.

'Yes, thanks. You?'

'Very well. Thanks.' His spoon tinged against the bowl.

'So. I'll be off this morning,' she said as calmly as she could manage.

Tony slammed down his mug. 'Already? Zu!'

'It's time for me to go,' she said firmly. She'd practised this line until dawn broke and she'd finally fallen into disjointed sleep.

Upstairs, Rohan and Josie dreamed on. Tony sat back in his chair, his arms raised above his head. 'Why are you being like this?'

'Like what?' she asked disingenuously.

'So *angry*. I thought you wanted me to be happy.'

'I did. I do. But Josie's not making you.'

'Yes, she is.' Tony wasn't making eye contact. She was sure he was lying but what was the point of arguing when he was determined not to listen?

'That's great. But I'm not going to be able to stay here any longer. It's just all too . . .' She forgot her lines. 'I can't cope with it,' she finished.

'But where will you go?'

'Back to Anjali's.'

Tony looked at his hands, then up at her. 'Zu. You're my daughter. I love you and the boys more than anything. But I need –'

She held up a hand to silence him. 'I know, Dad. I know what you need. But *I* need to go. Let's just leave it at that.'

The Tube platform at Edgware was deserted. Zu shivered and stamped her feet as she sat in the empty train carriage waiting for the engines to crank up and start it moving. Even the Monteverdi Choir thundering out Mozart's *Dies Irae* failed to calm her.

Her father was in love, she told herself for the thousandth time as the train finally lurched off. She was just going to leave him to get on with it. But she was in almost physical pain. Her face felt bruised, her body taut as if she were sunburnt, her stomach tilted and tipped.

He couldn't spend the rest of his life with Josie. All right, so Zu had been unable to cope with life at home any more and had run away, but she loved her father. He couldn't waste the rest of his life with this . . . slag.

She'd just have to get through the next couple of days and then she'd be off to Odessa – escaping again. She'd have to use the time productively, she decided, as the train started moving south. She could re-read *Anna Karenina*; she could watch some film classics like *Battleship Potemkin* – that had a famous section set in Odessa; do more job applications so they were sitting in aid agency inboxes when they returned after the New Year. As she got off the

Tube and walked briskly across the park, she added more and more virtuous goals to her list.

There was no point trying to have a social life. Everyone else she knew would be with their families, squabbling over the remote and trying to think of another thing to do with leftover turkey. Really, she was better off out of it.

By the time she reached the mews house, she was more positive. She'd survived far worse and so had millions of other people. She'd get through this. She reached into her satchel for the keys.

They weren't there.

But of course they were. Zu frisked through her possessions. Not much: fags, lighter, sunglasses, Oyster card, keys! Yes! Her heart lifted hydraulically but then she realized they were the Temperley set that she kept on the metal keyring she'd bought at Moscow airport. She carried on searching: phone, book, iPod, fags, lighter, sunglasses, Oyster card . . . She moved on to her pockets. A memory tugged at her sleeve. Christmas Eve in Farthingdale Road, removing them from her jeans, depositing them on the bedside table.

Damn.

What could she do? The thought of returning to the Tube, of making that journey back to Edgware, of having to encounter Josie and/or Dad again, was unbearable. She'd have to call Ro and beg him to bring them to her. Zu shivered. Behind the triple-locked purple door her warm coat was hanging on Anjali's Ikea coat rack. When she'd set off for Tony's two days ago, the weather had turned freakishly warm and she'd thought she'd only need her long, woolly cardigan. But now the wind was gnawing at her. It was hat, gloves, scarf and padded jacket time.

She called Anjali. Voicemail. Zu left a message asking her if there were spare keys anywhere and then she phoned Ro. Voicemail too. Zu asked him to call her as soon as possible and then wondered how to keep warm. She could go sales shopping, she supposed; people spent their Christmas night in sleeping bags outside Next, of all places, to bag a cheap fake-fur gilet, but that was about as appealing as a Hollywood wax. She could sit in a pub or café with a newspaper but she knew she'd take nothing in, just brood about Dad and Josie.

She decided to walk briskly to the office. It would be warm there and possibly Masha and Gary had left a selection of coats that she could borrow in the cupboard. She could use the computers to do that CV-ing, she could even have a kip on the sofas – Zu was an expert at grabbing sleep whenever she had the chance. Ro could come and meet her there and, assuming it was open, she could treat him to lunch at the steakhouse on Marylebone Lane where she'd once gone with Masha. They'd drink a couple of carafes of red wine and plot how to overthrow Josie.

Cheered again, Zu began walking back through the park.

Her phone rang as she turned into Luke Street.

'Ro, hi! What took you so long?'

'Hi, Zu, I got your message.' Ro didn't sound like himself, but official, distant. 'Listen, I can't see those keys. But –' he took a deep breath – 'to be honest, even if I could I wouldn't bring them to you. You're behaving like an arsehole. Why can't you be nice to Dad? I know Josie isn't perfect, but nor was Mum.'

It was like being punched in the face. Zu stood very still. Her little brother was speaking to her with something in his voice that sounded like hatred.

'But, Ro, I –'

'He just wants to be happy and you're making it so difficult for him. Why don't you just come home and say you're sorry and stop being so fucking selfish?'

'There are things about Josie you don't know,' Zu tried, but he'd already hung up.

She clutched the railings with one hand and with the other rubbed her eyes in disbelief. This couldn't be happening. All she'd wanted was the best for Dad but now he hated her. A fat salty tear trickled down her face, then another. Zu stuffed her hand into her mouth to contain a sob.

What was wrong with her? She'd cried more in the past week than she had in years. But blubbing in the street would be the limit. Thank God no one was around. She wiped away some snot with her sleeve but the tears continued to fall down her stiff, locked face. First Dad had been conned by Josie, now her brother. At least she still had Anj, though she hadn't called back either. Probably she and Josie were on the phone to each other right now, swapping beauty tips.

'Forbes!'

She swung round. There, peering through the wound-down window of a BMW, was Jack.

Zu swallowed. 'Henchie, you're stalking me, you freak.'

'Excuse me but you're obviously stalking me. Are you OK?'

'Fine,' Zu growled. 'Something in my eye.'

'Very keen of you to be going to work on Boxing Day.'

'Same to you.'

'I'm not working.' He nodded over his shoulder and Zu noticed a small dark child in the back seat. 'I was just showing Xander where my office is.' He pulled a pious face. 'For I believeth in a work–life balance. Unlike you, you daft muppet.' He leant over and opened his passenger door. 'You look freezing. Climb in.'

'I was going into the office.'

'Climb in and don't argue.'

Zu climbed in. It was blissfully, fuggily warm in the car. She reached her hands towards the hot-air vents.

'So, Zu,' Jack said mischievously, 'this is Xander. Xander, this is Daddy's friend Zu. She's been dying to meet you.'

'Zoo?' said Xander. 'With tigers?'

He had a ringleted face and molten brown eyes, just like his father. In ten years' time he'd be another no-good heartbreaker but once again Zu remembered her brothers when they were tiny. She smiled at him.

'No tigers. Sorry. I'm not nearly as exciting as London zoo.'

'We went to the zoo,' Xander told her cheerily. 'Lots of times. I like the meerkats best. They like small snakes to eat. Some work as lookouts and tell the others when eagles are coming to eat them and then they shout out when they all have to take cover.'

'Really? I never knew that.'

'And owls can't move their eyeballs. But they can turn their heads almost all the way round so they can still see everything.'

'I didn't know that either.'

'Nor did I,' Jack said. 'He's much cleverer than me.'

'Not hard.'

'Ha ha.' Jack looked at Zu. 'Where's your coat?'

She sighed. 'I had a row with my dad about his new girl-friend. I walked out. And now I can't get into Anjali's house because I left my keys behind and I can't face going back to fetch them.' She decided to leave out the conver-sation with Rohan because that might set off the waterworks again. Instead she said, 'I was thinking about staying the night on the Temperley sofa. But maybe a hotel would be a better idea.'

'Don't be ridiculous, Forbes. You'll stay at mine.'

She'd sort of hoped he'd offer, but she still gave him her best Lady Bracknell look. *No sex*, it implied. He smiled at her with mock innocence.

'But there's one condition.'

She raised an eyebrow.

'First you have to come on an outing with us.'

'I haven't got a coat,' she squawked.

'I've got a spare one in the boot. You'll be just fine.'

They were going to the Winter Wonderland in Hyde Park. The place was heaving with excited day-trippers, families and couples. Lights sparkled against the darkening sky, music boomed, the giant observation wheel turned over-head and the air smelt of hot oil, frying sausages and mulled wine. Zu found herself smiling at the festive atmosphere.

'Do you like it?' she said, bending down awkwardly to Xander's ear level. She had no idea really what you were supposed to say to five-year-olds. With her brothers it had been different – she'd been too busy getting them in and out of the bath, feeding them, reading them stories and all the things their mother neglected to do to think about conversation. But Xander just grinned at her and then slipped his gloved hand into her bare one. She stood stiffly for a moment, then he squeezed it. Tentatively, Zu squeezed back.

'What an adorable sight,' Jack teased.

'Henchie!' she said warningly.

'Just sayin'.'

Xander said something to her she couldn't hear over the screaming from the rides. 'Sorry?' she said, bending down so her mouth was at his ear again.

'I said, where's Sasha?'

'Who's Sasha?' said Zu, though she had a pretty good idea. OK, that was fine. Henchie was never going to change, was he? It was funny that another woman was on the scene. She was amused, yes, definitely amused, even if she did suddenly shiver and wrap her arms tightly round herself.

'Sasha's Daddy's friend,' Xander told her. 'But I like you.'

Henchie smiled, obviously oblivious to what they'd been discussing.

'So! Who's for the big wheel?'

They all squeezed in a capsule and were whisked up in

the air. The sun was falling in a palette of pollution-enhanced orange, pink and blue. London was like a jewellery box: the London Eye was a fragile diamond bracelet, the BT Tower a ring-laden finger with a ruby flashing at the top. And above it all there was a sliver of brand-new moon rising.

When they came down, they went skating on the crowded ice-rink. Zu was hopeless and wobbled along clinging to the barrier as if she were throwing up over the side of a cross-Channel ferry. She slipped. She slid. Meanwhile, Jack and Xander cut straight across the middle, hand in hand, skates scattering powder behind them like glitter.

'Show off,' Zu teased, as Jack grabbed her hand.

'All those years skiing in Klosters, darling. You should try it some time. Funny, I always had you down as co-ordinated.'

Zu pushed him and he wobbled dramatically.

'Waagh, aagh, aagh. Save me!'

'Dad.' Xander pulled at his hand, already embarrassed. 'Let's go round again.'

Afterwards, they had mulled wine while Xander drank a carton of orange juice and munched on some candy-floss which he'd claimed he wanted, but which he quickly declared he'd 'had enough of', and they watched a puppet show in a little tent theatre.

'He's a nice kid,' Zu said, nodding at the child, his face upturned and alight with wonder at Punch and Judy's antics.

'Well, of course. How couldn't he be with these genes?'

'Oh, silly me!' Zu slapped her head.

'I wish I could see more of him. Philippa and Rodrigo have said not a chance of increasing my access for another year. I've been speaking to my lawyer about it but she says we shouldn't push things. I don't know, I couldn't do more. I'm not travelling, I'm living like a monk . . .'

'You!'

'Yes, me,' Jack said with fake injured innocence. 'I've been a model citizen. But still no dice.' He looked at his child and Xander, sensing eyes upon him, looked over his shoulder and grinned and waved jauntily. Jack waved back and, after a second's hesitation, so did Zu. She was about to say, 'What about Sasha?', but then she thought – why? Just leave it.

'He's the love of my life,' Jack said. 'If I'd known how crazy I'd be about him, I –'

'Cue hankies,' Zu said, hoping to stem the soppy smile that was threatening to spread across her face.

'I despair of you, Forbes.' He looked her straight in the eye. 'I'm sorry about you and your dad.'

The tears stung again. 'It's fine. Crap happens.'

'You should call him.'

She shook her head.

'Have it your way.' Jack glanced at his watch. 'Anyway, our time's running out. We need to get Xander home before curfew or my chances of custody will be eternally fucked.'

They dropped Xander off at his grandparents' house near the Angel and then drove the short distance along Upper Street to Jack's place. It was a first-floor flat in a Victorian terrace and it wasn't what you'd call a cosy place: all beige carpeting and matching Ikea furniture. Still, Zu had a new and disconcerting sense of Jack as a domestic being. Two T-shirts hung over a radiator and there were a couple of pans in the sink. She'd never imagined him in such a context. The living room was dominated by an enormous telly, there were three bedrooms – at least she thought there were, she didn't investigate – a bathroom and a small kitchen with a table in the corner.

'Where were you?' she asked, indicating a photo, stuck to the fridge in the all-white kitchen, of Jack and Xander on a pebbly beach.

'He looks just like me, doesn't he?'

'Much more handsome. Luckily for him he must take after his mother. I asked where you were.'

'Day trip to Brighton. It was fun. Next time you should come with us.'

'Maybe.' She grinned. 'I enjoyed today.'

'Good. I'm sorry it took a bust-up with your family to get you to join forces with mine, but it was worth it.' Jack took a bottle of whisky from a crowded drinks tray.

'Can I have some ice in that?' she asked.

'You used to take it neat.'

'People change.'

'Some do. You haven't. You're still as prickly as ever. A regular hedgehog.'

'And you're as shy and retiring as I recall you.'

He handed Zu a tumbler and then, putting his hand on the small of her back, steered her into his living room. 'Sit down,' he said, nodding at the leather sofa. 'Have a drink and then have a bath to warm yourself up. Then we can watch a DVD if you like and order in. Do you fancy Chinese?'

'I prefer Indian.' Zu sat down. Normally she'd have suspected a seduction was being planned, but now she knew about Sasha she felt safe. All right, Henchie might still try it on but she'd have the ammunition to resist him – ammunition which, she admitted to herself, had been dwindling rapidly until Xander's remark.

'Indian it is.'

'How cosy,' Zu said, intending sarcasm, but it came out sounding like golly-gosh enthusiasm. 'Can I smoke in here?' she asked.

'The question is not *can* you, but *may* you. No, you may not. Look. You're still cold. Instead of nicotine, why don't you have a bath and I'll pop down the road and pick up an Indian.'

'All right,' Zu agreed.

After a quick bath (she was never one for wallowing in tubs), Zu was even more desperate for a cigarette. Wrapped in a towel, she went into the spare room, which was a bland box containing an Ikea bed, an anthracite duvet, an Ikea table and an Ikea chest of drawers. She opened the window and leant out. Jack would never know. The street far below was deserted with only the occasional car passing by, the first trickles of people returning from family Christmases. She hoped they'd had a better time than her. Suddenly she was exhausted. She stubbed out the cigarette on the window sill, lay down on the bed and shut her eyes.

When she opened them, Jack was standing at the door. He was holding a purple carrier bag in one hand, two flutes in the other and a bottle of Dom Perignon tucked under his arm.

'What's going on?' Zu asked groggily.

'You fell asleep.'

'And?'

'I've brought you a Christmas present.'

She peered at the bag. 'Isn't that the Indian?' But it was tied up with a black ribbon and – the biggest clue of all – had a white Liberty logo. 'Does Liberty's have a food department?' she asked, confused.

'Nope, the Indian's from Emni round the corner. I ate mine hours ago. It's nearly midnight.'

'What?' She sat up, pulling the towel round her.

'You've been asleep for ages. Don't worry, your curry's in the fridge, I can microwave it.' He sat down beside her. 'But first, open the bag. Go on.'

Zu couldn't help being infected by his excitement. 'You sound like Xander,' she said as, gingerly, she took the bag from him. She pulled the ribbon and was confronted by a frothy layer of tissue paper.

'Is this some kind of a joke?' She was sure she'd find a stink bomb or a whoopee cushion.

'No.' He leant over, delved in and pulled out the red dress they'd bought on their shopping trip, the colour of the dusk sky in Siberia.

'Try it on.' He smiled. There was no sound from the street outside.

'This isn't for me. It's for . . . whoever.'

'You said I needed to buy something for my lady.' Jack looked at her, then glanced away. Zu's stomach backflipped.

'Dresses don't suit me.' She tried.

'Come on, Forbes. Humour me. Put on the dress,

320

we'll toast Christmas and then you can go back to sleep.' Through the ceiling came a burst of wild laughter. For a second she wondered if it was mocking her before she realized it was the neighbours' television.

'Please?'

'Out of the room,' she said.

Jack went into the hall. Heart thudding, though she wasn't quite sure why, Zu dropped the towel and pulled the dress over her head. It fell to her knees, had no sleeves, and was glaxy cold against her goose-pimpled skin.

'Can I come back?' Jack was peeking round the edge of the door.

'All right,' Zu said gruffly.

'Stand up.' Jack shut the door behind him as if hordes of onlookers were fighting to be granted entry. He gave Zu a long, appraising look.

'Fits you. Glad I asked your size.'

'Fuck off, Henchie.' Zu sat down again. She felt vulnerable. 'Why don't other women feel the cold?' she asked.

'Have a cigarette,' Jack said. 'I know you want one.'

Gratefully, she crawled across the bed and pulled her Marlboros out of her bag. 'Want one?' she grinned over her shoulder.

'Oh, what the fuck. The in-laws'll never know.'

He took two from the packet and put them in his mouth, took her chunky silver lighter from her hand and lit them both. He handed one to her, not taking his eyes from her face, then, cigarette hanging out of the corner of his lips, he popped the champagne cork and filled the flutes. They clinked glasses.

'Merry Christmas, Forbes. Again.'

'Same to you, Henchie.' Zu felt a new sensation, low in her stomach, as if something was pulling her. Her senses were on alert like a hunted animal, her mouth was dry, she was aware of her nipples rubbing against the dress and of her ancient black knickers with the elastic half gone. This was what being sixteen was supposed to have felt like. She had to keep her head. She put down her flute on the bedside table and cleared her throat, just as he took her hand in his.

'No!' she yelled, standing up and snatching it away. 'What's going on?'

He laughed. 'You're sweet, you know that?'

'No.'

'Forbes. Zulekha. Zulekha Forbes. Zu. I love you.'

'Henchie, you've lost it. Anyway, you have a girlfriend.'

He looked shocked. 'No, I don't.'

'You do! Xander told me.'

'We finished months ago . . . like, back in the autumn.' He reached out and grabbed her hands. 'Mainly because I was falling for you.'

'Oh.' Zu's mouth was dry.

'You know why you're responding like this?' Henchie said. 'You've never been loved.'

'That's crap. My naani loves me. My cousin loves me. My mum . . .' Zu faltered. 'She loved me too, she just got sick. And my dad and my brothers . . . they . . .'

Thank God he kissed her because she would have cried. And because Zu had absolutely no intention of crying again she kissed him back. He tasted of honey.

He swept her hair back from one shoulder and dipped his head to kiss her neck, then he picked her up and carried her across the room, like a bride being carried across the threshold. He laid her down on the bed and carefully removed the dress, as if from a doll, bending his head to kiss every centimetre of her. He laughed at her tattoo, which was a bad rendering of the Chechen flag, on her pubic bone, then licked it. By the time he kissed her mouth again, she was completely naked, finally oblivious to the cold rushing in through the still-open window. He tasted salty. He pushed back her hair from her face and looked into her eyes and In felt liquefied.

Afterwards, Zu was curled in a ball, her head on his chest.

'You have no idea how long I've wanted this,' he whispered.

'Fool,' she laughed.

'Maybe.' He placed his hand on her bottom. Zu slapped it away and fell asleep. She dreamt that she and Mum and Dad were at the zoo and Kieran and Rohan were in their double buggy. Everyone was laughing.

Her phone woke her. It was just after eight and there was a text from Anjali apologizing for having had her phone switched off all Boxing Day and saying the spare keys were in the drainpipe at the back of the house.

Zu looked at the phone and looked at Jack fast asleep. Then she caught herself. She was behaving like a teenager: entertaining thoughts about how cute and vulnerable he looked.

All the same. He'd said he loved her. He'd said he loved her! Her nerve endings were wired up to the national grid. She was a dark, cold house whose lights had suddenly been turned on and fires lit.

'I love you too,' she whispered.

She jumped up and pulled her clothes from their crumpled pile on the floor. She went into the hall where Jack's keys were lying on a small table. She grabbed his coat from the rack and opened the door. She was going to go down the road, find a deli, buy croissants and fresh coffee and orange juice, and she was going to surprise Jack when he woke up. She was going to be one of those women you saw in adverts, reading the papers in bed, laughing with her lover. The kind of woman she'd always despised. Until now.

She opened the door and went down to the communal hallway. An old lady was coming through the front door – not a hairy-chinned old lady but an elegant, coiffed one in shiny leather boots and what looked suspiciously like a real fur coat. Not that Zu had any problems with fur, in Russia everyone wore it.

'Hello,' the lady said. 'Are you a friend of Jack's? Or Sasha's?'

Ice gushed down Zu's spine. 'Jack,' she stuttered.

'Ah.' The lady looked put out. 'Of course. Sasha is away at the moment. Always travelling, that one. Sorry for the inquisition but I like to know who's in the building.' She headed towards the stairs. Zu watched her. Black spots danced before her eyes. She wanted to be sick.

Sasha is away at the moment.

She opened the front door and walked out on to the

road, knees buckling. She looked at Jack's keys in her hand. She opened his letterbox and pushed them through.

Halfway to Angel Tube, her phone began to ring. Jack's number flashed up. She stuffed it in her pocket and hurried into the station and on to the escalator. Her signal vanished and she turned off her phone. There was no way she was answering it to Henchie ever again.

43

It was awful but actually, with Zu gone, the mood back in Farthingdale Road was transformed. Ro and Josie had both stumbled down an hour or so after she'd left. Wearing their pyjamas, they had a relaxed brunch of leftovers accompanied, at Josie's suggestion, by a bottle of Cava. Afterwards they played various games on the Wii and laughed continuously and then they watched three stupid movies back to back. Much the same as yesterday but without Zu's disapproving presence.

Tony was reeling. He understood it must be strange for Zu having another woman in the house and he could see Josie might sometimes wind her up. But Zu didn't live there any more. What business was it of hers? And for all Josie's flaws she still could be so sweet and fun and understanding. He'd been so happy when Zu said she'd come home, then so secretly devastated when Kieran said he wouldn't, so chuffed at the sight of Rohan – more grown-up after just a term away. Now he'd hit a new low. Would the rollercoaster ever end?

'Josie's all right, Dad,' said Rohan, when Josie disappeared up to the bedroom to Facebook her friends about what a lovely day she'd had.

'She is, isn't she?' Tony was hugely encouraged.

'Yeah. So try not to get too worked up about Zu. She

disappeared as soon as she could get out, so she can't tell you what to do now.'

'Do you think Mum would be OK with it?' Tony asked, desperate for absolution.

Rohan rolled his eyes. 'For God's sake. Mum put you through enough. Don't you think she would just want you to be happy?'

Domestic harmony reigned for precisely fifty-seven more hours and then Josie broached the question of New Year's Eve.

'I want to go out,' she said, quite reasonably.

'I'm pretty sure there's a band playing at the Bricklayers,' Tony said. 'I could book us a table.'

Josie looked at him with faint pity. 'I wasn't really thinking of that. I was thinking of going to a rave with the old crowd. And then maybe you and me could go to the Bricklayers for a New Year's lunch. How does that sound?'

Behind her back, Rohan pulled a face.

'I think I'd rather we saw in the New Year together,' Tony tried.

She bent over and kissed the top of his head, just on the bit where the hair was most meagre. 'Bless you, you sweet, sweet man,' she said. 'But I have to do New Year the Josie way. And I don't think you'd really like to be around to witness that.' She frowned. 'I wonder if the salon on the corner's open tomorrow because my roots need doing.'

She left the room. Tony looked at his son. Rohan looked back.

'The Josie way,' he repeated incredulously.

'She just wants to have fun,' Tony replied lamely.

'Look, don't get me wrong. I've told you I like her. I'm not going to go all Zu about her. But she needs to show you a bit more respect, Dad.' His phone rang. 'Oh, wicked, that'll be Kai telling me what the plan is for the big night.' He smiled as he answered. 'Yo!' Putting his hand over the mouthpiece, he added, 'You can come with us, Dad. If you don't want to be alone.'

Josie headed out at about noon on New Year's Eve wearing a bright pink basque, an orange feather boa and a flouncy net mauve skirt over stripy tights and chunky brown clogs. 'We're going to spend the afternoon in the pub, tank ourselves up for a night in the clubs,' she explained. She chucked Tony under the chin. 'We'll have our own celebration tomorrow,' she whispered in his ear and planted a kiss on his cheek. 'Have a good one,' she yelled upstairs to Ro and the door slammed.

Through the window, Tony watched her tapping along the street. She didn't look back. He sat down heavily in his armchair and after a second picked up his copy of the *Radio Times* (Ro and Josie had teased him for buying it). He'd usher in the New Year, like so many previously, with a glass of Merlot and Jools Holland's *Hootenanny*. Nothing wrong with that, of course, he'd just hoped this year would be different.

He went to the window again. It was a bright, sharp winter's day but only another hour of it remained. He'd make the most of it: he'd drive to Hampstead Heath and park by the Spaniards, then walk all the way down to the

Lido. Welcome the New Year with lungfuls of fresh air and endorphins.

The Heath was busy with dog walkers, families on the footpaths helping children ride their new Christmas bikes, couples holding hands and stopping to kiss. Tony would have liked to have gone on this walk with Josie.

He was striding past Kenwood House when he saw her approaching, red in the face as she tried to keep pace with a boisterous black dog.

'Gillian!'

'Tony,' she said, trying to smile.

'How are you? How was your Christmas?'

'Um, I've known better. I had a big row with my daughter. She walked out.'

'Me too!' Tony almost laughed, though it wasn't funny.

'Really?'

'So where is yours now?'

'She's kipping on a friend's floor in his disgusting flat on the Holloway Road. With about thirty-six other people, as far as I can see. It's not great but, as she's told me about a hundred times, she's sixteen and can do what she wants.'

'Oh, Gillian.' Tony's heart twisted. Whatever he was suffering in regards to Zu, this must be a trillion times worse.

'And what about you?'

'Nothing like as bad. Zu's really an adult, she really *can* do what she wants. We just had a row. She doesn't like Josie.'

'The woman you were with at Leela's party?'

He nodded. Gillian nodded too. 'And where is Josie now?'

'She's gone to a New Year's Eve party.'

'Without you?' Now Gillian couldn't hide her surprise.

'I don't think I'd have fitted in. It's fine. I'll be happy watching Jools Holland with a glass of red.'

'That's what I'm going to do.' She smiled.

They looked at each other.

'Maybe we should watch Jools together,' Tony said.

The Rivoli Ballroom, Brockley, was a riot of plush red-velvet, Austrian crystal chandeliers and oversized Chinese lanterns. The men wore suits with huge lapels and had slicked-back hair while the women were in flowery prom dresses with elaborate beehives. Gillian was entranced.

'Do you, er, do you come here often?'

'Haven't been for about twenty years,' Tony said. He felt nervous confessing but then he added, 'Actually, I used to play here in my band.'

'Really? You didn't tell me you played in a band.'

'It was a long time ago.'

'I mean . . . I guess running an instrument repair shop, it makes sense. What do you play?'

'Violin, normally, but in the band it was mainly guitar. Sometimes the sax.'

'Wow. I had no idea you were so talented.'

Tony was going to say something modest, but in the end he just smiled at her. She looked very pretty in her black velvet dress with a tasselled hem. Long earrings dangled from her lobes and she wore a bright pink lipstick that emphasized her generous mouth. As they'd strolled along the Heath, they'd agreed that they could do better than Jools Holland, and he'd suggested this alternative. So he'd gone back to her place in Kentish Town while she fed the dog and changed, and had waited in her cosy sitting room with its colourful kilim and quirky framed postcards on the wall and bowl of winter roses on the window sill, inspecting her CD collection which was impressively eclectic – everything from Bob Dylan to Abba, from Hawkwind to Kraftwerk. She'd never told him she was a Kraftwerk fan.

He'd never told her he played in bands. He realized that that first date had really been a wasted opportunity, that he'd been too fearful of moving on to give Gillian the opportunity she deserved, to really try to get to know her.

But now they had another chance. He remembered Josie and guilt flooded over him. *She* was his girlfriend, not Gillian. But she was in the East End somewhere, dancing on a podium, surrounded by bodybuilders. She swore it was innocent, so why couldn't he enjoy some innocent fun too?

The band struck up 'Rock Around the Clock'. Couples whooped as they ran on to the floor. Skirts whirled around legs, hips swivelled. He held out a hand to Gillian.

'Shall we?'

Two hours later, his legs ached and Gillian said her feet were sore. Both were sweaty and dishevelled.

'I haven't had so much fun in ages,' Gillian said, gulping down a pint of water. 'I can't remember when I was last on a dance floor.'

'Tragic, isn't it?' Tony agreed. 'At one time in your life you're out dancing every night, then it's once every six months. And then at some point you must hit the dance floor for the last time, without even knowing it.'

'Well, that won't be the last time for me,' Gillian declared. 'I'm going to get back in the habit now.'

'Me too.' They glanced at each other. The question of whether they might dance together in the future shimmered over them like a heat haze.

'You don't think it's bad to want to go dancing when my daughter's a drug addict and living in a squat?'

'What difference would it make if you sat at home every night feeling sorry for yourself?'

'That's what my sister says. It's just that as soon as you become a parent you feel guilty ever afterwards for enjoying yourself.'

'Too right.'

'Did you come here much with your wife?'

'Oh, only once or twice a year after Zu was born. My sister-in-law would babysit. After the twins, it was impossible. That was the end of life as we knew it.'

'But the twins have left now.'

'And so's Holly. I mean, I know that sounds heartless but you need to look after yourself now . . .'

The band was striking up 'Auld Lang Syne'. The motley crowd of revellers returned to the floor and linked arms.

'Should old acquaintance be forgot . . .'

Tony thought of Zu. So many New Years worrying about where she was, what she was doing, the dangers that surrounded her. This year she was just a few miles away but the worry was the greatest ever – the fear that he might never see her again.

'And never brought to mind . . .'

He glanced sideways at Gillian. She looked unspeakably sad; thinking of Holly, clearly. Ah well. For now all they could do was carry on singing.

> 'We'll tak a cup o' kindness yet
> For auld laaang syne.'

It was kicking-out time and it had started to rain. The street was full of cars, their lights reflected in puddles, but taxis were there none.

'We'll have to walk a bit,' Tony said. 'Try to find something.'

Gillian looked around dubiously. Her hair was already wet, her mascara had streaked slightly. She gestured at her flimsy shoes.

'I'm not sure how far I can go in these.'

'OK.' Tony looked around desperately. She shivered. Suddenly the night didn't seem quite so fun any more. 'Look,' he said. 'There's a station just up there and there's bound to be a few cabs around. People will be returning from the West End.'

'OK.' They started to walk. 'Do you mind if I lean on your arm?' Gillian asked.

'Of course not.' The rain continued to fall. 'Are you sure the station was in this direction?' she asked after a few minutes.

'Um . . .'

They looked at each other. They began to laugh.

'Lost in the rain in Brockley on New Year's Day.'

'When I woke up yesterday I didn't see myself here.'

They looked around. 'Maybe we should go back to the ballroom?' Gillian suggested. 'Start again.'

'Good idea.'

'Wow. Man accepts advice from Woman after getting lost. That's a first. Hang on a second. Sorry, but my shoes.'

Tony looked down. The strappy suede confections now looked as if they were rotting. 'Your feet must be freezing!'

'Well . . .'

'We can't have this.' He bent down and removed his shoes. 'Here!'

'I can't wear those, they're like boats.'

'Wear my socks then. They're good and thick. Remember, my original plan was a walk across the Heath.'

'They'll be ruined.'

'They're from Primark. Go on, put them on.'

Leaning against him for support, she removed first one shoe and pulled on a sock. She did the same with the other foot. 'I think that's the nicest thing anyone's ever done for me.'

'Please!'

They were on a quiet, suburban street, very similar to Farthingdale Road. The front door of one house was open and a crowd of people stood huddled in the porch smoking cigarettes. Music boomed, jerky, electronic. A tinny, German-accented voice sang faintly above the beat.

'"The Model". Kraftwerk,' Tony said.

They looked at each other again.

'The night's not over yet then,' Gillian smiled.

44

It was twenty past seven in the morning when Tony unlocked the front door of Farthingdale Road again. His chin prickled with a new beard, his eyes ached, his legs were heavy and inside him lager mixed with vodka mixed with a breakfast of bacon, eggs and fried bread (no tomatoes, Tony couldn't bear fried tomatoes) eaten at a transport café with formica tables and a prehistoric yellowing pin-up of Samantha Fox on the wall, (who was now a born-again Christian lesbian, as he had informed a sceptical Gillian).

He was exhausted but buoyant; guilty that he'd been out all night and at the same time the most cheerful he'd been in years. That had been quite a party. A crowd of them had ended up trying and failing to breakdance to 'Walk this Way' by Run DMC. One man, tall, skinny, inoffensively dressed and with an enormous Adam's apple, had been doing a passionate solo dance to Bonnie Tyler's 'Holdin' Out for a Hero' when he'd suddenly roared like a lion, picked up an aspidistra and taken an enormous bite out of it. The hostess, who'd seemed quite relaxed about the two couples having sex on her bed and the cigarette ash in the bath, went nuts and demanded everyone left.

They were giggling at the memory as they made their way — she in his socks again — back to the station. The dawn chorus was cheeping, the edge of the black sky was lighting up, the stars were going out one by one and it seemed as if the rest of the city was in a coma.

'Thank you for dragging me away from Jools Holland,' Gillian had said as they swiped their way through the ticket barriers.

'The pleasure was all mine.'

Smiling now, Tony pulled off his coat and walked into the kitchen. Rohan was sitting at the table, nursing a cup of tea.

'Dad?' he said incredulously.

'Good time last night?' Tony tried and failed to assume a nonchalant expression.

'Where have you been?'

'I went out.' He cleared his throat. 'Is Josie back?'

'No.'

'Ah.' Well, why should she be? He'd just got back himself. But why hadn't they spent the evening together?

'Call her,' Rohan said.

'Do you think she's all right?' Tony asked, suddenly guilty he hadn't been thinking of her more.

'She's probably just got shit-faced and crashed at someone's house. As did you, by the looks of things, you stop-out! I don't believe it. I was back by four.'

Tony pulled out his phone and called up Josie's number. After two rings, she picked up.

'Hello, gorgeous. Happy New Year.'

'Hi, Josie. Where are you?'

'I'm at Vivi's.'

'Vivi's?'

'Yeah, you know. He does manicures at Gor-Jus. The old biddies can't get enough of him, can they, Veeves?'

'OK. Well, see you later.'

'Oh, Tonio. Don't be like that.'

'I'm not being like anything,' he said, hurt. 'I just wanted to check you were OK.'

'I'm fine. Vivi's going to make some breakfast and then I'll be on my way. Shall we have pizza later? I could pick one up when I come out of the Tube. I've a real craving for spicy anchovies and lots of gorgonzola.'

'You do that,' Tony said and hung up, more confused than ever.

45

Gillian tottered home from the Tube, bits and pieces of last night's adventures flashing through her head. It had been so much fun, especially when she and Tony and the skinhead had attempted to breakdance. She'd thought she'd never laugh like that again.

Being with Tony was so liberating. The Holly problem which dominated her every second didn't diminish, but at least with him she felt a degree of understanding. She didn't know the details of what had happened with him and Zu but she knew he wasn't judging her for failing with her child.

She still felt guilty about enjoying herself, but Tony was right. What else was she supposed to do? Holly had left. She was alive and well; she'd called and said she was never coming back. Gillian had told her daughter that she loved her, she missed her. She told her what she'd had for supper, what she'd watched on telly. She didn't tell her how she cried every night, even though the tears barely scraped at her pain and just as well because if she removed the top layer, she feared the tears would never stop.

She had to look on the bright side. Life was so much more peaceful now. Just her and Waffle. No more yelling. No more angry voices on the phone saying *my fucking mother, fuck her, fuck you*. No one sneering, no one making Gillian feel sad or inadequate or furious. No more being woken in the middle of the night. No more cooking meals that were never eaten. She could put down her purse on the kitchen counter and next morning it would still be there.

Tomorrow she'd have the same old problems, but today she'd pretend she was twenty-three again. She'd sleep for a few hours, then take Waffle for a walk. Later she'd do an online shop and buy all Holly's favourite things – Jelly Babies, chocolate HobNobs, Ice Magic, Fluff – to help lure her back from the squat. She'd Google boarding schools, residential courses, boot camps – last resorts. It was a new year and she would sort this.

She unlocked the front door. Waffle bounded towards her, barking hysterically. From upstairs, music pounded. The house smelt like a dodgy pub from the olden days when you were allowed to smoke in them. The hall was littered with bottles and cans; cigarette butts and ash were everywhere.

'Gillian!' said a voice behind her. She twirled round. It was Amanda Cribbins, head of the residents' association, in a tracksuit, hands on hips. 'What has been going on here? We had to call the police four times.'

'What?'

Holly appeared at the top of the stairs, wobbly on her legs, eyes glazed, a large spliff in her left hand.

'Holly!'

'Hi, Mum. Happy New Year.'

Gillian stepped towards the living room. Holly ran down the stairs and jumped in front of her.

'No! Don't go in there.'

'Don't be stupid.' Gillian pushed her aside. The room

was dark; bodies were writhing all over the place. Three teenagers were slumped on the sofa, smoking spliffs and watching a porn DVD. The light fittings had been torn from the ceiling. Books and CDs were all over the floor.

'Get out! All of you! Out! Now!'

No one paid any attention to her. She turned and headed upstairs. There were black marks all along the stairway walls and someone had scribbled FUCK OFF in what looked like lipstick. She opened her bedroom door. Her clothes had been ripped from the wardrobe and lay scattered all over the floor. She picked up her blue silk Isabella Oliver dress. Someone had pissed on it. There was a used condom on top of her favourite grey velvet jacket. Her mirror had been smashed.

'Why didn't the police stop this?'

'They told us to turn the music down. We did.' Holly didn't look remotely repentant. In fact, she looked amused.

Gillian marched across the hall to the bathroom. The bath was full of vomit. She opened Holly's bedroom door. Two teenagers were asleep on the floor. Gillian started shaking them.

'Get out! Get out now!'

It was going to take all day just to get some semblance of order. She tried to make Holly help but she was too stoned and eventually Gillian had to send her to bed.

'But when you wake up, you are scrubbing every room on your hands and knees,' she warned her.

'Whatever.'

'And then I will sell whatever gadgets of yours you

haven't sold already or your guests haven't stolen to pay for a cleaning firm.'

Holly slammed the door.

Gillian went back into the kitchen, Waffle whining at her feet. Those bastards! Had they hurt him in any way? Her head throbbed and her hands shook from a combination of anger and exhaustion. She should be sleeping but she couldn't until she'd at least brought some order back to the place. She'd make a cup of tea and then start. Tears boiled down her face as she filled the kettle. The cupboard doors were hanging off. The microwave door was open. She looked inside. There was the TV remote, nuked.

Waffle rubbed comfortingly against her legs. She sat down and pulled him on to her lap. Without him, she thought, she would truly have lost her mind. Waffle licked her face. She buried her face in his fur and howled.

'Oh, what are we going to do, Waff? What are we going to do?'

She decided to tackle her bedroom first – bundle all the clothes in the washing machine. The dry-clean ones were chucked in a plastic bag. With rubber gloves, she picked up the condoms and put them in a bin bag. She collected the pieces of broken glass. She thanked God for the safe under the floorboard. At least all that was intact and so was her laptop and her camera.

As she was changing the bed linen, a thought struck her. Maybe she shouldn't touch anything. She needed to call the police, let them witness the mess, see if there was any redress. At the very least they'd give Holly a bollocking that might finally frighten her into behaving.

But not yet. She had to sleep before she saw the police, otherwise she'd be so exhausted she'd cry in front of them and that would be another humiliation.

She climbed into bed and Waffle jumped up beside her.

It was a long time before sleep came. Furious thoughts churned in her head of tracking down every single guest via Holly's Facebook account and going round to their houses in the middle of the night and wrecking them, of what she'd say to the police. Eventually she drifted off and dreamt she and Tony were daubing graffiti on the walls of the Rivoli ballroom.

She woke groggily because Waffle was whining, needing to be let out. She rolled off the bed and they went downstairs, walking over the cigarette butts. She opened the door into the garden. Her rose bush had been ripped out of the flower bed. A new surge of anger tore through her. She turned and marched back into the house and up the stairs. The little cow was going to sort this out.

'Get up now and start cleaning,' she roared, flinging open Holly's door. She pulled the duvet off the bed.

It was empty. Holly was gone again.

46

The nine men in the Close Encounters group met at Terminal Two at six in the morning. At first sight they were all much older than Zu had expected, about forty-six an average – and a couple of them clearly in their sixties. They were neither handsome nor ugly and none was an obvious weirdo. In the centre of their group stood Masha, looking like the heroine of a nineteenth-century novel in a white fur coat and hat, waving a clipboard.

'OK, so everyone has passport, yes? Everyone has boarding pass? Then let us go on the adventure of our lifetime!'

'Yes, Miss,' said Keith, who was very tall with a beerbelly and a white beard. Everyone sniggered.

Zu tried to raise a smile. She'd been so excited about going to Ukraine, even with this bunch of idiots. But now her tolerance for men had hit another all-time low. Henchie had said he loved her, for God's sake, and all the time he'd been living with 'Sasha'. She shook her head in disgust.

So far, Zu had managed to have as little as possible to do with Close Encounters. Sometimes she'd spoken to Nadia, the cheerful employee in the Odessa office, about a particular client one of the women had wanted to know more about. Once or twice, she'd clarified instructions on what type of flowers a client wanted delivering to a lady he corresponded with. Twice, she'd spoken to the British embassy in Kiev about visas when a client had wanted to bring over a lady. But, overall, she was still largely ignorant of whom Close Encounters attracted and what the trip would involve.

'Are you OK?' said one of the men gently at her side. His name was Spencer and he was in his late thirties, with a rubbery bald head and heavy eyelids behind round glasses that made Zu think of one of the pieces of furniture come to life in a Disney movie.

'I'm fine. Just tired.' She tried to smile. There was a naive air to Spencer. He was a farmer from Herefordshire and had told her that he'd joined Close Encounters because there were simply no single women living within a hundred miles of him.

'We're all tired. It was an early start.' He hugged himself in anticipation. 'But this should be a fun trip.'

'I hope so.'

'I've made dates to meet some of the women I've been emailing. The first is tonight. Her name's Elena. I mean . . . obviously you never know, but she looks perfect on the website. Right age, schoolteacher, loves cooking. I don't think I could do better.'

'Let's just hope the chemistry is there,' Zu said.

'She looks so pretty in her photograph,' Spencer said. 'She's wearing a lovely flowery dress – some of the girls are in their underwear! I don't think that would go down very well in Hereford.'

'I think they just wanted to look their best for the cameras,' Zu said. She had tried not to look too much at the pictures on the website: girls pouting, girls sucking their fingers, girls in negligees – and then other girls in sensible suits and pretty dresses. Those girls received far fewer hits. But British dating websites were hardly any better, she kept telling herself. Just because she didn't like wearing skimpy clothes herself didn't mean others weren't happy like that.

'Look at the last email she sent me.' Spencer handed Zu a piece of paper. 'She sounds just up my street.'

Dear Spencer,

Love cannot be controlled and it is hard to find, like a diamond in the earth. But when we do find it, like a diamond, it is ineffably precious. I want to find that diamond, find a man who will treat me the way I deserve to be treated. In return I will be the woman of his dreams. I will mould myself in whatever way he requires to make him happy.

Yours,
Elena

Zu looked up. 'Does Elena speak English?'

'No. Do you think that matters?'

Zu was staggered. 'Yes, I think it does! How did she write this?'

'An interpreter did it for her.'

'Right.' Zu wondered how many of these emails had been pinged off by Elena to every man who had contacted her. Her heart was already breaking for herself, but a tiny corner of it began breaking for Spencer too. She really hoped Elena would live up to his dreams. Having been let down so badly herself, the thought of it happening to anyone else was intolerable.

On the plane to Prague, where they changed planes, she sat next to Keith with the beer-belly and beard, who was a former lorry driver from Portsmouth.

'Have you been to Odessa before?' he asked.

Zu shook her head. 'You?'

'Nine times,' he announced proudly.

'*Nine?*' Zu had heard of repeat offenders, guys who went back again and again, but this was ridiculous.

Keith laughed. 'And twice to Kiev, four times to Moscow, twice to St Petersburg. But Odessa is the best. The girls are growing too sophisticated in the big cities. They're pickier about the guys they choose.'

'Right,' said Zu, stunned.

Keith shrugged. 'Ultimately, I'd like to get married again and I know I will. One day I'll just walk round a corner and bump into her, we'll look at each other and we'll know. But in the meantime, there's nowhere better on God's earth just to have some fun. I'm addicted. The problem is, the girls are just too beautiful. You want to pick just one but then another approaches you and the stakes keep going up.'

'Really?' piped up over-keen Al Wyatt behind him, or Al-the-Overkeen as they'd renamed him at Temperley for his habit of inviting girls to meet his mother, or go on holiday with him, within days of their first encounter. Gary had eventually persuaded him that he'd be better off on a Close Encounters tour because Odessan women

346

didn't like to string men along and wanted to seal their deal as soon as possible.

The plane taxied up the runway, the engines revved, and with a great roar it left the ground. Within seconds, England was obliterated by fog. Usually Zu loved this moment, knowing that once more she'd effected her escape, that perhaps – far away from home – she'd find some answers.

Now she knew better. There were no answers and there was no such thing as true love. The men, however, were still full of hope. Perhaps she should stop thinking mean thoughts about them and instead go easy on them for still being conned by this big illusion.

Odessa airport was the usual gloomy Stalinist bunker. Scrawny men with gold teeth jostled to sell their taxi services. Bulky men in cheap suits held up signs with foreigners' names on them. Once out of the terminal, it was cold, but not stupidly so – no more than a British winter.

'I was expecting snow,' Matt Billen whined.

'This is seaside city,' Masha pointed out. 'Odessa is famous for its temperate climate.'

A coach took them along a potholed road, past concrete high-rises, and then swooped down to the port. Zu sat next to Robert. He was in his fifties, with cropped grey hair, a craggy, handsome face and a very cross expression.

'So have you been a member long?' Zu asked politely.

'Just joined,' he barked.

'Oh? Well, good luck. Ha ha.'

'It's not about luck,' he snapped. 'It's about control. It's about having a relationship that's entirely on my terms. When you've let a woman take your life and everything you've achieved and rip it out of your guts and then use the kids to keep screwing you over for the next three years, then you won't want luck.'

'Right.' Now Zu really was shaken.

'Sorry,' Robert said. 'I'm feeling weird. Even now, the divorce is still fresh in my mind. I'm not sure I did the right thing coming on this.'

'I'm sure you'll have a great time,' said Zu, edging as far away from him as the narrow seat allowed.

They were staying at the Hotel Odessa, which was a huge monolith at the end of a pier jutting out into the icy Black Sea, with views back to the Potemkin Steps, the wide granite staircase that rose up from the port to the old town. Having checked in, the group became increasingly raucous.

'We're going to hit the town tonight!' yelled Keith. 'I can show you guys a few places you'll never forget.'

'Meet in lobby at six to go out to dinner,' Masha yelled. 'Then see you all at ten tomorrow for the induction meeting.' To Zu, she said: 'We need to get organized. Come.'

Close Encounters' headquarters for the trip were in a meeting room just off the bar. There were stacks of folders containing pictures of every woman on their books, together with a brief blurb about each one. Neatly laying them out was Nadia, their woman in Odessa. She was in her thirties, with long blonde hair in a tight ponytail, huge blue eyes and rosy cheeks. She wore a fitted red leather jacket and tight jeans. Next to her, Zu felt like a dung beetle beside a gazelle.

'Zu!' Kiss kiss. Perfume up the nostrils. 'So nice to put a face to a voice.'

'Likewise.'

Pleasantries over, Nadia turned to Masha. 'So what do you think of men? Which is best? I look at list: some good jobs . . . accountant, financial adviser, doctor.'

'You're way too pretty for any of them!' Zu exclaimed. 'And too young.'

Both women laughed kindly.

'Nadia is always looking for the pick of the bunch,' Masha explained, ignoring what Zu was saying. 'She has two boys. She needs to support them.'

'I was married but it didn't work out for me. My husband drank, he made me do all the work. Typical Odessa story. So I left him. I got engaged to Australian. But then I discover he have three children he didn't tell me about.' Nadia sighed. 'Plus he lived on a sheep farm two thousand kilometres from Sydney, and I am a city girl. So now I'm looking again. You never know, if I'm lucky I'll find a man to fall in love with. Worse case – he's kind and respects me.'

'The only girls who insist on love haven't yet been married to an Odessan,' Masha agreed sagely. Zu's head was starting to ache with the cynicism.

Masha looked at Zu appraisingly. 'I think you're tired,' she said. 'You go lie down for a while.'

'I'm fine.'

'We had an early start. Go and take a nap. We'll see you at the welcome dinner.'

'Honestly, I'm fine.'

'Go!'

It was the 'don't argue with me' voice. 'OK, then.'

Zu's room was on the sixteenth floor: big and utterly soulless. A bed, a telly, a desk, a wardrobe, an en-suite with no windows. Outside it was dark already. Her phone rang. She picked it up – probably Masha, having changed her mind – but instead she saw HENCHIE.

She rejected the call. A few seconds later a text arrived.

> Zu, what is going on? Why did
> you leave like that? Why won't
> you speak to me? Am I that
> crap a shag? :-) Please call.

She turned her phone off, took off her shoes, climbed into bed and dreamt about snow falling over Farthingdale Road while she, Jack and Josie all built a snowman together.

At breakfast time, the hungover Close Encounters clients sat next to the fish tank at a table covered in brown-and-white checked oilcloth. Only angry Robert sat alone, staring morosely into congealed scrambled eggs. Zu was heading for a corner table as far away from everyone as possible when Spencer saw her and waved.

'Hey! Come and join us.'

'Good night?' she asked resignedly, sitting down.

'Some of the women we saw . . .' said Matt Billen. He rubbed his hands together. 'Now this is what I've been talkin' about.'

Keith had been interrupted from holding court. He looked put out. 'The great thing about Ukrainian ladies,' he continued, not caring if she was listening or not, 'is they're kinda the best of both worlds. I mean, I've been to Thailand and the girls there are great, know what I mean? But they're Thai. Bring one home and you're going to get funny looks. Ukrainian girls, they're even more gorgeous, even more home-loving and they're European too. They look just like your neighbour's wife – only fitter because they take more care of themselves.'

Spencer was quiet. 'How was your date with Elena?' Zu asked him discreetly.

'Good. Until she said she was looking for a man with a full head of hair.'

Zu shook her head. 'Silly girl.' Then she remembered. 'Hadn't she seen a photo of you? Isn't the rule that you send one before you meet?'

Spencer shrugged. 'I was wearing a hat in my photo.' He held up his hands in self-defence. 'I know what you say about showing a true picture of yourself. But I wanted to look my best.' He wrinkled his nose. 'You know when she said all that stuff about diamonds, I thought she meant it specially for me.'

'You can't trust anyone,' Zu said meaningfully.

'I know. But you always hope.'

A coach carried them across the city to the first social – or party – which started at two. The sky was bullet grey, the Odessans walked with heads bowed, faces obscured by their huge fur shapkas. Exhaust fumes billowed from the backs of cars in white clouds. Nadia stood at the front with a microphone briefing the men, who, as one, gazed at her adoringly.

'You must keep your expectations reasonable. Stay within the parameters of what is going to improve your life. You are looking for a woman to share your life with. You're *not* looking for a picture to hang on your wall.'

The men nodded obediently.

'I have to tell them but they never listen,' Nadia muttered in Zu's ear as she sat down beside her. 'They say they are looking for serious woman and then they arrive and see the eighteen-year-olds and all that is forgotten.'

'Eighteen-year-olds?' Zu asked, but she was drowned out by Matt behind her, addressing Al-the-Overkeen.

'Odessan girls are gorgeous. But that's not why I'm here. There are gorgeous girls at home too. Odessan girls are more cultured – these women have degrees; they've read the classics; they love opera. They've grown up in a far less materialistic society than our women. They're perfect. That's what I'm looking for!'

'As well as a nice pair of tits and a tight bum,' Keith sniggered from the opposite row. Matt loftily ignored him.

The Palladium nightclub was a modern building near the station. The men trooped off the bus and in through the lobby, pushing through the turnstiles that led into the club itself. It was early afternoon but it seemed like midnight: techno music boomed, glitterballs twirled and neon lights flashed.

Groups of women were standing around the bar or sitting on the red velveteen banquettes. A few were matronly types, frumpily dressed in calf-length skirts and crocheted cardigans, but the majority were very young – barely out of their teens in many cases – and wore skimpy dresses, tight jeans, low-cut tops and towering heels. Their hair was teased, their make-up thick. Many were very beautiful indeed with shiny manes of hair, high cheekbones and full, sensuous mouths.

'Wow,' gasped Spencer.

Keith nodded proprietorially. 'Told you so.'

'How will I choose?' asked Al, eyes opening in wonderment. He reached into his pocket for a notebook and scribbled something as his eyes scanned the room.

Zu turned to Masha. 'I didn't know they'd be this young.'

'You saw the catalogue,' Masha said, her face closed. 'You know how they look.'

'I thought they were just . . . pictures taken in good light. It's horrible.'

'It's all legal.' Masha shrugged. 'They are not here to marry these men. They just want a nice time – dinner, maybe a gift or two.'

'So they're prostitutes.'

'Shhh.' Masha looked really angry. 'They are *not*. They are just young girls. Their lives are hard, boring. They just want little taste of fun. If these men are vain enough to think they like them for their looks or personality, that is their problem.'

Zu stared at her, unconvinced.

'I know what you see is not beautiful,' Masha said in a low but firm voice. 'But what is the alternative? When I was their age, I wanted the same. I tell you before. My father is always drunk, he die aged forty from lung cancer. My mother work thirty years in a factory. She spend all her spare time in queues for bread, for milk, for toilet paper. I don't want this life. I can't escape. Ukrainian girls can get visas to go nowhere. The only way out is to marry. And while you are waiting for a man who can be your husband, why not go out for a meal in one of the smart restaurants, where you've watched other girls eating caviar all these years?'

She took a deep breath. Nadia smiled sympathetically.

'Is hard situation,' she said, her tone more emollient. 'Girls don't like doing this but what else do they do? Men don't want to live alone for rest of their lives but they don't have courage to meet a wife in their home town. Nothing is black, nothing is white. Everyone is just trying to find happiness.'

Zu bit her lip. Henchie had said something similar. Masha waved an imperious hand. 'Go. Circulate. Introduce people. Translate if necessary. Look out for obvious prostitutes.'

Zombie-like, Zu headed over to two of the dumpier women who were standing at the bar, scanning the men. They eyed her warily.

'Hello, I'm Zulekha. I work with Close Encounters. Just wondering if you are OK? What kind of man are you looking for? Is there anything I can do to help?'

They smiled, a touch warmer now they knew she wasn't competition.

'I'm looking for husband,' said the slightly older, more faded woman. 'Mine has left me. I have a daughter. I work long hours. I want better life.'

'Me too,' chipped in the other. She wore gold strappy sandals and had orange toenails. 'My friend married a Canadian man. She went to live in Montreal and at first her husband want her to cook and clean, so she said: "I'll divorce you." He hired a cleaner the next day. Now she lives like a queen. Shopping all day, hairdresser, manicure. When she comes back here she says: "How can you live like this?"'

Zu thought of the men's fantasies of a woman who would cook and clean for them.

'I don't mean to be rude,' said the first woman. 'But we are wasting our time talking to you. The bus from Mariupol arrives in a minute and those women are serious competition.'

'I could introduce you to someone,' said Zu, looking round for Spencer. 'There's one man in particular I think would make a wonderful husband. There.'

They narrowed their eyes, then shook their heads. 'Not handsome enough.'

'No hair.'

'But he's kind.'

'Maybe.' They were clearly unconvinced.

It didn't matter. Within half an hour, the women were still alone but Spencer was sitting in a booth with a girl with frizzy blonde hair, dressed in hot pants and a leopard-skin boob tube, stroking his egg-like head. On his other side, a girl in a tight white vest had her arm round his shoulder. Tina Turner was hollering that he was simply the best. The girls threw their heads back laughing, gazing into Spencer's eyes and whispering in his ears.

A bottle of Ukrainian champagne sat in a bucket in the middle of the table. It would have cost him around two-hundred dollars. Temperley would take twenty-five per cent.

Al was sitting in another booth, flanked by two girls

who looked about fourteen. One was in a floaty floral dress with endless blonde hair; the other was a stockier type with brown hair pulled severely back off her face, emphasizing her big nose. She, Zu noticed, wore an Interpreter badge.

'Everyone all right?' Zu asked.

'He is asking what she can cook,' said the interpreter.

'Tell him anything he wants,' said the waif. Al smiled beatifically.

Moving between the tables, Zu picked up other exchanges. 'Don't tell him about my children yet – it might put him off.' 'Does he still live with his parents?' 'What does she like to cook?' 'Does she do any exercise?' 'Does he drink?' 'Does she cook many vegetables – tell her I don't like vegetables. Plain meat and potatoes man, me.'

The DJ cranked up the music and a pass-the-balloon game started. Spencer was in the middle of it, gamely bending his knees. All around him girls giggled. He swayed happily, arhythmically, as the girls danced circles round him.

'This remind me of when I meet Gary,' said Masha as they stood watching at the sidelines. 'He looked the kindest of them all. Ten minutes to know I should marry him, though it took longer to fall crazily in love.'

Keith gestured at a group of girls gyrating. 'Look at this! This is the biggest ego trip a man can ever imagine.'

So far, Zu had been delighted to be back in a country where you could smoke indoors. But suddenly the atmosphere was suffocating. She had to have air. She hurried through the lobby and on to the road and began walking, though where she didn't know.

'Watch out for the manhole!'

'Shit.' She stopped herself just in time. She looked round.

Angry Robert smiled gingerly at her. 'It wouldn't have been much fun, falling into an Odessan sewer.'

'Thanks, I was miles away.'

'Are you OK?' he asked her.

'I'm absolutely fine.' She didn't want to talk to the man, he was a nutcase. But Robert shook his head.

'You're not OK at all. Come. I'll buy you a drink.' He nodded at a bar across the street. 'Come.'

'Really. I have to go back.'

'You can spare five minutes.' He pulled a mock woeful face. 'Seriously. I'm having a crisis. It's your duty as a member of staff to help me.'

'One vodka,' Zu said crossly, although the prospect was appealing. She wasn't allowed to drink at the socials and it was quite a challenge staying sober while the men floundered all around her.

The bar was empty save for two teenage boys in battered leather jackets and Coldplay T-shirts. They ordered two vodkas from the weary-looking bartender and sat down. Zu offered Robert a cigarette. He accepted.

'You think we're all losers, don't you?' he said, taking her lighter.

'Not at all!'

'But we are.' Robert exhaled. 'Why can't we get a woman in our own country? None of us are deformed. We can't be penniless or we wouldn't be here. So what's wrong with us?'

'Everybody's different,' Zu said, employing the legendary

yes—no Indian head waggle that she always used to get her off the hook.

'I've seen you look at us once or twice. You're very young. I'm not sure that you've understood that what we all have in common is fear. Some of us are so shy, we're terrified of being laughed at. The fact the girls here can't understand a word we're saying makes it easier. Some of us have no confidence in our looks and even being able to talk to a beautiful girl gives us a rush like you can't believe. But most of us are just in terrible pain. Our wives and our girlfriends have left us because we worked too hard, or didn't buy them flowers regularly enough or because we were too grumpy or they just met someone hotter, and it's like having a knife repeatedly twisted in your gut.'

Zu looked at her hands. Robert was pretty much describing how she'd felt ever since the encounter in Jack's hall. She had believed something was there but it had all been a lie. Another shaft of empathy pierced her barrier of scorn. If she felt like this after one night, how would you feel if you'd had years, decades with someone, only to see it all collapse? No wonder the men were so willing to be taken for a ride.

No wonder Dad was.

As if reading her thoughts, Robert said, 'We need to start afresh. We lost most of our old friends when our wives went and now we want someone who has absolutely no preconceptions about who we are. We want someone to spend the second part of our lives with. I think we deserve it. I think we deserve a second chance at love.'

The vodka warmed her blood. She was feeling better. All the same . . .

'You're young and beautiful,' Robert continued. 'It may never happen to you. I hope it doesn't. But you never know what life's going to throw at you.'

'Life's thrown plenty at me,' Zu said, standing up, just as 'It Must Have Been Love' started playing on the radio. Roxette. Her embarrassing all-time favourite. A memory of her belting it out at a karaoke bar with Jack ran through Zu like a coin dropping into a slot machine. Her throat tightened as the Swedish woman sang about being in love, but it was over now. That's what she'd thought.

'We should get back now.'

Robert looked stricken. 'I'm sorry. That was stupid of me. You may be young but stuff can still happen.'

'Yes. Well . . .'

'Was it a man? We're all idiots, you know.'

'I know.'

'Your boyfriend?'

'Well.' Zu sat down again. The temptation to talk to someone was overwhelming. 'He wasn't even a boyfriend. But there's also my dad.'

And so, in this tiny bar with a grubby floor and a poster of the Caucasus mountains on the wall and a new background track of 'Alejandro', Zu told Robert about Tony and Josie, about the dominatrix secret. She even told him a little bit about Deepika. Robert listened without interrupting, except occasionally to order another vodka.

'It's really hard, isn't it?' he said. 'I'd be angry with my dad if he was dating a dominatrix – well, I'd be amazed, actually, given he's eighty-four, but anyway. Zu, remember your father doesn't know about her past.'

'Josie's horrible, anyway.'

'I'm sure she is. But your father must be very, very lonely.' Robert sat back in his plastic chair. 'That eats you up inside, it rips your guts out. You talk back to the radio. You scare off the postman with your witterings when he delivers a parcel. You long for your colleagues to invite you for a drink and then if they do you worry you'll bore them, that you'll have nothing to say to them. So you end up doing stupid things – like falling for silly girls. Like coming here.'

Zu looked into her glass. She remembered what Naani had said about loneliness. She'd always despised people who couldn't cope on their own, but maybe she'd been too hard.

'You don't need to like Josie. But, please, don't lose touch with your father. Call him. See him on his own. If he knows he has you he's far less likely to stick with her. God knows, if my son didn't live in Tasmania I'm pretty sure I wouldn't find myself here.'

'Right.'

'Want to talk about the not-even-a-boyfriend?'

But that would have been a step too far. 'No thanks. We really should get back now.'

47

Tony's phone rang at six just as he was waking up. He grabbed it, adrenalin pounding round his body as if he were an electrocuted rat. Zu! Rohan! Kieran! Beside him, Josie mumbled something and turned over.

'Hello?'

'Tony,' said a woman's voice. Oh Christ. A police-woman calling to say something had happened to the boys, or Zu.

'Yes?'

'It's Gillian. Look, I'm really sorry to call so early but I didn't know who else to turn to. My sister's in the Mal-dives and Holly stormed out yesterday after the latest big row and she hasn't gone back to the squat in Holloway. I need a car to look for her and mine's in the garage because she wrote it off and . . .'

'Have you called the police?' Tony was alert now.

'What?' Josie opened her eyes.

'I have. They say she hasn't been missing long enough for it to be a concern. Give it twenty-four hours. She's left before, they say she'll be back again. But I just have a feel-ing. I've called all her friends – well, the few she has left. No one's seen her. I'm terrified, Tony, she's probably off her head and something could have happened to her.' Gillian started to cry.

'Don't worry.' Tony was already out of bed and fumbling

for a T-shirt. 'I'll come over. We can drive around and look for her.'

'Oh, thank you! I know it's looking for a needle in a haystack but I can't just sit here.'

'Keep it down!' Josie grumbled.

'There's a problem, Josie. I have to go and sort it out. I'll see you later.'

Dawn was breaking, hazy orange and pink dissolving into a sharp blue sky. Tony saw early-morning London: bins overflowing, street cleaners mopping, delivery lorries reversing outside restaurants, shops and pubs – their doors open to release the sour stink of last night's boozing. After the Christmas break, life was resuming. Commuters trudged to the Tube, Tony braked behind buses stopping to let crowds on and off, cars honked, bicycle riders swore as they darted past. Mothers yanked children in uniform behind them, other mothers, bleary-eyed, bumped buggies down their front steps. Holly must be amongst the crowd – but where? Gillian had knocked on the doors of everyone she could think of and everyone claimed ignorance.

'She must have friends you don't know about,' Tony said as they sat in a parking bay off the Holloway Road, vainly watching the pedestrians.

'I don't think so. I've been pretty brutal about pillaging her mobile. I copied all the numbers off it, just a couple of days ago, and I called every one last night. I really don't think any of them were lying. Most of them said they weren't speaking to her any more because she'd stolen from them. She snorted, 'Not that that stopped them coming to her party.'

Tony turned on the engine. 'Well, we can keep driving but really you might be better off going home and waiting for her. I'm sure she'll be back soon. It's just too cold to stay out.'

'That's what I can't bear,' Gillian said. 'Knowing she's out there in the cold. She must be freezing.' She started to cry, just as her phone bleeped. She snatched at it.

'Oh God,' she said. 'A message. I don't know who it's from but they're suggesting I try a place in Loughton.'

'Let's go,' Tony said.

As they drove, Gillian biting her nails, Tony realized that – although he was terrified for Holly – he also felt good about himself. He was helping someone he liked. He was doing something useful. He liked it. Because this was his thing: helping women in distress. He'd spent so many years trying and failing to save Deepi. He'd been – he saw with startling clarity – trying to rescue Josie from something, he didn't know what. Now Gillian needed him and he was happy again.

It was a pattern. A pattern he needed to break. He needed to learn to love a woman for who she was, not for all the baggage she brought with her.

The street they were directed to was made up of low terraced houses with shabby front gardens. One in particular was full of Coke cans, crushed cider bottles and crisp packets.

'This'll be the one.'

'I'll come with you,' Tony said.

They banged on the door. A dog started barking. Eventually a girl opened it. She was in her twenties, wore dirty brown baggy trousers and a red sweatshirt, and was obviously wasted. The dog, a crossbreed, growled at them.

'Is Holly here?' Gillian said.

The girl paused just a second too long before saying: 'Holly? Er, no.'

Gillian pushed past her into the kitchen. There was a table covered with dirty glasses and empty beer cans with cigarettes stubbed out in them. Dirty cutlery lay on the filthy rug, the wall was splattered with graffiti and what looked suspiciously like bloodstains. In the corner was a threadbare orange sofa. A stained brown horse blanket hung over the window. A boy in baggy jeans sprawled in a threadbare armchair. The room reeked of old takeaways, dope and rancid clothes, of apathy, of hopelessness.

'Where's Holly?'

'She's not here.'

'I want to see her.'

The girl sighed. 'Just a minute.' She disappeared into the next room. They heard low voices. Gillian gasped and grabbed Tony's wrist.

'It's her!'

The girl came back.

'Let me see her.'

'She doesn't want to see you.'

Gillian pushed past her into the next room. Tony followed her. There was a mattress on the floor. Lying on it, fully dressed, was the girl who must be Holly. So pretty, though she was obviously stoned, thin and dirty, her hair matted. Lying next to her was a boy – well, a young man – even skinnier, even dirtier, wearing just his underpants, head on his arm, fast asleep. Even in this sepulchral light he looked alarmingly pale.

'Fuck off, Mum. What the fuck are you doing here?'

'Charming,' Gillian said. 'I wanted to know where you were.'

'Well now you know, so fuck off.'

'Delightful. I'd just like a number so I can keep in touch with you,' Gillian said calmly.

'I haven't got a number. Lost my phone.'

'A landline?' Gillian asked, still sweet. Tony was impressed. He'd have lost it by now. Holly just snorted in derision.

'OK,' Gillian continued. 'What about Jarmon? He always has a phone. He needs it for his deals. What's his number?'

'I dunno.'

'Well, ask him.'

'He's asleep. He's been asleep for ages.'

'Wake him up,' Gillian whispered. 'Or I swear, I will carry you out of here and drive you straight to boarding school.'

'I'd run away.'

'Get Jarmon's number.'

Holly sighed heavily and pulled herself up on to her elbow. 'Jarm,' she said, prodding the sleeping boy. 'Jarm. What's your number? Jarm.' She prodded again. 'Jarm! Jarm? Jarm!'

'Is he OK?' Tony stepped forward.

There was a bit more prodding, some mouth-to-mouth resuscitation, the arrival of paramedics, a lot of screaming, and much barking from the dog, before it was finally ascertained that Jarmon was dead.

Tony didn't return to Farthingdale Road until late in the afternoon. There'd been endless police interviews before he'd been allowed to go. Gillian and Holly were still there when he left, Holly sobbing in her mother's arms.

He drove home, shell-shocked, but also fantastically grateful for all his blessings. He felt desperately sorry for Jarmon's parents, but Holly was fine. His children were fine. Zu might not be talking to him but she wasn't lying somewhere in a filthy squat. Life could be very, very cruel but it could also be wonderful – he needed to focus on that side of things.

He'd been planning to pop in briefly to the workshop but he changed his mind. He'd go home and surprise Josie, who was no doubt Facebooking or napping or doing her hair in some peculiar new style. They could go to a movie. Out for a lovely meal.

He parked outside the house, excited. He hurried up the path and unlocked the door.

'Honey, I'm hoooome!'

He opened the living-room door. He stopped. Standing there was Josie in a black-leather corset, a studded dog collar round her neck, fishnet tights and black leather thigh boots. A man in a suit was kneeling in front of her covered in what looked like spaghetti bolognese. A broken plate lay beside him with pieces of spaghetti all round it. There was a puddle round the man, which Tony initially took for piss but at second glance realized was wine.

'What is this?'

The man looked round.

'Oh, fucking hell,' he said.

48

Zu was desperate to leave Odessa there and then, but it was impossible – she was booked on a flight at the end of the week and to change it would have cost her three thousand pounds. So she had to stay on and, after a frosty conversation with Masha, had to carry on working – phoning the girls after every social to arrange dates, watching the men flick through the catalogues and pick out their favourites.

She watched them sitting in the lobby with their dates, who were dressed up to the nines and reeking of perfume. The men showed them their photo albums which Close Encounters suggested they bring along: 'This is my house,' 'This is my car,' 'This is my office.'

Sometimes the dates would approach Zu in the toilets: 'Is two hundred thousand pounds a big mortgage? If he dies would I have to pay it off?' 'Is Colchester a good city to live?' 'What exactly is IT consultant?'

One day they went to Kharkov, which was a town a few hours' drive away. The coach took them past people at the side of the road huddled around tiny fires with pitiful stands in front of them, one for turnips, one for biscuits, one for matryoshka dolls, one for straw brooms, one for food cans. Four by fours with tinted windows overtook them and so did ancient Fiats. They passed ravaged factories and decaying apartment blocks. Zu felt painfully sorry for the Ukrainian people. But the men loved it. The girls were even more beautiful in Kharkov and, as Keith so charmingly put it, 'even more desperate'.

By the time they finally found themselves flying home in the Czech Airlines Boeing, everlasting friendships had been sworn between the men, business deals had been mooted, email addresses had been swapped and there'd been much talk of reunions.

From her aisle seat, Zu glanced around the plane, noting how each of the men had fared. Matt was no longer with them – he had dated a different girl every night and had decided to stay on for another fortnight. She just hoped his crabs had really been cured.

Robert, who had barely spoken to Zu after their heart-to-heart, had got very serious with a girl called Olga and been out with her every evening. Al had a long list of addresses of women he was going to correspond with. Keith appeared to have dated no one, but seemed completely unbothered by this and was already planning his next trip in the spring.

As for Spencer, he was sitting beside her.

'So how was it in the end?' she asked him.

He smiled shyly. 'Not a success. I'm so sorry. The girls were very beautiful and they were kind. They came out with me for dinner. They laughed at my jokes. But I could tell they weren't feeling what they should have been feeling. I don't know how you make anyone fall in love with you.'

He looked at Zu, as if hoping for an answer, but she could only shrug.

'Ladies and gentlemen. The captain has now put on the seatbelt sign. Please return to your seats.'

Zu watched the Home Counties emerging through the clouds. The sight filled her with dread. What was she returning to? She wasn't speaking to her father, though Robert had made her see she needed to get over that. The only guy she'd ever properly liked – well, loved – in her life was living with another woman and hadn't told her about it. Henchie had been texting and calling her continually but she'd deleted his messages without reading or listening. What a nerve he had!

Worst of all, she no longer had a job. Whatever Masha said about her being young and naive, whatever Robert had explained about loneliness, she just couldn't be part of this any more. She felt sorry for the men, and women, but she knew for sure now that marriages needed love.

'Pizza Hut, here I come,' she muttered to herself.

'Sorry?' said Spencer.

'So guys, see you all!' Zu said brightly, once they were standing in the baggage hall, suitcases around their feet.

'Aren't you coming with us on the Tube?' Keith was hopeful.

'Sorry. I've booked a cab,' she lied.

'A cab?' Keith perked up. 'Could you give me a lift?'

'Afraid not.' Zu pulled her best apologetic face. 'My cousin's come to meet me. And her husband and her . . . her son and daughter! There's no room.'

'OK. Well, then.' Keith stepped forward and kissed her on both cheeks. He smelt of pine and amber. 'Be in touch, Zu. Thanks for being such a great hostess. You were miles better than the last one. What was her name? The one before was good, though. She –'

'You're welcome.'

One by one, they said their goodbyes, apart from Spencer who just vanished into the crowd. Some headed to the Tube, some to the Heathrow Express, some to the bus station, some to the long-stay car park. Zu looked around for Masha but she had disappeared into the loos.

'Zu!' a voice said behind her.

She knew who it was. Slowly she turned round.

'Zu.' Henchie stood there. He looked as if he hadn't shaved for a week. He stepped forward. 'I was hoping I'd catch you here. I have to talk to you.'

'What's there to talk about?' she said, turning on her heel and heading towards the glass doors.

'What do you mean? We had our night together then you went all weird and ran out on me.'

'Yes, and do you wonder why?' Zu began walking briskly towards the taxi rank. Forget sneaking on to the Tube, now she'd have to spend hundreds of pounds on a black cab to escape Henchie. Just the sight of him made her feel sick and shaky. She could see the taxi rank, in fact she could see Robert climbing into a cab. Not too many people waiting. Henchie was walking alongside her, talking breathlessly.

'Did something happen? Did someone say something? What was it?' Zu ignored him. 'Zu! C'mon.'

'How can you pretend you don't know?' she snapped as she reached the head of the line.

'I don't!'

'Where you going to, love?' asked the driver.

'Regent's Park,' she said, opening the door. Henchie tried to follow her.

'Fuck off!' she snapped, pushing him backwards.

'Just tell me what it was!'

'This guy bothering you?'

'Sasha!' Zu snapped. 'Sasha is bothering me. And the fact you're still living with her and you told me it was all over.' She slammed the door in his face and the cab pulled off. The temptation to look back and see his expression was almost overwhelming but Zu resisted.

Her phone bleeped. Reluctantly she looked.

Sasha is a man, you dork!

Just as she was taking this in, another arrived.

Now will you call me?

All the way along the M25, the M40, the A40, she was paralysed with indecision. Should she call? Shouldn't she? What would she say? She felt like an idiot. She, better than anyone, should have known that Sasha was a unisex name – why hadn't it occurred to her?

They were almost at the house when she finally found the courage to call him back.

'Yes,' he said. He sounded angry. Her stomach flopped.

'I'm sorry . . . Jack. I should have believed you.'

'Who told you about Sasha?'

'Xander, then your neighbour. So I ran off. I –'

'Zu,' he said, still sounding angry. 'I wouldn't lie to you. I know I've not always behaved that well to some women but with you . . . Why didn't you ask me?'

'I don't know,' she said in a small voice. But she did

371

know. She'd thought what she had with Henchie was too good to be true and she'd been looking for any possible excuse to destroy it.

'What we had was so amazing and then you —'

'Can we meet?' she begged. 'Can we talk about it?'

'I don't know.'

'Please!'

A long, long pause. Zu's heart drummed.

'Meet me at Eros. Seven.'

'OK,' she said and hung up, heart singing. She was seized by an utterly unfamiliar urge to order the taxi to go straight to Anj's favourite beauty parlour so she could have her hair and nails done. But then Jack would think she'd lost it completely. *Concentrate, Zu. Concentrate. You've a lot to think about.* But then her phone rang again. This time it was a number she didn't recognize.

'Hello?'

'Zulekha Forbes? This is Benedict Agnew from Help Worldwide. Do you remember? We met in Grozny at the aid-workers' cocktail party.'

Benedict? Zu thought. *Oh God, yes.* Tall, mop of black hair, round face, slanty eyes, fondness for cravats. She'd snogged him in the embassy kitchen. What did he want? A girlfriend? A one-night stand? 'Hi. How are you doing?'

'I heard you were on the market,' he said. 'Which is good news for me. Because there's a job going if you're interested. Do you want to meet and talk about it. Tonight?'

Zu slammed the front door of the mews house and called up Jack's number on her phone. She was meant to be meeting him in twenty minutes but she was going to have to beg him to wait just another hour. A job was going in Kazakhstan. It sounded right up her street and Benedict was keen to pin her down as soon as possible.

Voicemail. 'Jack. It's me. I'm really sorry but I'm going to be a bit late, something's come up. Could we meet at eight maybe? Or nine would be even better. Sorry. Call me when you get this message. Sorry.'

She hung up, throat dry. She didn't like this. She'd wanted to see Jack. But a job was a job. She almost ran across the park and over Euston Road, headphones singing Haydn's *Missa Brevis*, through the Marylebone backstreets, lined with faceless mansion blocks, across Harley Street and on past Portland Place, crossing the road in front of the BBC.

The hotel Benedict had chosen to meet in was a shabby nondescript place near Tottenham Court Road, with coaches parked outside and a grey-lit marble lobby filled with miserable-looking pensioners sitting on suitcases, huddled in anoraks. Zu looked around for the bar, as her phone rang in her pocket. She pulled it out. Voicemail. A missed call from Jack. She mustn't have heard the phone ringing above all the traffic noise.

'Sorry, Zu, but I can't take any more of being messed around. I'll be at Eros at seven. Either meet me there or I'll know it's over. OK?'

Zu's stomach was cold. He sounded seriously angry now.

'Zulekha, hi! Great to see you!'

Benedict stood there grinning in a brown suit, hair in a weird buzz cut. Zu stared up at him.

'Benedict, I'm really sorry but I have a problem. I'll call you later. Sorry. Sorry.'

She ran towards the glass revolving doors. They spat her out into the cold street. She started running down New Oxford Street, across the north end of Charing Cross Road and down it past the bookshops, the sandwich shops, the tourist tat emporiums, past *Big Issue* sellers and ambling tourists, workers hurrying to the Tube and ravers embarking on their night. She turned into Shaftesbury Avenue passing *Les Misérables* – God, she loved that musical. She ran past the Curzon cinema, the shop that Anjali loved that sold hair products at trade prices, the Trocadero.

Get out of the way! There was Eros with dozens of people from every corner of the world sitting on its steps. The lights of Piccadilly Circus flashed above it. Zu glanced at her watch. Five past seven. Shit, he would have gone. She'd have to call him and beg him to return. And then she saw him, scarf wrapped round his face, hands deep in his pockets, eyes fixed grimly straight ahead, heading down into the Tube.

'Jack!'

He didn't hear. She ran to the steps, stumbling slightly as she hurried down them and into the tiled ticket hall with its orange pillars – which way were the barriers? She ran round to the left and saw him beeping his Oyster card. She fumbled in her pocket for hers. Where was it?

'Jack!'

He disappeared down the Bakerloo Line escalator. Where was her fucking card? Ah, here. She ran to the escalator and began running down it. Rust-red, white, dark-green, brown tiles flashed past, on to the next level, round the corner on to the next escalator. A busker was playing at the bottom.

'Jolene, Jolene, Jolene, Jo–leeeene . . .'

Two female tourists, middle-aged, in fake-fur jackets, stood abreast, chattering vivaciously and blocking her way. Zu couldn't believe it.

'Excuse me!'

The woman in front of her glanced over her shoulder and smiled uncomprehendingly.

'Excuse me!'

The other woman tapped her friend on the shoulder, explaining her crime.

'Ah!'

She moved to the side, smiling sweetly. Zu squeezed past her. Jack had turned round the corner. Was he going south or north? Surely north to change to the Victoria line to Highbury and Islington. Or maybe south to change on to the Northern Line for Angel.

She stood in the tiny space between the two platforms, head spinning first this way and that, while tutting commuters squeezed past her. 'Jack Henchie!' she yelled at the southbound platform and two hundred curious faces turned to look at her then – being nonchalant Londoners who would only be temporarily diverted if a T-Rex lumbered on to the platform – looked away again.

On to the northbound. 'Jack Henchie!' she bellowed but a train was roaring out of the tunnel, no one could hear her. She scanned left and right and then saw him a couple of carriages along, standing in an impatient group waiting to board the train.

'Jack!'

He was shuffling into the carriage, his face a picture of sadness. The doors began bleeping. She jumped into the nearest carriage and began squeezing past the strap-hanging commuters immersed in their *Standards* down the narrow central aisle. 'Sorry,' she said as she stood on an already cross-looking woman's foot. 'Sorry, sorry.' She opened the doors into the next carriage. Heads turned nervously, anticipating armed robbers or – worse – a beggar. Zu kept on squeezing.

'What are you doing?' a red-faced man in a suit asked.

'I'm looking for someone.'

'Aren't we all?' said a fat man who sounded dangerously like Keith from Odessa. There were subdued titters.

'The carriage is full, wait until the next stop to move up,' the man chastised her.

'He might get off there. Just let me past.'

'There's no room.'

'The next station is Oxford Circus,' intoned the recorded announcement.

He'd be changing trains there. Zu felt tilty and tunnel-visiony.

'Jack Henchie!' Zu yelled. 'If you are in this carriage, please wait for me on the platform.'

A rustle from the crowd, then everyone's heads returned to their books and papers. The train entered the station. The doors opened. A mass of people disgorged on to the platform. Zu followed them. A young blonde woman in a charcoal suit tapped her on the arm.

'I hope you find him.'

'Thanks.'

On to the platform. The doors closed behind her. People were everywhere, moving in all directions. She looked around and suddenly she saw him just a few feet away, smiling.

'You certainly know how to draw attention to yourself, Forbes.'

'Oh, shut up, Henchie.'

They stood, grinning at each other. Zu heard the tannoy booming in the background, people muttering as they stepped around them, the roar and squeal of a train arriving on the opposite platform. She stepped forward.

'I'm really sorry. I wanted to see you more than anything. I've missed you.'

'You're an idiot, Forbes.'

'I know.'

Zu moved her arm a millimetre towards him, a microscopic twitch. The next thing, as if shot from a cannon, they were in each other's arms, Jack's legs were pressed against hers, his arms were wrapped round her back and they were kissing the living daylights out of each other.

49

Tony waited until Beth was on her lunch break before he picked up his phone.

'Gillian, hi, it's Tony!'

'Tony! What's up with you? How are things?'

'Fine.' Of course that wasn't strictly true. But it wasn't the time to tell Gillian the events of the past couple of weeks . . .

Coming home to discover Josie in her Madame JoJo outfit. Discovering that Madame JoJo had had a very busy career in Nashville until immigration discovered her lack of green card. Finding out that she'd begun to work in an upstairs room at Gor-Jus as a 'masseuse', but then they'd thrown her out in a row about what percentage of earnings she should pay the owner.

How she'd been meaning to go straight, but she was short of cash after Christmas and she thought she'd just do a couple of jobs and really, Tones, what was the problem? Because dominatrixes didn't shag the clients. They just enabled their fantasies. And this particular client's fantasy had been to pretend he'd come home from work to a lovely meal of spag bol and a bottle of wine, only to have Madame JoJo start yelling at him for being late, chuck the plate at him and then pour the wine over his head.

'What was that all about?' Tony had asked, temporarily diverted.

'God knows, must have happened with some ex he was hung up on. Honestly, Toney-wones, they ask you to do the funniest things, bless them.'

Later, Tony would regret not asking for more details. But at the time he said: 'Whatever. You've been using my house as a knocking shop.'

'I *told* you, Tones, we don't shag them.'

'Josie, we've got to call it a day.'

'How about you?' he asked Gillian now.

So Gillian gave him a potted version of recent events.

Of course Jarmon dying was the most dreadful tragedy. But – I know it sounds awful – for Holly it was the kick she needed. Not that I'd wish him dead, but it gave her such a terrible shock. She's been crying and crying and we've really talked for the first time about how she felt about her father leaving. I'm just so bloody happy she wasn't harmed. So now we're trying to work out what to do next.'

'Which might be?'

'I've made a long list of terms and conditions. She's started a new school to finish her GCSEs. No drugs, no boozing, no smoking in the house. She has to be home by ten in the week, midnight at weekends. She has to tell me where she's going. She sticks to the rules or she's out on the street again. We'll talk about A levels later.'

'Good luck.'

'Thank you. It's scary. I have no idea if it's going to work or not. I just have to hope. How are your kids?'

'Well. Kieran says he's not going to uni any more, he wants to stay in Africa forever. I suspect a girl's involved. I'm planning a visit. Rohan's loving Salford. And Zu and I are speaking again.' He couldn't help smiling as he said this.

'Tony, I'm so glad!'

'Me too. She called when she'd got back from a trip to Ukraine and said she understood a bit better now about why I'd been so lonely. We met, had a drink. She was pleased I'd split up with Josie, obviously . . .'

'You split up with Josie!'

Was he imagining it – probably he was – but didn't Gillian sound just a teeny-weeny bit pleased?

'Mmm hmm. Anyway, Zu is still at Temperley but not for long. She's been offered a job in Kazakhstan and she's heading out there in a month or so.'

'Kazakhstan? That's great. Not too dodgy, is it?'

'So she claims. She's actually asked if I'd like to come and join her for a holiday. Amazing architecture, apparently. Beautiful mountains to walk in. Great food.'

'You should go!'

'I will. I can't wait. So, yes, it's all good. Just one snag.'

'Oh?'

'Zu's met a guy. Fantastic bloke. But she's going to have to leave him behind.'

'He couldn't go with her?'

'Not really. What could he do in Kazakhstan? Anyway, he has a son here. It's tricky. Zu wants the job but she's clearly not so thrilled about leaving him.'

A pause. *Say it, say it.* But he just didn't know how to phrase it. Maybe he'd text her later. But then Gillian blurted. 'Tony?'

'Yes?' His heart began to hammer.

'Would you like to come round for supper one night soon? We could talk more about it.'

'I'd love that,' he said. A bright winter sun as crisp as an apple was shining through the window and warming his neck. He picked up the almond croissant Beth had brought him from the deli mid-morning. He bit into it. Creamy almond filling exploded in his mouth and he felt a dusting of sugar coat his chin.

In the past few weeks, alone again, he'd finally begun to embrace life as a widower. He'd subscribed to Sky Sports, something Deepi had always forbidden. He'd sold the stodgy family car and replaced it with a two-door number. And he'd started not just repairing violins, but playing his old one again. Some classical, some blue-grass. He was looking at adverts for bands to join.

Maybe life wasn't always going to be so hard.

Shall I move in with new boyfriend? April 19 2012

Kentishfailure 23:11

OK, ladies, so we move on. As mentioned before, I've met a new man. It's very early days – just three months – but he's asking if I'll move in with him. What do you think?

Underthesea 23:14

Aww, Kentish, that's amazing. Big hugs to you. Is three months too early? Not if you believe in love at first sight, which I do. Hugs, hun.

NewYorker 23:16

Kentish, glad you're happy but I'm going to sound a note of caution. Three months? Way too early in my opinion. What's the rush? The other day you were on here saying how great it was to have some personal space again. Why be in a hurry to lose it?

Underthesea 23:19

NewYorker, she's nearly 44. Why wait? If you know, you know. I feel sorry for you, I really do, leading your life in such a state of caution. Go for it, Kentish, you'll have to change your name soon as you're deffo not a failure any more. (And you'll probably be leaving Kent, where I guess you live, LOL.)

Leosmama 23:24

Sorry, Kentish, I know it's another topic but how is your dd getting on?

Kentishfailure 23:38

Thanks for your enquiry, Leosmama, she's getting there. She's actually been revising hard for her GCSEs and I think they won't be an utter disaster.

Deardiary 23:45

Same old story. Mothers more interested in their personal life than their kids' welfare. Take your pick. Then they come on here complaining about their terrible relationship, how their children don't respect them etc. Can't they see if they gave up work and prioritized their children's needs rather than their own selfish desires, none of this would happen?

Kentishfailure 23:47

Underthesea. I live in Kentish Town, not Kent. Diary, with the greatest respect, go fuck yourself :-)

50

Zu and Jack were in bed. They'd just been out for dinner to a Korean restaurant and when they got back to his place they'd leapt on each other. Now they were playing their new favourite game of tapping out a tune on the other's back. The other one then had to name it.

'Old Macdonald?' Jack tried.

'Don't be silly.'

'Twinkle Twinkle.'

'You've been spending too much time with Xander. Look, I'm going to sing a bit to you. Ooh ooh ooh, yeah.' She clicked the fingers of her right hand and continued to strum with the left.

'Oh, it's coming, it's coming . . . I . . .'

'Too late. Time's up. "Stray Cat Strut" by the Stray Cats.'

'Shit! I knew it.'

'You did not.'

'How do you know that song? You're way too young.'

'My dad used to play it. We used to dance to it together, clicking our fingers.'

'I'm going to miss this,' Jack said suddenly.

'I'm going to miss it too,' she said after a second.

Jack rolled from his front on to his side and took her face in his hands.

'I don't want you to leave me. Xander won't be too thrilled either.'

'Now, Henchie, don't pull the emotional blackmail on me.'

'Just sayin'. You've got to realize, Zu, if you make a connection with someone, they're sad when you break it.'

'I know that,' she said indignantly. 'That's why I never do . . . never did . . .'

'After your mum, I can see why you didn't want to get close to anyone,' he said gently. During the past few weeks she'd told him bits and bobs about Deepika. Not the whole story, she wasn't sure she could ever bore anyone with that, but enough for him to understand far more about her.

'I'm trying to change that. I just have to make this one last journey. There's email, there's Skype and it won't be for long.' She burped loudly, but for once, Jack didn't tease her.

Instead, he cleared his throat. 'You know I'd come with you in a second if I could. But Xander –'

'I know. It's fine. It's probably better I go alone.'

'Marry me when you get back,' he said, his tone so light it was impossible to tell if he was joking or not. 'It might finally stop you running off.'

'Don't be a dick, Henchie.' His hand started creeping up her naked thigh. 'What are you doing?' she asked in pleasurable anticipation.

'Getting ready to ravish you. Again. After which you won't ever want to leave.'

'God, you've got a big head.'

'It's not the only big thing I've got.'

'Ooh, matron,' she giggled and then there was silence for a while until she gasped, 'Please don't stop.'

'Only if you say you're not going.'

'Jack. I have to go. You know why I do. Oh! Please don't.'

'Damn. You're just too sexy for me to stop. OK, I give in. I give in. Do what you want, just let me ravish you.'

So now she was standing in the queue at Heathrow, Terminal Three, a rucksack at her feet. The flight was leaving in an hour. Tony was looking anxiously at his watch.

'Don't sweat it, Dad. We've plenty of time.'

They'd been late leaving because the farewells with Anjali had been emotional and prolonged. Then the M25 traffic had been terrible. Tony had twitched with anxiety, while Zu had turned the radio dial to Classic FM and the volume on to high.

'You've still got to get through security and to the gate, which they'll close forty-five minutes before departure.'

'Chill. Once my bag's checked in, they'll wait. And I won't dawdle. It's not like I go browsing round Duty Free for perfumes.'

Despite himself, Tony grinned.

'But what about Leela? Where's she?'

'She'll be here. She's always late.'

They inched forward. A middle-aged, Indian couple – him stocky in a check suit, her small and skinny in a shearling jacket with hair down to her bottom – were involved in an animated discussion with the check-in lady.

Zu didn't understand it. When she checked in, they swiped her passport, asked if she'd packed her bags herself and gave her a boarding card. But every other passenger seemed determined to spend hours leaning against the desk, exchanging recipe tips. Maybe it was something else she'd master one day.

'Shall I ask someone if we can jump the queue?' said Tony.

'When the moment comes to queue jump, we'll queue jump. Until then, don't worry.'

Actually, she was less relaxed than she sounded. But she wasn't going to have Dad freaking out. She thought of saying goodbye to Henchie that morning. He'd almost pushed her out of the door, saying he couldn't deal with farewells. At the memory of his mouth brushing across hers, Zu swayed slightly and shut her eyes. When she opened them, the couple and the check-in lady were still gassing away. Tony shuffled and glanced at his watch.

'Five more minutes, Dad, then I'll kick up a fuss. So. What are you going to do tonight?'

Tony's face turned a soft shade of pink.

'Seeing Gillian?'

He nodded.

'That's great.'

'You were right about Gillian all along. I should have listened to you more.'

'Maybe you should have.' Zu smiled. She wasn't making a song and dance about her father and Gillian. Obviously she was delighted, not to mention a little smug that her hunch they'd be good together had been proved correct, but if there was one lesson her time at Temperley had taught her it was that it was pointless to meddle in other people's love lives. She'd leave them to get on with it.

'You will be careful, won't you?' Tony asked.

'Of course I will, Dad. I'll email all the time to let you

know how I'm doing.' They'd had this conversation so many times before, but this time it was proving much, much harder. Something was scratching at the back of her throat.

'I know you think I'm mad to worry so much. But you'll be a parent one day. Perhaps,' Tony added hastily.

A plastic-faced flight attendant was patrolling the queue. 'Passengers for the Delhi flight, please make yourselves known immediately!'

'That's you! Where's Leela?'

'There!' Zu smiled as an enormous trolley approached them. A porter – where the hell did Naani manage to find proper uniformed porters in the twenty-first century? – was pushing it. Leela bustled beside him in a pale green pashmina and a darker green salwar kameez, issuing commands out of the side of her mouth. Tony stepped forward.

'Leela, they're calling your flight. You need to check in now.'

Leela waved a hand. 'Tony, Tony, calm down. They'll wait for the first-class passengers.'

'First?' Zu tried to hide her smile of delight. 'I thought we were travelling business.'

'Ach, Baccha. Always first.' She waved at an airline employee. 'Are you checking us in, please?' She leant towards Zu and hissed loudly, 'Is Gillian here?'

'No, she's got some parents' thing at Holly's new school.'

'I am so pleased about this. I always said they were perfect for each other.'

'I know, Naani.' Zu had endured a lot of boasting on this subject. She declined to mention that she too had thought so. Why not let Naani take all the credit?

They were waved forward to a hitherto unmanned desk and suddenly it was all passports and luggage labels and Naani nodding imperiously.

'This flight never takes off on time, we've ages,' she asserted.

'Ma'am, I suggest you make your way straight to the gate,' said the anxious-looking man behind the desk.

'Zu!' She whirled round at the sound of her name. Wiping sweat away from his forehead, stood Jack.

'You're still here. I had to come. The last goodbye wasn't enough.'

The corners of Zu's mouth twitched. 'You numpty. I'll be back in a fortnight.'

'I know. But I still had to say goodbye again.'

They held each other for a moment, foreheads close.

'You can come to India with me another time,' Zu said. 'But it's better if it's just Naani and me in Haridwar, saying goodbye to Mum where her ashes were scattered in the Ganges.'

'But then you'll be off to space.'

'Not until Xander's grown up and you can come with me. For now, I'll just be at the space research agency down the road.'

She'd had to think hard but in the end there'd been no real choice but to turn down the Kazakhstan job. She'd run away too often. She wanted to stay in London – to be there for Tony, for her brothers should they need her, for Anjali, for Naani . . . and, of course, for Jack and Xander. She wanted to put her family first, her wanderlust second.

But then, as luck would have it, an opportunity had landed in her lap. Robert from the Odessa trip had called up out of the blue one day and offered her a job. A Russian oligarch who was desperate to beat Richard Branson and launch the first passenger space flight was in need of an assistant. It was a combination of translating and logistics, and – if all went well – it meant Zu might make it on to the first ever civilian trip to the moon without having to remortgage Naani's house to do so.

'Anyone else for Delhi?' the airline official yelled, very red in the face.

'Come on,' Zu said to Naani. They took each other's arms and, with one more wave at Tony and Jack, walked towards security.

He just wanted a decent book to read ...

Not too much to ask, is it? It was in 1935 when Allen Lane, Managing Director of Bodley Head Publishers, stood on a platform at Exeter railway station looking for something good to read on his journey back to London. His choice was limited to popular magazines and poor-quality paperbacks – the same choice faced every day by the vast majority of readers, few of whom could afford hardbacks. Lane's disappointment and subsequent anger at the range of books generally available led him to found a company – and change the world.

'We believed in the existence in this country of a vast reading public for intelligent books at a low price, and staked everything on it'
Sir Allen Lane, 1902–1970, founder of Penguin Books

The quality paperback had arrived – and not just in bookshops. Lane was adamant that his Penguins should appear in chain stores and tobacconists, and should cost no more than a packet of cigarettes.

Reading habits (and cigarette prices) have changed since 1935, but Penguin still believes in publishing the best books for everybody to enjoy. We still believe that good design costs no more than bad design, and we still believe that quality books published passionately and responsibly make the world a better place.

So wherever you see the little bird – whether it's on a piece of prize-winning literary fiction or a celebrity autobiography, political tour de force or historical masterpiece, a serial-killer thriller, reference book, world classic or a piece of pure escapism – you can bet that it represents the very best that the genre has to offer.

Whatever you like to read – trust Penguin.